Christine Rimmer came to her profession the long way around. She tried everything from acting to teaching to telephone sales. Now she's finally found work that suits her perfectly. She insists she never had a problem keeping a job—she was merely gaining "life experience" for her future as a novelist. Christine lives with her family in Oregon. Visit her at www.christinerimmer.com.

For my dear friend Carol Sue Ell,
who loves books as much as I do
and is always ready with a kind word.
Thanks for the smiles, Carol Sue,
and for making every day just a little bit brighter.

CARTER BRAVO'S CHRISTMAS BRIDE

BY
CHRISTINE RIMMER

Published in Great Britain 2015
by Mills & Boon, an imprint of Harlequin (UK) Limited,
Eton House, 18-24 Paradise Road, Richmond, Surrey, TW9 1SR

© 2015 Christine Rimmer

ISBN: 978-0-263-25190-6

23-1215

Harlequin (UK) Limited's policy is to use papers that are natural, renewable and recyclable products and made from wood grown in sustainable forests. The logging and manufacturing processes conform to the legal environmental regulations of the country of origin.

Printed and bound in Spain
by CPI, Barcelona

Chapter One

It all started three days before Thanksgiving with a silly magazine quiz.

Paige Kettleman and her best friend and business partner, Carter Bravo, sat in the plush Denver offices of Leery International Drilling. They were waiting to meet with president and CEO Deacon Leery, who had already commissioned five big-ticket custom-redesigned cars from their company, Bravo Custom Cars.

Carter was getting fidgety. He spent most of his working life in old jeans and T-shirts, with his head stuck under the hood of one of his soon-to-be beautiful custom creations. He'd never enjoyed taking meetings.

But Deacon was a major customer. And Deacon liked Carter to come to his gorgeous office and listen to him ramble on about classic cars for a while before getting around to the dream ride he wanted Carter to build for him next. As far as Deacon was concerned, Paige didn't really even need to be there. But she ran the business end of Bravo Custom Cars. She always went along to visit Deacon for that special moment when they started talking money.

Carter had already taken off his sport coat and tossed it across the back of his chair. Now he sat forward, elbows on his spread knees. He braced his square jaw on his big fist and tapped his booted foot impatiently.

Paige watched him and tried not to grin.

He sent her a quick, challenging glance. "So what? I hate sitting around. That's a crime?"

She stifled a chuckle. "Who said a word about crimes?"

He grunted. "Smug. You know you are. Sitting there all cool and calm in your preppy little suit, tap-tap-tapping on your tablet."

She gave him a bland smile. "I'm sure it won't be long now."

He grumbled something. She wisely did not ask him what. And then he grabbed one of the glossy magazines from the low table in front of them. Hitching one boot across the other knee, he slumped back in his chair and began thumbing through it.

She returned her attention to her tablet and her email correspondence with Kelly Cobb, the Realtor they'd hired a few weeks before. Bravo Custom Cars was looking to expand. Electric cars were the future, and Carter wanted to start building custom electric cars along with the gas hogs most of his clients favored.

Carter and Paige had their eye on a new location. They'd made one offer and been turned down. The owner had rocks in his head. Nobody else in town wanted that property. The building and large fenced concrete yard had been sitting on an ugly stretch of Arrowhead Drive on the outskirts of their hometown for over a year with a big For Sale sign on the gate. Paige and Carter were waiting for the seller to get real and lower his asking price a little before they tried again.

Carter nudged her with his elbow. "You got a pen?" She took one from her black leather tote and handed it over. "Thanks. You listening?"

"Um."

"Good. Because you'll love this. 'Is he really your best friend or are you secretly in love with him?' It's a quiz and you need to take it."

She zipped off the email to the Realtor. "No, I don't."

"Yeah, you do. It's all about us."

Paige reached over and snagged the corner of the magazine so she could get a look at the front of it. "*Girl Code*? You're reading *Girl Code*?"

"I'm broadening my horizons, trying to understand women better. Everyone says I need to."

She stifled a snort and pointed at the other magazines on the low table. "There's a *Car and Driver* right there."

His broad shoulders lifted in a dismissive shrug. "I've read that one. First question. 'Do you compare all your dates to him?' You know you do. So that's a yes." He scratched at the page with the pen she'd foolishly given him.

"It's obvious you don't even need me here," she wryly observed.

He actually had the nerve to smirk. "You're right, I don't. I know all the answers. Because, face it, I know you better than *you* know you—which proves I know a thing or two about women, after all."

"So then shut up," she muttered out of the corner of her mouth. "Take the damn thing silently if you just *have* to go there." A text popped up from Mona, who ran their front office. Mona was closing up for the night. Paige sighed and replied Still @ Leery's. C U 2morrow.

And Carter went right on to the next question. "'Can you tell him anything without feeling at all uncomfortable?' Oh, hell to the yes." He scratched on the page again.

"That's not fair. You have no idea the things I *don't* tell you." There weren't a lot of them, to be strictly honest. But he didn't need to know that right now.

"Oh, come on. You tell me *everything*, Paige. That's how you are with me. Constant oversharing. A thought pops in your head and I'm the only one there? Comes right out your mouth." She elbowed him. Hard. He snickered, leaned away from her so she couldn't do it again and asked, "'Do you care about his happiness more than you do the happiness of your other friends?'" Another snicker as he checked the answer. "'Do you think about drunk-texting him every other weekend?' I'm going with yes for that, too, because if you were drunk, you *know* it would be me you drunk-texted."

Best to just ignore him, she decided. So she did—or at least she pretended to.

And he kept right on, asking the questions and answering them for her. There were twenty in all.

When he finally answered the last one, he announced, "You scored twenty out of twenty. Hate to break it to you, Paige. But you're desperately in love with me."

She considered taking off one of her high-heeled shoes and bopping him on the head with it. But if she hit him once, she would only want to hit him again.

He tossed the magazine back on the table. "I gotta ask."

"No, you don't."

"Why does every woman I meet just *have* to fall in love with me?" he went on as though she hadn't spoken. "I don't get it."

She scoffed, "You're not the only one."

"Wait a minute, hold on. We both know *you* get it. We just found out you're hopelessly in love with me like all the rest of them, remember? So, what is it that you adore about me?"

"Not a thing."

"I think we need to make a list."

"Carter, stop."

He was wearing that smile now. The one that drove all the women right out of their panties—except for her. As his best friend, Paige reminded herself, she was totally immune to that smile. And he was still talking. "Yes. Definitely. Let's make a list."

"Let's not and say we did."

He started ticking off his supposed lady-killing qualities. "Okay, I'll admit it. I'm better looking than most. And I have a great personality. I'm a god in bed—not that you would know that. And I'm well off, but come on. Half the time, I'm covered in axle grease." He gave her one of those looks, serious and teasing, both at the same time. "Paige."

"What?"

"We both know I'm not really all that."

"You think I'm going to argue with you and tell you you're wonderful and not to run yourself down? Ha. Think again."

He spread his arms wide and she had to jerk back in

her chair to keep from getting smacked in the chest with a rock-hard forearm. "Why can't someone explain it to me? What is this thing I have?"

Before Paige could manufacture a suitably quelling reply, the receptionist said pleasantly, "Mr. Leery will see you now."

So they got up and entered the inner sanctum where another plum project was waiting for them.

An hour later, they shook hands with Deacon Leery and wished him a happy Thanksgiving. It had gone well. Carter was excited about acquiring and redesigning his next four-wheeled masterpiece. Paige felt pleased with the deal she'd struck. A satisfying transaction in every way.

Except for that damn quiz. For some reason, she couldn't stop thinking about it.

Ridiculous. Why even worry about it? It was nothing but fluff. Silly, meaningless fluff.

"You're quiet," Carter said about midway through the hour-and-a-half drive back to their hometown of Justice Creek.

She made a sleepy noise, closed her eyes and leaned against the passenger-side window, hoping he'd assume she must be napping and leave her alone.

It worked. But Paige was not napping. Far from it. Her brain was packed to bursting with that absurd *Girl Code* quiz.

Let it go, she told herself. *It's no big deal. Forget about it.*

But she couldn't forget. It was stuck in her mind and it wouldn't go away. It was like the avalanche that killed her parents, a snowball rolling downhill, quickly gaining speed and mass until it buried everyone and everything in its path.

They weren't even her answers, she reminded herself. They were Carter's.

But unfortunately, his answers were the ones that she would have given. And for a silly, meaningless magazine quiz, well, they were kind of good questions, she had to admit.

They were *telling* questions.

And that was why she couldn't put it out of her mind. Carter *had* answered the questions just as she would have. And that meant she couldn't stop thinking that it might actually be true, that she'd gone and fallen secretly in love with her best friend.

And now just look at her, with that totally unacceptable secret loose and wreaking havoc in her mind and heart.

The only good news?

Nobody else knew. Not even Carter. He had no clue. She was dead certain of that. Thank God. He'd only been messing with her, taking that ridiculous quiz for her. He had no idea what he'd done.

The next morning, when he stopped by the house to walk the dogs and then fix breakfast for her and him and her younger sister, Dawn, he seemed totally oblivious. And then at work that day, he mostly stayed in the shop and she managed to stick to the office, so he had no chance to notice if she acted strange and preoccupied.

Mona, who worked side by side with her, caught on, though. "You okay, Paige? You seem kind of far away."

"Christmas on my mind, I guess," Paige outright lied. "And you know, it's kind of quiet today. We should get out the decorations, get them up. You think?"

Mona loved Christmas. She zipped right out to the shed by the back gate and hauled the boxes of decorations up front to the office. They spent a couple of hours setting up the fake tree and tacking sparkly garland on every available surface. Mona already had her old iPod loaded up with Christmas favorites. She stuck it in the dock at the end of the service counter. Holiday tunes filled the air. Mona hummed along under her breath, thrilled to have the office full of Christmas and no longer worrying about what might be bugging Paige.

Wednesday morning when Paige followed the tempting smells of frying bacon and perfectly brewed coffee downstairs, she found the dogs—her beagle, Biscuit, and Carter's hound, Sally—sprawled contentedly on the kitchen floor after their morning walk.

Carter stood at the stove. He had his back to her. She hesitated in the doorway in her flannel pj's and plaid robe and watched him cooking up the bacon nice and slow.

He liked to come over before she and Dawn got up, especially lately, since he'd broken up with his last girlfriend, Sherry Leland. Lately, Carter ended up at Paige and Dawn's a lot of the time. He would take Biscuit out with Sally, then let himself back in and start breakfast.

And even when he had a girlfriend, Carter still found time to walk Paige's dog and brew her morning coffee two or three days a week. Most Sunday nights, he came over for dinner and stayed on to play video games or stream a movie.

That he spent so much time at the Kettlemans' always bugged his girlfriends eventually. They didn't really like that his best friend was a woman and his business partner. They also didn't like that his best friend's teenage sister was kind of a cross between a daughter and a little sister to him. Paige got why it bugged them. She wouldn't like it, either, if her special guy spent most of his working life and half his free time with another woman. Paige used to suggest to him that maybe he should focus more on the girlfriend of the hour and not so much on hanging with her and Dawn.

He wouldn't listen. He said he liked being with her and Dawn, and if his girlfriend was jealous, she needed to get over that.

Paige always felt kind of sorry for Carter's girlfriends. Somehow they all fell so hard for him. And the deeper they fell, the more he pulled away from them. And the more he pulled away, the more upset they got. There would be scenes. Carter hated scenes, mostly because his childhood had been one long, dramatic scene.

His mother, Willow Mooney, had loved his father, Franklin Bravo, to distraction. Franklin was already married when he met Willow. But Frank Bravo didn't let a little thing like a wife get in his way. He set Willow up in a house on the south side of town. Willow kicked Frank out of that house on a regular basis. But she always took him back, remaining his mistress for over two decades, giving Frank five children while he was still married to his first wife, Sondra, who gave him four.

Yeah. Falling for Carter? Not a wise move.

This can't really be happening, Paige thought for about the fiftieth time since Monday and that awful, terrible, silly, pointless quiz. *This can't be happening to me.*

But if it wasn't, then why was she lurking in the doorway to the kitchen, staring longingly at Carter's broad, thick shoulders and fine, tight butt?

It just made her feel sad. Beyond sad. Carter's shoul-

ders and butt had never mattered in the least to her before Monday. Why should they mean so much now?

He sent her a quick smile over one of those far-too-
fine shoulders of his. "Coffee's ready."

As if she didn't know. Carter was a great cook. And
he had a way with coffee. She would know a Carter-
brewed cup of coffee blindfolded. All it took was one
sniff. Heaven in a cup.

"Thanks." She shuffled over and filled a mug with the
hot, wonderful brew. And then she stood there, leaning
against the counter, sipping it slowly, her heart breaking at the hopeless absurdity of it all as Carter cracked
eggs into her mother's favorite cast-iron pan.

Carter woke on Thanksgiving morning to the sound
of his cell ringing. He stuck out a hand, snared the damn
thing off the nightstand and squinted at the display. It
was 5:49 and his mother was calling.

When had Willow Mooney Bravo ever climbed out
of bed before six in the morning? Never, that he could
remember. Even when he and his brothers and sisters
were small they knew not to bother Ma too early in the
morning. She tended to throw things if you messed with
her beauty sleep.

His sweet redbone coonhound, Sally, lifted her
floppy-eared head from the foot of the bed and blinked
at him questioningly.

"Hell if I know," he said to the dog, and put the phone
to his ear. "Ma? What's going on? Did somebody die?"

"Happy Thanksgiving, darling. Everything is fine
and no one has died. But I know you're an early riser
and I wanted to catch you before you left the house. I
want a private word with you—today, I hope. I'm leaving

for Palm Springs tomorrow and I'm not sure when I'll be back." Since his father had died four years ago, you could hardly catch his mother at home. She traveled the world, flitting from one luxury destination to the next. "I wonder if you could drop by for a drink before you join the rest of the family at Clara's."

His half sister Clara Bravo Ames had invited the whole family to her house that afternoon for a big Thanksgiving dinner. Paige and Dawn were coming, too. "Won't you be at Clara's?"

"It was sweet of Clara to include me, but no. Big family gatherings exhaust me and I have an early flight tomorrow morning—and besides, I want to speak with you alone."

He didn't really like the sound of that. "About what?"

"Darling. Honestly. Don't be so suspicious. I'll explain everything when we talk."

"We're talking now." At the foot of the bed, Sally picked up the tension in his voice and whined. He snapped his fingers and she slinked up the bed, slithered in a circle and settled beside him where he could throw an arm around her and scratch her silky red head.

His mother went on, sounding way too casual for his peace of mind. "How about this? I know you're expected at Clara's at three. So let's say two o'clock at my house, just you and me." Her house was the Bravo Mansion, which his father had built for his first wife, Sondra. The mansion was full of beautiful things that used to be Sondra's. When Sondra died, Frank married Willow and installed her at the mansion. By then, Carter had been twenty-three and on his own. He'd never had to live in the house he still considered Sondra's, and he was damn

glad he hadn't. He didn't want to go there today, either.
"Carter. Are you still there?"

He patted Sally's smooth flank. "Yeah."

"Two o'clock, then?"

He reminded himself that she was his mother and
he really didn't see her all that often these days. "Yeah,
Ma. See you then." Disconnecting the call, he tossed
the phone on the nightstand. Then he turned to Sally.
"Walk?"

Sally let out a happy whine of agreement and lifted
off her haunches enough to give a wag of her red tail.

"Let's go pick up Biscuit and get after it, then."

Ten minutes later, he stood on Paige's front porch
and stuck his key in the lock. Biscuit was waiting on
the other side. He grabbed the beagle's leash from the
hook by the door and clipped it to Biscuit's collar. Then
he clicked his tongue and Biscuit trotted out the door to
wiggle over and butt against Sally, who waited patiently
for Carter to lock up again so they could get going.

Half an hour later, he was back in the kitchen at
Paige's, getting the coffee going, trying to decide between French toast and oatmeal. He settled on the
oatmeal because of the huge dinner ahead of them at
Clara's. Paige and Dawn came down together as he was
turning off the fire under the oats.

Through breakfast, Dawn chattered away as usual
about the afternoon dinner at Clara's, about how she
and her best friend, Molly D'Abalo, were going to the
movies with friends in the evening.

Dawn was a great kid. Not an ounce of bitterness in
her, though she'd lost her mom and dad suddenly when
she was only ten. Erica and Jerry Kettleman had been

buried in an avalanche while off on a twenty-fifth anniversary skiing trip. Paige had come home from college to take care of her little sister. Together, they'd made it work. And now, at eighteen, Dawn had boundless enthusiasm and a smile for everyone. She was an A student and first chair clarinet with her high school band.

Babbling away happily between bites, Dawn inhaled her oatmeal. Once her bowl was empty, she jumped up, carried it to the sink, ran water in it and rushed off upstairs to get dressed.

Carter turned to Paige, who wore her heavy plaid robe, with her brown hair loose and uncombed on her shoulders. Her eyes looked kind of puffy. She'd hardly said a word since she came downstairs. "You okay?"

She blinked and seemed to shake herself. "Uh. Fine."

"Sure?"

"Positive."

He couldn't really get a read on her, couldn't decide whether he ought to keep pushing her to tell him what was going on with her or let it go. It was odd. As a rule, he never had to push her to tell him if she had a problem. She always came right out with it and asked his advice.

Okay, so maybe this time she needed a little encouragement. He was just about to try that when she jumped up. "Thanks for the breakfast, Carter. You're the best."

"Gotta keep my girls fed." He watched her bustle to the sink, rinse out her bowl and bend to stick it in the dishwasher.

"Well." She shut the dishwasher door and straightened. "Better get after it. The day's not getting any younger. Leave everything. I mean it. I'll clean up."

"Will do."

"Quarter of three?"

"I'll be here."

And then she darted to the door and took off down the hall.

He didn't get it. They always spent a few minutes together in the morning after Dawn went back upstairs. But today—and for the past couple of days, now that he thought about it—Paige couldn't get away fast enough.

Her rush to leave the kitchen right after breakfast hadn't bothered him much yesterday or the day before. Today, though, he'd really wanted to tell her about the weird call from his mother. He wanted to get her take on Willow suddenly asking him to come to the Bravo Mansion and have a drink with her, alone.

But so much for wanting Paige's input.

"So, okay, then," he said to the dogs, because there was no one else there to hear him. He rose. "Come on, Sally. Time to go."

Built less than forty years ago on top of a hill at the west end of Grandview Drive, the Bravo Mansion seemed a product of a much earlier age. Georgian in style, with big white columns flanking the front door, the mansion bore a striking resemblance to the White House. Let it never be said that Frank Bravo didn't dream big.

The housekeeper, Estrella Watson, must have been told to watch for him. Before he was halfway up the front steps, she pulled the wreath-hung door open and gave him a big smile of greeting. "Happy Thanksgiving, Carter." She reached for a hug.

He wrapped his arms around her. "Good to see you." He'd always liked Estrella. She'd been the mansion's housekeeper for years, from before Sondra died and

Carter's mother moved in. Well into her fifties now, Estrella kept the house and grounds in great shape, hiring and supervising maids, gardeners and repairmen. She lived in, cooking for Willow whenever his mother was at home. She seemed to enjoy her job and treated everyone kindly.

A jumble of boxes filled the front hall, most of them opened, bright decorations and shiny ornaments spilling out. "It's a weeklong job, getting the house ready for the holidays," Estrella explained. "And I'm not preparing Thanksgiving dinner this year, so I thought I might as well get a head start."

What for? he couldn't help wondering. Only she and his mother lived there, and his mother was leaving for California. But Willow liked the mansion just so, whether she stuck around to enjoy it or not. And Estrella had a gleam in her eye, as though nothing pleased her more than decking the halls of the big, empty house.

She took his coat. "Your mother's in the library."

He thanked her and went on through the formal living room to the large book-lined room behind it, where a fire crackled in the ornate fireplace and the mantel was already done up in swags of green garland studded with shiny ornaments and twinkling lights.

"Carter." His mother rose from a silk-covered chair. She looked beautiful as always, in snug black slacks and a fitted green cashmere sweater, her chin-length blond hair combed back from the classic oval of her face.

He kissed the smooth, pale cheek she offered. "Ma. How are you?"

She fiddled with the diamond stud in her left ear. "Perfect. Thank you. How about a martini?"

He looked at her patiently. "Got a beer?"

She sighed. "Of course." She had a longneck waiting in an ice bucket on the fancy mirrored drink cart, right next to the Bombay Sapphire and the Vya vermouth. She also had a chilled glass for him.

"Just give me the bottle."

Another sigh. His mother had been born with nothing. Her own mother ran off when she was three weeks old and Willow grew up in a double-wide, just her and her father. Gene Mooney, deceased before Carter was born, had had trouble holding a job and drank too much. It probably wasn't all that surprising that, over the years, Willow had developed a passion for elegance and gracious living. The way Willow saw it, if a man insisted on drinking beer, he should at least use a glass.

Too bad. Carter took the beer, sat in the chair across from hers and watched as she skillfully whipped up her martini—stirred, not shaken.

Willow took her seat again and raised her glass. "To happiness."

Happiness? His mother had never struck him as a person who put a lot of store in happiness. She'd wanted Frank Bravo and the good life he provided for her. And she'd fought tooth and nail to get both.

But hey. She was getting older. Maybe she missed the happiness that had never seemed all that important to her while Carter was growing up.

"Happiness it is." He lifted his bottle in answer to her toast and resisted the urge to come right out and ask her why she'd summoned him here. It wouldn't kill him to try a little friendly conversation. "So, what's happening in Palm Springs?"

"The usual. Shopping. Spa time. And the weather is lovely there now."

"Well. Have a great time."

"I will, darling."

Ho-kay. So much for cordial conversation. He took one more stab at it. "We'll miss you at Clara's."

She smiled her cool smile. "Somehow I doubt that."

Annoyance gnawed at him. His half siblings had made it more than clear that they wanted to forgive and forget. Her decades-long love triangle was seriously old news. "You're wrong. We *will* miss you." He took care to say it gently. "And I think you know that."

She sipped her drink. "I didn't ask you here to talk about dinner at Clara's."

"Well, all right. What's going on?"

Willow lounged back in the chair and crossed her legs. "Notice I made a toast to happiness?"

"Yeah, Ma. I heard you."

"That's because lately I've been thinking a lot about happiness, about what makes a man—or anyone, really—truly happy." She paused. Just to be nice, Carter made an encouraging sound low in his throat. She said, "Take your brother."

"Which one?" He had two full brothers, both younger than he was—Garrett, thirty-three, and Quinn, thirty-one. And then there were also Sondra's sons, Darius and James.

"I'm talking about Quinn," his mother said. A former martial arts star, Quinn had retired from fighting last year and brought his little daughter, Annabelle, home to Justice Creek. Now he owned a gym and fitness center on Marmot Drive. Just recently, he'd gotten together with gorgeous Chloe Winchester, who'd also grown up in town. "Now that Quinn's married Chloe, he's a truly happy man."

Carter wasn't sure he liked where this was going. "Can't argue with that," he answered cautiously.

"I want that for you, too, darling. I want you to find happiness."

Okay, now. He *definitely* didn't like where this was going. "What are you up to, Ma? Just spit it the hell out."

"Love, darling. I want you to take a chance on love."

He really wished he hadn't asked. "Oh, well, sure. I'll get right on that."

"Don't give me sarcasm. You're thirty-four years old. When a man reaches your age and he's never been married, the likelihood that he'll find someone to be happy with is…" Another sigh. God. He hated her damn sighs. "It's not looking good for you. You have to know that."

Carter sat very still in the silk wing chair and reminded himself not to say anything he would later regret. But she pissed him the hell off. She acted as if he didn't want to get married. He *did*. Very much.

But somehow the whole romance thing never worked out for him. And it wasn't as if he hadn't tried. He had. Repeatedly.

There was just something about him, something *wrong* with him. Because he always attracted the drama queens.

Things would begin well. Lots of fireworks in bed, yes, but otherwise the woman would seem like a reasonable person, someone he could talk to, someone easygoing and fun. Early on, his girlfriends reassured him that they wanted what he wanted, a solid partnership and a balanced life. He always explained up front that he expected an exclusive relationship and he planned someday to get married, but if they were after passionate declarations of undying love, they should find a different guy. The woman would say that was no problem; she completely understood.

But every woman he'd ever dated had eventually told him she loved him. He never said it back. And his silence on the subject never worked for them. The downward spiral would start. There would be heated accusations, generally irrational behavior and a messy breakup at the end. He hated all that.

Truthfully, deep down?

Carter thought the whole love thing was pretty damn stupid. The way he saw it, falling in love was a good way to lose your mind.

His mother said, "I know, darling. I understand. I wasn't a good mother."

"Did I say that? I never said that."

"You don't have to say it. It's simply the truth. There were way too many big dramatic scenes. I loved your father to distraction and I wanted him to leave Sondra. Every time I kicked him out, I swore I would never take him back."

"But you always did."

"I loved him." She said it softly, gently. As though it explained everything.

Carter kept his mouth shut. It was stupid to argue about it. To some people, love excused the worst behaviors. All you had to do was call it love and you could get away with anything—steal someone else's husband, make your children's lives an endless series of shouting matches and emotional upheavals.

His mother set her empty martini glass on the small inlaid table by her chair. "I want you to take a chance on love. I may be a bad mother, but I do love you. And a mother knows her children. At heart, you're like Quinn.

A family man. I won't have you ending up alone because of my mistakes."

She wouldn't *have* it? You'd think he was ten, the way she was talking. "Ma, you really need to dial this back. It's not all about you. I'm a grown man and have been for quite a while now. It's on me if I can't make things work with a woman."

"Not entirely. I know very well that my actions when you were growing up have made you afraid of strong emotions."

He looked at her sideways. "Have you gone into therapy or something?"

"No. I've only been thinking—as I've already told you. These days, I have plenty of time for thinking."

"Well, think about something other than me and my supposed need for true love and a wife, why don't you?"

She didn't answer, only sat there in her chair, watching him for about fifteen seconds that only seemed like an hour and a half. He was just about to jump up, wish her a safe trip to California and get out of there when she said, "I asked you here to offer a little something in the way of motivation, a little something in the interest of helping you get past your fears."

He stood and set his empty beer bottle on the drink cart. "You never suffered from a lack of nerve, Ma. I gotta give you that. Look, this…whatever it is you think you're pulling here is more than I'm up for, you know? You really need to mind your own damn business."

His mother didn't seem a bit bothered by his harsh words. She gave a shrug. "I can that see you're ready to go."

"More than ready."

"Just listen to my offer before you leave. Please."

"Offer? You're kidding me. There's an offer?"

She draped an arm over the chair arm and crossed her legs the other way. "Yes, there is. I know that you and Paige have been eyeing a certain property on Arrowhead Drive, with a large cinder-block industrial building on it."

"What the...? How do you know that?"

She waved a hand. "It was all really quite innocent."

"Innocent," he repeated. Not a word he would think of in connection with Willow. "Right."

She fiddled with her earring again. "I drove by there a few weeks ago and saw the two of you standing outside the gate. And then I recalled how, several months ago, you said something about wanting to expand Bravo Custom Cars. I added two and two. Voilà. Four. Tuesday, I paid a visit to the owner. He had a price. And I have paid it."

"You're not serious."

"Oh, but I am. I've bought that property."

"What for? What possible use can you have for a fifteen-thousand-square-foot cinder-block building and a concrete yard rimmed in chain-link fence?"

"None, of course."

He wanted to pick up his empty beer bottle and hurl it at the garland-bedecked fireplace. "I'm going to leave now, Ma. Happy Thanksgiving and have a nice trip to Palm Springs." He turned to go back through the formal living room and out the way he'd come in.

And she said, "The property is yours, free and clear. But only as a wedding present."

Keep going, he thought. *Don't give her the satisfaction of taking her seriously.* But then he just couldn't let it go at that. He halted and turned back to her. "Reassure me, Ma. Tell me you *didn't* just say that if I get married, you'll give me the property."

"But that is exactly what I said."

Unbelievable. "What if you've got this all wrong? What if Paige and I have zero interest in that property?"

"Ah, but I'm not wrong, am I?"

He could strangle her. He'd probably get the death penalty and go to hell for murdering his own mother. But right at that moment, murder seemed like a great idea. "Just curious. Did you have any particular bride in mind for me?"

"Of course not. It has to be someone you choose for yourself."

He made a low, scoffing sound in his throat. "Wow. I get to choose the woman myself."

"I wouldn't have it any other way."

"I gotta say it, Ma."

"Go ahead. Whatever you need to tell me, I'm here and I'm listening."

"The way your mind works?"

"Yes?"

"It's always scared the hell out of me."

"Don't be cruel. Can't you see that I'm doing this for you? It's a nudge, plain and simple, an opportunity for you to start thinking about giving love and happiness a chance. I just want you to entertain the idea of making a good life with the right woman. The property is an incentive, that's all."

He laughed. Because it was funny, right? And then he said, "You have a great holiday, Ma."

She granted him her coolest smile. "Thank you, darling. I will."

He turned on his heel then. This time, he didn't pause

or turn back. He strode fast through the front room and into the giant foyer, where he collected his coat from Estrella and got the hell out of there.

Chapter Two

Not only was Carter's mother a manipulative nutcase; his best friend had checked out on him.

Carter sat between Paige and Dawn at the long, white-clothed table in his half sister Clara's formal dining room and wondered what was the matter with Paige. She'd hardly said two words to him all afternoon. At some point between the time she'd left the breakfast table that morning and two forty-five in the afternoon, when he picked her and Dawn up to bring them to Clara's, Paige had gotten dressed, combed her hair and put on makeup. But her eyes still had that strange vacant look.

If someone spoke to her directly, she would lurch to life and pretend to be interested. But as soon as the focus moved elsewhere, she'd settle back into the weird funk she'd been in for days now.

Twice, he leaned close and asked her if she was okay.

Both times, she lied. "Fine," she said the first time. "Great," she answered later.

He left her alone after that. They could talk about it when they got back to her place.

For now, he enjoyed his family. The food was always good at Clara's house. Plus, Clara was a truly sweet woman and happily married to a banker from Denver named Dalton Ames. They had a six-month-old daughter, Kiera.

Carter liked hanging around Dalton and Clara. Just seeing them together made him smile. They'd had some difficulties when they first started out, but they'd worked through them and come out strong on the other side.

Same thing with his brother Quinn and Chloe Winchester, who was now Chloe Bravo. Truthfully, Willow might be full of crap about a lot of stuff, but she was right about Quinn and Chloe. Quinn and Chloe had that thing—whatever it was. They shared that special connection, same as Dalton and Clara.

And then there was his cousin Rory and her fiancé, Walker McKellan. Rory Bravo-Calabretti was an honest-to-God princess from the tiny Mediterranean principality of Montedoro. She'd moved to Justice Creek last winter. She and Walker, who owned a guest ranch not far from town, were getting married on Christmas Eve.

And yeah, Rory and Walker had it, too. Same as Clara and Dalton. Same as Quinn and Chloe.

Hanging around at Clara's house on Thanksgiving, watching those three couples interact with each other, Carter could almost start to think that love and forever were actually possible.

At least for other people.

Once the meal was through, they all helped to clear

the table. Then a little later, Dalton turned the game on in the great room. Some of them—Carter included—gathered around the big screen mounted over the mantel.

Most of the women headed for the kitchen area, which shared the high-ceilinged great room space. Carter could hear them back there, bustling around, laughing and talking over each other, having a fine time. He heard Paige's distinctive husky laugh. Apparently, whatever was bothering her didn't stop her from having fun with his sisters.

Dawn came and sat on the sofa arm next to him. He glanced up at her and she sent him a quick smile. Then Quinn's daughter, Annabelle, who'd recently turned five, wandered over. She was the cutest kid, with a plump little pixie face. Chloe must have done her hair. It was curled and held back with big sparkly barrettes. She wore one of those puffy, lacy dresses that little girls liked to wear, complete with white tights and shiny black Mary Janes. She whispered something to Dawn.

Dawn said, "Absolutely," and swung the little girl up on her knee.

Annabelle leaned back in Dawn's arms as if she belonged there. She caught Carter watching her and said, "I *like* Dawn, Uncle Carter. She's very pretty."

"Yes, she is," he agreed.

Dawn, who'd always been good with kids, cuddled Annabelle closer.

Carter felt a little better about everything, with the two happy girls sitting next to him. He liked his family—his mother excluded, at least at the moment. He liked that Dawn felt comfortable here at Clara's with his siblings and half siblings.

Now, if only he could get Paige to get real about whatever was bugging her. Once they had that out of the way, he could tell her all about the stunt Willow had just pulled and break the bad news that they needed to find another property for the expansion.

After the pie and coffee, Carter drove Paige and Dawn home in the '61 Lincoln he'd taken out of the shop for the day. He was looking forward to being alone with Paige so they could talk.

"Gotta hurry." Dawn was out of the car the second he pulled up to the curb in front of their house. "I'm meeting Molly at the Gold Rush in twenty minutes." The Gold Rush was the movie theater on Golden Drive. She leaned in the rear door she'd just jumped out of. "Thanks, Carter. It was fun."

Paige said, "Home by—"

"Midnight, promise," Dawn finished for her and pushed the door shut.

Carter started to turn off the engine, but Paige said, "I'm really tired. And me and my Visa card have a shopping date tomorrow." Bravo Custom Cars would be closed. It was a BCC tradition to give everyone both Thanksgiving and Black Friday off. Paige went on. "Nell and Chloe and Jody are picking me up at three a.m." Nell and Jody were his sisters. "We're driving into Denver to check out the deals. I need sleep to get ready for a day of serious shopping, so I think I'll draw a hot bath and call it an early night."

He turned off the engine and shifted in the seat to face her. "You mean you don't want me to come in."

She cleared her throat. "Well, as I said. I'm tired and it's going to be a long—"

"Stop it. Tell me what is going on."

"What are you talking about? There's nothing—"

"Paige, you've been dragging around like the world's coming to an end for two or three days now, all the time constantly telling me there's nothing wrong. What's up?"

"Nothing. Really."

"Come on. It's something."

"Nope. Uh-uh. Nothing. Like I said, I'm just really tired."

He gave in. "Fine. Great. Later, then." It was only a ploy. He honestly expected her to hesitate, to say she was sorry for brushing him off, to ask him not to be annoyed with her—something. Anything.

But she only chirped out a quick "Night, then. And thanks. I had a great time," and leaped out of the car.

He watched her run up the front walk and disappear into the house. He just didn't get it. Paige told him everything. In detail. Way too much detail, as a rule.

What could be bothering her that she couldn't talk about it with him?

The next morning, Carter decided he would walk Sally alone. He was kind of pissed at Paige for shutting him out. Why in hell would he want to walk her damn dog for her?

And she was in Denver anyway, right? She wouldn't be there to eat any breakfast he cooked for her.

But then what about Dawn? Paige hadn't mentioned whether Dawn was going, too. What if Dawn was home alone? She'd need breakfast.

And what about poor Biscuit? Biscuit liked his morning walk with Sally.

So Carter and Sally went over to the Kettlemans', after all. He got Biscuit and walked the two dogs. On the way back, he called Dawn on her cell.

She answered with a big yawn. "Yeah, what?"

"You still in bed?"

"How'd you guess?"

He grunted. "Just checking to see if maybe you went to Denver with Paige."

"Uh-uh. Too early for me. You coming to make breakfast?"

"I'm on my way."

He made French toast and tried to be subtle when he asked Dawn if she'd noticed anything different about Paige in the last few days.

Dawn groaned. "Oh, yeah. Something's on her mind. But every time I ask, she tells me there's nothing."

He felt instantly vindicated. And then he frowned. "So...you don't know what it is, either, huh?"

"I'm clueless. Seriously. But how awful can it be, really? I mean, she got up at two-thirty in the morning to spend the day shopping. I don't think it's an incurable disease or anything."

"A disease?" That kind of freaked him out. "It didn't even occur to me she might have a disease..."

"Carter. Pull yourself together."

"Well, I'm worried about her, okay?"

"She's just feeling down about something."

"It's not like her," he grumbled.

"Everybody feels low now and then. Eventually, she'll tell you. She always does."

"Yeah," he said, feeling marginally better. "Of course she will. She always does." He knew everything about Paige, all the little things—that she thought she looked bad in purple and she liked '70s rock.

He knew that she'd been in love with a loser named Jim Kellogg when she was in college. She and Jim had been talking marriage, but he dumped her when her parents died. He said he didn't want to follow her to some Podunk small town and help her raise her sister. Since then, she'd only dated casually.

He asked Dawn, "What time did she say she'd be back from Denver?"

"Five or six—and, Carter?"

"Yeah?"

"Let it go. She'll tell you when she's ready to tell you."

"You're right. I will…"

After breakfast, he took Sally home and then headed for Bravo Custom Cars, thinking about Paige the whole way. About him and Paige, about how they'd hit it off from the start.

He'd met her at Romano's Restaurant, where she'd started working after her parents died. He'd liked her right off and he used to eat there at least a couple of times a week, partly because Romano's had the best Italian food around. But mostly because he loved to sit in Paige's section and give her a hard time. He'd asked her out more than once. She'd turned him down over and over, but he kept trying.

Finally, she'd told him gently and regretfully that she was never going out with him.

She hadn't told him why she wouldn't date him. Not then. The truth had come out later, as their friendship grew. About how she was happier on her own, that her heart had been stomped on but good by that Kellogg creep when she was already in bad shape from losing her parents.

But that was later.

He could still remember her way back at the beginning of their friendship, still see her so clearly, standing by his favorite booth at Romano's, her hands in the pockets of her waitress apron. "I don't need a date, Carter. But I could sure use a friend."

"Then you got one," he'd said.

The overhead fluorescents had brought out red lights in her dark brown hair, and her soft mouth kicked up at the corners. "Does my friend need another beer?"

When he opened BCC, she'd answered his ad for an office manager. He hired her on the spot and she got right after it, moving the furniture around in the office for better "work flow," as she called it, setting up the front counter and the customer waiting area so she could see everything from her desk. He knew cars. Paige knew a whole lot about systems and how to set up the front of the shop. Not only did she seem to have a knack for running the place; she'd been a semester away from getting a BA in business when her parents died and she quit to come home.

The woman knew her way around a spreadsheet. He'd figured out within the first few weeks that he needed to keep her around. So every year at Christmas, he gave her a percentage of the company as her Christmas bonus. Five years after they opened BCC, they were best friends and she owned 25 percent of the business.

They had a good thing going. And somehow, now that she'd cut herself off from him, suddenly everything in his life seemed all wrong. Best friends were supposed to communicate. Paige knew that. Or at least, she always lectured him about communication whenever he got feeling down and wouldn't say what was bugging him.

He unlocked the gate at BCC and sailed onto the lot. Stopping the Lincoln in front of one of the bay doors, he climbed out and went around to the shop's side door, where he turned off the alarm and let himself in. A button by the bay sent the accordion door rumbling up. He pulled the Lincoln into the open bay, got out again and shut the bay door. It was sunny out, but only in the midthirties, so he turned on the heat.

The Lincoln, which he'd customized in a number of pretty cool ways, needed a little fine-tuning. *He* needed to let all this worrying about Paige go. She would talk when she was ready to talk. And when she did, he'd be there to listen.

In the meantime, BCC was closed for Black Friday and he had the whole place to himself. He could get the Lincoln purring like a kitten and ready for the day trader from Boulder who'd commissioned it from him. And then he might even get started on the already cherry '68 Shelby Cobra GT-500 Fastback that Deacon wanted pimped out with a whole new sound system and all the modern conveniences, including GPS. Deacon also wanted a rear spoiler, a modified grille and monster wheels with some really garish rims. It kind of seemed a shame to do that to a work of art like the Cobra. But Deacon didn't pay him the big bucks to suddenly get squeamish over messing with the classics.

Carter had a killer sound system in his shop. He turned on the radio to a hard rock station. As ZZ Top roared out, he zipped up his overalls and got down to it.

He didn't notice he had company until about an hour later, when he rolled out from under the Lincoln and headed for the inner door to the office and the little table in front of the window, where Paige kept one of those K-Cup machines. He had a nice hot mug of coconut mocha on his mind and had all but forgotten that he'd failed to relock the side door to the shop when he came in.

Whipping a rag from his rear pocket, he wiped the worst of the grease from hands and switched off the radio. He loved vintage Bruce as much as the next man, but sometimes a little silence was good for the soul.

As he turned for the front-office door, he registered movement out of the corner of his eye.

And then he saw her: Sherry Leland, his ex-girlfriend.

Sherry had taken the cover off the metal-flake candy-apple-red '67 Firebird just back from the painter's on Wednesday, and draped that killer body of hers across the hood.

"Hello, Carter." She gave him one of her come-and-get-me smiles. The smile matched her outfit: a red thong, a Santa hat and sky-high stilettos.

It was a testament to how over Sherry he really was that his first thought had very little to do with her being nearly naked. His first thought concerned how those pointy heels of hers had to be screwing up the Firebird's high-dollar paint job.

"Sherry," he said and tried not to sigh.

"I thought you'd never come out from under that car." She stuck out her plump lower lip in a sexy pout and tossed her long blond hair. "I'm starting to get kind of chilly." She fluttered her eyelashes and glanced down at her bare breasts. Yep. She was chilly, all right. "Come on over here, baby," she cooed. "Come here and warm me up."

"Sherry, I..." He really wanted to ask her to please get off the hood and be careful while she was doing it. But showing concern for the paint job right at that moment would only send her through the roof.

Her pout started to get kind of pinched looking. "What is the matter with you? I *missed* you. I'm here in this smelly garage of yours practically naked and it's all for you." The big blue eyes suddenly brimmed with fat tears. "I'm here to get past this little problem we've been having. I'm here to prove to you how much I want to work things out."

There was nothing to work out. They were done and she knew it, *had* been done for months now.

He spotted her black trench coat. She'd tossed it on top of the cover she'd whipped off the Firebird. So he stuck his rag back in his pocket, crossed to the coat, grabbed it and held it up for her. "Sherry, come on."

She sniffled. "How can you be so cold? You're breaking my heart. How can you do this to me?"

"Put your coat on," he coaxed.

"Fine. Sure." Sharp heels digging in, she scrambled off the hood. He tried really hard not to wince at the sight. She tossed her hair some more. And then she came at him, hands raised in frustration. "I hate you, Carter Bravo!"

"Sherry, there's no point in—"

"Hate you!" And she hauled back and bitch-slapped him right across the face. That shocked him. She'd never physically attacked him before.

Then all the fight went out of her. She crumpled, burying her head in her hands. The sobs started.

He gently wrapped the coat around her. "It's over," he said quietly. "You know it is."

She sobbed harder. "But I *love* you…"

He took her to the counter at the window between the shop and the office and whipped a few tissues from the box there. "Come on, now. Blow your nose."

She snatched the tissues and swiped at her cheeks.

He said sincerely, "I'm sorry, Sherry. For everything. Let me drive you home."

"Forget it." With a furious sniff, she shoved her arms in the trench he'd draped on her shoulders and tied the belt, hard. Then she raked her acres of hair off her face and aimed her chin high. "I'm not going anywhere with you."

He had no idea what to say next, so he said nothing. She wheeled on one of those pointy heels and stalked toward the side door, flinging it wide when she got there. That door was made of steel. It banged good and loud against the wall. "That does it, Carter. I am through. Finished. I hope I never see your face again."

He kept his mouth shut. He had a feeling that even the sound of his voice right then could have her storming at him all over again. Uh-uh. Better to keep quiet and stand still.

At his extended silence, she fisted both hands at her sides, threw her head back and let out a yowl of frustration. A second later, she disappeared from sight.

Carter stayed right where he was, hardly daring to breathe, until he heard the Camaro he'd rebuilt for her start up. She gunned it and then roared from the lot. He gritted his teeth, hoping against hope that she wouldn't run into anything, wouldn't hurt herself or anyone else.

As the sound of the engine faded into the distance, he let himself breathe again. And then, reluctantly, he took a good look at the Firebird.

Yep. Dents and gouges all over that hood. Resigned, he whipped the cover back in place. Monday, he'd get it back to the paint booth and tell the customer he'd need a few more days before the car would be ready.

It would be okay. Sherry would get over him and eventually move on.

He just wished he knew what was wrong with him. He just wished he could someday find a sane woman to get involved with. His mother had it right about one thing. He'd always known that someday he wanted a family.

Well, the years were going by. And someday was starting to look a whole lot like never. But what the hell was a guy supposed to do? He'd tried over and over and it always ended up the way it had with Sherry. This time, he had zero desire to find someone else and try again.

Chapter Three

Paige had a great day shopping in Denver with Carter's sisters and sister-in-law. She found a bunch of fabulous deals, giving her a serious head start on her Christmas list. The stores were all decked out for the holidays, and Christmas music filled the air, so the day really kind of put her in the holiday spirit. It was good to get out of town and it helped her achieve a little much-needed perspective.

She realized she needed to stop avoiding Carter. It wasn't his fault if she'd suddenly started thinking she might be in love with him—*might* being the operative word.

It was a magazine quiz, for God's sake. What fool took a magazine quiz seriously?

The next morning, there he was as usual when she came downstairs. Her heart leaped at the sight of his handsome face and sexy smile. She thought of how good he was to her and her sister, showing up to walk the dog and fix the breakfast even when she'd been avoiding him for days. That made her misty-eyed.

But Paige didn't let a leaping heart or misty eyes keep her from trying harder that morning. She made an effort to join the conversation, remembering to thank him, to praise his cooking and his coffee. More than once, she caught him glancing her way, questions in his eyes.

She waited until Dawn went back upstairs to call Molly and make plans for their Saturday, before she said, "I'm sorry I've been moody the last few days. Hormones. They drive me crazy sometimes." Yeah, it was a stretch. But not a total lie. She *had* been on her period.

"But you're okay now?" He looked so hopeful.

She promised him that she was. He poured himself more coffee, sat down beside her—and his cell rang. It was Mona, already at the shop, with some unexpected issue that needed his okay.

He said he'd be right over and hung up. "Gotta go. You coming in today?"

"I wasn't planning to." Paige had Saturdays off. Mona took Mondays and they were closed Sundays.

He was already reaching for his jacket. "Talk later? We've got lots to catch up on."

Paige answered him vaguely, "Yeah. Later. Sounds good." Did that mean he'd be over that evening? Was she ready for that? And speaking of talking, she needed to talk to someone about all this, get her head on straight when it came to Carter—and keep it that way.

He clicked his tongue for Sally. "Come on, girl. Time to go." Leveling those clear green eyes on her, he said softly, "Glad you're okay."

"Thanks." She gave him her brightest smile.

Sally at his heels, he left through the back door. Biscuit watched them go from his favorite throw rug at the end of the snack bar, dropping his head to his paws when they were out of sight.

With a grim little sigh, Paige got up and started clearing the table. She was busy wiping counters when Dawn reappeared, fully dressed this time in jeans and a thick blue sweater patterned with a band of snowflakes across the front.

"Molly's coming over in half an hour. We're going to practice together for the Christmas concert." They were both in the school band and in the orchestra, Paige on B-flat clarinet, Molly on flute.

Paige tossed the sponge in the sink—and made a decision. Dawn might be only eighteen, but she had a level head on her shoulders. Paige trusted her absolutely. Who better to confide in than her own sister?

Half an hour should be plenty of time.

Dawn was frowning. "You okay?"

Paige went ahead and answered honestly, "No, not really."

Dawn leaned her head against the doorframe. "You've been acting strangely for days now."

Paige marched to the table and pulled out a chair. "Got a few minutes?"

Dawn joined her, taking the chair next to hers. "Want me to call Molly, tell her to come later?"

"Nah. Half an hour should do it…" Where to even begin?

Dawn braced her chin on her hand. "I'm here. I'm listening."

Paige waded in. "So, last Monday Carter and I went to Denver to meet with one of our biggest customers.

We had to wait awhile to see him and Carter decided I needed to take this stupid quiz…"

Dawn made a sound in her throat, a little grunt of encouragement.

It was all Paige needed. She let the story pour out, about the silly quiz and how Carter answered all the questions for her and then announced that the quiz proved she was hopelessly in love with him. "I know it's ridiculous. He was just giving me a hard time the way he loves to do. But all his answers? They were the answers *I* would have given. And since then, I can't stop thinking about it. Can't stop thinking that the stupid quiz was right, that I'm actually in love with him, with Carter of all people. It's driving me crazy, Dawn."

Dawn reached over and gently squeezed her arm. "I can see that."

"So I want you to tell me the truth now. I want you to tell me that of course I'm not in love with Carter, that I've just gotten hung up on some meaningless magazine quiz and I need to let it go and move on."

Dawn made a pained sound and looked away.

Hesitantly, Paige reached out and ran her hand down Dawn's straight golden-brown hair. It was the same color and texture as their mother's hair had been. Dawn also had their mother's warm hazel eyes. "Dawn?"

Dawn looked at her then—and winced. "Really? I mean, seriously?"

Paige tried a laugh. It came out more like a sob. "Ridiculous, right?"

Dawn clapped both hands to her head, as though she was worried her brains might escape. "Ugh." And then she dropped her hands to the table, slapping her palms flat. "Dude." She rubbed the tender skin beneath her eyes. "I'm just not gonna lie to you. I think you need to get real, you know? I think it's better if the two of you just face the truth."

Paige's stomach lurched and sweat bloomed on her upper lip. "Um, what truth?"

"You've always been in love with him."

Paige gasped. "What the...? No. Uh-uh. Just no."

"Oh, come on, Paige. He practically lives here. You work together and you're best friends and he'd rather be with you than any of those smokin'-hot girlfriends he's had. Paige, come on. Everybody knows—everybody but you and Carter."

Paige slumped in her chair. "I don't believe it. You think I'm in love with him."

"I don't just *think* it, I know it. And he's in love with you."

That had Paige scoffing. "Oh, please. Carter doesn't do love."

"Carter doesn't *admit* love. It's two different things."

Paige let her head drop back and groaned at the ceiling, because honestly, how could this be happening to her?

"You actually wanted me to lie about it straight out." Dawn sounded hurt.

Paige sucked in a fortifying breath and faced her sister. "I'm sorry. Come here." She reached for Dawn, who resisted at first, but then swayed in her chair and finally let herself lean on Paige. Paige stroked her hair. "You're incredible."

"Yeah, right."

Tenderly, Paige admitted, "Okay, I confess. Sometimes it's a little scary to have such a brilliant and perceptive baby sister."

"I wouldn't have said anything," Dawn muttered. "I never have. But you asked me straight out."

Paige rocked Dawn a little, the way she used to do so often during that first terrible year after they lost Mom and Dad. "Please don't be insulted, but I need to ask you not to tell him."

"Of course I won't tell him," Dawn grumbled. "Have I said a word up till now?"

"No, you haven't. You're an angel."

"Hardly." She pushed free of Paige's embrace and said, "*You* need to tell him."

Paige only blew out a hard breath and slowly shook her head.

At 2:10 that afternoon, Carter was in his office off the shop studying engine schematics for Deacon's Cobra.

Someone tapped on the door.

"It's open." Carter glanced up from his laptop as the door swung wide.

Murray Preble, one of Carter's top auto parts vendors, stuck his head in. "Got a minute?"

"Sit." Carter gestured at the empty chair across the desk. Murray closed the door before folding his long, thin frame into the offered seat. Carter frowned. Murray never shut the door when he stopped in to say hi. "Is this a secret meeting, Murray?"

Murray, who was usually a pretty cheerful guy, didn't even crack a smile. "I guess you could say that. I need this to be just between you and me."

Carter shut his laptop. "Is there a problem?"

Murray scraped his hand down his narrow face and smoothed his thick black hair off his forehead. "Well, Carter, it's about Sherry."

Sherry? Murray wanted to talk about Sherry—with the door closed? Cautiously, he asked, "What about her?"

Murray shifted in the chair. And then he straightened up and put it right out there. "I'm in love with her."

This was news. And maybe good news. If Murray and Sherry got together, she would leave Carter alone. "Well, great. I hope you'll be very happy."

"See, that's just it." Murray hitched an ankle across the other knee and wrapped his long fingers around his shinbone. "I've been patient, I really have. But she just won't believe that you're never coming back to her." Murray's brow crumpled with his frown. "You're not, are you?"

"Hell, no. It's over with Sherry and me."

Murray didn't look encouraged. "She won't give me a chance."

"Murray. What do you want me to say? It's over. I've told her several times. I don't know what more to do."

"She spent last night cryin' on my shoulder over you." Murray glowered at him. "I waited long enough, you know? Months. It's time I got my chance with her. She's…"

"What?"

"I'm telling you straight, Carter. Telling you more than you got any right to know. She's a passionate person, as hotheaded as she is beautiful. I love that about her. I want all that fire directed at me."

Carter put up both hands. "More power to you, buddy. I'm not standing in your way."

"Yeah. Yeah, you are."

"Oh, come on."

"Carter. You are. You're standing between me and my future happiness."

"I don't know what to say to you. Sherry and I broke up a long time ago. It's as over as it gets. I don't see how I can make it any more clear to her."

"Move on, Carter."

"I *have* moved on."

"Choose someone new. As long as you stay unattached, Sherry can tell herself that you're coming back to her and I don't have a prayer of showing her that I'm the man she needs."

Carter shook his head. "I'm sorry, Murray. I can't help you with this. I hope you get through to her. But there's no way I'm up for trying again with someone new anytime soon. As long as we're putting it right out there, Murray, the truth is, I always make a mess of it with women somehow. I'm losing heart, you know? I'm about done."

Murray jumped up. He turned to the side wall and stared at the Prime Sports and Fitness calendar hanging there. November had an image of a gorgeous woman's back and shapely arms as she executed a lat pull on a Universal machine. "Well, how about Paige?" Murray asked without taking his eyes off the calendar.

It took Carter a moment to make sense of Murray's question—and even then, he didn't really understand it. "What do you mean, how about Paige?"

Murray faced him then. "I mean, why the hell don't you just settle down with Paige? Everyone in town can see that you two are meant for each other. And come on, you practically live together already. You sure you're not *already* with Paige and just keeping it a secret for some reason known only to the two of you?"

"Already with Paige? Have you lost your mind, Murray?"

"No, I have not. What I've lost is my heart. To Sherry. I want her to get over you and love me back."

"And I sympathize with that. I would *love* for her to forget about me and be all about you. I've told her it's over more times than I can count. I don't take her calls or answer her texts or her emails. If she drops in on me, I send her away. I've done everything I can to—"

"No. No, you haven't, Carter. You haven't shown it's over by moving on. And if you think about it a little, you'll see I'm right. You and Paige are a great match. And frankly, if you choose Paige, Sherry will definitely wake up and smell the coffee. She's always gone on about Paige, always believed that you're secretly in love with Paige."

Carter made a strangled sound. "Are you crazy? Of course I'm not secretly in love with Paige."

Murray grunted. "Sherry would never admit it, but we both know she sees Paige as the rival she couldn't beat."

"Uh, we do?"

A firm nod from Murray. "You bet we do. So if you and Paige finally get together, finally couple up and admit what's really going on between you, Sherry will have to accept that she's never getting you back."

Carter cleared his throat. "Murray."

"What?"

"I'm sorry, Murray, but no. Just…no."

Murray glared at him. "I'm only asking you to think about it."

"There's nothing to think about."

"What is the matter with you?" Murray practically shouted. "Why can't you see?"

"Murray, whoa. Chill."

But Murray did not chill. "Open your mind, Carter!"

He turned and flung the door open. "Open your mind and see the light." Murray left, slamming the door good and hard behind him.

Carter stared at that door for several very long seconds. And then he shrugged and opened his laptop again and put Murray Preble out of his mind.

Or tried to.

Unfortunately, Murray's weird visit stuck with him, made the Cobra engine schematics blur in front of him, made it so all he could think about was Paige.

"Open your mind!" Murray had yelled at him just before he slammed the office door.

Carter kept thinking about that. About his mind opening.

Opening like a door, a door that hadn't really been there before. He looked through that new open door and saw everything he wanted: marriage and a family.

To a sane and even-tempered woman.

A woman like Paige.

Because Murray was right. Paige was perfect for Carter.

No. Of course, he wasn't in love with Paige. He wasn't in love with anybody. Carter had no intention of going to the stupid place, thank you very much. But now that he'd opened that door, he could clearly see that Paige was just about as good as it got for a man like him.

How come he'd never realized it before?

Paige was smart and fun, and he loved being with her. She was completely reasonable, no drama, not ever. He worked with her and he hung with her and her little sister was family to him. Even their dogs were best friends.

He couldn't imagine his life without Paige. And to marry her and have kids with her...

Hot damn. That could work out. That could be good.

Carter got up from his desk and stared at the fine back and arms of Miss Superfit November as he worked out the kinks in the plan he was formulating.

Kinks like the fact that to have kids together, he and Paige would have to have sex with each other.

That could be weird. He'd never considered sex and Paige in the same sentence before—or wait. Scratch that. He *had* been attracted to Paige way back at the beginning. But then they'd decided to be friends without benefits and he'd accepted that.

So the idea of having sex with her didn't gross him out or leave him cold. It had just always seemed like a bad idea to go there, to take the chance of messing up a great friendship—not to mention a successful business partnership.

However, now that he'd let himself consider the concept of Paige as a bed partner, well, it didn't strike him as awful. He could get into it. He was sure that he could. And sex didn't necessarily have to screw up what they had. If they got married, that would only make their friendship and business partnership stronger.

Oh, yeah. The door was open, all right, open wide and showing him everything. It all fell into place.

He didn't have to be alone. He could get married and have a family, after all.

A family with his best friend.

A family with Paige...

Talk about huge.

Carter left BCC at a quarter after five that night. He'd planned to go home and shower, then take Sally and head over to Paige's.

But after opening that door in his mind and seeing a family with Paige on the other side, well, he wasn't quite ready to spend the evening with her. It was all too new and also a little bit scary.

He had to find just the right way to bring it up to her.

And he needed to find out for sure if they had the necessary physical chemistry together.

And hey. What if she just said no?

Uh-uh. He wasn't ready to see Paige. He could blow this whole thing before it even got started if he didn't handle it right.

So that night he stayed home.

Paige spent the day on household stuff. She bought groceries and baked a casserole, vacuumed and dusted the downstairs.

And the whole day she kind of dreaded the evening, when Carter would show up and she'd have to deal with him while knowing that her sister—and apparently most of the people they knew—believed that Paige was in love with him.

And that he was in love with her.

Awkward. Embarrassing. Too strange for words.

She hardly knew what to say to him—to Carter, of all people.

But then, as it turned out, he didn't show up.

And that just made her sad. So she put on some old yoga pants and a baggy sweatshirt, streamed a tearjerker on Netflix and ate a quart of Ben & Jerry's Chunky Monkey.

The next morning, Sunday, Carter considered chickening out again and not showing up at Paige's to walk Biscuit with Sally, not being there to get the coffee going.

But if he bailed on their usual routine again, he'd have to admit to himself that opening the door in his mind had freaked him out just a little—hell. Who was he kidding?

Opening that door freaked him out a *lot*.

But freaking out was no excuse to turn wimp and bail on his girls.

So he walked Biscuit with Sally as usual and then let himself back into Paige's quiet house and made the coffee.

He was standing at the fridge, staring inside, trying to decide what to make for breakfast as his brain kept insisting on circling back to the mind-altering concept of Paige and him and a houseful of baby Bravos, when he heard a soft sigh behind him.

A hot bolt of lightning seemed to surge across his shoulder blades and the hair on the back of his neck stood to attention. Bizarre.

He shut the door and turned around.

And there she was: Paige, leaning in the doorway, wearing that old plaid robe, flannel pajamas and silly fuzzy slippers he'd seen a hundred times. She'd tried to comb her hair, but she must have slept on it hard, because it still stuck up on the left side.

"Hey," she said. The single huskily spoken word seemed to hit him in the chest and then curl around him like a hug.

"Mornin'." Damn, she was cute. With those big brown eyes and that soft, pretty mouth. Not aggressively sexy, not showy like most of the women he'd dated. But hot in her own down-to-earth, *real* sort of way. The more he looked at her, the more he thought he could definitely tap that.

And wouldn't it be great to live here with her in the house she grew up in, to stop going back and forth between their houses? Her house was homier than his, a perfect place to raise their family.

If she would have him.

She was so smart. And she could be intimidating with that steady, unruffled way she had of looking at a guy. Since that bastard in college broke her heart, she didn't give her trust easily—not to men, anyway.

But he had a head start on that, being her best friend and all.

"What?" She straightened in the doorway.

"Nothing." It came out nice and calm, giving zero hint of the nervous energy churning inside him. "I was thinking eggs Benedict. I didn't make muffins, but I see you have some store-bought."

"Sounds wonderful." She went to the coffeepot and filled a mug, turning back around the way she did almost every morning, leaning on the counter for her first sip. A pleasured sound escaped her.

Would she make sounds like that in bed?

He realized he really wanted to find out.

The big brown eyes were soft and shadowed. He couldn't really read them. She said, "You're good to us, Carter. Thank you."

"I never did anything I didn't want to do." It came out gruff, low. It wasn't what he'd meant to say and he wondered where the hell it came from.

But those soft lips turned up in the beginning of a smile. "I know that."

"I like it here, with you. With Dawn."

"I'm glad."

He was maybe three steps away from her. It would have been so easy, to close the distance, take the mug, set it on the counter. Draw her into his arms…

"Carter, hey!" Dawn chirped from the doorway, shattering the moment. She joined him at the fridge, pulling the door open again and taking out a carton of orange juice. "What's for breakfast?"

"Eggs Benedict," said Paige.

"Yum. Just what I was I hoping for." Dawn edged around Carter, set the pitcher on the counter and opened the cupboard to get down the juice glasses.

Paige and Dawn got the table ready and he cooked the food. They sat down to eat. Things started getting really strange about then. He kept having the feeling that something was going on at that table between the sisters, as if they knew something he didn't and both of them were on edge about it.

They told him repeatedly, way more times than necessary, how much they loved his eggs Benedict. Then they started in on Christmas stuff—on how they were looking forward to Rocky Mountain Christmas, Justice Creek's big holiday shopping event next Saturday.

Next Saturday was also the date of the Holiday Ball at Justice Creek's world-famous Haltersham Hotel. It was a charity event to support the local children's shelter. Carter had bought a bunch of tickets at a chamber of commerce auction months ago and passed them out at the shop. He'd given some to Dawn and Paige, as well. At the time, he'd planned to take Sherry. When they broke up, he'd gotten Paige to agree to go with him.

He asked Dawn, "So, are you going to use those tickets I gave you for the Holiday Ball?"

She nodded. "Me and Molly and a couple of other friends are going together."

"Sounds good." He turned to Paige. "We still on for that?"

Her eyes looked enormous suddenly. She stammered out, "Uh, yeah. Sure. Of course, we are."

Dawn chimed in way too brightly, "I think it's going to be cool!"

Paige started talking again—as if she couldn't get away from the subject of the ball fast enough. Suddenly, she was all about how she needed to bring the Christmas stuff down from the attic. Dawn said she wanted to go to Molly's after breakfast, but she promised that later in the day, she'd come back and help with hauling the boxes down, and then they could maybe start on the tree.

Carter said, "I'll bring it all down for you, soon as we're through with breakfast." All the girlie chatter ceased abruptly. He looked at Paige and then at Dawn and then back at Paige again. "What did I say?"

"Nothing," said Dawn.

"You *didn't*," added Paige. "You didn't say a thing."

None of this made sense. They kept shooting each other looks. "What's going on here?"

"Nothing, really," Paige insisted. She and Dawn traded frantic glances that told him there was actually a whole lot going on here.

Women. He knew he had to give it up, that if they didn't want to tell him, he was never going to know.

He shrugged. "So, then…I'll get the Christmas stuff down before I go?"

"Um, great," said Dawn.

"Thank you," said Paige. "I'll help. It won't take long."

After the meal, he cleared off while Paige and Dawn ran upstairs to get dressed. Paige came down a few minutes later in jeans and an old flannel shirt, her hair tied up in a ponytail. He followed her back up to the attic, admiring the view the whole way. She filled out those worn jeans real nice.

At the top of the stairs, she hustled along the landing to the door at the end where a narrow set of steps led up to the area under the eaves. They went up. Paige pulled the chain on the bulb that hung from the rafters, and light filled the dusty space.

"Over here." She pointed at the stacks of plastic bins and cardboard boxes grouped together near the one small attic window that looked out the front of the house. Her eight-foot tree was there, in three sections, wrapped in heavy plastic for protection.

They went to work hauling everything down to the living room. It took several trips up and back. The whole time, he kept on the lookout for his moment—to try a first kiss, maybe.

Or to catch her arm, turn her toward him, tell her that he had something important to say...

But somehow the moment never came. She seemed in a really big hurry. And she actively avoided meeting his eyes. Whenever they happened to face each other in the process of turning to the stairs or grabbing for another box, her gaze would slide on by, not once connecting with his.

When he set the last bin down in the living room, she suddenly couldn't get rid of him fast enough.

"Whew." She gave him a blinding smile, at the same time letting her gaze skitter away to some point past his left shoulder. "That was easy. Thanks to you—and you're excused, Carter. I've got it from here."

Excused.

He was *excused*?

What did that even mean? Excused for the day? For freaking ever?

Forget it. He wasn't even going to ask. Instead, he suggested, "How about you let me help you get the tree upright before I go?"

For that, he got a blinding smile, one that seemed more than a little forced. "That would be great..."

So she grabbed the stand and set it up, centering it in the bay window that faced the front yard. They peeled the protective wrapping off the tree sections and she guided them into place as he lowered them.

After that, he figured she could manage the rest. And by then, he couldn't wait to get out of there. He called Sally in from the kitchen, took her leash and his jacket from the hook by the door—and left.

At home, he kind of settled down a little. He started thinking that he'd let his nervousness about approaching Paige as a woman—as a prospective bride, for crying out loud—affect his judgment.

There was nothing going on with Paige. Or with Dawn, either. He was the one with the problem. He felt edgy and unsure. He didn't know how to kick-start a conversation about forever—not with Paige. He'd never expected to be talking about marriage with her.

He needed more time to think about it. Too bad that thinking about it, so far, had gotten him exactly nowhere.

One thing for certain, though, he'd lose what was left of his mind if he spent the day hanging around the house. So he went on over to BCC, which was closed on Sunday.

Alone in the deserted shop, he played heavy metal at mind-numbing volume and went to work bolting the stupid spoiler to the trunk of Deacon's Cobra.

* * *

Paige had the Christmas carols playing and was arranging strings of lighted garland on the mantel when Dawn and Molly came in at noon. The girls made grilled cheese sandwiches and heated up a couple of cans of soup, then called Paige in to join them.

After lunch, Molly and Dawn pitched in with the tree and the other decorations. It was nice, really, with the holiday tunes playing and the three of them humming along, dragging Christmas treasures out of the boxes and bins and hanging them on the tree.

Molly, fuller-figured than Paige, with thick black hair and big dark eyes, spent so much time at their house she counted as a sister, too. Her parents had divorced the year before and Molly said she felt more at home with the Kettleman sisters than she did at her mom's house or at the condo where her dad lived with his new girlfriend. Paige and Dawn had taken care to stay on good terms with both of Molly's parents, so her folks had no issue with Molly hanging at Dawn's a lot of the time.

It was lovely, that Sunday afternoon, a holiday memory in the making—Dawn and Molly and Paige, getting the house ready for the holidays. Really, life lately was just about perfect.

Or it would be, if not for Paige's problem with Carter. Since the damn love quiz, she found it hard even to talk to him. She felt so nervous around him.

And it hurt him, the way she was behaving. She could see the confusion and pain in his eyes. He didn't know what was wrong. He didn't understand.

And she didn't know what to do about that.

Hold steady and wait? Only six days had passed since

that day at Deacon Leery's office. She couldn't help hoping that maybe this crazy feeling would fade.

Or maybe honesty was the best policy. Maybe she should just…bust herself to him. Tell him she was in love with him and let the chips fall where they may.

Paige cringed at the thought. How could that possibly go well? The man couldn't get away fast enough when women started using the *L* word around him.

And surely it was too early for such a drastic move. Dear God. This was *hard*.

Why now? It didn't even seem fair.

She'd finally gotten over her parents' deaths—or as over it as a person ever gets after something like that. She loved her job and business was good. Her sister was happy, graduating with honors in the spring. She had Carter for companionship. And now and then, she went out with attractive men, but refused to get bogged down in the responsibilities of a committed relationship.

Everything was just right.

Until this.

"You need to go talk to him," Dawn said.

Paige realized she was standing at the tree, staring blankly into space, a misshapen clay star she'd made in second grade dangling from one hand.

Molly, hanging a crystal snowflake from a high branch, nodded in agreement with Dawn. Paige realized that Dawn must have told her about the love quiz.

Which was okay with Paige. If you couldn't trust your honorary other sister, well, who could you trust? And Molly was every bit as respectful of a confidence as Dawn.

Paige hung the ugly ornament, tucking it in among the branches where it wouldn't be too obvious. "Funny,

I love the ugly ones as much as the pretty ones. Each one is a memory, precious. To be treasured, you know?" Tears blurred her vision. She dashed them away.

And Dawn said, "I mean it, Paige. Go!"

A sad little whimper escaped her. "You think? Really?"

"Yes, I do," Dawn declared.

"He's probably at the shop—"

"Go," Dawn commanded again.

Paige freshened up a little, put on minimal makeup and changed into red skinny jeans, ankle boots and a raglan-sleeved red sweater over a tan tank.

Dawn was waiting at the door, holding her coat.

Fifteen minutes later, she pulled her SUV in next to Carter's dually at BCC.

Would he be annoyed with her for butting in on his private time with his latest four-wheeled baby?

Too bad.

Dawn was right. Paige needed to talk to him. Needed to tell him...

What?

Better not think about that. If she started thinking, she'd never get out of the car.

She shoved open her door and jumped out, taking off at a run for the shop's side entrance. She could hear hard rock blaring, even through the thick walls and steel door.

He'd left it unlocked. She pushed the door wide. The loud music got louder. She hesitated on the threshold, but only for a second. Then, on shaky legs, she went in, pausing to shut the door gently and turn the lock, too.

The shop went dead quiet.

She whirled back around just in time to see Carter toss the stereo remote onto a workbench.

"Paige." His voice was so rough, but in the most delicious way. He wore old jeans, a black tee and an ancient navy blue hoodie. And he had a black smudge in the middle of his forehead. Had any man on earth ever looked so hot?

Nope. Never. Not in the whole history of humankind.

And the way he stared at her—as if he'd missed her, as if he hadn't seen her in years.

Sparks flashed across the surface of her skin from that look in his eyes. He looked…determined somehow.

What in the world was happening here?

And then he started moving, started coming toward her across the concrete floor. Coming *for* her, with…

Could that possibly be desire in his eyes?

Please. She must be dreaming. She blinked several times in rapid succession, to wake herself up.

But she didn't wake up. And by then, well, if this was a dream, she hoped she *wouldn't* wake up. Because Carter still had all that thrilling fire in his eyes and he kept coming until he was standing right in front of her.

She gasped as he reached out to cradle her face between his big strong oil-smudged hands. "Paige."

And then he kissed her.

Chapter Four

Dear sweet Lord in heaven.

He smelled so good. Like gasoline and the air right before a thunderstorm. Gasoline and ozone and something else, too, something so very Carter it made her heart ache.

His big hands were rough and warm against her cold cheeks. Amazing, that kiss. Those firm, hot lips of his at first gentle, nudging, brushing…

And then pressing harder as her own mouth gave to him, opening, letting him in.

His tongue. Rough and soft and hot and slippery. It swept the inner surfaces of her mouth, slid in between her upper lip and her teeth, tasting her, *knowing* her.

There was a groan. Hers? His? She really couldn't tell.

Wherever that low, purring sound came from, it echoed deliciously inside her head as his fingers threaded upward, combing through the hair at her temples, tracing the shape of her ear. Oh, those fingers. They caused a series of shivers like hot, fierce electric shocks to arc across her scalp.

Another groan. That one had definitely come from her own throat, the sound rising from the center of her, all quivery with need.

And still, he kept kissing her, touching her so lightly, running those rough fingers down the sides of her throat, around the back of her neck, clasping her, holding her in place.

So that he could kiss her some more.

Breathless, she was, dizzy with the wonder and the heat of it. Had there ever, in the history of time, been such a slow, hot kiss as this one?

Their first real kiss…

My God.

Imagine that.

Her knees were actually trembling. She had the strangest sensation of falling. At the same time, she was soaring. And his mouth just kept on playing with hers.

She managed to lift her own two hands and grab on to his big rock-hard forearms. That was the only way she kept herself from slithering to the concrete floor, just melting downward, knees collapsing, into a quaking puddle of wonder, confusion and lust.

It ended from overload. The pleasure, the wonder, the total disbelief that this could be happening between her and Carter…

It all swirled together until her head was reeling and her knees were knocking.

With a soft, lost cry, she broke the kiss and swayed against him.

"Paige…" He whispered her name as he gathered her in, those bulging arms of his holding on, holding her up.

With a sigh, she let her head fall against his big chest. "I can't believe…"

He chuckled, the sound vibrating thrillingly against her ear. "What?"

"You. And me…" She took a minute to breathe. Just breathe. His scent was all around her, that wonderful smell of rain and heat and axle grease. "Can't be happening…"

"Oh, it's happening." He caught her chin and tipped her face up so she had to look at him. He was so beautiful. Moss-green eyes, finely cut cheekbones, thick, scruffy hair. And that mouth…

Oh, my. That mouth…

He rubbed at her cheek with his thumb. "I got grease on you. Sorry."

Like she even cared. "It's okay. It's fine, really…"

He looked at her so hungrily, a look that made her face feel hot and the core of her feel heavy and lazy and ready for anything. "But I had to do that," he said. "I had to kiss you."

She stared up at him, drinking him in with her eyes—drunk on him, really. Her mind felt so slow, so foolish and thick. "Uh, you did? You *had* to kiss me?"

"Yeah." Beneath the scruff on his lean cheeks, a muscle twitched. "And I'm *glad* I did."

Her heart beat faster. With happiness. With hope. "Yeah?"

He had that determined look again. "Paige, there's something I need to talk to you about."

At that, her heart bounced skyward and got caught in her throat. She swallowed hard to make it drop back into her chest where it belonged. "Ahem. Um. Sure. Yeah. Go for it."

He took her by the shoulders and set her gently away, all the while holding her there with his eyes. "I'll just wash my hands. We can go in my office."

"This is starting to sound kind of scary…"

His still held her in place with those big hands. "You're looking a little freaked. You're not going bolt on me, are you?"

"Of course not." It was just that, well, she'd come to talk to *him*. And now suddenly *he* had to talk to *her*? What about? She forced a trembling smile. "Go on. Wash up. I'll wait right here."

He gave her shoulders one final squeeze and then he went to the metal closet next to the concrete sink in the corner. He took off the hoodie and hung it in the closet. She watched the broad, powerful muscles of his back shift beneath the black T-shirt as he flipped on the taps, soaped up and rinsed his hands and then washed his face and neck, too.

When he came back to her, the T-shirt was wet at the neck and he smelled of borax and Joy dishwashing soap, the familiar combination they used in the shop to get the engine grease off without taking the skin, too. That smell, so familiar, made her suddenly teary-eyed. Borax and Joy and all the years that she and Carter had been friends.

From casual friends. To good friends. To best friends. It had been a natural development, an almost imperceptible progression. Over time, they grew closer, their lives meshing at home and here at BCC.

She really liked being his best friend.

But all of that would change now, which scared her to death and broke her heart, too.

"You okay?" He stood right in front of her again, so big and strong and hot and beautiful. No wonder his women always ended up falling too hard. The old T-shirt fit him like a second skin. She could see the heavily cut musculature of his shoulders and chest, see those washboard abs. She could see all the things about him that she'd never really paid much attention to until recently. The *male* things, the things that now made her want him way more than could possibly be wise.

"Paige?"

She shook herself. "I'm fine. Yeah."

He lifted a hand—slowly, as though he feared he might spook her—and he guided her hair back from her face on one side, following the long strands down, smoothing them over her shoulder. An encouraging smile pulled at those lips she really wanted to kiss again. "My office?"

"Sure."

He let his fingers trail down her arm to clasp her hand. And then he pulled her along with him, across the shop to the inner door.

His office had the basics: desk, laptop, guest chair, file cabinet. And an ugly brown corduroy sofa on one wall. He dropped to the sofa and pulled her down next to him.

"See, it all started with Murray Preble." He eased one big arm along the sofa back and hitched a knee up to the cushions.

She took off her coat and didn't know what to do with it, so she tossed it across the sofa arm. "Murray the auto parts guy?"

"Yep." His bronze eyebrows drew together. "But first, there was Sherry."

Paige sat up a little straighter when he said his old girlfriend's name. "What about Sherry?"

He raked his spiky hair back with his fingers. "You were out of it when that happened."

"Out of it? Excuse me?"

"Don't get all prickly. It was last week. Black Friday. When you were in Denver with Nell and Jody and having those hormone problems, remember?"

She reminded herself not to get annoyed with him for bringing up hormone problems, the way men always did. After all, she'd *told* him it was hormones. "Right. I remember."

"I wanted to tell you all this sooner, but you haven't been talking to me—or even wanting me around."

She felt contrite then, she really did. "I am sorry, Carter. That I haven't been available, that we haven't talked."

"It's okay." He looked at her so steadily. "We're past it, right?"

She gave him a shy smile. "Yeah. We are. Totally past it."

He was staring at her mouth. "I really want to kiss you again." And his gaze shifted up to meet her waiting eyes. "You better stop looking at me like that. It's way too distracting."

A wave of sweet pleasure washed through her. He wanted to kiss her. *Wow.* This could be good. Really, really good. "Sorry." She tried her best to look unkissable. "Go on. It was on Black Friday…"

"Yeah. I was here, in the shop, working out the kinks

in Terrence Bolger's '61 Lincoln Continental. Sherry showed up…"

He went on to tell her all about Sherry in her thong and Santa hat and killer high heels. Paige ignored the twinge of jealousy as he related the story. Sherry Leland was drop-dead gorgeous. But Paige knew Carter. He'd been over Sherry for a long time now. She even felt a little sad for the other woman when Carter told her how he'd put Sherry's coat back on her and sent her on her way.

Carter continued. "Then on Saturday, Murray comes by. He wants a private word with me. Turns out, he's in love with Sherry and he wants me to find another girlfriend. He said that if I found someone new, Sherry would finally have to accept that it was over between her and me."

Paige couldn't help scoffing. "Murray wants Sherry, so *you're* supposed to find another girlfriend. Just like that?"

Carter grunted. "Exactly. I told him no."

"Of course you did."

"He got a little worked up. And then he started talking about you."

"Hold on. What have *I* got to do with anything?"

Carter eyed her sideways. "Don't get pissed off, now."

"I'm not. I'm also not following. Could you just answer my question, please?"

"Fine. Murray said I ought to get together with you."

Her throat clutched. "Um. With me?"

"That's right. He said that you should be my girlfriend. He said everyone in town knows that you and me are meant for each other."

Oh. My. Golly. Weakly, she asked, "They do?" She

couldn't believe it. Murray had told Carter what Dawn had told *her*, that everyone "knew" about her and Carter—except her and Carter.

Carter nodded. "According to Murray, you and me have a secret thing going on—so secret, we don't even know about it ourselves. According to Murray, Sherry has always felt that you're the one rival for my, er, affections that she could never beat."

"Wow." So there really was hope, then, for the two of them, maybe? Cautiously, she asked him, "So…what did you say then?"

Another grunt from Carter. "What do you think? I told Murray *again* that I'm not getting a new girlfriend just so that he can have a better shot with Sherry."

"Of course you're not," she echoed numbly, all her bright, shiny new hopes dying a thousand deaths. "That would be a really bad reason to start a new relationship."

"Because I don't *want* a new relationship."

Pull yourself together, Kettleman. It's not his fault if he's not interested.

But then, why had he *kissed* her?

Why had he said she made him want to kiss her *again*?

He was looking worried all of a sudden. "Er, Paige? You still with me?"

She drew her shoulders back. "Of course. I'm right here. I heard every word and…well, okay, then. That's settled."

Twin lines formed between his eyebrows. "What's settled?"

"That you're not just getting some girl to go out with because Murray can't stand the competition."

"Damn straight I'm not. But Murray did get me thinking…"

"Ah." She tried to appear interested in the usual best-friend sort of way. "Thinking about…?"

"You. And me."

"Wait a minute. You and me? What do you mean, you and me?"

He was staring off toward the fitness calendar on the far wall. "I wish I could describe it, Paige. It was like a door, you know? A door opening up in my mind."

"I am just not following."

"A door that swung wide…and there you were."

"Me?"

"Yeah. You. And it, well, it just hit me, you know?"

"What hit you?"

"What I want, what I've been looking for all this time…it's you."

A strange, squeaky sound escaped her. "Er, me?"

"I have a proposal, Paige."

This was all so very confusing. "I don't…what?"

"Just listen. Just let me explain."

"I…okay. All right, Carter. You go ahead, why don't you? You go ahead and explain."

Carter jumped up so suddenly that she gasped. She stared up over his lean hips and the very tempting hint of package displayed by the frayed zipper of his jeans. She took in his corrugated abs and broad chest so lovingly outlined by that old T-shirt. She skimmed his big shoulders, his thick, powerful neck, let her gaze track on up, until she was looking directly into his shining green eyes.

That was when he said, "I want us to get engaged."

Paige swallowed. Hard. "Engaged in what?"

"*Engaged*, Paige. As in 'to be married.' I want us to get engaged right now, today, and I want us to get married within a few months. I want to move into your house with you and Dawn. Because I want to be together with you—really together. Completely together. And that means marriage. That means children. That means a family, Paige. I want us to make a family."

Somehow she managed to sputter out, "But I don't—"

He cut her off, with enthusiasm. "Open your *mind*, Paige." He dropped to the couch again and took her chin in his big borax-scented hand. "Just open your mind and you'll see that it's perfect, *you're* perfect." He said it so tenderly her heart kind of melted. "And you've been right there in the center of my life for so long now."

"Oh, Carter…"

"You're everything I want in a woman. You've got heart, Paige. And a great sense of humor. You're good at math. Easy on the eyes…" He let go of her chin, but he didn't stop talking. "You're sane and smart and reasonable."

"Uh, thank you. I think."

"There's never going to be any big emo drama with you because I'm not in love with you and you're not in love with me."

There. That. All wrong. Not surprising, not in the least, coming from Carter. But all wrong for her.

Because she *was* in love with him. Desperately, damn it.

And he was still talking. "We're best friends, plain and simple. And who better for any guy to marry than his best friend?"

"Well, Carter, I…"

"You what?" He scrunched up his forehead at her, as though *she* were the one saying crazy things.

She suggested gingerly, "Well, you have to see that this is pretty out there, what you're suggesting, don't you think?"

"Out there? No. Not in the least. Yeah, I was a little bit concerned that we might not have any sexual chemistry given that, until now, it's never occurred to either of us to even fool around a little, when we're together practically 24/7. But hey. Now I've kissed you. I think we can both agree that the chemistry thing won't be a problem." Paige opened her mouth to say…she had no idea what. And he just went cheerfully on. "Paige. Really. I get that this is a lot to take in."

"You do, huh?"

"What is that? Sarcasm? Come on, Paige. How 'bout this? You think about it for a day or two, okay?"

"A *day* or two?"

"Yeah, that ought to be long enough, right?"

"But I—"

"Paige. I have one important point left to make to you."

"Ah. Well. Good to know."

"And my point is this…" He reached across the cushion between them, pulled her close and kissed her again, those amazing lips of his settling on hers so perfectly, his clever tongue delving in, his big arms all hard and hot around her.

Wow! Who knew just kissing could feel like this?

She'd been missing out big-time on the sex front, that was for sure.

When he finally lifted that amazing mouth off hers and grinned down at her, her head was spinning.

She told him so. "Carter. My head is spinning."

"What'd I tell you? Chemistry." That wonderful mouth swooped toward her again.

"Stop." She brought up her hands and pressed them flat to his rock-hard chest.

"Stop?" He looked hurt. "I thought you said you *liked* kissing me."

She resisted the urge to reach up and tenderly lay her palm along the side of his too-handsome face. "I do like kissing you."

"Well, then, what's the—?"

"I have things to say and I can't say them while you're making my head spin with your incredible kisses."

He let her go then. And he looked way too pleased with himself. "Incredible? My kisses are incredible?"

"Yes." She did her best to look stern. "Now, can we move on, please?"

He flopped back to his end of the ugly couch, stretching that big arm along the couch back again. "Yeah. Shoot."

She tried hard to order her thoughts—no mean feat when he looked at her as though he'd like to gobble her up for lunch. "I think we need to slow this down a little."

He shook his head. "No. Bad idea. What we need is—"

"Stop." She showed him the hand. "Listen. *I'm* talking now."

"Sorry." The gleam in his eyes said he really wasn't sorry in the least.

She proceeded before he could start in again. "I think you're really rushing this and there's no reason to rush."

"Wrong."

"Am I speaking or not?" she asked sharply.

He made a disgruntled sound, but then allowed, "Go ahead."

She did, quickly, before he could run over her some more. "Why can't we just slow down a little? Let's just, you know, go out together, like people do. *Be* together like two normal human beings. We can take it one day at a time, and see how it goes. Why do we have to get instantly *engaged*, for heaven's sake?"

He grinned his cocky, way-too-charming grin. "You know me, Paige. Go big. Or go home. I'm thirty-four years old. Now that I know what I want, I don't want to waste another day. I want to get going on this—and here's a thought. How about you just look at it as sort of a test-drive engagement, if that makes you feel better?"

"A *what*?"

"A test drive," he said, clearly tickled pink at the thought. "We'll test each other out, get a solid sense for whether or not we want to seal the deal."

"You can't be serious. Did you *have* to make a car analogy at a time like this?"

Those fabulous shoulders lifted in a lazy shrug. "Say you'll marry me, and we'll be together—I mean, *really* together—through the holidays. We'll let the whole town know that we're engaged. Then on New Year's Day we'll evaluate the situation and decide if we want to say I do."

"Evaluate?" Surely he hadn't actually said that.

Oh, but he had. "Yeah. Evaluate. You know, the way you always make me do when we have to come to a decision for BCC. We'll make a list of pros and cons and see which side is longer."

"Carter. I have to ask. What planet *are* you from?"

"Okay, yeah. It sounds a little crazy, I know."

"Crazy is too sane a word."

"I'm thirty-four, Paige."

"You said that already."

"And I'll say it again. I'm thirty-four and I want a family. And I've finally realized that you're the one I want my family with. I want to get moving on that. I see no reason at all for us to drag our feet—plus, hey. We'll be helping Murray out in the bargain. Now come back here." He reached for her again. She should have resisted. But somehow, well, it just felt so good when he put his arms around her.

"Don't you dare," she whispered, but it was really hard to mean it when she was all wrapped up in his embrace, feeling breathless—and suddenly yearning.

His lips were only an inch from hers. "Come on, Paige." He was so big and solid and he smelled so good. "It's just a kiss."

"I don't—"

"Just one?" he coaxed, all sweet and charming now. "Please?"

Somehow her hand had slid up to clasp the back of his neck. Her fingers brushed the blunt ends of his hair. "Oh, Carter…"

"Yeah?" His eyes were tender now, golden light gleaming within the green.

"Maybe just one…" She tightened her grip on the back of his neck. He let her do that, let her pull him down to her, until his mouth covered hers.

She moaned at the contact. He made a low, rumbling, satisfied sound in response.

His big hands roamed her back, and his hot tongue invaded her willing mouth.

Why, oh, why, did he have to be so good at kissing? It wasn't fair. No wonder the women who fell for him always had trouble letting him go. He got them all sexed up until they couldn't think of anything but his big hands and that plump mouth, so soft and pliant in comparison to the rest of him.

He lifted that mouth a fraction, whispered her name, "Paige…" and slanted his kiss the other way. She moaned again and his hands slid down to cup both cheeks of her bottom.

It felt so good, his hands holding her, palms spread, fingers digging in, his mouth taking hers. She lifted herself toward him, pressing her body closer, harder…

Really. Truly. This *had* to stop.

Gathering every ounce of will she possessed, she shoved him away again and scooted back to her side of the sofa.

"Paige, what the hell?" he demanded, rough and low.

They stared at each other across the width of the center cushion, both of them breathing raggedly. A hot flush burned on his cheeks, and his eyes were green fire.

She got up fast, before he could reach for her again. "Look, I…I don't know what to say."

But he did. "Say yes."

She smoothed her hair, tugged on her sweater, then snatched up her coat from the end of the couch. "I can't do this right now."

"When, then?" He growled the question.

"I…I don't know. Really, Carter. It's all too much. I have to go. We'll talk about this later."

"But when?"

"I don't know. A few days. I…need to think."

He started to say something else but then seemed to change his mind. He sprawled back against the cushions, all big and handsome and way too manly. "There's no point in running away, Paige. You have to know that."

Maybe not. But right at the moment, running away seemed like the only option.

She whirled and got out of there before he could try again to stop her—before she could weaken and admit to herself that all she wanted to do was stay.

Chapter Five

Dawn and Molly were putting the last ornaments on the tree when Paige got back to the house. Pentatonix sang "Mary, Did You Know?" in perfect harmony from the living room speaker dock.

Paige hung her coat in the front closet. Biscuit appeared, wriggling in ecstasy at the sight of her. She bent down and gave him a nice rub around the collar. He followed her to the open arch between the living room and the front hall, where she paused to admire the girls' work. "You two have a gift. It looks so beautiful."

Dawn got right to the real question. "What happened? Was he there?"

"Oh, yeah."

"And?"

"Ugh." Paige headed for the sofa, where she dropped to the cushions. "I cannot even tell you." She planted her face in her hands. With a whine of sympathy, Biscuit dropped to his haunches at her feet. Both girls ran to her. They nudged Biscuit out of the way and sat on either side of her, each throwing an arm around her so they shared a group hug.

Dawn asked, "Bad?"

Paige pulled her face out of her hands. "I just… I can't talk about it now."

Molly asked, "But are we *mad* at him?"

Dawn chimed in with "Molly's right. We need to know whether to yell at him or ignore him the next time we see him."

In spite of all the strong emotions roiling inside her, Paige couldn't help chuckling. "No, we're not mad at him. We're not ignoring him. We're not yelling at him—well, *I* might, eventually. But not you two. He hasn't done anything bad. Much."

"Well, now. There's a mixed signal," Dawn groused.

Paige hooked an arm around her sister's neck and kissed her cheek. "Just treat him like you always treat him. Remember, he loves you and he's always been good to us."

"But did he *reject* you?" Molly demanded.

"Far from it."

Both girls brightened. Dawn said, "So…it's good, then? You two are going to be together?"

"I don't know what's going to happen yet. I really, truly don't. You're going to have to let Carter and me work this out between ourselves."

"No fair." Dawn made a show of sticking out her lower lip. "I want details."

"Well, you're not going to get them. Just believe me when I say you don't have to worry. I'm okay, really. Carter and I are…just fine." Sort of. Maybe. "And I just want you to continue treating him the way you always have." She wrapped an arm around each of them and gave them both a squeeze. "Please?"

Reluctantly, they agreed.

An hour later, the empty boxes and bins were stacked in the front hall, ready to be stowed upstairs again until it was time to put everything away after the holidays. Dawn and Molly had a date with Molly's mom for Sunday dinner, after which the two girls would do homework and practice their music together. They gave Paige more hugs as they left for the house around the block where Molly had grown up.

Once they were gone, the place seemed too quiet. Not so great to be left all alone with nothing but her thoughts for company. She should fix herself dinner.

But she just didn't feel up to cooking right then. So she started hauling the boxes back up to the attic, Biscuit at her heels.

The doorbell chimed as she was coming down for the third time. At the sound, she got that butterflies-in-the-belly feeling. It might be Carter. He usually showed up for dinner Sunday night. And, except in the mornings when he walked the dogs before she got up and often came back and made breakfast, he always respected her privacy and rang the bell.

Definitely him. She could see the sleeve of his black leather jacket through the left sidelight. Sally peered in on the other side, tongue lolling, tail wagging. Biscuit scuttled right over there and sniffed excitedly at the bottom of the door.

Was she tempted not to answer? Definitely. She really wasn't ready to deal with him again.

But she longed to lay eyes on him. If felt like forever

since she'd last seen him, last kissed him, last felt those strong arms around her...

Oh, she had it bad. And really, how could that be good? She wanted his love—and he thought a test-drive engagement was a superfine idea.

Head up and shoulders back, she opened the door.

What do you know? The man of her dreams: Carter, big, bemuscled and hot as ever, dressed all in black, holding an extralarge Romano's pizza. "I come in peace." His hair was still damp from his shower and he'd actually shaved. "Got plans for dinner?"

She muttered defensively, "I was going to figure something out."

"But you haven't yet." He held out the box and the delicious smell grew stronger. "Sausage and mushrooms. Your favorite."

Sally slithered around her as Biscuit chuffed a happy greeting. "Your dog's already in. I guess I have to be nice and let you in, too."

He gave her that grin, the one that made women's panties spontaneously combust. "You want the pizza, you have to put up with me. Package deal."

"Why is it that everything good seems to come with conditions?" She stepped back and gestured him in.

"Dawn?" he asked as he handed her the pizza.

"She's at Molly's till ten."

He hung his jacket on the peg by the door. Underneath, he wore a black, long-sleeved Henley. He shoved the sleeves up those fine corded forearms and tipped his head at the empty Christmas boxes stacked by the stairs. "You want these put away before we eat?"

She was trying so hard to think bad things about him.

But no, he just had to be his usual thoughtful, generous, helpful self. Too bad he was also a man who never really let his girlfriends get all that close, a guy who came up with totally out-there ideas like a test-drive engagement.

"Thank you," she said sweetly. "Getting these boxes to the attic would be wonderful."

"So stash the pizza and let's get after it."

She took the pizza into the kitchen and left it on the snack bar, then rejoined him in the front hall, where she found him leaning in the arch to the living room, one hand stuck in a back pocket. "The tree looks great."

She went and stood beside him. "Yeah. It's that time of year again…"

Now he was watching her. "You're a sucker for Christmas."

"My mom was, too." Paige tried not to stare too long at his mouth, tried not to think of how fine it felt locked on to hers. "My mom collected every last decoration and ornament we ever made in school."

"And you still have them all."

"Oh, yes, I do." The glance they shared had gone on for way too long.

Finally, he said softly, having heard all this before, "And you miss her most this time of year."

"Yeah." Her last memories of her parents were of that final Christmas. They did all the best Christmas things that year, cut down a live tree, made dozens of cookies and way too much divinity and fudge. They'd decked the house up right. There was snow. They all went sledding. "I can still see us, the four of us and Granny Kettleman." Granny had died two years later. "I see us all sitting around the candlelit table in the dining room for

Christmas dinner, holding hands as Granny says grace. In my memories, it's all so perfectly corny and wonderful, like one of those old Norman Rockwell paintings." Actually, her then-fiancé, Jim Kellogg, had been there that Christmas, too. But somehow, in her memories, she'd managed to blot that jerk right out of the picture.

That year, Paige and Jim had gone back to school two days before New Year's. A week later, her folks went skiing for their anniversary, just the two of them. Dawn had stayed with Molly's family so Mom and Dad could have a special romantic getaway...

Carter's hand brushed her shoulder. "Hey."

She blinked and brought herself back to the moment, to Bing Crosby singing softly in the background, to the Christmas lights on the tree in the bay window. Carter's finger brushed up and down the side of her neck.

Shivers sparked and burned where he touched her. She shouldn't encourage him. Still, it seemed the most natural thing to step in closer. He tipped up her chin with his thumb and lowered his lips to hers.

Paige sighed when his mouth touched hers in a beautiful, sweet kiss. A kiss of comfort and understanding, with just a hint of fire beneath the careful tenderness.

Too soon, he lifted his head. "So. The boxes?"

She nodded. "The boxes. Please."

Once the work was done, they headed for the kitchen. Carter put down fresh kibble for the dogs and then they took the pizza and some beers into the living room. She flipped the switch beside the fireplace and cheery flames licked the fake logs.

They shucked off their boots and got comfy on the sofa, the pizza box open on the coffee table in front of them. He grabbed the remote and turned on the in-progress Broncos game.

Half an hour later, after two fourth-quarter touch-downs, the Broncos were a game up on San Diego in the division race and the giant pizza was all but decimated.

"'Nother beer?" she offered, feeling pretty good about the evening, really. If she didn't let herself think about his outrageous proposal and smoking-hot kisses of that afternoon, she could almost pretend that they were back to the way they'd always been, Carter and Paige, best friends forever.

He nodded. "'Nother beer would be good."

So she took the empties to the kitchen, returning with two fresh ones. She set his on the coffee table in front of him and dropped to her end of the sofa, drawing her stocking feet up yoga-style and assuming either he would change the channel or they would now watch the after-game talking heads.

But Carter only turned off the TV and tossed the remote on the side table next to him. "Come here," he said, leaning back against the sofa arm and actually crook-ing a finger.

She stayed right where she was. "What? You think I'm Sally all of a sudden?"

He chortled. Apparently, he found her so very amus-ing. "You're always so cool, Paige. Lately, I've been thinking that your being cool is damn hot." He gave her a long, low-eyed look. She felt his gaze tracking, down over her red sweater and jeans, to the Christmas tree socks she'd put on to feel festive—and then right back up again until he once more met her eyes. "There's so much I never realized about you before, so much I want to do with you."

Speaking of hot, maybe she ought to turn off the fire…

"And *to* you," he added in that low, rough voice that made her want to do things to him, too. He lightly nudged her knee with his toe. "Come on over here so I can show you how much I like you."

She chewed on her lower lip for a moment, truly torn. She *wanted* to go there. She wanted it bad. "You're supposed to be giving me time, remember?"

He said a swearword under his breath—and then, lightning quick, he sat up, reached out and grabbed her arm. She smacked at him with her free hand.

That didn't stop him. He just held on and hauled her back with him, pulling her on top of him, stretching out with his head on the sofa arm and her all over him like a blanket.

She glared down into those gold-flecked green eyes. "This is not fair."

He lifted himself up, but only enough to catch her lower lip between his white teeth. She gasped at how disgustingly good it felt. He worried the tender flesh briefly and then let it go. "Where'd you ever get the idea it was going to be fair?"

Her lip tingled where he'd bitten it—not hard, oh, no. But sharply. Excitingly. Her hips were pressed to his, her breasts to his chest. It was like stretching out on a flesh-covered slab of rock—hot rock. All of him, chest, belly and lower down, all hot. And under the fly of his black jeans, things were not only hot, but getting harder, too.

Before she could remember that she needed to stop him, he eased a hand up under her hair to cradle the back of her head. And then, so gently, he guided her down until her lips settled over his.

She groaned—a groan of protest that somehow came out like a moan of pleasure instead. He smelled all showered and fresh, and he tasted of beer and the promise of great sex. And then there was all that rock-hard hotness going on.

His hands roamed her back, sliding down and cupping her bottom the way he'd done at the shop, cupping her and pulling her closer, making sure she could feel every inch of that hardness beneath the fly of his jeans.

She wanted to drag him up the stairs to her bedroom and have her way with him. Repeatedly.

But she was not going to do that. No way. She was *not*.

"Not, not, not," she moaned as she made herself pull her mouth free of his. She glared down at him and tried to come up with the right words to make him see how wrong it was for him to keep taking advantage of her like this.

But then he said, "So, then. I'm thinking tomorrow I'll take you to Denver to pick out the ring."

"What did you just say?" She gaped down at him. Since this afternoon, she'd been doing a whole lot of gaping.

"The ring, honey. We need to get you an engagement ring."

Honey? Oh, no way. With a cry of frustration, she scrambled off him, sliding her feet to the floor and bouncing to a standing position. Bracing her fists on her hips, she glared down at him. "May I remind you— *again*—that you're supposed to be giving me time to think over whether any good at all can come from this crazy idea of yours?"

He laced his hands behind his big fat head. "And I've decided that you've got it all wrong."

"Wrong?" She made a few sputtering sounds.

And he blithely continued. "Yeah. You're wrong. It's not time yet for you to think it over."

"Not *time*?" She raised both hands, palms to the ceiling, and then let them flop in complete frustration to her sides. "What are you even *talking* about?"

"Very simple. First, we have to get through our trial engagement, see how it goes, you know? And *then* is when the thinking part comes, meaning that's when we consider whether or not to actually get married."

"But I haven't even decided if I—"

He put up a hand. "Hold on a minute." He winced as he sat up, and then he cast a rueful glance at the obvious bulge in the front of his jeans. "Look what you did to me, Paige."

"What *I* did?"

He had the nerve to nod. "Sex is important, Paige. And we need to start having some. But you gotta agree that it wouldn't be a good example for Dawn, if I'm in your bed and we don't have any kind of formal commitment."

"Formal commitment?! It's a fake engagement you're talking about here."

He dared to look wounded. "It's not fake, no way. Just because we're testing the waters, that doesn't make it fake."

That did it. "I can't do this right now. You've got me so turned around, I can't think straight. You need to go."

Shaking his head, he reached for his boots and put

them on. She stepped back as he rose. Sally, by the fire, got up and followed him into the front hall, Paige trailing after.

He took his jacket from the peg and put it on, grabbed Sally's leash, then wrapped those long, strong fingers around the doorknob.

But then, instead of pulling it open, he reached for Paige again.

This time she was ready for him. "Oh, no, you don't." She jumped back before he could grab her.

"Let down your guard, Paige." Now his voice was rough and low. He coaxed, "Come on. Have a little faith. It's going to work. Just give it a chance and you'll see it's the right thing for both of us."

God, when he looked at her like that—eyes all hot and full of feeling, as though there was no other woman in the world but her…

It wasn't a good idea, this wild plan of his. But she really, really wanted to go with it anyway. She wanted to have sex with him. She wanted to *be* with him, desperately, be his woman, his fiancée—even if it only lasted till Christmas.

Which was most likely just what would happen. She'd be crying by Christmas, her life a complete mess.

She tried to make him admit that. "You're refusing to see the whole picture here. We work together, we're best friends. This idea of yours could ruin everything. It could completely destroy what we have."

"No way."

"Carter. Come on, think about it. *Really* think about it. What if it doesn't work out? What if…one of us falls in love and the other doesn't?" *What if one of us is al-*

ready in love? "What if it ends up destroying our friendship, our partnership, everything? Then what?"

He just wouldn't listen. "That's not going to happen."

"You can't be sure of that."

"Yes, I can. Nobody's falling in love. That's the beauty of it. We know who we are with each other. We're going to have a great life together, Paige, a *happy* life. That falling-in-love crap isn't going to happen to us."

But it's already happened to me.

And yes, she should simply tell him that. But she couldn't make herself do it. She knew what would happen if she did.

He'd be out the door in an instant. How sad was that? She was in love. And she wanted a chance with him. She couldn't stop thinking that this ridiculous test-drive engagement of his was the only way for her to get her chance.

Her chance to have everything—and also, her chance to lose it all. "I mean it, Carter. You have to give me some time. You have to let me think it over."

"How long?" he demanded. He clicked his tongue at Sally. She trotted over and he bent to clip on her leash.

"You've got to give me a week without pressuring me." Sally looked up at her as she spoke—and then turned to Carter when he said, "A week's too long. We need to move forward."

"Not until I have time to think about it."

"Two days." Carter glared at her as if he wanted to strangle her—strangle her or grab her and tear all her clothes off.

She glared right back at him. "I can't believe I'm bargaining with you about this."

"Two days." He growled the words. "And then we're on."

"Two days and then *I* decide."

"You always have to have it your way." His voice was hard. Cold.

Her heart ached. But she stood her ground. "Two days. Absolute minimum."

"Fine. Two days. And then you decide."

Chapter Six

The next morning when Paige went downstairs, there was no sign of Carter. No perfect pot of coffee brewing, no delicious bacon sizzling in the pan. Just Biscuit whining at the door to get out.

She walked Biscuit, made the coffee herself and fixed breakfast for her and her sister.

Dawn had questions. "How come Carter's not here? Is this about you and him? Is he having trouble dealing with your telling him how you really feel?"

Paige debated explaining everything. But no. Her baby sister didn't even need to hear it. And Paige certainly didn't feel like telling it.

She evaded Dawn's questions.

At work, Carter kept his promise. He was civil and distant. She hated it, the distance. Yes, he was only giving her what she'd asked for. She knew that. Still, she missed her best friend.

The next day, Tuesday, he was out of town trying to track down a car for another rebuild. His absence made things a little easier. She could almost pretend that everything was as it used to be. Except for the ache in her heart, which wasn't as it used to be at all.

That night, Paige was no closer to knowing what to say to him than she'd been when she asked him to give her some time. Tomorrow, she needed to give him an answer. Unfortunately, she didn't have one.

Thus, at two in the morning, she remained wide-awake, tossing and turning in her bed.

If she'd been asleep, she might not have heard the tap on the window. That probably would have been for the best.

But she did hear it. And instead of ignoring it, she shoved back the covers and went to investigate. Biscuit jumped down from the end of the bed and followed her over there. Slowly, she eased the blinds open.

The window overlooked the side yard. In the faint gleam of starlight and the soft spill of the streetlamp bleeding in from the curb near the front of the house, she saw that a light snow was falling. She also made out the shape of a man hunched on the slope of roof right beyond the glass.

Carter.

Of course.

His eyes gleamed through the slit in the blinds. "Let me in, Paige." The window muffled the words. Still, she heard him.

So did Biscuit. He whined in delight at the sound of Carter's voice and his tail got going like a metronome, slapping at the back of her calf.

Serve the man right if she just shut the blind all the way again and went back to bed.

But knowing Carter, he would only keep tapping, calling her name louder, until she gave up and let him in.

She yanked the blind up. The window opened to the side. She pressed the latch and pushed it wide. Cold air and the smell of a winter storm had her wrapping her arms around herself and shivering.

His white teeth flashed with his grin. "For a minute there, I was afraid you'd tell me to get lost."

The screen remained between them. "I'm still debating that," she muttered. "What are you doing on my roof?"

"Getting to you."

"Maybe you've forgotten." She ladled on the sarcasm. "I'm supposed to have till tomorrow to give you an answer."

"It *is* tomorrow," he announced way too loudly. "Get rid of the screen."

"Shh!" She cast a glance at her bedroom door, which was shut. But still. Noise tended to carry in the middle of the night. "Keep your voice down. You'll wake up Dawn."

"Sorry." He didn't sound one bit contrite, but at least he'd lowered his voice again. "The screen…?"

She gave in, grabbed the little tabs at the base and eased it out of the frame, pulling it into the room and propping it against the wall, then stepped aside to make way for him. He extended a long leg over the sill, turning his thick shoulders sideways so they would fit through the opening. For a moment, she dared to hope the window was too small for him. But with a little maneuvering, he was in. "Brrr," he said, turning to slide the window shut. "Brisk out there." He seemed to fill up the room with his big self and the cold, wet smell of the snow that clung to his shoulders and dusted his hair. Biscuit whined again. "Hey, buddy." Carter dropped to a crouch and started scratching his ears. "Turn on a light. It's dark in here."

She trudged to her tangled bed, dropped to the edge of the mattress and flipped on the lamp.

Carter rose again. She watched as he shrugged out of his heavy jacket and tossed it on a chair. "Biscuit. Lie down." He snapped his fingers and pointed at the doggy bed on the corner. The dog trotted right over there and flopped down, which totally annoyed her. She could never get that dog to go to his bed, but Carter made it happen on the first command.

"You look cute in those pajamas," he said. "What are those, dogs?"

"Dachshunds," she muttered glumly. "Dachshunds in Christmas sweaters and holiday beanies."

He came to her then and sat down beside her, bringing the tempting scents of winter and manliness and a faint hint of aftershave right along with him. "Cute." He fingered the soft flannel of her sleeve.

She pulled her arm free. "It hasn't been two whole days and you know it."

"I couldn't wait." He nudged her with his elbow. Gently. And then, low and hopefully, he asked, "So, what's the verdict?"

She stalled, like the big fat chicken she was. "Why couldn't you just come in the front door like a normal person?"

He frowned. "I don't know. It seemed kind of wrong to just let myself in at two in the morning. And I didn't want to ring the bell and wake Dawn up, get her all freaked out, wondering what's going on…"

"Right." She wanted to stall some more, get all up in his face for disturbing her in the middle of the night, insist that he could have waited for daylight, at least. But instead, she stared into his wonderful, beloved face and admitted the awful truth. "God, Carter. I missed you."

Which, of course, had him smiling that knee-melting smile. "You did?"

She gave it up completely. "Yeah. A lot. I missed you a lot." And then she hung her head and scowled down at her flannel-covered thighs.

"Hey," he said so softly, so coaxingly. And he caught her chin with a gentle finger and made her look at him. His eyes twinkled much too brightly and he teased, "Merry Christmas to me."

She made a snorting sound, but he didn't let that stop him. He just eased his other arm around her shoulders and drew her close to his side. She went without protest. After all, close to him was exactly where she longed to be. She lifted her chin for him when he guided it higher so he could claim her mouth.

A kiss ensued. A fabulous, wet, hot, very long kiss.

Still kissing her, he eased her back across the bed. She gave in to his urging, lifting her arms and wrapping them around him, kissing him some more.

However, when he started unbuttoning her pajama top, she caught his hand. "Stop." She opened her eyes and waited.

Eventually, he lifted himself away from her just enough to demand, "What now?"

She put on her sternest expression. "Carter. I mean it. You have to slow down…"

"Whatever you want." He sat up.

She sat up, too. Tugging her pajama top back into place, she made a halfhearted attempt to smooth her tangled hair.

When she looked at him again, he was holding out the most beautiful diamond ring she'd ever seen. Even in the dim light from the bedside lamp, the gorgeous thing really sparkled. "What in the…?" Words failed her. That happened a lot around him lately.

"Be my fiancée, Paige." He caught her hand and slipped it on. Perfect fit, wouldn't you know? The enormous oval diamond winked at her from the bead-set platinum band.

"My God, Carter." She held it toward the light and the big stone glittered madly. "This looks like the real thing." She glanced at him accusingly.

His fine mouth flattened out. "Of course it's the real thing."

"It must have cost a fortune. Did you ask them what kind of return policy they had?"

"Will you for once in your life not worry about the damn money?"

"Someone has to. You never do."

"Only the best for my fiancée." He slid over nice and close again and went back to work unbuttoning her jammies.

Paige looked down at his big hands as he slipped the first shiny red button free of the button hole—and just like that, it all came painfully clear to her.

She knew exactly what she had to do.

"Carter." She took off the ring, removed his hand from the second button of her pajama top and placed the beautiful diamond in the middle of his calloused palm.

"Damn it, Paige. What's your problem?" He shot her a hot, wounded glance. "It's a no? How can it be a no? I thought you said you missed me. I thought—"

She put a finger to his warm, beautiful lips. "Shh. It's not a no."

Twin lines formed between his eyebrows. "I don't get it."

Her heart trip-hammered against her ribs. "There's something I have to tell you before I can give you a yes."

A relieved sigh escaped him. "Fine. Go for it." He waved the diamond at her. "And then take this damn ring back so we can get on with the plan."

Slow, careful breaths, she reminded herself. It had to be said. He really needed to know. "Remember that silly magazine quiz you took for me the Monday before Thanksgiving, when we were waiting for Deacon Leery to see us?"

"What's that got to do with anything?"

"Bear with me. Do you remember?"

"Yeah. What about it?" He gazed at her blankly, waiting for the punch line.

She delivered it. "Well, Carter, you were right. You answered every one of those question just as I would have. And they were excellent questions, really. Which is why that was the day I realized I'm in love with you."

His eyes widened—and not in a good way. "You... *what*?"

She took another slow, deep breath and said it again. "I'm in love with you, Carter."

He shot off the bed, turned and backed toward the window. Shaking his head, he accused, "You're lying," in a low, furious whisper. "And that quiz? I was only messing with your head, only having a little fun, that's all."

Sadness weighed her down. Yeah, she'd known he hated it when women said the *L* word. Still, she'd kind of hoped he might react differently if the words came from her. So much for hope. Stifling a sigh, she rebuttoned her top button. "I know it was only a joke. To you."

"Uh-uh. No." He stuck the ring in his back pocket. "You're not in love with me, Paige. You're too smart for that crap. This is just your way of getting me to back off."

Was there ever a man as thickheaded as this one? "I'm not lying, Carter." She made herself look him straight in the eye. "I'm in love with you and if I did say yes to you, it would be because you, um, fill up my heart and make my world better. Because you're hot and I want you. A lot. Because I love to be with you and you make me laugh and I can always count on you. Because you make my coffee just the way like it. Because you're both a stand-in dad and a big brother to my baby sister." She tried a wobbly smile. He didn't return it. "But I *would* be dishonest to go into this, er, engagement plan with you if I didn't tell you upfront how I feel. So I'm telling you. I'm in love with—"

He threw up both hands. "Stop saying that." He scooped up his heavy jacket from the chair where he'd tossed it. "I…can't tell you that back. I'll never tell you that. I don't believe in that, you know I don't."

She did know. The guy just wasn't going to the love place. He'd always been perfectly clear on that.

And what did he think? That this "awful" revelation had been easy for her? It hurt to see that horrified, get-me-out-of-here look on his face. It hurt a lot.

Still, she'd done it. She'd told him the truth about the state of her heart. Now they could move on. "Well, all right, then. We can give up this crazy test-drive engagement plan and go back to the way it's always been."

"No," he argued, for no possible reason that she could see. "Did I say I wanted to call it off? I never said that."

"But, Carter—"

"No, Paige. I mean it."

"You mean what?"

"I just need a little time to deal with this information, okay?"

"Um, sure." Had she ever in her life had such a bizarre conversation? Not that she could recall. "Take all the time you need."

He shoved his arms in his jacket. "You know, you're acting really...sane about this, I have to say."

"Uh. Thanks."

"You're amazing, Paige. One of a kind."

"Wow. Great," she replied without much enthusiasm.

"I just need to think this over a little."

"No problem."

He turned and slid the window wide. A gust of wind and snow swirled in as he faced her again. "We'll talk."

"Sounds good." Paige wrapped her arms around herself against the sudden chill.

He actually attempted a smile. "Well, all right. Night, then."

"Night, Carter."

And he turned again, squeezed his big self out onto the roof and disappeared from sight.

Biscuit woke her before dawn. He stood at the bedroom door, whining to be let out. She crawled out of bed and opened the door. He left.

But not fifteen minutes later, he was back again, sitting at the side of the bed, his tail sweeping the rug, panting and staring up at her hopefully. She knew what that look meant. Carter had not come by to walk him.

"Fine," Paige grumbled. Biscuit wagged his tail harder. "I'm coming, I'm coming..." She shoved back the covers and got dressed.

Outside, beyond the front porch, a thin blanket of white covered the yard and the walk. Snow dusted the hedge tops and clung to the branches of the evergreens.

"Pretty, huh, baby?" she asked the dog. Biscuit whined and tugged the leash. "Heel," she said firmly.

For once, he obeyed, falling back to his place at her side. They went down the steps and out to the sidewalk. She walked him around the corner, down three blocks, and then back home, stopping to let him take care of business, her plastic bag at the ready.

The neighborhood looked so beautiful all covered in white. Most of her neighbors already had their lights and wreaths up, some had even left the lights on all night. So cheery and Christmassy. It really lifted her spirits.

She was smiling when she got back to the warm, cozy house. She went straight to the living room and turned on both the tree and the mantel lights.

Dawn came down as she was scooping coffee into the coffeemaker. "No sign of Carter, huh?"

Not since about two-thirty this morning. "Nope. Poached eggs?"

"Sure. Don't ever tell him I said so, Paige. But I miss him when he's not around."

"Your secret is safe with me."

Dawn went to the cupboards to get down the plates,

mugs and flatware. "Looks like we got about three inches of snow."

"Yeah. It's gorgeous out there."

Dawn carried the plates over to the breakfast nook. "So, are you two going to work out this, um, whatever it is that you're not explaining to me?"

"We definitely are," Paige replied with a lot more confidence than she felt. "Eventually."

At nine, when Paige walked into BCC, Carter was already busy in the shop. He hardly spoke to her that day. She returned the favor. Friday was pretty much the same.

By Friday evening, all the snow had melted. Paige drove home through the snow-free streets, telling herself that it was all for the best. She'd done the right thing, to lay all her cards on the table with Carter. In time, she would get over him. He would stop feeling he had to avoid her. They might have a nice, straight-ahead talk about how foolish they'd both been.

And then their relationship could go back to the way it used to be.

In the meantime, she would be fine. Tomorrow was her day off. She didn't even have to set eyes on the man. She would go to Rocky Mountain Christmas on Central Street and shop until she dropped.

That night, Dawn and Molly went to a party at a friend's house. Paige raided her DVD stash and found *Love Actually*, *While You Were Sleeping* and the Wynona Ryder version of *Little Women*. She watched them back to back, with a carton of Ben & Jerry's and a jumbo bag of peanut M&M's for company.

She told herself how great it was that Carter wasn't there. He would have insisted on watching *Bad Santa* or something equally gross, guy-centric and R-rated.

She didn't need him. Uh-uh. She and Ben & Jerry were doing just fine on their own.

Dawn came in at midnight. They watched the end of *Little Women* together. When they went upstairs, Dawn took Biscuit to her room. The dog was a total bed hog, so Paige could look forward to tossing and turning without him in the way. She washed her face and brushed her teeth and donned her other Christmas pajamas—green flannel with dancing elves. Ho-ho-ho and all that jazz.

The last few nights had been awful. She'd hardly slept at all, her mind on Carter and her hopeless love for him and the best friendship she missed so much. That night, she assumed, would be pretty much the same, probably with a little indigestion thrown in from all the ice cream and candy.

But she climbed into bed and turned off the lamp— and must have fallen asleep right away. The next thing she knew, she heard a sound at the window.

"Huh?" She gaped at the bedside clock. It was ten after two.

Tap-tap-tap. "Paige?" *Tap-tap.* "Come on, let me in…" *Tap-tap-tap…*

Paige popped to a sitting position. *Carter.* At the window.

Again?

She blinked away sleep and raked her hair out of her eyes and refused to get excited at the prospect of seeing him.

"Paige." More tapping. "Come *on*…"

"Fine." She turned on the lamp, pushed back the covers and took her time crossing the room. Drawing up the blind, she slid the window back.

"Hey." He gave her a happy grin.

"This has got to stop, Carter."

"Don't be cranky. I needed to see you."

"I was sound asleep."

"Sorry."

"You're out of control, you know that?"

Now he put on his pitiful face. "The screen. Please?"

She gave in and pulled it free of the frame. Once he was in, she folded her arms tightly across her middle and ordered, "Shut the window. It's cold out there."

He shoved it shut and shrugged out of his big jacket. "Don't be mad at me."

"What are you doing here?"

"We need to talk."

"*You* need to talk, apparently. And always in my bedroom in the middle of the night." And why did he have to look so totally manly in old jeans, older boots and a frayed BCC Grand Opening T-shirt from five years ago? It just wasn't fair.

He gave her the sexy eyes. "You look so cute."

"I look like I was sound asleep. Probably because I *was*."

He gave her a slow once-over. "I think I like the elves better than the wiener dogs."

She refused to soften toward him. "You've barely said a word to me since the last time you climbed in my window, and now suddenly you're all about my festive pajamas and how we *have* to talk? Uh-uh. You are not making me feel any more kindly toward you."

He looked at her sideways and asked in a voice both rough and way too tender, "But you still love me, right?"

She made a scoffing sound. "And you wonder why all your women turn into drama queens. You drive them to it."

"Be nice, Paige." He reached out and wrapped his big fingers around her upper arm.

Even through the fuzzy flannel of her sleeve, heat sparked and sizzled across the surface of her skin. She pulled her arm away. "Start talking."

"Can we maybe sit down?"

"Sure." Head high, she marched to the bed and dropped to the edge.

He eyed her warily for a moment, but then came and sat beside her, just as he had two nights before. A weird and awkward silence ensued—because no way was she starting the conversation when *he* was the one who just *had* to talk at two in the morning.

Finally, he opened with "So…you're okay, right?"

"Other than my annoyance with you for interrupting the first sound sleep I've had in days? Yeah. I'm fine." She flashed him a sharp glance. "And if your needing to talk consists of you asking me questions and *me* doing most of the actual talking… No, Carter. Or, as you would say, *Hell to the no.*"

He grumbled, "So, then you're really pissed at me, huh?"

"And there you go with yet another question."

He shot her a glance both bewildered and contrite. Really, for a man who couldn't run away fast enough at the mere mention of the word *love*, he was altogether too lovable.

And then he glumly confessed, "I don't know how to start."

And she couldn't just leave him there, hanging, all on his own. She put her hand over his big, rough, hot one. When he turned it palm up, she laced their fingers together.

He gave her a sweet little squeeze. "As far as you being in love with me…?"

Her heart rate accelerated and her mouth went dry. "Yeah?"

"Really freaks me out."

"I noticed." She made herself look directly at him. His beautiful tawny eyes were waiting.

He lifted their joined hands and brushed those amazing lips across the backs of her knuckles that peeked out, just barely, between his big fingers. "But it's okay."

"What's okay?" Her breath had kind of snagged in her throat. She made a conscious effort to suck in air and let it back out slowly.

"I mean, if you can be in love with me and be okay with it, so can I."

Okay? He said it was *okay*?

That was…very, very *not* okay. "Carter, I have to tell you. When I get married—*if* I ever get married—I want the man I marry to be more than just 'okay' with me."

"But I *am* more than just okay with you."

She shook her head. "Sorry. Not feelin' it."

"But it's true. I'm gone on you."

A burst of laughter escaped her. "Oh, come on."

His eyes darkened and his jaw hardened. "Don't laugh at me, damn it. It's really…kind of a stunner for me, too, you know? I'm not sure what to make of how I feel about you now. But whatever this is, I do feel it. I've got a real thing for you. You're something special, Paige. Special and drama-free and wonderfully sane."

Sane. How romantic.

Not. "Carter, I just think…" Her sentence trailed off into oblivion.

Because he messed with her concentration by leaning closer and nuzzling her ear. "Plus, I gotta ask…"

A lovely shiver went through her. One she tried to make light of. "Oh, great. More questions."

"Don't get all judgey. This is a *good* question. I think you're going to like it."

"Of course you do."

He nibbled on her earlobe. And then he pulled his hand free of hers—but only in order to wrap his arm around her and tuck her in close to his side. He stroked her hair, pausing to free it from where it was all tangled up in the collar of her pajama top. His touch and his closeness felt so good, so right. And she kind of loved the way he touched her, fussed over her. So much so that she couldn't quite make herself push him away.

And then he leaned even closer. "The question is—" he nuzzled her temple and his warm breath teased her ear "—how'd you get so damn hot, Paige?"

She made the mistake of turning toward him. Now she looked directly into those molten green eyes. And had he always smelled this good—like pine trees and mountain air and a hint of high-grade motor oil?

He captured her mouth.

She moaned. She couldn't help it. His tongue pressed the seam where her lips met. And she gave in without even token resistance, gave in to him instantly, sighing in welcome.

Oh, that kiss. *His* kiss. She should have known better than to let him put that mouth of his on hers. His kiss weakened her everywhere—her shaking knees, her quivering belly, her yearning heart and definitely her mind.

He guided her back to the bed the way he'd done two nights ago, so she lay across the mattress, her bare feet dangling just above the rug. The whole way down he kept his lips locked to hers, kissing her about as close to senseless as she could possibly get without actually losing consciousness. She sighed some more and clutched his thick shoulders and fervently wished that she would never have to let go.

But then he lifted up enough to ask, "Well?"

Her eyes popped open and she stared at him blankly. "Um…" Her mouth tingled from that kiss of his. Oh, who was she kidding? Every inch of her tingled. "What was the question?"

"How come you're so hot?" He went to work on the little green buttons of her pajama top.

"I think it's your fault." It came out breathless with yearning. "You do it to me."

"Paige, sweetheart…" Oh, that voice of his, so deep and rough and wonderful. His voice touched her, stroking her, arousing her every bit as much as his big hands and his clever mouth did. He kissed the tip of her nose, and one button slipped free. He moved on to the next and the next after that. She didn't even pretend to try and stop him.

And what do you know?

In seconds, he had all those little green buttons completely undone.

Undone. Yeah. Exactly. He'd undone her buttons. He'd undone *her*.

She gazed up at him, dazed and way too willing, her hands still clasping the hard curves of his shoulders. He took them—one hand and then the other—and guided them back onto the mattress to either side of her head.

And then he got hold of her unbuttoned pajama top and peeled it wide. She felt the cool air of the shadowed bedroom on her bare breasts.

"So pretty," he whispered as he lowered his head. He sucked her nipple into his mouth.

Paige gasped and then she moaned. She tried to lift her hands again to hold him, pull him closer to her.

But he didn't let her. With a low chuckle, he caught both her wrists and pressed them into the mattress.

"Fine," she complained in a breathless little whisper. "Be that way."

He made a rough sound, a knowing sound. That sound vibrated against her willing flesh as he suckled her breast, flicking her aching nipple with his tongue, nipping it lightly with his strong teeth.

Surely this couldn't be happening, she and Carter in her bedroom in the middle of the night, doing the things people do when they're a lot more than friends. Surely this couldn't be real.

Oh, but it was.

He kissed her other breast. She shuddered in delight and lifted her body toward him. He let go of her wrists then—in order to undo the little satin bow at the top of her pajama bottoms. She lifted her head off the mattress and watched in heated awe as he eased them down and tossed them away.

"Carter, I—"

"Shh, Paige. It's okay…"

She blinked and stared down at herself. Naked. Except for her pajama top spread wide against the sheet, she was naked.

She was naked and Carter, still fully clothed, was sliding to his knees by the side of the bed. He guided her legs apart and moved in between them, taking her by the waist, pulling her closer to the edge of the bed, then easing her thighs up onto his shoulders. She let him do all that, let him position her just where he wanted her. She didn't make a peep of protest, gave him nothing but a willing sigh. She let him see all of her, and she felt not even a hint of reserve or shyness.

"Relax," he whispered.

She did relax. She let her head drop back to the bed as she felt his breath across her skin. Her body hummed with pleasure as he laid a burning trail of kisses up the inside of her right thigh.

And he didn't stop there. He pressed that clever mouth of his to the eager flesh stretched over her hipbones, brushed those lips in places she knew she shouldn't let him go.

Ah, but she did let him. She more than *let* him. She welcomed him, opened wide to him. She surrendered. To his hot kiss, to the heat that seemed to roll off his big, hard body in delicious waves.

To the magic in his hands.

Oh, he was good at this. So good that she cried out more than once and he had to reach up and press his fingers to her lips and whisper, "Shh. Shh, now, sweetheart…" before he went back to driving her crazy with his lips and his tongue and even his teeth.

And did she mention those hands?

Oh, my, those hands. It so wasn't fair what he did with those hands. He had her completely at his mercy.

And at his mercy, as it turned out, was a great place to be.

She felt her body rising, the tide of pleasure cresting. And she rode it joyfully, spreading her arms wide on the bed, clutching the pillows, the blankets, the sheets, grabbing tight and holding on, tossing her head, moaning his name, trying to keep from shouting out loud as her climax rolled through her.

In the middle of it, as she came apart completely, he rose and joined her on the bed again. He kissed her, taking her mouth as his fingers continued making magic down low. His lips were so warm. He tasted of her own arousal, and he kissed her so deeply as the waves of pleasure pulsed and shimmered all through her. She hit one peak, dared to think it was over…

But it wasn't over. She faded down a fraction, started to catch her breath—and it was happening all over again. The pleasure receded only to bloom hot and glorious once more.

When it finally ended, she just lay there, body limp, little sparks of giddy light flashing pleasantly on the insides of her eyelids.

"Paige?" He kissed her name onto her slack lips.

She sighed. "What now, Carter?"

"Say yes, Paige."

She opened her eyes and looked at him as he stared down so intently at her. His mouth was swollen, red from kissing her. She could feel his erection, hard and hot, against her side, pressing at her through the fly of his jeans. And his eyes were so green right then, green and deep. And way too determined.

All at once, she felt very naked. She fumbled for the sides of her pajama top to gather it around her.

He caught her hand. "Don't hide from me. Just say yes. Just say you'll be my fiancée, say we'll be together. *Really* together. Say I can stay with you, here, tonight, in this bed."

"Oh, I don't think that's a very good idea."

"Will you stop with the negatives? Show me the positive. Give me my yes."

"Carter…" She reached up then and touched the side of his face. "Tonight I ate a carton of ice cream, watched a bunch of girlie movies and told myself I was licking my wounds, moving on…"

He turned his mouth into her hand and kissed her palm. "Say yes, Paige."

She knew she should remind him again of all the ways his crazy plan would be flirting with disaster. But really, he was such a terrific man. He'd always been so good to her, generous, caring, there at her side whenever she needed him.

And now that she'd had a taste of him, well, she really didn't want to stop.

He said, "We can be good together, better than ever. I know we can. I just want my chance with you."

That got to her. After all, she wanted the same thing. *Her* chance with *him*.

Why *shouldn't* they try it? Why assume it would all go to hell in the end?

After all, it was the season of miracles. Maybe the miracle she wanted most of all would happen. She and Carter would work it out and end up making a life together, building a family, having it all.

He bent close and rubbed her nose with his. And he didn't stop there. He pressed soft, tender kisses on her cheek, along her jaw and then on her mouth.

Generous. Yes. He was a generous man. Even in bed.

And she couldn't hold out against him any longer, didn't *want* to hold out.

"Say yes." He breathed the words into her hair. "Have a little faith, Paige. Take a chance on me."

By then, she'd all but forgotten all her very good reasons for telling him no.

She just wanted what he wanted, the two of them, together. To be his through the holidays, to get her chance to show him that love didn't have to equal insanity.

"Yes, Carter," she whispered. "All right. I accept your proposal. We'll try your Christmas engagement and see how it goes."

Chapter Seven

Carter could hardly believe it. "You just said yes." At last. It was happening. They were on. "Tell me I'm not dreaming."

Paige gave him that beautiful, soft little smile of hers. "You're wide-awake. And we're in this."

He kissed her, hard and quick. And then he sternly instructed, "Do not move."

She laughed. "Carter, what—?"

"Stay right there." He cut her off before she could get rolling. "Stay just as you are. Don't move and don't say a word." She looked amazing with her clothes off, all soft and so touchable, with all that velvety pale skin, her dark hair wild against the white sheet, those fine breasts with their dusky nipples that fit his hands just right...

Paige Kettleman. Naked for him. Who knew?

And the way she'd come apart for him? That had been

something special. All signs were good they would share a smoking-hot sex life.

She pressed her sweet lips together and widened her eyes at him to let him know that, okay, she would be quiet and she wouldn't move. Maybe for thirty seconds—a minute, tops.

That should do it.

He got up, fast, and reached back to get hold of his T-shirt, whipping that puppy over his head and off in an instant. He jumped on one foot and then the other, pulling off his boots and getting rid of his socks. After that, there were only his jeans and his boxer briefs. He reached in a front pocket and pulled out the three condoms he'd brought because a man who knows what he wants needs to be prepared to get it.

A flick of his wrist and the condoms landed on the bedside table next to the lamp. Paige was still quiet, still all eyes. Other than the wide eyes and the pressed-together lips, she hadn't moved a muscle. That wouldn't last long.

He ripped his fly wide. Careful of his damn close-to-painful erection, he took both jeans and boxer briefs down in a single motion, stepping clear of them, giving them a kick toward the bedside chair.

Paige's eyes had gone wider than ever. And his minute of silence was up. "Carter…" She said his name on a soft exhalation. And then she slipped her arms out of her pajama top and held them out to him.

He couldn't get back to her fast enough, going down to the bed and gathering her into his hungry arms. She snuggled right in.

Damn, he did want her. He wanted her bad.

He tipped up her chin to take her mouth.

And wouldn't you know? Being Paige, she started talking again. "Wait. I need you to promise me…"

He groaned. "Did you happen to notice I'm about to explode here?" She laughed. And he grumbled, "Right. I suffer. You laugh."

She lifted her mouth and gave him a quick, sweet little kiss. "I just need your agreement on one thing."

He teased, "As if I could refuse you anything in this condition."

She snuggled in closer. She felt really good there, her head tucked in against his chest. "It's about Dawn."

"What about her?" He kissed the top of her head and then ran a hand down the silky skin of her outer arm.

She tipped up her chin then and he looked down into those coffee-brown eyes. "As long as we're test-driving our relationship, we're going to be discreet for Dawn's sake."

"Discreet…" Did anyone but Paige even use words like that?

She pinched up her mouth at him. "Yeah. Discreet. You've got to be out that window before daylight. And whenever we spend the night together, we have to work it out so she doesn't have to know."

"How's that going to happen? She's eighteen and not in any way an idiot."

"We're going to *make* it happen, somehow. I need your word on that, Carter."

He combed his fingers through her hair. It smelled like vanilla and flowers. He wanted to bury his face in it, rub it on his chest, wrap it around the part of him that was getting very impatient to continue what they'd started. "I don't like sneaking around."

"Says the man who keeps climbing in my window in the middle of the night."

He traced the indentation of her spine. Slowly. With pleasure. "You're not going to budge on this, are you?"

"Nope."

"All right. Have it your way. I'll be gone before daylight and we will be discreet."

She gave him a glowing smile. "I appreciate that."

He thought about the ring then. "I didn't bring the ring tonight. I started thinking that maybe I was pushing it, choosing it for you. That maybe you wanted to pick out your own ring."

"I *love* that ring." She said it fast, without taking time to think about it.

He knew she meant exactly what she said. "Well, good, then. You got it."

But then she started thinking. Paige *always* started thinking. "You know, maybe we should pick out something a little bit—"

"Don't you dare say 'cheaper.'" He gave her a lowering look meant to signify that she shouldn't poke the bear.

"Well, really, now, Carter, I don't need such an expensive—"

"Stop. You like it and I chose it for you. It's yours. Discussion over."

"I cannot believe that we're sitting here naked, arguing about an engagement ring."

"So stop arguing. Let's go back to the part about how we're naked and take it from there."

Her answer came softly, almost shyly, "Okay."

His mama had caused no end of trouble for her children, but she never raised a single fool. Carter swooped down and captured Paige's fine mouth, pushing his tongue right in, loving the taste of her as much as the feel of her in his arms.

As he kissed her, he scooted them both around so they could stretch out on the pillows. He kicked the blankets down all the way, trailing kisses over her soft, strong little chin and into the sweet-smelling curve of her throat where the skin was so delicate and tender. He couldn't resist sucking that softness against his teeth, knowing it would leave a mark, forgetting already that they were being *discreet*.

Paige wrapped her slim arms tight around him and pushed her beautiful breasts against his chest. She whispered his name urgently, encouraging him to kiss her some more.

He was just working his way downward over her delicate collarbones when all at once, she had him by the shoulders and she pushed herself up. She pressed him back against the mattress, dark eyes shining with intent to take the lead.

Hey. No problem. She drove him crazy with her bossy ways a lot of the time.

But in bed, he could be flexible. He liked to run things, yeah. He also enjoyed it when his woman stepped up and demanded a little control.

She looked down at him through lazy, shining eyes. "Oh, Carter. So many muscles. I might have to kiss them all."

He didn't object and she got right to work on that, scattering kisses across his chest, over his shoulders, along the side of his neck. And then down. She wrapped her soft hand around him. He gritted his teeth and tried not to embarrass himself.

And then she took him in her mouth. He closed his eyes and gave himself up to the pleasure she offered.

But it had been a while. After the disaster of Sherry, there'd been no one else. And Paige's mouth all over him, well, that brought him to the brink way too fast.

He reached out, fumbling for the nightstand. She glanced up and met his eyes as his fingers closed around one of the condoms.

Now, there was a great view. Paige with her soft mouth all around him, that silky hair falling to one side and tickling his thigh, those big, dark eyes so soft and sexy...

"Can't last," he confessed with regret.

And she reached up and took the condom from him, getting it out of the wrapper and down over his aching hardness in no time.

"Come up here." He took her by the shoulders. She let him pull her up so they were face-to-face. And then he kissed her. He really, really liked to kiss her, to spear his tongue in and taste her, so sweet and wet and open to him.

At his urging, she straddled him. He reached down between them to hold himself in place.

And then, so slowly, she lowered herself onto him.

Oh, yeah. That was something special, Paige taking him in. He sucked in air slowly, letting it out with care, keeping his eyes open so he could watch her move on him. He drank in every line, every curve, every sigh and sweet shudder as she took all he had.

When she was almost there, he couldn't resist. He caught her soft hips and yanked her down harder.

She let out a hot cry.

"Shh." He reached up, touched her mouth in tender warning. "Shh…"

She started to move then, staring straight in his eyes, her hair falling forward, her pretty breasts swaying, her hands braced at his chest. She started to move…

And then he was the one making noise, groaning so loud and deep she bent right down close and teased, "Shh," against his mouth.

That was right before she kissed him again, her clever tongue slipping between his parted lips, sweeping the inside of his mouth, driving him wild as she kept rising and falling above him, pushing him to the limit, taking him right to the edge.

He hovered there, just barely keeping himself from going over, determined to feel her go first.

But she went on kissing him, went on moving so perfectly, lifting and falling, driving him closer. He was losing the battle, and he knew it. He wouldn't be able to hold out.

So he wrapped his arms around her and rolled them.

On top, he had a chance to outlast her, to hold on to control long enough to feel her shatter around him— Paige, all around him.

For the very first time.

She gazed up at him, eyes hazy with need, a tiny knowing smile curving the sides of her mouth. He lowered his head and covered her mouth again, taking that smile for his own, rocking into her as she lifted her legs and wrapped them good and tight around his waist.

After that, sensations rolled over and through him so fast, he lost all control. Heat sizzled and burned along every nerve. He surged into her and she took him, rocking beneath him, holding him tightly, just as he held her. He felt the end coming.

And then, just before he lost himself inside her, she cried out, sweet and lost and beautiful. He still had his mouth on hers and he drank in that cry.

Her body tightened around him in the first wave of her climax. So good, so right. He pushed into her harder. And then he held it, held still within her as her body pulsed around him and she moaned into his mouth.

That did it. He lost it. He threw his head back and groaned at the ceiling as the finish plowed through him, mowing him down.

He got up long enough to deal with the condom and then he returned to gather her close. For a while, they just lay there, all wrapped up in each other, drifting. He stroked her back and she cuddled in close. Her breathing evened out.

She'd fallen asleep.

Worn out, poor baby. The past several days had been hard on her and he knew he was to blame for that.

Because she loved him. Because she knew the way he was, not going for the love thing, no way. Because she'd tried so hard to hold out against him and he wouldn't let her do that.

But things would be better now. They were together just the way he wanted it. He would take care of her and she would be fine.

Had he rushed her to bed?

Maybe a little.

But he'd felt driven to seal the deal with her. And he was glad that he had. He wanted this, with her. He wanted it a lot. Wanted it so much that he had to be careful not to overthink it. His mother had been right, though he would never admit that out loud. He distrusted strong emotions, especially when he felt them about a woman.

But then again, the woman in question here was Paige. Paige could keep a level head even when the *L* word was involved. She'd always amazed him, the cool she had at her command.

Except in bed. She really came apart in bed. Which was the one place he didn't care how touchy-feely and explosive things got.

Yeah. He just knew it would all work out fine.

One thing nagged at him, though.

With all the tension between them, they hadn't been talking much in the past several days. He'd yet to tell her that Willow had bought the property on Arrowhead Drive, that she'd offered it to him as a bribe, an incentive to get married.

He needed to let Paige in on that, ASAP.

But who knew how she'd react? She could get cold feet, start wondering if he only wanted to marry her for the deed to the property. He could lose the ground he'd finally gained.

Maybe he should hold off on telling her. Just for a little while. She'd said she wouldn't be checking in with the Realtor again until after the holidays, so he had some leeway. He could wait a few days before he brought it up.

Right now the top priority was showing her just exactly how good they would be together.

In his arms, she sighed and a cute little snoring sound escaped her. Grinning, he tucked the covers over her and then slid carefully from the bed so as not to disturb her. She had her own private bathroom, a good thing, or he'd have to take a chance on wandering the upper hall, maybe disturbing Dawn.

When he came back to Paige, she was still sound asleep. The clock by the bed showed five minutes of four. He knew he should leave.

But damn, she looked so sweet and peaceful. He wanted to wrap himself around her, snuggle in tight and close his eyes. Just for a little while. He could sleep with her for an hour, then get up and go, come back and get Biscuit, take him out with Sally for their morning walk.

Then he'd make breakfast for the three of them, just like always. All nice and discreet, the way Paige wanted it. Dawn would have no clue of where he'd spent the night…

Carter woke to morning light shining in the window he'd climbed through the night before.

Paige slept on, sprawled on her stomach, one slim, soft arm thrown across his chest, her head turned toward him. So tempting, her hair tangled across the pillow, lips softly parted, totally conked out. He wanted to turn her over and kiss her awake.

But no.

She wouldn't be happy if she found him in her bed when he'd promised to be long gone by now. He needed to get out of there before she realized he'd blown it.

It took a lifetime, easing out from under her arm and inching his way toward the edge of the mattress. He took a lot of care not to let any cool air get in under the blankets. At one point, she sighed and stirred. He froze with one foot on the rug and the other still on the bed, holding his breath, certain he was about to be busted.

But she only turned her head the other way and went on sleeping.

She didn't even move after that. He made it out of the bed and into his clothes. Shrugging his jacket on, he turned to the window and slowly, carefully, slid it wide.

Cold morning air flowed in. He worried that the change in temperature might wake her.

But she didn't stir. He hoisted himself over the sill and out to the roof. As quietly as possible, he eased the window shut. Crouched outside, his breath a white mist, he peered through the glass.

No movement from the bed. Excellent. But she'd be waking up any minute now. Time to get the hell out of there.

He considered leaving the way he'd come, going up the gable and dropping to the roof of the garage, crossing it and using that big tree in the far corner to climb down into the front yard.

But going out through the backyard would be safer. He could slip out the side gate and avoid the possibility of one of her neighbors coming out to grab the morning paper and spotting him wandering around on Paige's roof.

So he went the other way, staying low to avoid detection, moving quickly to the covered porch that ran along the back of the house. He scuttled down the porch roof to the edge of the shingles, which was only about ten feet from the ground.

He could make that jump, no problem. So he launched himself outward, staying clear of the guttering, neatly landing and rolling, coming up in a crouch.

At which point, from behind him, Biscuit started barking.

He whirled, rising, as the beagle zipped out the kitchen door that Dawn had just opened for him.

Busted.

"Hey." Carter gave Dawn a sheepish wave, then dropped to a crouch again to greet the panting dog.

Dawn, looking half-asleep in pajamas, a giant sweater and heavy socks, folded her arms across her middle and tipped her head to the side. "Carter, what's going on?" she asked on a yawn.

He scratched Biscuit's floppy ears. "Thought I'd drop in."

"From the roof?"

He tried for humor. "I considered the chimney…" When she just looked at him, he made it worse. "Ho-ho-ho?"

For that he got a hard sigh and a definite eye roll. "Where's Sally?"

"Sally?"

"Yeah, Carter. Skinny red dog? Lives at your house?"

"Right. Sally. Well, see, I, uh…" He cast about for a plausible lie. Nothing came to mind. And then Biscuit took off, sniffing his way toward the back fence. Carter still had nothing, so he offered, "How 'bout some coffee?"

Shaking her head, Dawn turned from the doorway. At least she left it open for him to follow her in.

Paige entered the kitchen to find Dawn sitting at the breakfast bar watching Carter make the coffee.

She knew instantly that things weren't quite right. The dogs were not sprawled on the floor as usual after their morning walk; Carter still wore the same jeans and T-shirt he'd worn when he climbed in her window five hours earlier; and Dawn was too quiet—she had a strange, thoughtful look on her face as she watched Carter spooning grounds into the filter.

Dawn glanced over and spotted Paige in the doorway. She squinted and frowned. "What's that on your neck?"

"Where?" She pressed her hand randomly to the left side of her throat.

"No, the other side…"

By then Carter had started the coffeemaker and turned around so Paige could see his face. The guilty look he wore said way more than Paige wanted to know. He cleared his throat nervously. "Ahem. It kind of looks like a bruise…"

"Oh. My. God." Dawn blinked as disbelief slowly turned to understanding.

Paige slapped a hand over the spot. She couldn't believe it. Damn Carter and that sexy mouth of his. She glared at him.

He muttered, "Sorry…"

And Dawn accused, "Down the chimney. Right." She swung her gaze to Paige again. "I just caught Carter jumping off the roof."

Paige sent her brand-new fiancé another dirty look. He'd not only given her a hickey; he'd failed to keep his promise and go home before daylight. "What am I going to do with you?"

Dawn was the one who answered. "Have sex with him, apparently." She snorted. "I just might be scarred for life, knowing that."

Paige went on glaring at Carter, who responded with "Come on, Paige. We need to tell her what's going on."

"Yeah," Dawn agreed. "The truth. Novel concept."

Paige left the doorway and went to sit on the stool

next to Dawn. When Dawn sent her a grumpy look, she wrapped an arm around her and pulled her close. "I wanted to be discreet for your sake."

"With Carter involved?" Dawn gave her a fond head butt. "Good luck."

"Hey," Carter groused. "I can do discreet."

Paige and Dawn made identical scoffing sounds. And then Paige said, "Carter's asked me to marry him…"

It was really pretty sweet the way Dawn's eyes lit up. "And…?"

Carter stood a little straighter. "She said yes."

Dawn threw both arms wide, almost whacking Paige across the face. "At last!" And then she grabbed Paige and hugged her. "Oh, I knew this would happen eventually. Finally! This is totally amazing. Not to mention wonderful, terrific and just about perfect."

Was it? Paige hugged Dawn back and slid a warning glance at Carter over her shoulder. He'd better not start in about how they were test-driving their relationship. Dawn didn't even need to hear that.

Either he took the hint or didn't want to get into that part of their arrangement any more than Paige did, because he only said proudly, "I am one lucky man."

Dawn let out a giddy squeal of laughter, flew off the stool, zipped around the end of the snack bar and headed straight for Carter. He opened his arms to take her in.

She hugged him as hard as she'd hugged Paige. "You're moving in here, right?"

He caught her face between his hands and dropped a kiss on her forehead. "That's the plan. Eventually."

She looked at him sideways. "Did you actually climb in my sister's bedroom window last night?"

He busted to it. "Yeah. I kinda did."

"Because you didn't want to freak me out, right?"

"Yeah, pretty much."

"From now on, just pick a door, will you?"

"Okay, sunshine. I can do that."

"Good."

He let her go. "So, what do you want for breakfast?"

"Pancakes?"

"You got 'em."

Dawn asked, "How long has Sally been at home alone?"

"Too long."

"We should go get her."

"I'll do it." Paige slid off the stool. She was still in her pajamas and robe, but she'd only be out of the car long enough to run up and down Carter's front walk.

She headed for the garage, grabbing her purse from the closet in the front hall on the way.

So much for total discretion around Dawn, she thought as she drove to Carter's house. But then, why sneak around, really? It wouldn't work with Dawn, anyway. She was too smart for that. And she'd taken the news of the engagement well.

Better than well. Dawn had been so happy for them.

How bad would it be for her if things didn't work out, if the cons outweighed the pros when Paige and Carter evaluated their "test drive"?

Oh, please. Dawn would be fine. She'd survived and thrived even after losing both her parents way too young. She could no doubt rise above her big sister screwing up with Carter.

And was this a screwup?

On the rational level, it certainly felt like it. A try-out engagement? Pretty much a big helping of ludicrous drizzled in crazy sauce.

But on that other level, the level that had to do with Paige's hungry heart and her yearning body, with all the parts of her that *felt*, the parts that wanted and needed and burned, the parts of her she'd been denying ever since Jim Kellogg cut out her heart and then walked all over it?

On that level, desire had the lead now. She'd let Carter in her bedroom window and taken him to her bed.

It was done. She had loved it. She wanted more.

And she wouldn't focus on the negative, she promised herself as she pulled up in front of Carter's house. She was in this now. She was Carter's bride-to-be.

If she ended up crying by New Year's, so be it. She was going to love every minute of being Carter Bravo's Christmas bride.

Chapter Eight

That day was the annual Justice Creek shopping bazaar known as Rocky Mountain Christmas. Then, in the evening, they were going to the Holiday Ball at the Haltersham Hotel. Carter decided to take the whole day off work and spend it with Paige. He called Mona to tell her he wasn't coming in, then he went home to shower and change.

He was back within the hour and he brought a suitcase. Paige came down the stairs to meet him wearing her favorite soft white sweater, skinny jeans, knee boots and a bright red scarf.

He held up the suitcase. "I thought I'd bring a few things over. You know, for any time I stay the night..."

Was he pushing things too fast?

Without a doubt.

Did she care in the least?

Heck, no. She was *glad*. She smirked, "Moving right in, huh?"

"Oh, you bet." He was looking at her mouth. Something flared in his eyes. He dropped the suitcase and reached for her, dragging her close and nuzzling her neck. "You smell amazing."

She went to mush, just at the feel of his hard arms wrapped around her.

Dawn and Molly were already over on Central Street enjoying Rocky Mountain Christmas, so Paige didn't pull back when his kiss turned hot and deep.

And wonderfully slow.

When he finally let go of her mouth, he asked, "Dawn?"

"Gone with Molly."

"Perfect." He grabbed the suitcase in one hand and her in the other and dragged her back up the stairs to her room, both dogs following behind.

In the bedroom, he ordered Sally and Biscuit to lie down by the window. They did, without him having to say it twice.

He turned to her. "Now, where were we?"

"Why don't you tell me?"

"How 'bout I show you, instead?"

And he did. He took off everything she'd just put on and they spent a very satisfying hour doing what came naturally.

Then she pulled on a robe and helped him put his stuff away. There were empty drawers in the bathroom and plenty of space in the walk-in closet, including an empty bureau that had once been her dad's. The unpacking accomplished, he took the dogs downstairs and she got ready all over again to go to Rocky Mountain Christmas.

When she went back downstairs, she followed the

close harmonies of the Puppini Sisters singing "Santa Baby" and found him sitting in the living room with the fire going, looking at the tree.

He rose when she entered the room. "There you are. Close your eyes."

What was he up to now? "Why?"

He chuckled. She did love the sound of his laughter. In some ways, he didn't have a clue. But in others, well, he was one of a kind in a very special way. "Come on, give me some trust, Paige. Work with me here."

"Oh, all right." She shut her eyes. He moved behind her and put both his hands over her closed eyelids. "What? You think I'll cheat and peek?"

"You just might. You're sneaky that way."

She laughed and tried to elbow him.

But he only dipped out of range—and kept those big hot hands of his covering her eyes. "Behave."

"Okay. I surrender. Do with me what you will."

"Now you're talkin'."

"Except not right here in the living room. Dawn may be open-minded, but that doesn't mean she needs to see us cavorting naked in the parlor."

"I can't believe you just said 'cavorting.' And 'parlor,' too."

"Cavorting can mean either leaping and dancing around excitedly or applying oneself enthusiastically to sexual or disreputable pursuits."

He grunted. "I may not have gotten past junior college, but I do know what cavorting means."

"Just so you also know, we're not doing any of that here in the living room." Right then she felt his lips on the back of her neck, and a delicious shiver skittered down her spine and bloomed sweet and hot in her belly. "Stop that."

He chuckled. The sound was so lovely, rich and low and rough. He advised, "Then stop talking and let me do this thing—or I'll be forced to carry you back upstairs where we can cavort in private."

The idea of going upstairs again held great appeal. But they couldn't spend *all* of their time in bed. "Do the *thing*, then. Whatever it is."

He still had his hands over her eyes. "Turn around slowly." She did. He stayed behind her, covering her eyes. "Stop." She obeyed. "Now move forward."

"Toward the tree?"

"Are you peeking?"

"Of course not. But it *is* my living room and I know you turned me around a hundred and eighty degrees and that would mean I'm now facing the tree."

He laughed again.

"Why is that funny?" she demanded.

"It's just…*you*, Paige. Always with the calm and reasonable deductions." She would have asked him what, exactly, he meant by that. But then he added, "And I mean that in the best possible way."

She decided to be mollified. "So, then. Move forward, you said…?"

"Yeah. Move forward toward the tree until I tell you to stop."

She started walking. He came right along with her, his hands over her eyes.

By her estimation, they were maybe a foot from the tree when he said, "Perfect. Stop." She stopped, the shin of her right leg just brushing the sharp tip of what she recognized by feel as a lower branch. "One step to the right."

She stepped. "That's too far. Take half a step back." She did. "Bingo." His hands dropped away. "Now open your eyes."

She opened them and found herself staring directly into the brightly lit and heavily ornamented branches of the tree. "Wow. My Christmas tree. Who would have guessed?"

He put his hands on her shoulders. She felt his warm breath in her ear. "You're not paying attention."

Of course she was paying attention. She was staring right where he'd told her to look…

And then she saw it—her beautiful engagement ring, on which she knew very well he'd spent altogether too much money. It hung from a branch a foot from her face, spinning and sparkling on a short length of red satin ribbon. "Oh!"

He pressed his cheek to hers. "Merry Christmas, sweetheart."

Sweetheart. It sounded really good coming out of his mouth. "Carter…" She turned her head and kissed him—a short, sweet one. And then she took the ribbon off the branch and eased the end from the loop that held it to the ring.

When she had it free, he took it from her, caught her left hand and slipped it on. "Looks good," he said, his voice just gruff enough to make happy tears scald the back of her throat.

She twined her arms around his neck and kissed him again, a slow one this time, tangling her tongue with his, sighing when he reached down and pulled her in good and close so she could feel how much he wanted her, even with no actual cavorting likely again for hours and hours.

When he lifted his head, he asked, "Rocky Mountain Christmas?"

"Oh, yes, please."

They shopped and then shopped some more—well, Paige shopped. Carter went with her into just about every festively decorated store. He carried her bags for her and didn't complain once.

They ran into lots of friends, two of his brothers and three of his sisters, all of whom congratulated them when Paige showed off her ring. At a little after two, they met up with Dawn and Molly, who both squealed in delight at the sight of the ring.

All four of them were hungry, so they went to Carter's half sister Clara's restaurant, the Library Café, where they ate club sandwiches with steak fries. Carter had a beer and Paige, Dawn and Molly all had cappuccinos because they were the perfect drink for a cold, clear almost-winter day.

Carter dropped Paige and the girls off at the house at a little before five. He wanted to check in at BCC and he hadn't thought to bring a suit over, so he would return to his house to get ready for the Holiday Ball. He left Sally with Paige.

Sally was a sweetie. She kept Biscuit company. The two of them would sniff every inch of the backyard together. Inside, they spent most of their time sprawled on the kitchen floor side by side, drooling on chew toys.

Paige and the girls got to work primping for the big night. They showered and did each other's hair and helped each other get that smoky-eye look just right. Molly and Dawn gave Paige a bad time about the bruise on her neck, but both assured her that, once she'd dabbed on concealer, you couldn't even see it. Paige pinned up her hair and wore a vintage '50s emerald-green taffeta creation. The dress was ankle-length, sleeveless, with a draped collar, a fitted top and a giant full skirt. She'd found it on Etsy and fell hard in love with it, one of those dresses Christina Hendricks might have worn to the office Christmas bash on *Mad Men*.

The girls had already gone off with their friends when Carter arrived. He looked fabulous in his dark suit and he whistled at her and made her spin around so he could admire her '50s splendor from all sides.

And then he took her in his arms and he kissed her.

She clung to him and he didn't seem to mind. "You look so handsome." She brushed her fingertips through the short, coarse hair at his temple. "And I feel so happy…"

"Merry Christmas to us." And he kissed her again.

Right then she believed with all her yearning heart that it was all going to work out for them, that their test-run Christmas engagement could lead only to a walk down the aisle and happily-ever-after.

All the lights were blazing at the white, red-roofed Haltersham Hotel. Twin rows of beautifully decorated trees lined the walk up to the famous front portico where the ghost of Olivia Haltersham was still said to wander sometimes late at night. The frail and unstable Olivia had been the pampered wife of steel magnate Thor Haltersham, who had built the hotel back at the turn of the twentieth century.

Carter passed the car keys to the valet and ushered Paige between the glowing trees and up the walk to the wide front steps. She gave her short black velvet cape to the coat-check girl. They followed the crowd up a series of pink marble steps, beneath a heavily carved mahogany arch and then down a wide hallway to the entry hall that led to the ballroom with its giant windows topped by elegant fanlights. Those windows offered breathtaking views of the mountains. Accented in gorgeous dark woodwork like the rest of the old hotel, the ballroom's burnished floor gleamed in the light of the original Tiffany stained-glass chandeliers.

It was a magical evening, Paige thought. She danced with Carter, both of them laughing and swaying to the beat, having a great time. And when the band played slow songs, she went into his arms, her taffeta skirt rustling softly against the dark wool of his trousers.

He whispered such lovely things in her ear. He said she was beautiful and he'd always liked dancing with her—never more so than now, when he knew he would get to go home with her and stay the whole night.

Whenever they took a break, they were instantly surrounded by friends and family. Paige didn't mind at all being hugged and congratulated by Carter's siblings and half siblings. More than one friend said how they'd always known the two of them would end up together. Carter grinned and complained that he'd had to use all his powers of persuasion to get Paige to give him a yes. Paige laughed and said she'd tried her best to resist him.

Carter said, "In the end, I convinced her to give me a chance." He pulled her in closer, brushed a kiss at her temple and Paige couldn't help thinking that the evening had turned out just about perfect.

But perfection never lasts forever.

At a little after midnight, Paige and Carter were standing near the ballroom's gorgeous old rosewood bar, chatting with Carter's youngest sister, Nell. Carter had just told a silly joke. The three of them were laughing— and, then, in the space of an instant, Carter's face went blank and his eyes went flat.

Paige frowned up at him. "Carter, what…?" She let the question die unfinished because by then she'd spotted the problem.

Sherry.

Carter's ex, in a tight red velvet dress that showed off her lush curves, came right for them. She had her blond hair piled up high, tumbling in little curls along the graceful column of her neck.

Carter caught Paige's arm and pulled her behind him. He did it so fast, Paige didn't think to protest. Sherry kept coming, her wide red lips a grim slash and her eyes sparking fire.

The outspoken Nell remarked, "Oh, come on. Seriously?"

Carter sent his sister a quelling look as Sherry stopped short in front of him. He took a crack at civility. "Hi, Sherry. Merry Christmas."

But his ex wasn't having it. Sherry tossed her golden head. "You don't have to look at me like that, Carter. You don't have to put Paige behind you like that. I'm not going to *do* anything."

Paige wasn't sure she believed her. The blonde was a human explosion just begging to happen. Still, it felt more and more wrong to hide behind Carter, to peer over his shoulder as if he were her shield in case the bullets started to fly.

So she stepped out into the open and took his arm.

"Paige," he warned darkly. But at least he didn't try to drag her behind him again.

She aimed a smile at Sherry and said the first mundane thing that popped into her head. "Beautiful party, don't you think?"

Sherry never once took her gaze off Carter. "I only want to say that I hope..." She seemed to lose her train of thought. Her eyes had started glittering, filling with tears. One got away from her and trailed down her cheek.

Paige slid a glance at Carter. He looked miserable. Paige knew he saw the big scene coming. He hated big scenes and he had no idea how to keep this one from happening.

Paige tried, "Listen, Sherry. This is neither the time nor the place to—"

"Please." Sherry sniffed. She tipped her chin toward the art glass chandeliers overhead and announced furiously, "I hope you'll be happy, Carter. Very, very happy. Congratulations to you both. Long life and...a big family and everything you ever wanted."

Carter said carefully, "Thank you."

Sherry turned to go. Paige dared to hope that the worst was over—until Sherry threw her head back and let out a wild cry. Then she buried her face in her hands and started sobbing.

That was when Murray Preble materialized out of the crowd. "Sherry, I'm here," Murray said, his voice low and gruff, his eyes hot with passion. "I'll always be here."

Sherry sobbed all the louder and started walking—straight into Murray's open arms. "Oh, Murray," she cried. "It's happened, just like I always knew it would. He's with Paige now. Hold me, Murray. Help me. Please..."

Murray cradled her close and whispered something in her ear. Then he gazed over her golden head straight at Carter and gave Carter a slow, solemn nod. Carter didn't nod back. He stared at nothing, his eyes a million miles away.

Tenderly, Murray tucked a thick blond curl behind Sherry's ear. "Come on, now, honeycup, it'll be all right. Just give it time and you're gonna be fine." He turned her and ushered her toward the exit. She clung to him, staggering in her high heels like a crash victim reeling away from a horrible accident, until they disappeared through the open doors.

As if on cue, the music started up again.

Nell groaned, "Honeycup? Did he just call her honeycup?"

Carter muttered, "Murray's a good guy."

"Yeah. But…*honeycup*?"

"Looks like it worked for her. She went with him, didn't she?" Carter took Paige's hand. "Let's dance."

She hung back, worried about him. "Are you all right?"

"Yeah." He didn't really seem all right. His tawny eyes were distant. "Dance with me."

What else was there to do but let him lead her onto the floor?

They danced a couple of fast ones and then the band started playing a Christmas ballad. He pulled her close and wrapped both arms around her. They swayed to the music.

Eventually, he asked, "You okay?"

She pressed her lips to the side of his throat and breathed in the scent of his aftershave. "I am. I'm having a wonderful time."

He nuzzled her ear. "I hate big scenes."

"I know," she whispered. "Look at it this way. It's over and she's gone. There'll be no more drama tonight."

* * *

Half an hour later, Paige left Carter chatting with one of their customers from Boulder. The ladies' room in the entry hall had a line out the door, so she went looking for a better option.

The clerk at the front desk sent her down a hallway that branched off the lobby on the opposite side from the one that led back to the ballroom. It was a narrow hallway, and rather dim. The milk-glass wall sconces gave only muted light and the carpet was thick underfoot, muffling sound. The sign for the restrooms glowed greenish way down at the far end. And the holiday music from the ballroom? It seemed to be coming from some other dimension.

It really was kind of spooky. Paige shivered a little and a nervous giggle escaped her. People often claimed that the Haltersham was haunted. She might run into frail Olivia's ghost. Or the ghost of that woman who'd jumped from an upper floor back in the forties when she learned that her fiancé had died on the beach at Normandy...

She'd almost reached the green glow of the Ladies' Room sign when a woman's voice behind her said, "Paige. Wait a moment. I've been hoping for a word with you." Soft, cool fingers closed around her arm.

Paige stifled a thoroughly ridiculous shriek and froze in midstep. Turning her head slowly, not sure what to expect, she found herself staring into the ice-blue eyes of Carter's mom, Willow.

"Willow!" She eased her arm free and pressed her hand to her racing heart. "You surprised me."

"I'm sorry." A charming smile lit up Willow's face. "I really didn't mean to startle you."

What was she doing here? She hadn't been in the ballroom—had she? If she had, wouldn't she have said hello, at least? And Willow had always avoided town events. No one had mentioned she was coming tonight.

"I had no idea you were here," Paige blurted. "We didn't see you in the ballroom," she added unnecessarily.

But she never knew what to say to Willow. Carter's mom made Paige nervous. Who knew what went on in Willow's mind? She always seemed a little antisocial, somehow, as though she didn't really like other people all that much. She stayed in the mansion her husband had built for his first wife. And when she wasn't at the mansion, she traveled the world.

Willow laughed her sexy, husky laugh. She wore a clingy, calf-length black dress, low-cut, with spaghetti straps, and she looked absolutely stunning in it. "I only wanted you to know how happy I am for you and Carter. My son's a lucky man and I know you two are going to be as wonderful together as you've always been—only more so, of course, now that you'll be *truly* together in the fullest way."

Well, that was nice. Wasn't it? "Thank you, Willow. We're...very happy."

"I'm so glad." She caught Paige's arm again. Paige resisted the impulse to jerk free. "And please say that you'll let me give you an engagement party."

What? Willow never gave parties. Did she? "I, um..."

"I really want to do this, Paige. Say that you'll let me. We'll do it now, during the holidays. So romantic, to be engaged at this beautiful time of year. A dinner party, at my house, two weeks from tonight. I'll take care of everything. I promise to make it special. All you have to do is say yes and give me a guest list. I'll see to the rest. It can be as large or as intimate as you'd like it to be. What do you say?"

Who are you and what have you done with the real Willow Bravo? "Well, that's so…kind of you."

"Good. It's settled, then. Two weeks from tonight."

"Ahem. Well, we should talk it over with Carter, don't you think? If you'll just hold on for a quick minute while I duck into the ladies' room, we can go talk with him about it now."

Willow waved a hand. The huge diamond Frank Bravo had given her when he finally married her sparkled aggressively even in the gloomy hallway light. "Oh, I've already spoken with Carter. He's totally on board."

"Um. He is? He never mentioned a party to me…" And if she didn't get into that restroom soon, she was going to embarrass herself. "Just…" She held up a finger. "One minute. Promise. I'll be right out and we can go find Carter."

Willow gave her another radiant smile and a tiny nod. Paige took that for agreement and darted beneath the glowing green sign, shoving the door wide and rushing through.

All the stalls were empty. She ducked into the first one, slammed the door shut and eased her aching bladder just in time. Once that was taken care of, she washed her hands and hurried back out to rejoin Carter's mom.

The dim hallway was deserted. "Willow?"

No answer. Willow had vanished as mysteriously as she'd appeared.

Chapter Nine

"You're serious?" Carter didn't get it. And he really didn't like it. "My mother was here, at the hotel, tonight?"

"Yes. Just now. In a hallway off the lobby. She stopped me on my way to the ladies' room."

"I thought she was in Palm Springs…"

Paige shrugged. "Well, if she was, she's not anymore."

Dread tightened his stomach. Was this about the property? Had his mother told Paige about her insane marriage-incentive plan?

That would not be good. *He* needed to be the one to tell Paige about that.

Soon.

"Come with me." He took her hand and led her out of the ballroom and over to one of the long sofas that lined the walls of the entry hall. They sat down. "Now, tell me what happened."

"It was weird. She popped up out of nowhere. She said

how happy she was for us and that she wants to give us a dinner party at the mansion to celebrate our engagement. She wants to do that two weeks from tonight. She said that you're already 'on board.'"

"What else did she say?"

"What do you mean, what else?"

"Who knows?" he lied. "With my mother, you never do. So, that's all she said, then?"

"That's all—and *are* you on board for a party at the mansion?"

"How could I be on board? I haven't seen her or talked to her since..." About then, he realized he'd never told Paige that he'd had a drink with his mother on Thanksgiving Day. If he mentioned it now, Paige would wonder why he hadn't said anything about it before. She'd want to know why Willow would have asked him to come visit her alone that day.

He wasn't ready to go there. He just wasn't.

Paige prompted, "You haven't seen her since when?"

"A while. It's been a while." That sounded lame. He waited bleakly for Paige to demand when, exactly, *a while* might have been.

But she let it go. She fiddled with her necklace of emerald-green stones and chewed on her plump lower lip. "Don't be offended, but your mother's so...strange, Carter."

"Tell me about it." He hooked his arm around her shoulders and pulled her close. She leaned into him with a sweet little sigh. "Don't let it bother you, okay? Just forget all about it. I'll deal with her."

Paige pulled back and scrunched up her face at him. "Wait a minute. What does that mean, forget all about it?"

"It means you don't have to worry. I'll get us out of it."

"Carter, no. I never said I wanted to get out of it."

"Well, *I* want to get out of it."

"Why?"

"Come on. A dinner party at the Bravo Mansion?"

"What's wrong with the mansion? It's a beautiful house and I'm sure a party there will be lovely."

"Paige, it was Sondra Bravo's house and my mom stole it from her, just like she stole Sondra's husband. I don't like it there and I don't want our engagement party there."

"You're just being pigheaded."

"No, I'm not. You said it yourself. My mother is strange. We don't want to go trusting her with our party."

"But I think it was really sweet of her to offer and we need to…" Her voice trailed off as something sad happened in her big eyes. "Wait a minute…"

He didn't want her looking sad. "What? What's wrong?"

"This is about the test drive, isn't it?"

Crap. "No."

"Yeah." Now her pretty mouth was all pinchy. She leaned closer, but only to accuse in a tense little whisper, "I get it. You don't want your mom to go to all the trouble of putting on a party for us when we still don't know where we're going with this yet."

"That's not it at all." He said it a little louder than he should have.

She darted a glance around the hall and nudged him with her shoulder. "Keep your voice down."

"Sorry." He leaned in and spoke softly. "Paige. It's not about the test drive. My mother just… I don't trust her, okay? I know she must be up to something."

"Something like what?"

"How would I know?" Well, all right. He knew more than he was telling. And he needed to get honest with Paige.

Soon.

She said, "I don't know what your mother does when she travels, but here at home, she's kind of a recluse."

"So?"

There was eye rolling, followed by scoffing. "God. Clueless much?"

"My mother is my mother. It's not my fault."

"But if a situation arises where you can help her get outside herself a little, don't you think you ought to go with it?"

"Outside herself. What does that even mean?"

"You're being purposely thick."

Yeah, well. So what if he was? "You're saying that her giving us a party is going to help her, somehow?"

"I think it might. I think she feels ostracized by her past. I think she feels that people don't like her much."

He grunted. "Now, why in hell would she feel that way?"

"Carter. Be nice."

"Face it. People *don't* like her. She stole another woman's husband. She had five kids with him while he was still married to the woman she stole him from. And now she lives in that woman's house."

"It's *her* house now and the rest of that is way in the past."

"But it *happened.*"

"And now it's over, and I've talked to your sisters and brothers."

"When?"

"Over the years—and don't look so suspicious. I'm

only saying what you already know. Your brothers and sisters want to put the past behind them. And your mother throwing our engagement party is a good way to help make that happen. Plus, I personally want to establish a good relationship with Willow. Saying yes to the party could be a nice start on that."

"Nobody has a good relationship with my mother. She's doesn't get close. It's not how she is." He spoke firmly, hoping she'd finally accept that he didn't want to do this.

Didn't work. "Well, I want to try. I agree that she and I will probably never be BFFs. But she's offered to do something nice for us, and I don't want to turn her down."

He knew that look in those fine eyes. It was the look she gave him when he insisted on paying more than he should for a car—multiplied by about a thousand. She was digging in her heels here and she wouldn't let it go until she had it her way.

She was way too damn determined about some things.

And apparently, his mother throwing their engagement party was one of those things.

Carter decided to look on the bright side. If he said yes to the party, that didn't automatically mean his mother would blab to Paige about the property before he found the right moment to tell her himself. If Willow intended to bring up the property to Paige, she probably would have done it tonight.

Right?

As if he knew. When it came to his mother, who could ever say?

He gave it up. "All right. I'll call her tomorrow and tell her we're going for it."

Paige's mouth lost the pinchy look. She leaned closer. "Thank you." She smiled full out and her husky tone spoke of good things to come. "We have to give her a guest list."

Damn. All those years they'd just been just friends. What a waste. They needed to have a lot of sex to make up for all they'd missed. "How 'bout we put the list together in the morning, before I call her?"

"Perfect." She brushed her lips across his and pulled away much too soon.

He ached to gather her close again and claim another kiss. But if he did that, he'd never want to stop. "You want to dance some more?"

She tugged on his collar, brushed a soft fingertip down the side of his throat. His mind wandered to more interesting places than the entry hall to the ballroom at the Haltersham Hotel. He wondered what she had on underneath that pretty green dress and how long it would be until he got to find out.

Then she leaned close again. "I was kind of thinking it would be nice to go home…"

He leaned in even closer—close enough to nuzzle her silky hair. "Let's get the hell out of here."

In Paige's bedroom, he ordered the dogs to sleep on the floor. They trotted over to the rug not far from the door and flopped down with a matched pair of gusty sighs.

"How do you get them to do that?" Paige was fumbling with her necklace.

He moved behind her and undid the clasp. "Just call me the dog whisperer."

She snickered. "Right." And then she held out her hand. He put the necklace in it. "Unzip me?"

He took her zipper down and peeled the sides of the dress wide. "Red lace." He ran a finger along the back strap of her bra. "I was wondering what you had under here."

She sent him a teasing smile over her shoulder. "I'm all about the holidays. Green dress. Red satin and lace." She peeled the dress down to her waist. He admired the slim shape of her shoulders, the sleek curves of her back. She shimmied the dress the rest of the way down, taking her lacy, frothy slip with it. Then, stepping out of both, she scooped them up in her free hand.

"What time does Dawn get home?" he asked as he watched her walk away from him, looking way too damn good in those high heels, the red bra and that itty-bitty pair of lace-trimmed red satin panties.

"Dawn's staying over at Molly's." She disappeared through the bathroom door, no doubt headed for the walk-in closet on the other side.

He just stood there for a moment, staring after her, thinking how great it would be to see Paige in her underwear every night for the rest of their lives.

And even better to get it off her. Possibly with his teeth.

Then he remembered he had way too many clothes on. He got busy, tossing his jacket over a chair, taking off his tie and his shirt. Stripped to the waist, he sat on the edge of the bed and whipped off his shoes and socks.

Paige reappeared without the dress, the slip or the necklace. And now her feet were bare.

He rose, undid his belt, slid it from the loops and hung

it over the headboard. "So if Dawn's at Molly's, I guess tonight we can be as loud as we want to be."

She wrapped her arms around herself, which pushed her breasts together over the lacy tops of the red bra. Burying his face there? Definite priority. "You *are* kind of noisy," she said, completely Paige-like, all smug and pulled together, even in nothing but her Christmas underwear.

"*I'm* noisy? Last night, I thought you would scream the house down."

She smiled so sweetly. "You kept shushing me."

"For Dawn's sake. But tonight, I might just let you scream."

She laughed. "As long as it doesn't freak out the dogs."

He dropped trou and then threw them at the chair. "Come here."

"Bossy, bossy." But she came to him. "Can I help you with those boxer briefs?" She didn't wait for his go-ahead, but got right to it, slipping a finger under the elastic waistband, sliding it back and forth against his belly.

The only word that came to mind was "Please."

She peeled off his boxers, going down with them, very slowly, to her knees.

When she got there she tipped her head and glanced up at him. Those eyes of hers, they saw too much. He sifted his fingers through her silky hair, smoothing the dark strands on her shoulders.

And then she wrapped her hand around him. It felt so fine it hurt. A low growl escaped him as she took him in her mouth.

Oh, that was something. Paige all around him, using her hand and that sweet, wet, hot mouth of hers, her silky hair brushing his thighs.

He let that go on for as long as he could bear it, and then he took her arms and lifted her, pulling her close against him, covering her mouth with his, kissing her endlessly as he removed her bra and got rid of those pretty panties. They still stood by the bed and that was fine with him. He kissed her breasts, let his hand trail down to the wet center of her.

She moved against his fingers, moaning, crying out. He never once shushed her. He liked when she made noise, loved when she lost herself, gave herself up to him, shattering from just his touch, once.

And then a second time.

After that, she pulled open the bedside drawer. He helped her, getting the wrapper off the condom, rolling it down over himself.

Then he turned her around and bent her over the bed. She went down, sighing his name. He pushed into her softness from behind, bending over her slim body so he could slide his arm around her and touch her while he moved inside her. He played her slick wetness with his fingers, rocking into her with long, slow, deep strokes until he felt her climax yet again.

That time, she not only cried his name; she said she loved him. She said it loud. "Love you, Carter. Love you way too much…"

No, he didn't believe in that crap. But still, he ate it up. It sounded damn good, now that it was coming from Paige. He'd never thought he'd ever get to be with her like this, get to see her come apart for him, and then make her do it all over again.

He moved faster. She rocked in rhythm with him. It felt so good. Exactly right.

The finish rolled through him. He bent even closer,

his body curling over hers. She reached back and wrapped her hand around his neck, turning her head to offer her lips.

He kissed her as he came, groaning hard into her open mouth. She tasted every bit as good as she felt.

In the morning, he got up without waking her and took the dogs out for a walk. When he returned, he found her at the kitchen table in her robe and elf pajamas, her laptop open in front of her.

The dogs went for their water bowls. He came up behind her, bent close and nibbled her neck. "What's up?"

She reached back and pressed her fingers over his fly. "You. As usual…"

He blew in her ear. "If you mock me, I won't make you breakfast."

She leaned back and he kissed her upside down. Then she explained, "I'm putting together the guest list for our engagement dinner. I figure I can just email it to your mother, right?"

Damn. He'd almost succeeded in forgetting that he had to call his mother that morning. "That'll work."

"You have an email address for her?"

"I don't remember it offhand, but yeah. I'll get it for you." He kissed her once more before rising and going to the counter to start the coffee.

He made them omelets with cream cheese, chives and Canadian bacon. Afterward, he tried to tempt her back to bed.

But she said, "Uh-uh. You need to call your mom. Do it now."

"Bad idea. She won't answer—or if she does, she'll be pissed off."

"Because?"

"She never gets up until ten." It was just nine. "Come on." He grabbed her hand and pulled her out of her chair. "This won't take long. I promise. I'll be on the phone to her at ten sharp."

Paige hung back a little, but the soft, willing curve of her mouth told him it was only because she loved to give him a bad time. He kissed her. She gave right in and kissed him back, after which he coaxed her up the stairs and out of her pajamas. Nothing like getting Paige naked to put the right spin on the day.

And he was as good as his word. They were back in the kitchen, fully dressed, at five after ten.

He called his mother.

"Carter, darling. How nice to hear your voice." He heard her yawn. "I'm so glad you called because I've been longing to congratulate you. I know you and Paige will be blissfully happy."

So far, so good. She hadn't mentioned the property. "Thanks, Ma. I'm a lucky man."

"Did Paige tell you I want to give you a party?"

He glanced at Paige, who sat next to him at the table, laptop open, still working on the guest list. "That's why I'm calling. To tell you that Paige thinks a party at your house sounds great."

"Only Paige? What about you?"

He couldn't resist a jab. "Well, I was already on board. Right?" Paige shot him a sharp look for that remark.

But Willow only chuckled. "You certainly are."

He gritted his teeth. "So, thank you and we accept." Now Paige beamed up at him.

"Wonderful," said his mother in her best tea-on-the-veranda voice. She named the date and added, "Seven for cocktails, with dinner at eight?"

He repeated the information to Paige, who nodded agreement. "Sounds good, Ma. We're on."

"I'm so glad. I asked Paige for a guest list…"

"She's getting it together right now. We'll email it to you today, if that's all right?"

"Perfection, darling." She gave him an email address. Paige passed him a sticky notepad and a pen. He jotted down the address and his mother said, "I'm leaving for Cancún tomorrow." Of course she was. "But Estrella will take care of everything, anyway. I'm just the hostess. I'll be home the day before."

"Great," he said, and felt more relieved than he should have that Willow was leaving again and reducing the likelihood that Paige would find out about the property before he'd explained to her that yes, his mother had tried to blackmail him into getting married, but that had nothing to do with why he'd proposed their Christmas engagement. "Have a good time."

"I will, darling. I always do."

"Thank you, Willow!" Paige piped up, loud enough that his mother heard it through the phone.

"Tell her it's my pleasure."

"I will, Ma."

"You should thank me, too."

"I thought I already did."

"Not for the party, darling…"

His gut clenched when she said that.

She laughed again. "I knew you would choose Paige. You just needed that nudge we discussed at Thanksgiving."

Matricide. Illegal. He had to remember that. "Bye, Ma. Safe trip." He hung up fast.

Paige was watching him. "You okay? You look a little pissed off." Her expression was tender and definitely sympathetic.

Maybe right now would be the best time to come clean, explain everything and reassure her that what was happening between them had zero to do with the property.

But then, what if she didn't believe him? He'd only just managed to convince her to give their engagement a go.

Uh-uh. He needed more time with her before he went into all that.

Paige raised a hand and waved it in front of his face. "Carter? You in there?"

He caught her wrist and pulled her out of the chair. "Right here." He hauled her close and wrapped his arms around her. "God, you feel good." He gave her fine bottom a two-handed squeeze.

"You are insatiable."

"Insatiable." He bent down and bit her neck. "I like that word."

"I need to get the guest list finished," she groused.

"In a minute. Right now you need to kiss me." He tried to capture her mouth.

But she got her hand up between them and pressed her fingers to his lips. Tenderly, she instructed, "Let me go…"

"Kiss me first. Help me forget that my mother drives me crazy."

"One kiss is not going to solve all your issues with your mother."

"Stop talking about my mother."

"You're the one who—"

He didn't let her finish. Pushing her fingers to the side, he captured that sweet mouth of hers.

By the time he let her go back to her laptop, he felt a whole lot better about everything.

Wednesday, Carter took Paige to a tree-decorating party out at the Bar-N Ranch, where his cousin, Rory, lived with her fiancé, Walker McKellan.

Most of the family was there—his sisters and brothers, and his half siblings, too. Some brought dates. Clara came with her husband, Dalton. Quinn brought his wife, Chloe. There was lots of food and plenty to drink and Christmas tunes playing nonstop. They all worked together to get the ranch house decked out right for the holiday season.

With everybody pitching in, the work went fast. The day before, Walker and Rory had cut down a beauty of a tree and set it up in a stand in front of the great room window. In record time, they had the lights strung and the decorations hung. Then they stood around the fire, shooting the breeze.

Nell was the first to mention the engagement dinner. "Guess what I got in the mail today?" She sipped a Black Russian.

Clara said, "An invitation to Paige and Carter's engagement dinner at the mansion?"

"You guessed it."

*Me, too*s filled the room.

Carter glanced at Paige. Her eyes were waiting. She mouthed, "That was fast."

Elise, his other half sister, said, "Those invitations

are gorgeous. Estrella's an artist, I swear. I mean, you could frame mine, I'm not kidding." For the benefit of friends not in the know, she explained, "Estrella's the housekeeper. She's a great cook, a brilliant organizer *and* she does calligraphy."

Clara said, "I'm so glad about this. This is big. Willow never does stuff like this. I keep asking her to come to family things. She always says she'll be out of town." She nodded at Rory. "Rory asked her to come tonight."

Paige was still tucking shiny ornaments into the mantel display. She arranged a gold pinecone just so among the pine boughs and said, "She's off to Cancún. Right, Carter?" At his grunt of agreement, she went on. "The dinner party was totally Willow's idea. She caught me at the Holiday Ball and said she'd like to give us a party."

"Wait a minute." Ice cubes rattled as Nell swirled her drink. "Mom was at the ball?"

Quinn and Chloe exchanged a doubtful look. Quinn said, "We didn't see her."

Garrett, Carter's other full brother, shrugged. "I didn't, either."

So Paige went ahead and told them about Willow catching her in the deserted hallway. "She looked beautiful," Paige said, "in a low-cut black silk jersey dress. I swear she doesn't look a day over forty—if that."

Jody, Carter's other full sister, who owned a florist shop on Central Street and was two years older than Nell, asked, "Did anyone but Paige see her that night?" There was a lot of head-shaking and a chorus of nos.

Paige said, "I know. It was strange. When she first grabbed my arm, I thought maybe I was about to come face-to-face with one of the Haltersham's famous ghosts."

"Weird," remarked Nell. "Mom is just weird."

Nobody disagreed. Carter could have added that their mother was also diabolical and manipulative and sometimes he wanted to strangle her. But he kept that opinion to himself and headed for the kitchen to grab another beer.

Quinn followed him in there. "Get me one, too?"

Carter took two longnecks from the fridge. "I think I need a little fresh air."

Quinn accepted the beer Carter handed him. "Mind some company?"

"Why not?"

They tossed their empties in the recycle bin Rory had set out in plain sight and went through the dining room to the front hall, where Garrett, beer in hand, joined them. Carter led the way out to the front porch, his brothers behind him.

Garrett hooked a leg on the porch rail. Carter and Quinn took the matched pair of carved wooden chairs that Walker, a skilled carpenter, had made himself. It was pretty cold, but they all wore thick sweaters, jeans and boots against the chill.

Carter glanced from Quinn to Garrett, thinking how they all three looked kind of like their father—big and bulked up. Quinn was a couple of inches shorter than Carter, his brown hair a shade lighter. Garrett, a year younger than Carter, ran Bravo Construction with Nell. He had almost-black hair and was the tallest of the three of them at six-four.

"I'm happy for you," said Quinn, tipping his longneck in Carter's direction. Carter tapped the bottle with his and they drank. Quinn nodded. "Paige is a winner and you two have always had something good going on."

"You lucky dog." Garrett knocked back a long sip. "All the good ones are getting snapped up."

Carter and Quinn snorted in unison. It wasn't as if Garrett was falling all over himself trying to find someone to settle down with. He liked the single life.

Garrett braced his shoulder against the porch post and nudged Carter's leg with his boot. "Mom giving a family party? Never saw that coming."

Carter took another long pull off his beer. "Paige wanted it, wanted to help her get 'outside herself.' Paige's words, not mine."

Garrett and Quinn exchanged freighted glances and Garrett said, "Yeah. We get that there's no way you were driving it." Of the three of them, Carter had always been the most impatient with Willow. He openly admitted his resentment of the choices she'd made and the childhood she'd put them through. Back in the day, he and his brothers and sisters had been known as the Bastard Bravos. It was a small town. Everybody knew way too much about everybody else. People looked down on them because their mom wouldn't stop having kids with another woman's husband.

Quinn, who had fists of steel and a heart of mush, said, "Be patient with Mom, bro."

"I'm trying. It ain't easy." He considered how much he was willing to say, and then asked Garrett, "She been after you to settle down?"

Garrett looked mildly terrified. "Hell, no. Why? She been after you?"

"Yeah. She kind of was. It's all Quinn's fault."

His youngest brother made a thoughtful sound. "Because of me and Chloe?"

"That's right."

Quinn settled deeper into the chair. "Marrying Chloe is the best thing I ever did."

Garrett challenged, "What about your little girl?"

"That goes without sayin'. Annabelle. Chloe. I got it all. Never thought I'd be this happy."

"And I'm happy *for* you," Garrett said. "For both of you. But just leave me out of it. I like being single."

Carter couldn't resist ribbing him. "You watch. Ma'll be after you next."

Quinn frowned. "Wait a minute. I'm getting the feeling she did more to push you toward the altar than you're telling us…"

Cater knew he'd already said too much. Still, he was kind of tempted to go all in, to tell his brothers exactly what their mother had done, and to ask them what they thought about his waiting for the right moment to go into it with Paige.

But why? It wouldn't matter what advice they gave him. He was going to do it his way, pick his own time—the *right* time—to tell Paige everything.

No call to go dragging Quinn and Garrett into it.

So he only shrugged. "Ma just got on me is all. She got after me to find a wife and start a family."

"And look." Garrett chortled. "It worked."

Carter had a sudden burning need to punch his middle brother in the face. But he settled for giving him the evil eye. "Don't even think that. Ma has got nothing to do with me marrying Paige."

Garrett put up both hands. "Don't shoot, big brother. I take it all back."

"Smart move." Carter drained the rest of his beer and stood. "We should go back in and join the party."

Quinn looked up at him, worry in his blue-green eyes. "You sure you're okay?"

"I'm good." And he was. He had Paige. She was not only his best friend now, she was *his* in the best kind of way. He liked sleeping with her, being able to stay at her house pretty much all the time. He liked *really* being a family with her and Dawn. And the sex with Paige? He loved that. Damn, if he'd only known. He wouldn't have wasted so many years just being her friend.

But Paige was all his now.

And he wasn't going to lose her, no way. They'd get through the test drive and end up together. He'd find a way to explain to her why he hadn't told her about Willow's skeevy trick sooner. It would all work out just right.

He had nothing to worry about. Not a damn thing.

Chapter Ten

That Saturday, Carter took another day off from BCC and drove Dawn to Denver to Christmas shop. Over the years, the trip had become an annual deal for the two of them. They left early in the morning.

Paige had a few things to go over at the shop, so she went in at eight. She made herself a cup of coffee and started running the numbers again for their expansion plans. It all looked good. She was almost tempted to give the Realtor a call, have her go ahead and make another offer on the Arrowhead Drive property. They could afford to pay more than they'd offered before Thanksgiving.

But first, she really ought to touch base with Carter. Not that he would care. He would go along with whatever she decided. Carter was the car genius. She was responsible for making the numbers add up. If she said she wanted to offer more and do it now, he would just say she should go for it.

Still, it was only right to run it by him before she made another move.

It had started to snow, pretty white flakes drifting by the window to the parking lot, when Mona came in at nine. Paige had the door to her office open and Mona stuck her head in. "What are you doing here on a Saturday?"

Paige got up and grabbed her mug. "Number crunching. Carter won't be in. He took Dawn Christmas shopping in Denver."

"I know." Mona headed for the K-Cup machine and Paige followed. "He sent me a text. It's not a problem. Jake and Billy can handle whatever comes up." The two mechanics were already at work out in the shop.

Paige and Mona chatted about Christmas shopping and the weather as Mona brewed herself a mug of caramel vanilla crème.

"White Christmas coming right up." Mona raised her full mug toward the window where the snow was coming down. Paige popped in a pod for herself and pushed the brew button. Mona asked, "So. How's engaged life treating you?"

"It's good." And it was. Overall. It did kind of bug her that she kept saying she loved him—mostly in bed when she kind of couldn't help herself—and he kept *not* saying it back. She shouldn't let it get to her. She knew how he was.

And her coffee was ready. She pulled the full mug out from under the spout. "Are you and Dean coming to our party at Willow's next Saturday?" Dean was Mona's husband of twenty-odd years.

"Wouldn't miss it." Mona sipped her coffee. "Carter's a good guy."

"I know."

"You two are great together."

"Thanks."

"So smile and act happy about it," Mona teased.

Paige laughed. "I'll have you know I *am* happy."

Mona nodded. "Excellent. To you and Carter and a lifetime of happiness." She raised her mug and Paige tapped it with hers.

In Denver, Carter took Dawn to Cherry Creek Mall and Larimer Square. They each bought gifts for Paige. Dawn helped him choose presents for his brothers and sisters. She shopped for Molly and Molly's mom. And they bought each other presents, too. It was part of their yearly tradition. They gave each other painfully specific hints about what they wanted.

Hints like, "Hey, Carter," as Dawn gestured grandly over a minifridge in the Macy's Home Store.

Carter scowled back broadly. "What do you need with a minifridge?"

"It's *convenient* to have a few fresh snacks in my room," Dawn replied, playing it adorably perky. "Plus, college? It'll be a freshman at CU before you know it. I'm so gonna need this in my dorm room."

"Forget it. I'm not dragging a minifridge all the way home." Total lie. He was definitely dragging that minifridge all the way home.

Once they'd clearly telegraphed what they wanted from each other, they both sneaked around, ordering each other to go elsewhere in the store so they could each grab the thing the other wasn't supposed to know about—even though they both knew damn well what the "secret" things were, because they'd each told the other exactly what they wanted.

Yeah, it was silly.

It was also great fun, teasing Dawn, the two of them running around the stores like a couple of fools.

Getting the minifridge under the camper shell in the back of his dually without her seeing him do it? A tougher job than most years.

But he made it happen.

Once they both got all their Christmas shopping handled, Carter always took her for a late lunch at the Capital Grille.

They'd just been served the Grille's signature cheeseburgers with Parmesan truffle fries, when Dawn announced right out of the blue, "You know, if you hurt my sister, I might have to kill you."

He set down the truffle fry he'd been just about to pop into his mouth. "Whoa, Dawn. Where'd that come from? I thought you were happy for me and Paige."

"I *am* happy for you. Mostly."

"Mostly? What the hell, Dawn?"

She sipped her Cherry Coke. "I love you, Carter. Everybody does. But you know how you are."

"Huh?"

"You heard me. I worry about how you are."

He picked up another fry, dredged it in ketchup and ate it before daring to ask her what in the hell she was talking about. "Okay. I'll bite. How am I, exactly?"

She cut her burger in half. Slowly. "You're a great friend. You're totally there for Paige—and for me, too. As a friend. But you're pretty old to be suddenly deciding you want to marry my sister."

He tried to make light of it. "Old? I'm not *that* old."

"Yeah, you kind of are. I mean, come on. There are statistics about guys like you. When guys your age who have never been in a long-term, committed relationship finally *do* get married, the chances of it lasting are not good."

He wanted to tell her that was a bunch of crap. But hadn't his mother said essentially the same thing? And that was kind of spooky, the more he thought about it.

Which made him decide *not* to think about it.

Dawn demanded, "What changed your mind all of a sudden?"

"Nothing changed my mind. I just realized that Paige is the one for me, okay?" Did he sound defensive? He wasn't. Uh-uh. Not in the least. He got to work on his burger, guzzled some beer.

Dawn took a few bites, too. Then she jabbed a fry in his direction. "You should take advantage of this moment and make me feel a whole lot better."

"Yeah? How?"

"Tell me how in love you are with my sister."

Love. Right. She just *had* to go and bring up love. "Look, Dawn—"

"See that?" She wiggled the fry at him. "That right there? You're scared to say it. And that's not good."

"You don't know what you're talking about." He said that in his firmest, most mature tone.

But Dawn was not impressed by his firmness and maturity. "I know exactly what I'm talkin' about." She sat back in her chair and gave him a tight little smile. "And *you* know how to convince me I'm wrong, but you are not doing it."

He threw up both hands. "Okay. Now I'm lost."

"Oh, no, you're not. You know exactly what you're *not* saying." She was too damn smart by half.

"Your sister's everything to me. I just don't believe in all that hearts-and-flowers crap, okay?"

"No, Carter. It's not okay. You've got a love phobia and you need to get over it. A man needs to be able to tell the woman he loves *that* he loves her. Paige deserves that. You know she does."

"You're way overcomplicating this thing."

"No, I am not."

"Plus, there is no such thing as a love phobia."

"Oh, yeah, there is. You have an irrational fear of falling in love."

He tried a little scoffing. "You're eighteen years old. What do you know about my supposed irrational fears?"

"Being eighteen doesn't make me totally oblivious. Unlike *some* people I could mention."

"Now I'm oblivious?" That kind of hurt.

Dawn tipped her head to the side and studied him for several long, uncomfortable seconds. "Look. I told you already, you're a great guy. But you've had a lot of girlfriends and none of them have lasted all that long. I just worry, I do. I don't want my sister hurt. Especially not by her best friend in the whole world."

"But I don't want to hurt her, Dawn. I would never hurt Paige. I want to *marry* her, make a family with her."

She had her hands in her lap now, and she stared down at them, hard. "My sister is the best there is."

"You think I don't know that?"

"She's only been in love once before in her life." Dawn spoke more softly now. She still refused to look at him. "And you know what that low-down rat did to her, dumping her flat because of me..." The tightness in her voice spoke of tears about to fall.

"Dawnie. Hey. Come on, now. Look at me."

"Fine." Dawn jerked her head up and glared at him through tear-shiny eyes. She dashed away the moisture with the back of her hand.

He had a clean handkerchief and he passed it to her. She yanked it from his fingers and dabbed her eyes some more.

He reminded her, "That guy wasn't good enough for Paige."

"I know that." She sniffed.

"And it's not your fault that Paige came home when you lost your parents."

"Of course it was my fault. She had to come home and raise me or I would've gone to my dad's sister, Aunt Mary Frances, in DC. Aunt Mary Frances never got married and works for the State Department. She keeps plastic covers on the furniture and is allergic to pets. No way could Paige do that to me. So she came home for me. She had no choice."

He couldn't let that stand. "It was *not* your fault, no way, no how. And Paige did have a choice. There's always a choice. Your sister made the right one—to take care of you, to keep your family together. And because she made the right choice, she got to see who that Kellogg creep really was before she went and married him."

Dawn wiped at her eyes again. "Well, I guess you're right about that."

"Yes, I am. And I'm not going to hurt Paige."

She gave him her best tough-girl scowl. "You better not."

"I promise I won't."

"Good. Because you'll *really* be in trouble with me if you do."

"Point taken. Eat your burger."

She grabbed it off her plate and took a giant bite, chewing aggressively and swallowing hard.

He suggested mildly, "Please don't choke yourself."

She reached for her Cherry Coke, sucked down about half of it and set the glass back on the table with purpose. "I do love you, Carter. I'll probably always love you, no matter what you do. And so will Paige. But you really need *not* to screw this up, okay?"

"I won't screw it up," he promised, and thought about the property. His mother would be back from Mexico in six days and Paige needed to know everything by then. "You can count on me," he added strongly, because he *was* going to tell Paige before Friday. He would get totally straight with her, lay everything out. "I mean that."

"Great." Dawn tried a wobbly little smile and then ate more of the burger, chewing more slowly this time. He went to work on his food, too. Eventually, she offered in her best peacemaking voice, "Share the hazelnut cake for dessert?"

He grinned wide, relieved and grateful that she wasn't staying mad at him. "What's lunch at the Grille without hazelnut cake?"

By the time they got in the pickup for the ride back to Justice Creek, Dawn's usual sunny spirits had returned in full force. She cranked up the radio and sang along to the holiday tunes while he griped that if he heard "White Christmas" one more time he just might lose his mind. It had been snowing on and off all day. Halfway home, the snow started coming down again.

They reached Justice Creek at a few minutes of four.

The dogs greeted them at the door. No sign of Paige yet. She'd said she was going to BCC that day and probably wouldn't be home until five or six. He helped Dawn haul all her loot up to her room. She gave him a hug and then went to Molly's.

Carter drove over to his place. He transferred the minifridge from the back of the pickup to the floor of his garage, dropped off his bags full of Christmas stuff, grabbed a change of clothes and returned to Paige's, where he took the dogs out for a walk in the snow.

When he got back to the house, the outside lights were on. So was the tree in the living room window. Paige must be home. He walked faster, eager to get to her, impatient with having to pause on the front porch to knock the snow off his boots.

He was just reaching for the door when she pulled it open.

God, she looked good. The light behind her brought out the shine to her dark hair, and those brown eyes were bigger than ever. Her fine mouth curved up in a smile just for him. How was it that the house always seemed warmer and brighter when Paige was in it?

"It's freezing out there. Get in here." She grabbed him by his heavy jacket and pulled him over the threshold. The dogs whined in greeting and danced around them as she shoved the door shut, turned the lock and engaged the chain.

Then came the best part. She melted into his arms.

The woman could kiss. How could he have lasted all those years without ever once having her tongue in his mouth? He loved the taste of her, the feel of her body under his hands, pressing against him. The smell of her—vanilla and coffee, something a little spicy, just so damn good.

He was hard in an instant.

She laughed. "It's nice how glad you are to see me."

"And to *feel* you…" He buried his face against her neck, scraping his teeth there, then licking the spot, too. She moaned.

And the dogs kept whining. Biscuit went up on his hind legs, pleading for Paige's attention.

Sorry, buddy. Me first. He lifted his head long enough to tell them both firmly, "Down. Go." Biscuit dropped to all fours again. With one more whine each, both dogs turned away. Their paws tapped the floor as they trotted to the kitchen and a happy reunion with their water and food bowls.

She asked, "Good day shopping?"

"The best. And that's saying something, given that I'm a guy and guys hate shopping."

"Dawn called. She said she had a great time, too. And she's spending the night at Molly's."

He bit her neck again and then whispered against her soft skin, "Good. Tonight I can see you naked in front of the fire."

"Where you're going to see me naked always seems to be a priority for you."

The stairs were right behind him. He shrugged out of his jacket and tossed it over the newel post. "That's because I've got my priorities in order." She wore a soft blue sweater dress, belted, with black tights and tall boots. He went to work on the belt, getting it undone and off her in seconds flat.

She slapped at his wrist. "Handsy much?"

He gave her his best wounded look. "I can't help myself."

"Yeah, right."

"Because there are so many places I want to see you naked and so very few hours in a day…"

She laughed as he undressed her, lifting her arms so he could whip off the big sweater, turning obediently to let him unhook her lacy pink bra. He got a little distracted from his purpose when he started kissing her breasts. She wrapped her hand around his head and held him close and whispered his name while he bit her nipple—gently—and flicked it with his tongue.

Eventually, he realized he had yet to reach the main goal. "Sit here." He took her by the shoulders and guided her down to sit on the stair so he could pull off those tall, sexy boots. Then he took her hand and stood her up and got to work on the tights. When she stepped out of them, he hung them on the newel post over his jacket.

That left only her little pink panties. She took them down for him and tossed them over her shoulder. "Ta-da!"

He bent and grabbed her around the waist, lifting her in a fireman's carry and heading for the living room as she laughed, kicked those long, silky legs and pounded his back with her fists.

When he set her down in front of the fire, she went right to work helping him get naked, too. He took the condom from his pocket and set it within reach as they stretched out on the rug together.

It was so good, better even than he'd imagined it might be, lying with her in the glow of the fire, snow falling outside. He kissed her, top to toe, and then he buried himself in her. She wrapped her arms and legs around him, holding him close to her, whispering his name.

At the end, she said the *L* word. "Love you. Oh, Carter, love you so much…"

He didn't say it back to her. He couldn't, somehow. Even though he knew what he felt. Knew what he had with her. Knew without any doubt that she was the one for him.

And had been for a lot longer than he'd ever let himself admit.

He lifted himself up on his arms and stared down at her, rocking into her, loving the way her pale skin flushed burning pink.

"Love you…" She opened her eyes then, and she looked right at him. "Love you," she whispered, still contracting around him. She closed her eyes, turned her head to the side.

"Don't…" He bent closer then. But she kept her face turned away from him. So he caught her chin and made her turn to him. He covered her mouth and kissed her until she opened for him.

That did it, somehow. Her tongue came out and tangled with his and that tipped him over. He surged into her, kissing her so hard and deep as his climax shuddered through him.

It was all so romantic, Paige thought. Perfect really. Paige and Carter, all cozy, on a snowy winter's night.

But in spite of all that perfection, she wanted to cry. She really hated that she was starting to understand exactly, up close and personal, why all his girlfriends turned into drama queens eventually.

He was the greatest guy in the world—helpful, tender, smart. Funny, sexy, attentive.

But he just wouldn't let a woman get too close. And

that was beyond frustrating. It made her want to yell at him and start throwing things.

Carter whipped up some pasta with marinara sauce for dinner. Paige had brought home a fresh loaf of sourdough. She cut up a salad.

They ate in the breakfast nook, sharing a bottle of red, with candles on the table and the snow drifting down outside. The food was delicious.

And she was with the man she loved.

Perfect.

Except for that little problem he had with the word *love*. Except for how all of it was only a test drive with a plus-and-minus review waiting at New Year's.

Yep. She really got it now. Why all his girlfriends ended up throwing tantrums and calling him names. She felt more sympathy for them than ever lately. She thought of them fondly, wished them all well.

And she reminded herself that she'd gone into this knowing exactly what was up with him. She really did love him. And even if it didn't work out in the end, she was not going to regret this time they had together.

She was going to enjoy it, put her hurt feelings away and focus on the good stuff.

Because there was plenty of good stuff.

After dinner, they lingered at the table over second glasses of wine.

"I gave the books a good going-over at BCC today," she said. "We are so in the black."

"And that makes you happy." He gave her a relaxed smile. "I love it when you're happy."

"Good. Because I *am* happy." *About BCC's success, anyway.* "And I'm thinking maybe we should go forward with the Arrowhead Drive property. I can tell Kelly to up our offer, see if we can seal the deal before Christmas, after all. That way we can probably make the move by the end of January."

He had the strangest look suddenly. Vague and wary, both at once—and maybe just a little…what? Guilty? She was about to ask him what was going on when the look vanished and she wondered if she'd seen it at all. He drank some wine and settled back in his chair. "I don't know. What's the big hurry? Why not just wait like we planned? I don't want to pay more than it's worth."

She laughed. "You're kidding, right? You never worry about the money."

"Well, I just think our plan to wait till after New Year's is a solid one, that's all."

Good thing she'd checked with him before making a move. "It's always possible someone will come along and scoop it up while we're waiting for the owner to get reasonable about the price. You're okay with that?"

He looked out the dark bay window, where the snow was starting to pile up on the sill. "Paige, the property's been sitting there with no action for over a year. It's not going anywhere. And it's only a few weeks till the New Year."

"You didn't answer my question."

He stood, rounded the table and got behind her.

She tipped her head back to look up at him. "What are you up to now?"

Those gorgeous moss-green eyes held hers. He smiled a slow upside-down smile. And then he put his big hands on her shoulders, bent close and whispered in her ear, "Forget the property for now. It's all going to work out, you'll see…" He tucked a sweet kiss right there, behind her ear.

Her blood got thicker, her body felt warmer. Intelligent thought deserted her. "If you say so…"

"Um." He nibbled his way down the side of her throat. "Let's go upstairs."

"Why? You've already seen me naked up there."

"Exactly. And that's how I know it's something I really need to see again…"

Yeah, all right. Carter felt like a first-class douche canoe for not busting to the truth about the property when Paige had given him the perfect opportunity to tell all.

He could so easily have said, *We've already got the property. My mother bought it for us as a wedding present.* He *should* have said it, and then gone on to explain the whole truth.

But that was the problem: the whole truth didn't look so good.

What if she didn't believe him when he said the property had nothing to do with their sudden engagement? And already, he'd waited too long to tell her. That alone would make her wonder…

He decided not to think about it. Not right now.

He still had a week to figure out what to do.

Instead of getting honest, he took her upstairs and straight to bed, where he unwrapped her like a present—the best present ever. She was the gift that kept on giving. Every day, every hour, every minute he had with her only made him more and more certain she was exactly the woman for him, right for him in every way. Paige was totally no drama, the sanest woman on the planet.

Also, the sexiest in the most down-to-earth, *real* way. And funny and smart. He never got bored just hanging around with her. And now that she was his, he was never doing anything that might make her go away.

Sunday, they spent the whole day together, doing pretty much nothing. They walked the dogs, hung out with Dawn and Molly. They wrapped Christmas presents and piled them high under the tree. He stayed the night, same as he had every night since he'd finally gotten his ring on her finger. Daily, he moved more and more of his stuff to Paige's. Why would he want to be at his place, when he could be at hers, where it was cozy and homey—because Paige was there?

The week passed so quickly. He kept reminding himself he had to get honest with Paige before Willow got home. But then, all at once, it was Thursday and he still hadn't said anything.

And then on Friday morning, the day his mother was due home from Mexico, when time was seriously running out, Paige buzzed him in the shop. "I need a few minutes. My office?"

"Something wrong?"

"It's about the property." *Crap.* He and his two other mechanics, Jake Lindell and Billy McClesky, were pulling the original engine from a little bit of automotive history, the first of the muscle cars, a '49 Oldsmobile Rocket 88. "Carter. You there? I've got our Realtor holding on the outside line…"

"Uh. Right here. Sorry." Billy and Jake could manage without him. "I'll be right in."

Dread forming a hot, hard ball in the center of his chest, he got out of his coveralls and cleaned up fast at the sink.

Paige's office door was open. She was still on the phone, but she saw him and gestured him in. He hung back in the doorway, reluctant to find out exactly what was going on, as though by not entering the room, he could somehow forestall the inevitable. "All right," she said—to the Realtor, he assumed. "No, Kelly. Uh-uh. Don't even blame yourself. He *told* you he would let you know if there was another offer. It's on Kritinski that he didn't even bother to give us a chance at it and we didn't find out until now…" Alan Kritinski was the owner of the property on Arrowhead Drive. Or had been, anyway, until Willow made her move. "Yes." Paige slid another glance at Carter. "He's here now. I'll talk it over with him and then we'll let you know what we want to do next… Thanks." She hung up and gave him a distracted frown. "You're lurking. Come in and shut the door."

He obeyed, shoving the door closed behind him, dropping into one of the two chairs that faced her desk. "What's up?" As if he didn't know.

"You won't believe this. Kelly was checking the listings and discovered that the Arrowhead Drive property's been sold—and, Carter, you'll never guess who bought it."

And there it was. Yet another chance to come clean. He opened his mouth to tell all.

Nothing came out.

Paige said, "Carter, you're gaping."

"Uh, yeah. Just surprised." He ought to be ashamed of himself. And he was. But that didn't stop him from asking, "Who bought it?" as if he didn't damn well know.

"Brace yourself."

"Hit me with it."

"Your mother bought it."

"Wow," he said lamely, because he knew he had to say something. "That's bizarre."

Paige shook her head. "I don't get it. What could Willow possibly want with an empty factory building, a big parking lot and some office space?"

"Not a clue," he lied some more. Because why stop now?

She chided, "I told you we should move on it."

"And I guess you were right." He put on a regretful expression. It wasn't all that hard. "Sorry. I screwed up." In more ways than one.

But then Paige smiled. It was a real smile, an easy one. The knot of dread in his chest loosened just a little. She shrugged. "Yeah, but it would have been too late anyway. Willow bought it weeks ago, before Thanksgiving. She must have struck the deal just a day or two after Kritinski turned *us* down."

He rubbed a hand over the back of his head. "She's my own mother and still, I will never understand what drives that woman." That, at least, was true.

Paige nodded. "Totally concur. What was she thinking?"

And that was when it came to him. Right then, as Paige agreed with him about Willow. He finally saw the perfect solution to this sticky problem that had so far only kept sucking him down deeper and deeper into lies and evasions.

It was so simple. He should have thought of it before. *Paige never needed to know.*

Willow could give them the property as a wedding present, as promised—and keep her mouth shut about the rest of it.

Everybody wins.

Paige was already moving on to the next supposed

step. "So we'll have to start looking again. I'm sure Kelly can find us something that will work for us."

He spoke up then. "Before you turn the Realtor loose, let me talk with my mother." *And tell her she'd better not say a damn word.*

"What good will that do?"

"What good? You just said it yourself. What possible use could she have for that property?" *Except as a bribe to manipulate her own son?* "Whatever she bought it for, I can probably make her see that we need it more than she does. I'm hoping I can get her to sell it to us for a reasonable price." *A price like, say, nothing.* "So just tell Kelly to hold off until we have more time to think about it."

Paige templed her fingers and swiveled in her chair. "Why not? It's certainly worth a shot."

Chapter Eleven

Carter went straight to his own office off the shop and called the mansion. Estrella told him that Willow wasn't due home until the afternoon.

"Have her call me the minute she gets in?"

"Of course."

He tried Willow's cell. Straight to voice mail. He left a message for her to call him immediately.

And then he waited.

She never called back.

He tried the mansion again at two that afternoon. Estrella said Willow had called to say she'd run into an old friend in Denver and wouldn't be home until the next morning.

"Did you ask her to call me?"

"Of course. She hasn't called you yet?" Estrella sounded apprehensive. "I really did make it clear to her that you wanted to hear from her right away."

He soothed the housekeeper and told her not to worry. "We both know my mother. She does what she wants to do." *And to hell with the rest of us.*

"I'll be glad to call her again and remind her that you're waiting to speak with her."

"No, don't do that. It's not your problem. Thank you, Estrella. I'll take it from here."

He called Willow's cell again. This time he left her a detailed message explaining everything, that Paige knew Willow had bought the property but she didn't know why. And Carter had decided she didn't need to know. His mother was to keep her mouth shut about what she'd been up to. He ended with "And when you get this, call me back right away."

Willow never called.

That evening, Dawn and Molly had their Christmas concert at the high school auditorium. Both girls had solos. Carter and Paige sat close to the stage, and Carter tried to focus on the music, on both Dawn's and Molly's accomplishments. They were talented girls, each headed for great things, he was certain. He tried to forget about his damn mother and her games. He thought he did a pretty good job of that.

But later, when he and Paige were alone in her bedroom, she asked him why he seemed so jumpy. He lied and said he was nervous about the engagement party. She kissed him and promised him it was going to be fun, that they would have a great time.

He hardly slept all night. He kept his cell by the bed with the sound on, so desperate to make things clear to Willow that he didn't care that Paige would hear it when it rang.

He had his lies all lined up. If Paige asked him who

was calling at such a late hour, he planned to groan and gripe that it was Willow, who couldn't be disturbed until ten in the morning, but felt perfectly justified calling other people at any damn time of the day or night. Then he would take it in the other room. And once he'd dealt with his mother, he would get back in bed with Paige and pull her into his arms. If she was still awake and wanted to know what the call was about, he'd tell her the good news: Willow was giving them a killer of a wedding present.

But the phone never rang.

By morning, he felt as if he had ants under his skin, all jumpy and freaked. He did his best to hide it from Paige.

But she saw through him, knew him to his core. She knew that something was really bugging him. She just guessed wrong as to what. She caught his face between her hands and kissed him, slow and sweet, and then promised him that the party was going to be beautiful.

She tried to convince him to stay home from BCC. But he told her he needed to go in, even though he didn't. That was in order that he could take off at lunchtime without Paige knowing he'd gone.

He drove to the mansion, planning a stakeout. He would refuse to leave until he'd talked to Willow and she was on board with the plan.

Estrella answered the door in a chef's apron. Wonderful cooking smells drifted out around her. She said she was very sorry. Willow had called to check in at ten and explained that she wanted to have lunch with her "old friend." She wouldn't be home until five that evening.

"But I have it all under control, I promise you, Carter. Everything will be just right for tonight."

He reassured her, "I know it's going to be great, Estrella, because you're in charge and you are the best."

She beamed. "How nice of you to say—and while you're here, why don't you come in for a minute? Let me show you the table. You can have a look at the menu, take a quick tour through the public rooms. I've rearranged the furniture a bit to make it more comfortable for mingling. Plus, the house does look beautiful all done up for the holidays. And on your mother's instruction, I've stocked the wet bar with several bottles of Veuve Clicquot, which will be on ice when the guests arrive. There's nothing like good champagne to get the guests smiling. Especially when you're celebrating something as important as your engagement to that one special woman you want to spend your whole life with."

He could not have cared less about the menu—which Paige had approved after sharing it with him—or the table or even the fancy champagne. But Estrella was a total sweetheart, stuck on her own getting ready for *his* party. He couldn't refuse her. "I would love to see…everything."

She stepped back and ushered him in. He followed her through the rooms, oohing and aahing over the showy Christmas decorations and the table set with Sondra Bravo's gold candlesticks, monogrammed gold flatware and gold-rimmed dishes. He told Estrella it was all gorgeous. And it was. That table would have passed muster at the Prince's Palace in Montedoro, where his cousin Rory had grown up. And the food? Estrella's meals were always excellent. But she'd outdone herself, with a full-out prime rib feast. She had five large standing rib roasts all trussed up and rubbed with spices, ready to go into the mansion's three large ovens when the time was right.

When he'd seen it all, she walked him back to the

door and he thanked her again for everything. He returned to BCC and worked for another couple of hours.

And then he went home—well, actually, to Paige's house, which had been more a home to him than his own place for a long time now. He greeted the dogs and found Dawn and Molly in the living room, laughing it up, playing the Wii version of "DanceDanceRevolution." He stuck his head in and waved at them. They giggled, returned his wave and went right on dancing.

He made a circuit of the main floor in search of Paige. When he didn't find her, he climbed the stairs. No sign of her up there, either.

So he texted her. Where u @?

She answered right away. Hair & nails. Party, remember?

He wanted her there with him, didn't want to miss a minute he might have with her. Which was paranoid and he knew it. They had the rest of their lives together. I'm home. Miss u.

She sent back a heart smiley and B there in 1 hr.

He took a shower and then stretched out on the bed to wait for her. But his recent sleepless nights caught up with him. He must have dozed off.

When he woke, it was after five. Paige should've been home two hours ago. Mildly freaked, he groped for his phone. But then he realized that someone had settled the spare blanket over him: Paige.

He pushed back the blanket and swung his feet to the floor.

The sound of feminine voices led him to the shut door of Dawn's room. He knocked. "Dawn?"

"Don't come in here! No men allowed!" Dawn yelled back.

"Where's Paige?"

The door opened a crack and Paige stuck her head out. "Right here." Her silky hair was piled up loosely in pretty, soft curls. "Did you sleep well?"

"Great." He bent close and brushed her lips with his. She smelled like roses and some sexy spice, and he wanted her out from behind that door and into his empty arms.

She said, "I'll be out in ten minutes."

He leaned on the doorframe. "Why not now?"

Dawn called, "Eye makeup, Carter! We need Paige for that."

Paige explained, "It seems I have a talent for the gradient effect."

Which told him nothing. "Huh?"

"It'll be more like half an hour," Dawn called. "And the sooner you let her get back in here, the sooner she'll be done!"

So he left them alone and went downstairs, where he ate a handful of peanuts to hold him over until the prime rib and hoped that Paige would hurry. They could maybe slip in a quickie before they finished getting ready.

But when she met him in the bedroom twenty minutes later and he tried to kiss her, she wasn't going for it. "I just spent half the day getting my hair like this. Now you want to me to roll around on the bed with you?"

"Your hair looks beautiful." He eased her robe off her shoulders. "I'll be careful."

"Liar." She pushed his hand away.

He pouted. Even though men don't pout. Unless they have no shame…

"Poor baby." She relented then, and kissed him. And then she stepped back and shook a finger at him. "Don't you even touch my hair."

"I wouldn't. I swear it…"

And then, slowly, she sank to her knees.

Damn, she was amazing. Too many years they'd wasted. He would do anything to keep her, now that he finally had her in the fullest way.

He clasped his hands behind his back to keep them from going where they ached to go—which was directly into all those soft, silky curls. He made himself *not* touch her and watched her use her hands and mouth on him. It was so beautiful. He never wanted it to end.

But it did. Spectacularly. When he pulled her to her feet again, he tried to return the favor. But she only pressed her soft hand to his cheek and said, "We're out of time. I need to get ready."

Out of time. It sounded so…ominous.

Would Ma be back at the mansion now? Maybe he could sneak in a quick call to her.

"Carter?"

"Huh?"

Paige gazed up at him, her smooth brow crinkled in a frown. "You seem distracted. Are you all right?"

"Are you kidding? You just went down on me and I'm getting prime rib for dinner. What could possibly be wrong?"

He did try to reach Willow again on her cell while Paige was busy in the bathroom. Straight to voice mail. He didn't even bother to leave a message. And there was no point in calling the mansion again just to listen to poor, overworked Estrella make excuses for his mother.

Fine. If possible, he'd get Ma alone during the party. If not, well, he just hoped to hell he'd get lucky and she wouldn't tell Paige the real reason she'd bought the property right out from under their noses.

What a mess. His mother was a piece of work—popping up out of nowhere when you didn't want her around, never available when you needed her.

His hair was kind of scrambled after his nap, so he grabbed another quick shower and put on a good suit. Paige looked terrific in a black dress with one of those tops that tied behind her neck and left her pretty shoulders bare. It fit like a glove on top and flared out from the waist to just above her knees. Dawn and Molly were looking excellent, too, in party dresses and high heels. Most of the snow had melted from the week before, so he drove them in the '54 Cadillac sedan he'd restored years ago and had Jake bring over from storage at BCC that afternoon.

The mansion was lit up so bright you could probably see it from Denver. Holiday music flowed from inside. Family and friends were already gathering when he handed the keys to one of the parking attendants hired for the night. He ushered Paige and the girls up the wide white steps and inside where a giant tree blazed in the foyer, and his mother smiled and hugged people and said, "Welcome, welcome. So glad you could come." She wore sparkly white silk and looked half her age.

She hugged him, too. "Darling. You are so handsome. Welcome to your party. I think you'll agree that Estrella has outdone herself."

"We need to talk," he said, low, for her ears alone.

She acted as if she didn't hear him. "Paige!" she exclaimed over his shoulder. "You look just beautiful…"

He told himself to give it up. Now wasn't the time.

But he knew he wouldn't be able to stop himself from watching for his moment.

He filed into the front parlor with everyone else. The

large room was decorated to holiday perfection and the Veuve Clicquot waited on ice. A pretty woman in a red gown at the grand piano sang "Have Yourself a Merry Little Christmas" in a sultry alto voice.

Carter accepted a flute of the champagne and made the rounds, visiting with his brothers and sisters, telling everyone how great it was that they could come, while he kept an eye on his mother, waiting for her to duck out for a minute at the same time as he kept reminding himself that he was totally losing it. If she didn't want to talk to him, he should just let it the hell go.

About seven-thirty, he got lucky. He saw when Willow slipped out of the large parlor and into the foyer.

Paige, across the room laughing and chattering with Clara and Rory, had her back to him. He seized the moment and ducked out after Willow.

As his mother crossed the foyer, he trailed a little ways behind her. She smiled at the guests who lingered near the giant tree, and started up the stairs. He waited until she was at the top and then did the same, waving and nodding as he went by the group of friends around the tree. At the upstairs landing, he saw her ahead, strolling along the upper hallway. He rushed to catch up as she turned the corner into the master suite's private foyer. When he rounded that corner, she'd already crossed the foyer and was entering the suite. He caught up with her just as she was about to close the door.

"Hold on a minute, Ma."

"Carter!" She put her hand to her chest. "You startled me."

"We need to talk and you know that we do."

"Not right now, darling." She tried to close the door

on him. He stuck his foot in it. "Carter. Please. It has to be obvious to you that this is not the time." She kept pushing on the door, but he didn't move his foot.

Fine. It would only take a minute. They didn't need a long conversation. He just wanted her agreement about what *not* to tell Paige. "I know you got my messages," he whispered through the crack his foot was keeping in the door. "You know what I want. Just tell me you understand and you won't say a word to Paige about that little bribe of yours, and I'll leave you alone. My marrying her has zip to do with your ridiculous scheme and you know it."

Willow sighed heavily and let the door drift open. "Darling. I think you need to step back and take a deep breath. We both know that honesty in a relationship is always preferable to secrets and lies. I think you should tell Paige the truth. I really, truly do."

Carter saw red. It took all his willpower not to batter the damn door with his fist. Who was his crazy-ass home-wrecker mother to take the high road about anything?

And then she said, "But all right. I'll keep your secret if that's really how you want it. You may simply tell Paige that I'm thrilled to give you the property as a wedding gift—and leave out all mention of any *bribe*."

Paige had glanced over her shoulder in time to see Carter duck out after Willow.

She'd been worried about him all day. Something was up with him. Something was wrong.

And she had a very strong feeling that whatever it was, it concerned his mother.

Maybe she should have just left him alone to chase after Willow and do…whatever it was he seemed so determined to do. She could ask him about it later, when they were alone.

But she didn't like that he kept lying to her, telling her everything was fine when she knew in her bones that it wasn't.

So she left Clara and Rory chatting together, and followed him as he followed Willow out into the foyer and up the grand staircase.

When he turned a corner at the end of the hallway, she hesitated. Maybe she really should leave this alone, go back downstairs and ask him later what he'd been doing up here. She turned to go—and then couldn't quite give it up.

So much between them was so beautiful. And yet…

She loved him and she'd told him so and he had said nothing.

There were just too many games between them. She wore his ring on her finger, but she wouldn't know if it was real until after the holidays—and a totally ridiculous pro-and-con evaluation.

Uh-uh. She needed to know what was happening here.

She squared her shoulders and kept going, hesitating again at the end of the hallway. From there, she could hear Willow talking tightly about secrets and lies, about honesty in a relationship, about how Paige should know the truth. About the property being a wedding gift.

And how she would never say anything about a bribe.

A bribe? Paige didn't get it.

And she was eavesdropping, plain and simple. That wasn't right.

Anxiety building, her heart suddenly racing, she stepped out from behind the shelter of the wall and directly into a foyer area. About ten feet away, Carter stood with his back to her at a half-open door.

Willow, on the other side of that door, spotted her immediately. "Paige," she said softly, with a strange little smile.

Carter whipped around. The sudden stark misery on his face told Paige way more than she wanted to know. He whispered her name. "Paige…"

And her heart kept on beating frantically, as though it would punch through the wall of her chest. So many lies. Too many silly games. Where even to start?

But she was the levelheaded one, the sane one who never let her emotions get the better of her. So she only asked mildly, "What bribe?"

Carter blanched.

Willow said, "Carter will explain everything." She gave her son another of those weird little smiles. "Won't you, darling?"

Carter just said, "Paige, I…" And then ran out of words.

No drama, Paige reminded herself. No drama, no way. At least not until she had him alone. "How about this? Let's discuss it later. Right now we're the guests of honor at this beautiful party your mom has thrown for us." She held out her hand to him. "Let's go downstairs where we belong."

Paige felt oddly anesthetized for the rest of the evening. As if she were wrapped in gauze, looking at everything through a white fabric screen, feeling everything distantly, as though every inch of her skin had gone numb.

But even numb and wrapped in gauze, she could see that the party was a success. Carter's brothers and sisters all said that the mansion had never looked so warm and inviting, that Estrella had outdone herself.

And Willow, as it turned out, was an excellent hostess— Willow, who spent most of her time traveling, who rarely attended local events and seemed to consider family gatherings dangerous to her health.

Not tonight, not at this party. Tonight, Willow was someone else altogether, happy and chatty, her smile glowing and sincere.

When they took their seats at the table, Willow made a toast to the happy couple. Carter's mom said that she'd known the first time she met Paige, at Bravo Custom Cars three days after Paige had taken the job as office manager, that Paige was the one for her oldest son.

Willow gave a husky chuckle. "Though I have to say, I never would have guessed that it would take the two of them five more years to figure out what I knew the minute I saw them together."

A ripple of knowing laughter filled the room. Everyone seemed to know something Paige didn't really get. Across the table, Dawn and Molly were laughing with everyone else. Dawn leaned close to her best friend and whispered something.

Molly nodded and giggled some more.

Paige remembered the Saturday morning after Thanksgiving, when she'd confided in Dawn, and Dawn had told her that "everyone" knew she had a thing for Carter.

Now Willow was standing right there at the table, lifting a cut crystal champagne flute that had once belonged to her lifelong rival, saying that she'd been waiting five years for Carter and Paige to finally get together. And judging by the nods, the laughter and the grins on all their faces, everyone at the table knew what Willow knew.

They all knew everything.

Only Paige was left stumbling in the dark.

And what about Carter? How much did he know?

She wanted to turn to him and ask him straight out. But now wasn't the time. This wasn't the place. And besides, Paige didn't dare look at him. She had the strangest feeling that, if she looked at him, into his eyes, the numbness would fade and the gauze would fall away.

And she would be left there, seeing too much, every inch of her body burning and tingling in excruciating pain.

Willow continued talking, so relaxed, smiling and gracious. She said she was so glad that her son had figured out what he really wanted at last. She said that she adored her only grandchild, Quinn's daughter, Annabelle. And she wanted more grandchildren, please. She scolded Paige and Carter that they shouldn't take forever about it—she wasn't getting any younger, after all.

Through the rest of the evening, Paige kept her head up. That strange numbness kept her nice and calm as she played her part.

"Okay, what's going on with you two?" Dawn asked as soon as they were back in Carter's gorgeous old Cadillac and on the way home.

"Not a thing," said Carter.

"We're fine," Paige lied.

Dawn made a scoffing sound, but she left it alone. Molly was staying over. Paige dreaded the moment when she and Carter were alone. Things needed to be said and yet she didn't want to say them. And she really didn't want Dawn and Molly around for any of it.

Carter must have felt the same way. When he pulled into the driveway and sent the garage rumbling up, he said, "Paige and I have to go over to my place. You two go on in. We'll see you later."

Dawn leaned up between the seats. "What is going on?"

Paige had no answer for her, so she just said, "Go ahead. We're at Carter's if you need us."

Dawn gave her a long, searching look. Paige's stomach spurted acid as she waited for resistance.

But then Dawn only made a frustrated sound low in her throat and said, "Fine. See you later." She and Molly got out and went in through the garage.

Carter shut the garage door and backed out from the driveway.

Carter's house was cold.

He hadn't been there for weeks, except to grab more of his stuff to take over to Paige's. Even Sally was at Paige's. He hadn't put up any Christmas decorations— but he rarely did. It had always seemed pointless to him to put up a tree and spend all that time decorating it when he was the only one around to look at it and he would rather be at Paige and Dawn's, anyway.

He turned up the heat and asked Paige if she wanted anything. She shook her head and took the couch. He longed to sit beside her. But those fine, dark eyes said he'd better not try it.

He sat in the easy chair across from her.

For an endless five seconds or so, they stared at each other.

Finally, she said, "So tell me. About this *bribe*." She sat so still, her pale, pretty face way too calm. He had the strangest feeling that any second she would shatter.

But she didn't shatter.

Not Paige.

He told her everything, all of it. About the drink he'd had with his mother on Thanksgiving Day when Willow told him she'd bought the property—for him. That she wanted him married and when he *did* get married, the property would be his wedding present from her.

"I would have told you that day." He couldn't keep a hint of bitterness from creeping in. "But you would hardly talk to me. As it turned out, you were freaked over that silly love quiz, remember?"

She reminded him way too softly, "You've had plenty of opportunities since then to tell me all about it."

Something deep inside him twisted. "Yeah. I kept promising myself I would come clean with you. Soon. But, well, *soon* never came. We were together and it was so damn good and I didn't want to rock that boat, didn't want to take a chance I might lose you. I was afraid you wouldn't believe me when I told you that my wanting to marry you had nothing to do with the damn property. And then, the longer I didn't tell you, the harder it got to figure out how to tell you. Finally, the other day, when Kelly called to tell you my mother had bought the property, I..." Damn. He did not want to tell the rest of it. But Paige was waiting. And he knew she wouldn't let him get away with any more lies. "I decided there was no reason you ever had to know the whole story. I decided I would get my mother to do just what she planned to do, give us the property as a wedding present. But as far as her scheme to bribe me into marriage with it went, I would just tell her never to say a word to you about that." He paused for breath—and also, because he was kind of hoping she might say something.

Like maybe, that she understood.

Didn't happen. So he forged on. "Unfortunately, all of a sudden, my mother was unavailable. I kept calling and leaving messages. I even dropped in at the mansion, but she wasn't there. By the time we got to the party, I was frantic to get through to her. So when she went upstairs, I followed her. I caught her at the door to her room and I told her what I wanted from her. And could she just agree to do it my way? Oh, hell, no. Suddenly, she was all about honesty and how lies weren't a good foundation for a relationship. You walked in on her telling me that." He put up both hands. "And that's it. That's all of it. It was stupid and I was wrong and all I want is for us to get past this."

Paige drew a very slow breath. "Carter." She turned her head and stared into the dark fireplace. "I just..." Another slow breath. It seemed to be a huge effort for her, but she made herself look at him again. "I don't want to do this anymore."

He pretended not to understand. He couldn't *bear* to understand. "What are you talking about? Come on. You have to believe me. The property doesn't have a damn thing to do with why I want to marry you."

She smiled then. He'd never seen her look so sad. "I believe you."

Hope blazed in his chest, searing like a brand. "You do? Thank God." He stood to go to her.

She put out a hand. "No. Please. Don't."

He didn't get it. But his knees did, apparently. They bent and he sank back in to his seat. What was the problem, then? She'd just said she believed him. But still, she was pushing him away. He tried to make it clearer. "I didn't want to lose you. That's all it was…"

"Oh, Carter. Why can't you see? This thing with the property, this big secret you've been keeping from me, it's not the main issue, it's more the final straw. The problem is that I love you. And I went ahead with your ridiculous test-drive marriage plan thinking that somehow I would get you to love me, too. But you…you hold back. You know you do."

Okay, he got it now. And he didn't like it one damn bit. "This is all about *I love you*, isn't it?" he accused. "This is all just because I won't say the silly words." It came out angry. Because, damn it, he was getting mad.

And she just wouldn't cop to it. "No. It's not that. It's really not."

Bull. "Who's lying now?"

"I'm not lying. The words you won't say are just the symptom of the deeper problem. I've seen a true and happy marriage. My parents had one. I want that, what my parents had, I do. And I'm afraid I'll never have that with you."

He was getting that feeling. Like his head might explode. Like his heart might just crash its way out of his chest. "Don't talk to me about symptoms, about how perfect your parents were. This is about *us*, damn it.

About how good it's been since you finally agreed to wear my ring. You *know* how good it's been. I know you know. You and me, together, it's better than I ever dreamed it could be."

"Well, it's not good enough for me."

He wanted to yell at her, to shout the house down. But he kept it together, just barely. He braced his elbows on his spread knees and leaned across the table at her. "What in the hell do you want from me, Paige?"

She pressed her own knees together, planted her elbows on them and leaned right back at him. "What do I want? Well, let's see. How 'bout a *real* engagement? How about, if you're going to ask me to marry you, you do it straight out and let me say yes or no? You don't come up with some bat-crap-crazy idea about trying it out until the holidays are over and then *evaluating* the *situation* to see if we want to make it real or we don't."

Okay, yeah. Maybe the test-drive hadn't been such a great idea. And he should apologize some more, he knew it. He should drop to his knees and beg. Because it would kill him to lose her and she had a right to know the whole truth, the one he'd been hiding from her—and from himself—for eight damn years.

But he didn't beg. He was too furious at her. "What else was I supposed to do?"

She gasped as though he'd just said something so outrageous. And then she whispered hotly, "I just told you, you need to say what you want, to be honest about it."

"Honest. Right."

"Don't you mock me, Carter."

"How can I help it? You're so full of crap. All your talk about being honest, as though it's so simple. Just tell Paige what you want from her. Just be honest and straightforward. Yeah, sure. You mean like I was honest eight years ago when I first met you? Because I *was* honest and we both know it. I went right after what I wanted, and it was you. And you had one answer for me back then. That answer was no. You turned me down. Repeatedly."

"That was all I *could* do right then," she cried. "I'd just lost my parents. My fiancé, the guy who'd said he loved me more than his life, had dumped me flat the second things got tough. I had a little sister to raise. I wasn't in any condition to be going out on *dates*."

"Yeah. I got that. You wanted a *friend*. And I gave you what you wanted for eight long years. I went out with *strangers*, tried to make it work with women who ended up hating me because I wasn't really there for them. I even succeeded in convincing myself that I wanted what *you* wanted—for you and me to be good buddies, the best of friends. And then, a few weeks ago, with a nudge from my crazy mother and another from Murray Preble, I started to see the light, to admit again what *I* wanted. And it was still you. And so I went after you. And maybe I did it in a roundabout way. Maybe I did go about it all wrong, coming up with a test drive and then an evaluation. Because you're all about the damn pros and cons, Paige, now, aren't you? I thought, well, she can have one of her lists at the end and maybe then she'll finally see that we should be together, maybe she'll…" The words dribbled off into nothing and he was left wondering what the hell was the matter with him?

God help him. He was babbling like an idiot, revealing things he'd never let himself think all that hard about. They hurt, those things. He wished he hadn't said them.

So he shut up. He shut up and he stared at her across that low table, stared long and hard.

She stared back. She looked as if he'd punched her a good one right in the solar plexus, as if he'd knocked all the air clean out of her. "I don't… I just never…" She flopped back against the cushions, then strained forward again. "Oh, Carter, how could you not have known you didn't need that silly test-drive? I told you right out I'm in love with you."

"Oh, come on. Like talking about love is going to make anything clear to me. How many times have I told you that when people talk about love, all I see is my mother standing in the middle of the street, screaming at my dad while he peels rubber to get away from her? All I see is her crying and carrying on, wailing about how much she *loves* him—as she empties his underwear drawer onto the front lawn."

A low whimper escaped Paige. She covered her face with her hands. "Oh, God. What a mess…"

His head pounded in rhythm with his racing heart. He slapped a hand on the back of his neck and squeezed, hard, as though he could rub the pain away. "Terrific. This is a big mess and I'm still a liar, right? That's all you can see."

She dropped her hands and gaped at him. "No. That's not what I said. Carter, can we just dial it down a notch? I just need a little time to—"

"Stop." He lurched upright. "Just don't, okay?" He felt like someone had taken a belt sander to his heart. Everybody thought love was so damn great. He failed to see the wonderfulness. It just felt like torture to him. "I'm taking you home."

"But we need to—"

"No. No, we don't. I've had enough, okay? I get it now, Paige. It's not going to work with us. You've made that way clear. I want this to be done."

She stood, too, then, slowly. Her big eyes brimmed with tears. "What, exactly, are you saying?" She whispered those words.

"I'm saying you're right. Us, getting married? Dumb idea." He was lying. But what did it matter, whether he lied or told the truth? Either way, she refused to believe him. Either way, he'd messed everything up completely. They might as well get it over with. He might as well just do what she expected of him. "I want to take you home, pick up my dog and move on."

She looked at him so hard. As if those big eyes could bore a hole in the center of his forehead. Her soft mouth quivered. But she didn't say anything. He wanted to grab her and hold on so tight, she would never think of leaving him again.

But he just couldn't take it. All this hurt, all this *feeling*. This wasn't going to work. And he needed to end it. Now.

So he did. "Let's just stay away from each other until after the holidays. Tell you what. Don't come in Monday. Take a couple of weeks' vacation, why don't you? And then at the first of the year, we'll take a meeting, talk about BCC and whether or not it's really workable for you and me to be partners anymore."

She sucked in a shocked breath. He waited for her to argue, to do something impossible. Like maybe to fight for what they had.

But she didn't.

He watched, hating himself, already starting to see all the ways he'd blown it, as she took off his ring and set it carefully on the coffee table. "All right, Carter," she said. "Take me home now."

Chapter Twelve

At Paige's house, Carter waited outside.

Paige went in alone. The house was quiet. The light under Dawn's door meant the girls were probably still awake.

Quietly—so they wouldn't hear her, come out to investigate and start asking questions—Paige gathered up everything she could find of Carter's and stuck it in a duffel she dug out of the closet. Then she put Sally on her leash and took the dog and the duffel out the front door.

He was waiting for her, leaning against the driver's door of the Cadillac, making her ache with yearning just at the sight of him. He accepted the big bag from her and went to toss it in the trunk as she put Sally in the backseat. Then he slid in behind the wheel again. She stood in the driveway and watched his taillights until he turned the corner and they disappeared.

Inside, Biscuit was waiting by the front door. She took

him out for a few minutes, then let him come upstairs with her. He hogged the bed, as usual. He also cuddled up close and tried to lick the tears off her cheeks as she cried.

The next morning, when the girls came downstairs and asked where Carter was, Paige played it vague. "He, um, decided to spend the night at his house."

Dawn made a groaning sound low in her throat. "Have you *looked* in the mirror? You've been crying all night, haven't you—and where's your ring?"

The tears crept up the back of Paige's throat again and filled her eyes. "We're, um, having some problems. Taking a little break, is all."

Dawn wasn't buying that. "He broke up with you. That idiot. I'll kill him."

"No!" It came out on a sob. "It's at least as much my fault as his."

"No way."

"Yeah. It really is. I hurt him. I've *been* hurting him for a very long time. And I…oh, Dawn. I think we both really blew it and I don't know what's going to happen. He said it's over. He really seemed to mean it."

Dawn grabbed her and hugged her as Biscuit moved close and whimpered in sympathy. "I'll kill him," Dawn threatened in her ear.

"Don't say that. I love him."

"I know you do."

"I'll always love him. And…and *he* loves *me*, even though he can never make himself say it."

"Oh, Paige. I know that, too."

A laugh that was more like a sob escaped her. "Because everybody knows, right?"

"Yeah, pretty much."

Paige held on tight, breathing in the familiar smell of Dawn's strawberry shampoo, grateful beyond measure that she had her sister to hold on to.

Molly got up and joined the hug, too. The three of them just stood there in the kitchen, holding on to each other, as Paige let go and cried even harder than she had the night before, and Biscuit whimpered at their feet.

Later, when they sat down to Molly's special German pancakes, Paige told the girls what she'd planned. "Carter gave me vacation time till the first of the year. And I'm going to take it. I'm calling an old college friend, a travel agent, tomorrow. I'm seeing if I can book a last-minute trip to someplace where I can sit on a beach in the sun in the yellow bikini I bought last summer and never took the tags off of. I want to leave right away and I'll be back by New Year's, in time for your spring semester. Either of you want to go?"

Dawn and Molly exchanged a look. Dawn nodded. "I'm in."

And Molly said, "I'll call my mom and see if it's okay."

Carter was at the shop, alone, that afternoon, when Dawn pounded on the side door.

He let her in and then he grabbed her in a hug. She didn't seem to care if he got grease all over her, just hugged him back as hard as he was hugging her.

When she pulled away, she clutched his shoulders and glared up at him. "God, Carter. You look as miserable as she is."

What was he supposed to say to that? He settled for saying nothing.

Not Dawn. "I told you I'd kill you. I still kind of want to. I mean, all guys are stupid a lot of the time.

But you… I don't get it. Paige won't really talk about it. What *happened*?"

"I screwed it up."

"Well, then fix it."

He pulled free of her grip. "Just let it go, Dawnie. Just, you know, let it be, huh?"

"We're leaving, Paige and me and Molly."

"Huh? Going where?"

"I don't know yet, but we'll be gone until New Year's. Paige won't ask you, so I will. Would you take care of Biscuit while we're gone?"

"Of course."

"You should call her."

"Stay out of it, Dawn."

She pressed her lips together and muttered, "You are the king of stupid and I have zero sympathy for you."

Paige's college friend worked a miracle, though at a premium price. It was high season, but still, they got a two-bedroom bungalow in a resort on Saint John, Virgin Islands.

Dawn took Biscuit to Carter's on Monday night. When she got back to the house, Paige demanded, "Did you tell him where we're going?"

Dawn shrugged. "He didn't ask and I wasn't about to volunteer anything."

"Good," Paige replied, and tried to sound as though she meant it.

They left before daylight the next morning. Snow was falling when they boarded the plane in Denver.

On Saint John, it was eighty degrees under a cloudless sky, the sun beaming down on the blue ocean and the sparkly white sand. Paige got out her yellow bikini and cut off the tags and tried to care that she'd soon be basking in the Caribbean sun.

In Justice Creek, Carter shoveled his front walk and hung out with Biscuit and Sally. He wasn't good for much else.

In that final week before Christmas, business was kind of slow. A good thing, because for the first time since he was thirteen and Dobs Kelvin, the old biker who lived down the street, put a wrench in his hand, Carter couldn't work on his cars. They reminded him of Paige.

But then, everything reminded him of Paige. He had it so bad. Worse, even, than he'd realized on Saturday when he told her he was cutting her loose.

Cutting her loose.

Yeah, right. And while he was at it, he might as well cut out his heart.

And come to think of it, he kind of had.

Now that the fury had faded, he was starting to see the truth.

And it wasn't pretty.

He was worse than Willow had been back in the day. He might as well have emptied Paige's underwear drawer in the street, the way he'd carried on Saturday night, threatening to bust up their partnership at BCC, blaming her for all the times he didn't make it work with other women…

He wanted to go to her so bad.

But she was gone and he had no idea where to find her.

On Wednesday, he left the shop early and went to Romano's for dinner. He ordered the veal piccata, which was excellent, as always, though he barely managed to choke down a few bites. Because, come on. Who did he think he was kidding, to try to eat dinner at the restaurant where he'd met Paige?

Murray and Sherry were there, sitting in a booth in the corner, eyes only for each other. He wanted to be happy for them. But he kept asking himself why they got to be happy and he had to lose everything that mattered most.

Because you're the king of stupid, Dawn's voice echoed in his ear.

On Christmas Eve, his cousin Rory married Walker McKellan in a rustic chapel in the national forest. Carter went because he couldn't think of an acceptable excuse not to. Rory's parents, the sovereign princess and prince consort of Montedoro, were there. It was a beautiful setting, and the bride and groom looked so happy, and that just made Carter feel worse than ever.

His brothers and sisters asked him where Paige was. He said he didn't know. They all wisely left it at that—well, except for Nell. She took him aside and told him he was crazy if he'd let Paige go.

He told her to mind her own damn business.

She grabbed his arm and whispered, "Carter. Don't blow this. Don't throw away what matters most to you."

"Leave it, Nell." He jerked his arm free and got the hell away from her.

On Christmas Day, he got the visit he'd been dreading, the one from his mother. She came at seven in the morning, which shocked the hell out of him. He'd never actually seen her awake at that hour.

Willow told him she was giving him and Paige the property as a Christmas present. She petted the dogs and said gently, "Nothing is unfixable."

He admitted the disgusting truth. "I acted like a drama queen."

And his mother smiled. "Well, at least you come by it naturally."

"It's not funny, Ma."

"I never said it was. Now get your ass to wherever she's run off to, admit how wrong you were and tell her you're not leaving until she comes home with you."

He opened his mouth to order her out of his house. But the words that came out were "I messed up on so many levels. She's probably never going to speak to me again."

Willow hugged him. That was seriously weird. "She loves you and you love her," she said softly when he saw her to the door. "I know you'll work it out."

Half an hour later, he sat on the couch with Biscuit on one side and Sally on the other, channel-surfing like mad and telling himself that Paige *had* to come back eventually. She had a house and a dog—and Dawn and Molly had school.

His phone trilled three notes: incoming text.

It was from Dawn. She still loves you, you idiot. You need to come here and work it out.

The address of a luxury resort in the Virgin Islands followed, complete with a bungalow number.

At eight the next morning, it was seventy-two degrees on Saint John and the sun was shining bright.

Carter, his heart banging like a gong in the prison of his chest, stood at the door to Paige's bungalow and lifted his hand to knock.

The door swung open before his knuckles made contact.

Paige. She wore a gauzy sky-blue shirt that came to

midthigh. Her hair needed combing. Her cheeks were pink from the sun and she'd sprouted a few freckles across her adorable nose.

"My God," he said prayerfully. He'd never seen anything so beautiful in his life.

She scowled at him—but her eyes were shining. "What did you do with my dog?"

"My mother's looking after both Biscuit and Sally. Believe it or not, she's good with them. She also gave us the property as a Christmas present."

"Us? I thought there was no us. I thought you just wanted to be done."

"I lied."

She said nothing, only gazed up at him, waiting.

He knew he owed her more, so damn much more. "I... you were right. I messed everything up with that stupid test-drive engagement. I never wanted that. I was just afraid that if I came right out and asked you for forever, you might turn me down. And then I didn't tell you about my mother trying to bribe me with the property, because I was scared I'd lose you over that. Then the night of our party, when all my lies came back to bite me in the ass, I lied some more and told you I was through. That was the biggest lie, Paige. Because for me, you're the one. I'll never be through with you."

She swallowed. Hard. "I've lied, too—to myself. About you. About who you really are to me. I should have opened my eyes to the truth sooner. Jim Kellogg hurt me and I held on to that hurt for way too long."

"Are you...over that now?"

"I am, Carter. I really am."

"Ahem. Well, then. I know it's a lot to ask. Maybe too much to ask. Because I know I blew it, and I'm so sorry that I did. But still, I want to try again. I would give anything, if you and I could try again."

Her face seemed to light right up from within. "My mom always used to say it's not how bad you mess up, it's how hard you work to heal the pain you cause each other."

"I'm…I'm willing Paige. Whatever it takes, I'll do it. For you."

Her sweet mouth trembled. "I'm willing, too, Carter. For you."

"Paige?"

"Um?"

"I just need to get my arms around you."

She made a tight little sound, as if her throat had locked up on her. Her shining eyes had tears in them now. "Well, um, you'd better do that, then."

"Dear God. Yes." And he reached out and hauled her close, splaying his hands across her slender back, burying his face in the crook of her neck, loving the feel of her, so soft in all the right places, drinking in the scent of her, like soap and vanilla.

Like home.

"You're my home, Paige," he whispered idiotically.

"Carter." She pressed those sweet lips to the side of his throat. "I love you. I missed you so. I'm so sorry, that I couldn't be…with you sooner. I'm so sorry I hurt you, that I didn't understand."

He made his own confession. "I didn't let you see, didn't tell you the truth. I wanted you so much and I worked so hard for so long to tell myself that being your friend was enough. And in some ways, it was. It really was. It was a whole hell of a lot better than not having you at all. But…" His mind was a fog, with jet lag and longing, with the unbelievable wonder of her right there, breath and flesh and heart and soul, all held at last in his hungry arms.

She pulled back and looked up him through those big, misty eyes. "It's okay. You don't have to—"

He put a finger to her lips. "Yeah. I have to. I need to say it. I need you to know that I do you, that I always have. That I walked into Romano's that night eight years ago and I saw you standing there with an order book in your hand, wearing that white shirt and that short black skirt and that little triangle of an apron, with your hair pulled up in a knot on the top of your head, laughing at something a customer had said. I took one look at you and I thought, *Oh, yeah. Mine. I'll take her for the rest of my life...*"

She scanned his face, drinking him in, as though she'd been wandering in the desert and he was made of water. "Carter. You said it."

"Yeah, I did. And I'll say it again. I love you. You're the woman for me, Paige. You're the only one." He pulled her close again and he kissed her.

She let him kiss her.

She more than let him. She wrapped her arms good and tight around him and she lifted that soft, fine mouth to his.

When he raised his head, she took his hand.

He grabbed the suitcase he'd dropped on the step and let her lead him inside, through a simply furnished, sunlit living area, down a short hall to the open door of a bedroom.

"Dawn and Molly?" he asked.

"In the other bedroom, still sleeping." She entered the

room and pulled him in with her, pausing only to quietly shut the door and turn the privacy lock.

He barely had time to set the suitcase down again before she got to work unbuttoning his shirt. "I love you," he said as she undressed him. "I love you so much, Paige. I thought I would lose you. I couldn't work, couldn't sleep—"

"Shh. You haven't lost me. You never could. Not really. We would always find our way back to each other in the end."

And then she kissed him again and they fell across the bed together.

Make-up sex. Nothing like it.

Especially make-up sex with love, spoken freely, given honestly.

An hour later, she put her blue shirt back on and he got dressed again. They went out to the tiny galley kitchen. He made coffee.

"So good," she said, when she took that first sip. "Nobody makes it like you do." She let him fill his own cup, then led him outside to the small private lanai with its own perfect view of white sand and blue ocean.

They shared a chaise. It was cramped, but neither of them could bear not to be touching the other.

He held her close against him and drew lazy figure eights on the velvety skin of her arm. "Remember the love quiz?"

She groaned, "How will I ever forget? That was awful. It really was, Carter. You have to understand, it hit me hard, to realize out of the blue that I'm in love with you. And that I probably have been for a very long time. And I had no hope at all then that *you* might love *me* that way."

He gave a pained laugh. "But I did love you that way. I'd just been telling myself not to go there for eight long years."

"Because of me, because for so long that was all I could handle, for us to be just friends."

"Exactly—and didn't you ever wonder how I got twenty out of twenty to 'prove' you were in love with me?"

She turned in his arms, so she was half lying on his chest. And she pressed a kiss on the end of his chin. "I just thought it was what you told me, that you knew me so well, you'd guessed and you'd guessed right."

"Wrong."

"Well, okay. Then what?"

"There was no guessing involved." He cradled the side of her face, ran his hand down the length of her warm, silky hair. "Those answers were *my* answers. Twenty out of twenty."

She sighed. And then she tucked her head under his chin. "*Your* answers. I never had a clue..."

He kissed the top of her head. "Happy day-after-Christmas."

She snuggled in closer. "I missed you so much yesterday. Dawn and I agreed it was hardly like Christmas, without you standing at the counter mixing stuffing at the crack of dawn, getting the turkey ready to go in the oven. We left all the presents, untouched, under the tree at home..."

"When we get back, I'll roast a turkey," he promised. "We'll have Christmas all over again."

"And we'll do it right this time." She laid her hand over his heart. "Is it snowing in Justice Creek?"

"It was when I left."

"I missed that, snow for Christmas..."

He ran a hand down the sweet curve of her back. And then he asked, low and rough, for her ears alone, "Will you please come back to me, Paige? Will you give me one more chance? Come back and be my wife and my best friend and my partner at BCC. I swear to you that I'll never lie to you again, never hide the truth no matter how painful the truth might be, no matter how bad it makes me look. I'll never make a game of loving you, never hold you at a distance by not showing you my heart. Because you're everything to me, Paige. And life without you is nothing but a gray, depressing slog."

"Yes," she whispered without hesitation. "Yes, I will marry you and be your wife, your best friend and your business partner for the rest of our lives. Because you are the man for me, Carter Bravo. And no one else will do."

A long, coffee-flavored kiss sealed the deal.

After the kiss, he pulled her to her feet, slipped his ring back on her finger and took her into the bungalow, where they woke the girls and shared the news that they would be spending the rest of their lives together, after all.

* * * * *

'Stay,' she blurted.

It stunned him into silence.

'I'll hire you privately. . .to stay. . .here.'

With me, she couldn't quite bring herself to say.

Tiny lines appeared at the corners of both his eyes. 'I can't, Sera.'

She kicked up her chin. 'I'm not worth breaking a few rules for?'

'I'm not. . .I can't. . .' Breath hissed out of him. 'I don't want to hurt you any more than I already have, Sera.'

Just when she'd felt sure her newfound courage would be rewarded. Did the universe not realise how difficult it was for her to open herself up like this? But having started she couldn't stop. Too much rode on it.

'Then what's stopping you? Because it's not your job?'

'I think *I'm* stopping me, Sera,' he murmured.

It was the pain that got her attention; it shadowed his gaze and thickened his voice. His leaving would hurt her, but staying was hurting *him*. Somehow. She didn't want to hurt him. But she had to understand. And she would never forgive herself if she didn't try just one last time.

'Some things are more important than rules, Brad. Aren't they?'

BODYGUARD. . .TO BRIDEGROOM?

BY

NIKKI LOGAN

Published in Great Britain 2015
by Mills & Boon, an imprint of Harlequin (UK) Limited,
Eton House, 18-24 Paradise Road, Richmond, Surrey, TW9 1SR

© 2015 Nikki Logan

ISBN: 978-0-263-25190-6

23-1215

Printed and bound in Spain
by CPI, Barcelona

Nikki Logan lives on the edge of a string of wetlands in Western Australia, with her partner and a menagerie of animals. She writes captivating nature-based stories full of romance in descriptive natural environments. She believes the danger and richness of wild places perfectly mirror the passion and risk of falling in love.

She loves to hear from readers via www.nikkilogan.com.au or through social media. Find her on Twitter: @ReadNikkiLogan and Facebook: NikkiLoganAuthor

For Margaret Kruger
'White, no sugar, half a cup.'

And for the staff—and wildlife—
of Al Maha Desert Resort
who offered me such a transformative experience.

CHAPTER ONE

IT TOOK BRAD KRUGER all of three seconds to sift through the faces in the crowd of passengers disembarking from the pointy end of the flight from London and identify the one he needed. First, he filtered out anyone with a Y chromosome, then the women over forty or under eighteen, then the impeccably dressed locals returning to the pricey desert emirate of Umm Khoreem. That left only three priority passengers that could be his client and only one of them had her long hair out and flowing gloriously over bare shoulders.

There she was…codename 'Aspirin'—for the headache he was going to have for the next month.

Of all the gin joints in all the towns…

Brad glanced along the long row of immigration staff in their pristine robes and watched as Seraphina Blaise was subtly corralled to the entrance of a long, winding and empty queue that casually eased her away from the one filled with locals and towards a counter with double the staff. As she negotiated the maze of retractable belts, she seemed oblivious to the fact she'd just been selected for special immigration attention.

She might have left a British Christmas all rugged up, but somewhere over the Baltic she'd pared back into something more suited to a desert one—except that apparently she'd dressed for the heat rather than for the culture.

'Here we go…' Brad muttered under his breath, pushing off the ornately carved pillar he'd been leaning against and triangulating a course to bring him as close as possible to the official who'd flagged her.

Her inadequate dress had probably caught Immigration's

attention, but it was her arrest record that would likely *keep it*. Umm Khoreem issued visas on arrival for those who were just visiting. No visa, no entry; and people had been refused entry into the security-conscious state on much less than bad fashion choices and a fresh conviction.

A carefully blank official took her passport as Brad drew closer on the Umm Khoreem side of the immigration barrier, asked a few questions, frowned at her answers, and spent the next few minutes reading various pages on his touch screen while the leggy brunette shuffled awkwardly before him. She glanced around to pass the time, and Brad saw the moment she finally registered that she'd ended up in a queue for one while everyone else was being whisked through further along.

Her rounded eyes swung back to the official.

Yep. Just you, love...

Her whole body changed then. She lost the casual lightness with which she'd practically bounced along the switchback lanes, her bare shoulders sagged and her spine ratcheted straight. Remembering her last run-in with authorities perhaps...

Brad caught the eye of one of the other immigration staff, who took his time sauntering over but bowed his cloaked head and listened as Brad briskly murmured his name, credentials and purpose. The man nodded and returned to his post, then picked up the telephone. At the next aisle, the first immigration officer answered, flicking his eyes up to his colleague and then over to where Brad now stood before returning his gaze to the woman in front of him. The official barely acknowledged him, but barely was all he needed.

Whatever happened from now he'd just insinuated himself within the process.

And he could do a much better job from within than from without.

The official requested her bags and a customs officer

set about a professional but laborious inspection more designed to buy them time to run a series of immigration
checks than to fulfil any particular fascination with the
contents of her designer luggage. When the computer had
spat back everything they needed, the men stepped out
from behind their barrier and gestured for her to follow
them. Her feet remained fixed to the spot and she glanced
around for someone—anyone—to come to her aid. No one
did. After a moment, the larger of the two men returned
the few paces to her side and gestured, not unkindly, towards the interview room.

Perhaps it was the 'please' that Brad saw on his lips in
English that got her feet moving. Or perhaps it was the in-
tractable hand at her back that stopped short of actually
touching her. Either way the official achieved his aim, and
Seraphina Blaise took the first careful steps behind one official while the second flanked her from behind. Just before
they left the arrivals area, the man to the rear glanced his
way and jerked his head just once in permission.

Brad moved immediately.

Two was bad enough, now there were three. As dark and
neutral as the other officials but this one wasn't in the traditional robe and headdress of his people. He looked more
like a dark-suited chauffeur. Or a CIA agent. Or a chauffeur for the CIA.

All three men stood on the other side of the sound-
proof glass of her containment room talking *about* her
but not *to* her. The immaculately dressed officials listened
attentively—one of them even smiled, which had to be a
good sign except that he followed it up with a firm and
distinctly suspicious glare in her direction. The chauffeur
talked some more, his hands gesticulating wildly.

'Is there a problem?' she asked aloud, with more confidence than she felt, counting on the soundproofing being
one-way. Only the chauffeur bothered to look up for the

briefest glance before his attention returned to the airport officials and their intense conversation.

This wasn't her first run-in with authorities, but it was her first in such a conservative country where everything was done so differently from Britain. Still, the basic rule applied here as it did everywhere in life...

Show no fear.

But do it politely.

'Perhaps we could please begin?' she called out carefully, as though the only part of this bothering her were the delay. 'I have a service waiting to collect me.'

She threw in a winning smile for good measure. Hopefully, it would temper the *thump-thump* of her heart clearly audible in her voice. But the smile was wasted as the rapid, under-their-breath discussion continued without her. Then the largest of the officials shook the chauffeur's hand and crossed to the table where her documents lay spread out. He flipped her passport open and stamped it with the visa, then initialled it and passed it to him.

She jumped as the glass between the spaces suddenly snapped to opaque, then again a moment later, when the door to her half of the room was flung open and the chauffeur stood there, her bag in one fist and her documentation clenched in the other.

'Welcome to Umm Khoreem,' he said, with no other explanation or apology, wedging the door open.

He might have shared the same tan skin and dark hair as the other officials, but his accent wasn't Arabic. She stared at him, her feet still nailed to the floor as he spelled it out in clearer terms.

'You are free to leave.'

'That's it?' Her passion for natural justice started to bubble. 'Why was I detained in the first place?'

She had a fairly good idea—those few hours in a disguised medical research lab north of London were going to shadow her forever—but she just wanted to hear him say it. Plus, she wanted to narrow down his accent. But he wasn't in the chatty mood, it seemed; he slid his sunglasses on, turned and walked away from her with her suitcase. And her passport.

She hurried after him. 'Can I please have my—?'

'Keep walking, Ms Blaise,' he gritted, nodding towards the distant glass exit. 'You're not legally in the country until we get past that door up ahead.'

His tortured vowels gave her an answer—Australian— and the way he practically barked at her made her reassess him as airport security or some kind of translator. The other officials might have been obstructing her entrance but they were nothing but painfully and professionally courteous. He might have facilitated her release but he was curt and grumpy.

So, if he wasn't airport staff then who was he? Why should she follow a random stranger down some long dark corridor?

Though she had little choice as he marched off with all her worldly goods.

'Sorry, what just happened?' she puffed, hurrying up beside him as he strode along the passageway. Other than, clearly, she was almost refused an entry visa. 'Why did they let me go, just like that?'

He didn't deign to do more than angle his head slightly back as he answered. He certainly didn't stop or even slow. 'They had little option when the ruling Sheikh vouched for you.'

Her feet stumbled to a halt. 'You're a sheikh?'

His laugh ricocheted off the polished walls of the corridor. 'Do I look like a sheikh?'

How would she know? Maybe they were all neat-bearded, square-jawed types. 'Then how—?'

'Sheikh Bakhsh Shakoor is my employer. I therefore spoke on his behalf.'

Oh, everything was starting to make more sense now.

'And why exactly does Sheikh Whatsit care what happens to me?'

Or even know about it, come to think of it? It all happened so quickly. One minute she was happily arriving, the next she was unhappily interned.

'You are a long-stay guest in his most prestigious resort. He would not be pleased to hear you had been detained on a technicality.'

A criminal charge wasn't exactly nothing. That was why she'd declared it on her immigration form. Transparency and accountability and all that. But she was spending a fortune on her month at the Sheikh's desert resort and being booted out of his country bound in red tape would obviously be an expensive outcome for the resort. And since he probably also owned the airport...

'He has no idea what you just did, does he?' she guessed.

'The Sheikh does not have time for trivialities.'

Way to make a girl feel special... 'So, you just got creative?'

His lips pressed closer together as he lifted her suitcase as though it were empty of designer contents and pushed it ahead of them through the official exit into the Umm Khoreem side of the airport.

To freedom.

Kind of.

'I gave them a few assurances,' he went on. 'Nothing that should put a crimp in your sunbaking plans.'

Yep, he probably did think she'd come to bask under Umm Khoreem's toasty winter sun. Rather than for the sanctuary—from life and from her least favourite time of year.

'What kind of assurances?'

The pace he set across the polished stone of the airport terminal was almost hard to match, though it was fantastic to be moving her limbs again after nine hours on a crowded plane. She hurried after him as he wove in and out of the thick stream of passengers like a rally pro.

'While you are within the fenced bounds of Al Saqr resort, you are a guest of the Sheikh,' he said, back to her, 'and his protection extends to you. Under those conditions they were happy to overlook your recent…crime… and grant you entry into Umm Khoreem.'

'You make it sound like I was caught robbing a bank,' she huffed.

'You'd be surprised how much I know about you, Ms Blaise.'

She glanced up at him and tried to guess how serious he was about that. There wasn't much to know. Her criminal record was empty of anything but a shiny new conviction for trespass. For defending those who could not defend themselves.

On balance, that was a pretty good trade-off.

'Wow. Someone is a little judgey…'

It was all there in the frost in his tone and the grind of his jaw, but getting into a fight was not how she'd imagined starting her month-long exile. Then again, neither was being detained, and—once again—she reminded herself how foreign this culture was from her own.

'The resort's boundaries are massive,' he said. 'As long as you remain within them, you'll be fine.'

Being managed irked her as much as it always did. 'And what is to stop me from just taking my bag and disappearing into the glass and chrome of Kafr Falaj?'

She could see the tallest of the capital's buildings from here.

His locomotive surge across the terminal came to an abrupt halt, and she almost crashed into him. Impenetrable black glass swung her way.

'I am.'

Even without being able to see his eyes, she believed him. Her long legs might get her some distance in the short term but his hard build said he would easily best her on endurance. Plus she'd never been any good at running in sand.

'I gave them my own word, too,' he went on.

'So, now I'm beholden to the Sheikh's chauffeur as much as the Sheikh himself?' she tested.

Coral lips thinned between the neatly trimmed beard and moustache. 'I am not a chauffeur, Ms Blaise. I'm part of the royal protection detail.'

Was she supposed to be impressed that his title had the word 'royal' in it? Well, *snap*, *buddy*, she was celebrity royalty, and it had never done her any particular favours. Quite the opposite, really.

'Which makes me *your* protection detail for the next month,' he added blandly.

Immediately she regretted everything about the past fifteen minutes. It wasn't this guy's fault that she'd been dumb enough to be taken in by people she'd thought she could trust—a *man* she'd wanted to trust—or that it had all happened right before Christmas, a season she struggled with at the best of times. A forty-minute drive was one thing; the thought of spending the next *four weeks* butting heads with someone over baggage that wasn't rightfully his did not appeal. She'd come out here to lie low—and to do the right thing by her father—not to stir up the locals.

But she was more proficient in nurturing chasms than bridging them.

'Gosh, you drew the short straw,' she joked. 'Babysitting *me* for an entire month.'

She'd meant that to be self-deprecating, but she saw the word 'babysit' hit him as surely as the word 'chauffeur' had. His jaw clamped that tiny bit harder.

'On the contrary,' he gritted. 'I drew anything but a short straw. You'll understand when you see where I get to spend the next four weeks.'

She might be known for her questionable decision-making now and again but even she knew to back away from the edge, sometimes. And the stiff way that this man held his body told her that this was definitely one of those times. But retreating didn't mean she had to scramble, so she took her time setting off as he headed for the airport's exit and she swanned after him with as much grace as she could muster, even as the glass doors slid wide and the warm desert air slapped her full in the face.

Outside the window of Al Saqr's luxury SUV the region's capital, Kafr Falaj, whizzed past in all its expensive glory— a spectacular city that had sprung up out of the sand in just a couple of decades. A testament to man's supremacy over nature.

Except that Sera preferred nature's supremacy to mankind's any day.

The travel website had told her it translated as '*village of channels*', grown on the strength of the massive network of ancient irrigation conduits that rivalled the Roman aqueducts and that still funnelled water from underground aquifers and mountain foothills to the desert village's thriving agriculture. A village that had quickly grown into a city. Thankfully, this was as close as she needed to get to Kafr Falaj and its over-abundance of foreigners—living there, working there, visiting there. Where they were headed, the handful of foreigners would be vastly spread out.

Studying the city had killed some time, then the emerging desert, and, in between, she'd studied *him* while he'd concentrated on the fast desert highway. The neat cut of his dark hair, the crisp edges of his suit collar, the clip of his dark beard so close it had to be a professional job, the curious scar cutting down into his left eyebrow. He hadn't spoken since bundling her into the back seat of the massive SUV. She'd squeezed herself through the gap and into the front passenger seat before he'd even come around to his own door.

She hated the whole Miss Daisy thing. She never rode in the back if she didn't have to.

'So, we're going to spend four weeks in each other's company,' Sera said, simply to crack the long silence as they drove out of the city. 'What should I call you?'

'What did you call your last protection?' he finally grunted.

'Russell it is, then,' she said, smiling. 'What are the odds?'

Dark sunglasses turned her way, just slightly. 'You can call me Brad, Ms Blaise.'

'You know that Blaise is a stage name, right? First and last name all in one. Like Madonna. Or Bono. Apparently that was a thing in the eighties.'

'I assumed.'

But maybe he remembered the vast quantities of money that she was spending on this trip, because he spoke again and this time it was longer than three syllables. 'Would you prefer a different surname?'

'I'd prefer no surname at all, actually.' Ha! Like father like daughter.

'Okay. Seraphina.'

'God no! That's as much of a show name as Blaise. Pretty sure Dad's publicist picked it.' Forgetting that a little girl needed to live with it.

His lips pressed more tightly together within the architectural facial hair. 'What do you call yourself?'

'Sera.'

'Fine. How about we set some ground rules, Sera?'

She'd had a gutful of alpha-male types. They could tie her in knots way too easily. 'You know...you sure are shovey about how things need to be.'

'Establishing parameters is necessary. I have a job to do.'

She opened the console fridge between them in the back seat and cracked the lid on one of several frosty bottles of water she found there. 'I'm not sure how parameters are going to go with me. Didn't you read my file? There must have been a note.'

From her father. Or Russell. Or the security detail before him. Her tutor before that. Any of her nannies. How far back did he want to go?

'There were quite a number of notes, in fact.'

And he struck her as a man who would have read them all. 'I do like to think of myself as noteworthy.'

Again, no reaction to speak of. Just that steady, impermeable, infuriating, Polaroid regard pointed firmly at the road ahead.

'How about I set the first parameter, Brad?' she went on.

'Go ahead.'

'What say whenever any one of us has something to say to the other we remove our sunglasses and make actual eye contact? Like polite people.' She sweetened it with a smile.

Oh, well...start as you mean to continue.

The silence grew weighted—blue whale kind of weighted—but then Brad lowered his head just slightly, removed his glasses and folded them carefully into his breast pocket with the hand not steering, then turned back to meet her eyes square on. But his weren't contrite, and the act didn't weaken him. His regard burned into her as if he were scanning her DNA and, for just a moment, she wished she'd kept her big mouth shut.

Pale grey eyes—combined with his dark colouring they were stunning.

Yep, you're going to need to leave those glasses on...

'You do realise you're textbook, I suppose?' he said as he returned his focus to the traffic around them and she was able to breathe a little easier.

'Textbook what?'

'New client. Trying to control things.'

She glanced out at the eight lanes of pristine highway cutting south through the open desert on the outskirts of the city and thought about making light of it. But then some-

thing about the unfairness of his judgement pushed a few
of her natural justice buttons.

'Listen, Brad, I've lived my whole life in the care of
professional people. A couple of jerks, most of them nice.
Some of them completely lovely. But all of *them* were paid
to be there, too. I don't think it's too much to ask for a little eye contact when we speak. Just so I know you're real.'

He focused his grey gaze on the highway ahead—thinking, driving—until finally he came to some kind of conclusion. He swung his regard her way again, and a little puff
of heat formed at her collar.

'Parameter one,' he agreed on a single nod before turning back to the road. 'Courtesy in all its forms.'

Meaning...?

But, before she could finish the thought, he barrelled
onwards while he changed lanes to tuck their black SUV
in behind a huge silver one.

'Parameter two,' he continued mildly. 'I'll respect your
right to independence if you'll respect my responsibilities
as your specialist security detail.'

And if his responsibilities and her rights failed to
align...? 'Is that your way of asking me to do whatever
you say?'

'It's my way of asking you not to fight me just for the
sake of it.'

Hmm. Maybe he *had* read her file.

'Fair enough. Parameter three...' Time to really lay
down the law. 'I'm your responsibility, but not your friend.
You get to be annoyed but not disappointed if things don't
go how you'd like them to.'

Okay, so maybe that baggage wasn't really his to be en-
cumbered with but it couldn't hurt to knock it on the head
nice and early. The last thing she needed on her big desert
time out was anything that reminded her of her father's
not-so-quiet disappointment.

'I'm good with that. Very good, in fact. I'm not here for the conversation.'

She sat back straighter against the plush leather seat. 'Any final comments?'

He considered. 'Parameter four. If you need help—if you really need it—you come to me. No matter what else has gone down between now and then. I'll manage whatever it is.'

There was that word again...

She'd been *managed* her whole life.

'You really have a thing for control, don't you?' Which was tantamount to waving a red tea towel at the bull of her capricious nature.

He shrugged. 'I'm paid to control our environment.'

Her environment, for the next four weeks.

'Okay...' Four weeks was a long time, she needed to lighten things up a bit. 'Courtesy, cooperation, respect and emergency protocol. I think we've covered everything. Except maybe a safe word? I vote for "capsicum".'

His dark brows folded. 'Capsicum?'

'You know...in case either of us needs out of this arrangement at any time?'

If she thought the muscles of his face capable of it, she would have pegged that tiny twist on the right of his mouth as a smile. Probably just gas. Except then he really blew her mind by making a joke.

Kind of.

'What if you're ordering at a restaurant and you say it?' he queried, eyes fixed on the road ahead.

Her perception of him shifted just a little. In an upward direction.

'I'll call them peppers.'

'And if you're planting a garden?'

She matched his straight face. 'In the deserts of Umm Khoreem?'

'What if you're picking out wall colours?'

She laid her hand on her heart. 'I pledge to do no interior decorating until this month is up.'

His eyes returned to hers and—miracle of miracles—they were just a hint warmer than before. More *bark of oak* and less *Thames in winter*.

'Okay.' He nodded. 'Capsicum it is.'

Why did it feel good to have had a small win over this man, even in jest? And exactly when had it started feeling a little bit like flirting?

CHAPTER TWO

THE MORE SHE SPOKE, the more comfortable Brad felt about the month ahead. This wasn't some helpless princess who would flap her hands every time something didn't go her way. She wasn't the needy type. She might well end up being a pain in his butt but at least she wouldn't be looking to him for any kind of rescue. As far as he could see, this gig was more about protecting her from herself.

Still, she was celebrity offspring and he was a pro and so, out of habit, his eyes scanned the many expensive vehicles keeping pace with them at two hundred clicks on the highway away from Kafr Falaj. Each one with extra dark window tinting that obscured its occupants. Once, that would have made him twitchy, but this was Umm Khoreem—there was an oil-rich sea between here and any of the conflict hotspots he'd ever been stationed. And he was here keeping an eye on some rock star's kid, not enforcing sanctions or protecting UN personnel.

Those days were behind him.

He cracked his knuckles and slid his eyes back to his client. Sera had made quite a meal of studying the endless desert since the whole ground-rules conversation had limped to a civil halt between them, and her eyes were still fixed on the massive dunes in the distance as they sped along the Al Dhinn highway.

His mind flashed up the client sheet that her London-based security firm had provided.

Seraphina Blaise. Twenty-four years old, daughter of a middle-aged Goth frontman who'd been performing live for most of Brad's own youth and still was today. A punishing and relentless schedule that kept his band, The

Ravens, at the top of the charts whenever they released anything. Blaise didn't really seem old enough to have an adult daughter, but who knew with these rock types—they started their careers young, or made their mistakes early. Whichever.

His daughter's file was full of labels like 'ardent' and 'rash' but also 'committed' and 'loyal'. And 'damaged'. There were screenshots about her very public arrest earlier in the year mixed amongst older citations for volunteering, academic excellence and her talent as a photographer. So which was true? He had citations—a drawer full of them— and they didn't necessarily make him a better person.

Maybe he'd be better off ignoring what was in Sera's file and conducting his own assessment.

Her tongue might be a little sharp but it worked for a pretty switched-on brain; not everyone called him out as thoroughly as she had just now. It was hard not to respect a pre-emptive striker even if she was overly cranky. She'd just been detained by one of the toughest and touchiest governments in the world—he'd throw her a bone on that one.

She'd been carved by some kind of post-modern sculptor. A whole bunch of mismatched parts that came together into an intriguingly curious package. Everything about her was long. Her face, her jaw, her nose. Hair. Fingers. Legs. It reminded him of Al Saqr's best Arab horses but still managed to be feminine. It shouldn't really work together but somehow it did, leaving her more...striking than classically pretty. She didn't accessorise with copious amounts of jewellery the way most of her flight had; other than the silver clasps on her flimsy blouse, the treacle-brown hair tumbling down over her bare shoulders was all the decoration she needed.

On the other hand, she'd swanned into a conservative country with her arms and shoulders bare. Ordinarily, he would have chalked that up to cultural ignorance, but in Sera... He found it hard to imagine that she hadn't read up on the region she was visiting. It was almost as if she was challenging Umm Khoreem to a silent social debate.

Maybe she was. Her file was full of protests and causes and righteous indignation about one thing or another.

For the second time in forty minutes, Brad hit the indicator to change lanes, and he navigated the SUV around and under the highway to reach the start of Al Saqr's access road. He let the massive vehicle own the road; when the resort was as exclusive and private as Al Saqr, oncoming traffic was rarely an issue.

Sera sat up straighter to see what was ahead. The composed woman he'd seen at the airport was morphing, with every stretch of her long neck, into a different creature. A more excited, engaged, relaxed woman.

Or maybe the desert was just wielding its subtle magic already. It was good like that.

'Still fifteen minutes,' Brad murmured, and she slumped back into her seat like an impatient teen. He forced himself not to smile. 'Is this your first desert?'

'Not counting ones I've flown over? Yes.'

'Whatever you're expecting,' he murmured, 'you're wrong.'

Her eyebrows raised, but she didn't bite. She peered, instead, out the front of the vehicle at the vast…nothing… that was ahead of them.

Five minutes later, he pulled to a halt at Al Saqr's armed boundary checkpoint. Per the regulations, the guard came out and eyeballed the whole vehicle—including the empty back seats—checking Sera's name off the sparse guest register before waving them through the raised boom gate. In his periphery, Sera eyed the massive mesh fences stretching out in both directions as far as she could see and the casual way the guard's high-powered weapon was slung over his shoulder. For the first time, her confidence seemed to wobble. Just a little.

'Do you get much trouble out here?'

'The fences are to protect the wildlife,' he reassured. Though, in truth, they went a long way to making his job easier given the only people allowed past Al Saqr's checkpoint were registered guests, staff and suppliers. That lessened his field of professional concern from everyone on the Arabian Peninsula to just a comparative handful.

Although something told him that Sera, herself, would be dominating his field of concern for the next few weeks of his life.

That elegant neck started craning again as they left the asphalt and hit the compacted road gouged through the desert. Around them, the geometric shapes carved by wind into the sand and the occasional fire bush dominated. But as they crested a high dune she got her first glimpse of the resort far ahead, nestled in the middle of an enormous expanse of interlocking, golden blonde sand dunes.

Like the oasis it functionally was.

'It's gorgeous,' Sera breathed.

Yeah, it was. The resort stretched like a jewelled tiara along the top edge of a massive sand ridge.

Not that the desert needed any gilding.

The date palms that signalled the presence of shallow groundwater started to whizz by, first in singles, then in spikey clusters. Tucked away between small dune rises on their left and right were small, scattered buildings— service sites for the resort and their staff—but the road kept on moving past those, disappointing Sera visibly every time one was not part of the larger resort. Finally, the palm clusters merged into a proper croft and Sidr and Ghaf trees thickened up around them as neat herringbone pavers seemed to emerge from the graded sand like the yellow brick road in Oz.

Just as well, too, or Sera would have run out of seat to climb. He glanced sideways at her and tried hard not to acknowledge that curiosity did good things to her face.

'Oh, wow!'

He loved this part. The moment that someone saw Al Saqr for the first time. The luxury resort that she would be calling home for the next month.

He scanned the arrivals area ahead as they pulled into the paved circle in front of the resort's reception despite knowing that no one but authorised personnel and guests could have been inside the fences. Old habits died hard.

'Standby,' he instructed, levering his door handle.

Dry heat rushed past him as he climbed out, still scanning for threats, then crossed quickly in front of the SUV to open the passenger side door as two staff emerged from the heavy timber entrance of the resort's central hub. The shorter of the two was traditionally but comfortably dressed, smiling broadly enough to pop dimples, his hand outstretched. Behind him stood a taller man, ginger haired, dressed in khaki and boots.

They nodded briefly to Brad then stood at attention as he gave Sera his arm down from the high SUV.

She stepped forward enthusiastically as soon as her feet touched earth.

'Hi!'

Brad closed the SUV door quietly and stood in much the same pose as his colleagues—hands behind him, back straight—as they introduced themselves to Sera. There was little sign of the woman from the airport, now. This Sera had pulled her thick hair back in a desert-friendly ponytail while she was waiting for him to clear the arrivals area and wore undisguised excitement on her face. You had to be a real tough guy to remain unaffected by Al Saqr's unique beauty.

This Sera was more girl than woman, and the unfamiliar twist in his gut hit him again.

'Ms Blaise, welcome,' the shorter of the two men said in impeccable English, pressing an introduction card into her hand for her later reference. 'I am Aqil, your guest relations coordinator. Anything you need, do not hesitate to ask for me.'

Eric was taller, and he leaned around Aqil to shake Sera's hand and introduce himself before adding, 'I'm an Al Saqr field guide. You'll be doing your activities with me.'

Two more staff emerged with a guest trolley and quietly collected Sera's luggage from the SUV as Aqil and Eric ushered her beyond the main doors. Brad followed the arctic air that pumped out through the opening courtesy of air-conditioning powered by the ocean of solar panels tucked between the dunes out of guest view. No matter how many times he was assigned out here, stepping inside was always like walking into Aladdin's cave. Cool, dark and just a little bit mystic. Traditional Arabian architecture and furnishings had been put to good use in the resort's foyer, and the whole place smelled vaguely...herbal. It had an immediate impact on Sera.

'I wish I'd kept my camera out of my luggage,' she murmured, running her eyes from the labyrinthine floor tiles up to the ornate timber roof features.

Aqil turned a winning smile on her. 'It is beautiful, no? You will be in this building often over the coming weeks. Many opportunities. This way, please.'

They guided her into the receiving lounge off to one side of the foyer, filled with richly upholstered sofas and low, old tables. Old in a good way—an expensive way—not old like the beaten-up furniture he remembered from his UN days in the desert villages. Eric returned with a tall glass of tropical fruit juice for Sera.

'While you rest here I'll just have a word with your liaisons,' Brad murmured.

She might have heard him, she might not. Her attention was so thoroughly taken by the feel of the woven sheaves hanging over the arched doorway and the intricate wrought iron decorating the window looking back out to the foyer. But he took momentary leave to check in with Aqil and Eric.

Their focus shifted immediately once they were out of Sera's presence.

'What's the protocol?' Aqil said quietly.

'Close contact,' he briefed them, fast. Which meant he needed to be on hand nearby. Very nearby. 'Where have you put her?'

Aqil consulted the site map spread on his desk. 'Suite ten is vacant on both sides.'

Ten was good. Far enough away from other guests for privacy and quiet but close enough to the main buildings for a fast response if needed. And it meant he could set up camp in eleven, right next door. Al Saqr had multi-roomed suites, but an unrelated man and woman under one roof on the Arabian Peninsula…? Nope, not even if she was under serious threat. But better safe than sorry. Celebrity did weird things to people.

And he didn't take any risks these days. He'd come too close in the past.

'No one enters her suite when she's in it unless I'm present,' he ordered.

'Understood.'

He rattled off a few other need-to-knows and then turned back to the lounge where Sera had finished fondling the curtains and sat, happy as a clam, sipping her juice on the luxuriously padded traditional lounge. Her smile was as bright as the desert outside when he returned to her side.

'It's all so amazing,' she gushed.

His gut twisted that little bit more. He didn't want her softening. He didn't want bright innocence to start peeking out from behind the façade. He wanted the self-assured, cranky client to stay. Because she was easier to dislike.

And dislike was easier to manage.

'Ready for your room?'

She glanced longingly at the juice still half-full in her hand then back at him.

He caught the smile before it infected the rest of his neutral expression. 'Those are as common as sand out here.'

She took one final long, hard suck on her straw, then

placed the glass down on the carved coaster that had been
discreetly laid out for her.

'Let's go.'

Al Saqr must look a bit like a scorpion from the air, Sera
thought. Long stretches of treed pathway extended out from
the resort's main building like articulated legs, going in different directions along the bank of the massive dune the
resort was built on. Dotted along them at private yet ac-
cessible distances were the individual suites.

Not rooms exactly, she saw as they passed two that
weren't theirs, more like quasi-tents with the same plastered white walls and dark timber windows as the resort,
but with canopied canvas roofs sitting like a broad sun hat
over each hexagonal suite. With timber deck everywhere
its shadows reached.

She sighed as her eyes fell on every new and alien thing.
Nothing here would remind her of the media and their
scrabbling. Or of home. Or the season.

'Here we are,' Aqil advised, pulling the courtesy buggy
into the shade of a suite about halfway along the front leg
of the scorpion, facing all that empty desert.

The way the suites were staggered, it was easy to feel
that it was just she and the desert. No other human being
or work as far as the eye could see. She took her time getting off the buggy, knowing that Brad would get there before her and indeed he did, sweeping inside as soon as the
door opened and clearing the room before she was allowed
into it. She smiled awkwardly at Aqil, who just shrugged
and waited in patient, dimpled silence with her.

Stepping inside was totally worth the wait. Cool and
dim and fragrant. Just like the resort reception. But that
was where the similarity ended. This was a suite that managed to be simple yet more luxurious than anything she'd
ever stayed in before. The six-sided shape of the room was
countered by custom furniture in traditional style so that

everything fitted without making it feel cluttered. Long sofas, luxury coffee station, writing desk and an opulent, high, king-sized bed centred against it all. Three of the six edges of the suite were glass doors with thick light-controlling drapes of the same kind of silken weave she'd gone crazy patting earlier.

Until Aqil flung one set open.

Beyond the glass doors, the Arabian desert flowed golden and dramatic, its dunes laid out in all their glory all the way to the horizon where the shadows of mountains loomed. And immediately in front, between all that sand and her air-conditioned life-support system, a gorgeous, deep, blue plunge pool, half in desert sun, half in shade.

Sera pressed her hands to the glass doors and leaned into the heat soaking in through them. Hot desert. Cold pool. Espresso station. Massive *Princess and the Pea* bed…

Some of the tension she'd been carrying around for the past year shifted and broke away, turning to dust on the warm desert breeze.

'Your home for the next month,' Aqil murmured. 'Let me show you everything…'

It only took a few minutes, yet there was nothing she could need that Al Saqr hadn't thought of. Lazy luxury from top to bottom.

'Mr Kruger is in the suite immediately to your right,' Aqil said when the tour was done, handing Brad an old-fashioned, hand-wrought key that matched hers. 'His bag has been placed there already.'

On cue, hers was whisked in. Even with only one bag, she'd over-packed. Right now she would be entirely happy to spend the whole month in her swimsuit, though probably she'd need to throw on a dress to go for food now and then. She glanced at the table set up by the pool.

Unless she had dinner come to her…

Another knot in her shoulder unravelled.

'Aqil, thank you. This is…exactly what I needed.'

Silence. Beauty. Nature. Far enough from civilisation that even *she* couldn't cause a stir out here. The perfect place to lie low for a bit.

And not a hint of Christmas festivity.

'We pride ourselves on being what our guests need, Miss Blaise,' Aqil murmured. Then he excused himself, told her how she could contact him if she needed him and departed. She leaned back on the warm glass doors, closed her eyes and let even more of the tension soak away into that heat.

When they reopened, Brad was still there. Waiting quietly for instructions.

Kruger. Brad Kruger. A strong name for a strong man.

'I'm going to dig out my camera,' she said, pushing the thought away as firmly as she pushed herself away from the glass. 'And I'm going to take a swim. And lie on this day lounge. Possibly not in that order. Why don't you get settled in next door and come back when you're done? We can talk about how this is all going to work.'

He nodded—the only discernible part of his inscrutable expression—and departed, leaving just her, her heavy heart and the non-judgemental desert.

Brad tore himself away from the familiar view and got up off the sofa. Getting 'settled' had only taken him a few minutes—how long could it take to unpack one small bag and lay out basic toiletries in the obscenely large bathroom?

If Sera's UK security were paying for anything other than close contact then he would be back in his own apartment in the city, driving out to the resort every morning to supervise his client. But close contact meant *close* and so he'd be enjoying the resort's six-star facilities gratis for the next month. His eyes strayed back out to the soft, rich light falling onto the desert sands.

There were definitely worse ways to spend your Christmas.

He'd heard the distant splash of Sera lowering herself

into her pool a while earlier, so he trusted that she was too busy enjoying the view to be getting up to any early mischief. But he'd figured she could probably use a little mental space after her dramatic arrival in the country, so he'd cooled his heels for the twenty minutes after unpacking, then done a token perimeter assessment of both their suites to stretch it out a little more.

In his experience, protect*ees* never adjusted quite as well to the idea of close contact as the protect*ors*, even the ones whose lives depended on high-level guard. It was a skill, hitting that fine balance between too much and too little supervision. Relaxed enough to keep your client sane and compliant, but not so relaxed that it opened a window for the kind of risk that he was hired to protect them against. And not so much that the client became overly reliant on you and stopped listening to their own instincts. Overly reliant or overly fond—the small twist in his gut reminded him. That was just as dangerous. As he'd discovered the hard way.

The best balance was…indifferent acquiescence.

That was what he'd be pushing for with Sera.

His suite, which also meant hers, was unchanged from the last time he was assigned to Al Saqr—locked from the inside, glass doors on three sides, huge pair of timber doors on the public side, privacy fences all around but open to desert everywhere else. Rule of thumb here was that you kept your desert walks away from your neighbouring accommodations; a privacy thing. So staff wouldn't visit while Sera was in the suite and no one should be hauling themselves up the dune face and stumbling into her private pool area any time soon.

Though *shouldn't* and *wouldn't* weren't necessarily the same thing. His formal orders were to make sure Sera stayed out of trouble while the media attention from her recent legal troubles died down, but when your father was as rich and famous as hers, anything was possible. And he wasn't about to get caught out by letting his guard down.

Once burned, ten times shy.

Brad locked suite eleven's door behind him and jogged past Sera's to the neighbours on the other side to confirm nine was definitely empty. Then he checked his watch to ensure a full hour had passed and he presented himself back at her door, knocking firmly.

He counted to ten before trying again.

Still nothing.

'Sera?'

His chest filled with lead. *Please don't let her have gone exploring alone...*

Just because she'd agreed to ground rule number two in the SUV didn't mean she'd stick to it when faced with the seductions of this unique place. He stepped down off the decking leading to the front door and walked around the side of the suite where his own had a side opening for maintenance staff to use. He could hear a bunch of animal noises he didn't recognise—one of them a kind of gaspy hitch—so the wildlife around them could be just about anything.

'Sera?' Something about the desert silence made him not want to shout. 'I'm coming around.'

But as he stepped back up on to the decking within her back yard, his quick eyes saw exactly why Sera hadn't heard him. She floated at the deep end of her little pool, the water cascading over her arms that lay folded on its tiled infinity edge, chin resting there, staring out at the desert beyond. Her long hair looked even darker wet and it hung flat down her back between pale shoulders and blue swimsuit straps, which made it easy to see the headphones she had wedged into her ears. He followed the white wires over to where her phone rested on the flat, dry tiles of the pool edge.

Something about her posture stilled his feet before he reached the steps, though.

And then he heard it… The choked hitch he'd attributed in amongst the other desert wildlife sounds. It wasn't an exotic bird calling at all; it was Sera, crying—sobbing, actually, if only she weren't doing such a good job of muffling it in her folded arms. He stood, frozen, and stared at her heaving shoulders and back. Everything in him burned to go and check on her. The urge bubbled up and made his feet twitch.

But a single image fought its way through all the instinct and kept him utterly immobile—a young, glittery-eyed face, splotched red with distress, pressed up against the rear window of a hastily departing transporter, his little mouth open in a cry that Brad couldn't hear.

But he'd felt it down to his very soul.

He still did.

Sera's tears could be about just about anything. The ex-boyfriend her file said she'd parted ways with. Bad news from home. Work hassles, if not for the fact that she didn't have a job, at least, not a proper one. Her father's money had brought her freedom from the worries of ordinary people.

He stared at the soft lurches of her pale shoulders.

Clearly, money hadn't exactly bought her happiness.

Whatever it was, it wasn't any of his business until it put her at physical risk. His job was to keep Sera out of trouble for four weeks. Muddling around in her emotional well-being was completely outside his remit. He wasn't paid for it.

And he wasn't remotely skilled at it.

He took a backwards step, and then another, and vanished the way he'd come, leaving Sera to her privacy.

And her pain.

CHAPTER THREE

'HAVE YOU TASTED the bananas?' Sera burst out, answering his door knock a little later. 'They're amazing. God, I've missed bananas.'

Brad reeled a little at the sheer joy on her face. Quarter of an hour ago she was inconsolable. Maybe the desert with its ever-changing moods was a fitting place for her.

'Is there some kind of British banana shortage I'm not aware of?' he said, rather than obsess on things that were outside his purview.

She turned and walked back into her suite, leaving him to follow. 'I stopped eating them. All our bananas are flash-frosted and shipped in from West Africa or South America; it's been ages since I've had a fresh, locally harvested banana. Sensational.'

Somehow, she'd even managed to make fruit political.

'Are you okay?'

She smiled, and it appeared totally sincere. Obviously a quick rebounder, then.

'Sure. Are you?'

He narrowed his focus on her red-tinged eyes. 'Do you need some eye drops?'

Really, Kruger? You gotta keep snooping? Let it go, man.

She waved his concern away. 'The pool is lightly salted.'

A little bit extra now, given her copious tears. But her easy dismissal made it impossible for him to exercise the absurd Galahad complex she seemed to have triggered in him.

Seraphina Blaise did not need—or want—his help.

His attention tracked to her still-unpacked luggage. 'How are you settling in?'

Her mouth split into a smile as wide as the desert they

sat in. 'It's unbelievable, already. Have you seen the light? It changes by the hour. It's going to be amazing to photograph.'

'We'll be doing a bit of that, then?'

'I'm here for a month,' she murmured. 'I'll go mad without a focus. Besides, it's what I *do*. You know?'

Yeah. He knew all about her photography. It was what had got her in the papers in the first place. Taking photos of animals in confidential research labs. And getting caught doing it. Though that hadn't been quite the accident she'd first believed.

'I figure I'll be busiest in the mornings and late afternoon, when it's coolest and the light is richest,' she said. 'Do you…? Are you supposed to be twenty-four-seven?'

The settling-in phase was always clunky, but Sera managed to make it feel extra awkward. As if he were some kind of stalker and they were negotiating the terms on which he'd lurk around after her.

'I'll be seven days a week for the next month,' he confirmed. 'But I won't be in your face all the time.'

'There'll probably be three or four hours in the hottest part of the day when I'll retreat in here. That's time off for you.'

'Maybe,' he hinted. It all depended on what she got up to while she was alone. Complementary WiFi was a potentially dangerous thing. All it would take was one culturally bolshie blog…

'I'm your protection, Sera. My job is to be here when and if something happens.' And *something* could whip up like a sandstorm. 'I'm not going to be out having shots at the bar when you might need me.'

She stared him down and it reminded him much more of Sera from the airport. 'This place is like Fort Knox. What could possibly happen to me here?'

Any question whether or not she knew what he was truly here for evaporated on the warm desert air.

Okay, time to toss his cards on the table...

'My brief is to ensure you keep a low profile for the next month,' he admitted.

'Actually, that's my brief,' Sera said. '*You're* here because my father clearly doubts my ability to honour my promise to him.'

The politics of her family had no more place in his mind than her tears did. Nor the confused hurt that had just flashed across her bold gaze. He forced his natural empathy aside.

'Your UK security firm are taking no chances,' he said. 'I'm paid for close contact, which means twenty-four-seven.' Or as much as the culture here would allow. 'That will keep you safe from any crazies and—conveniently—means I'll be around to head off any...social issues that might emerge.'

'What if I pledge not to publish any manifestos while I'm here?' she joked.

He couldn't match her light laugh. That was exactly the sort of thing he was hired to restrict. 'I'll be resetting your device passwords daily. More often if I need to.'

'Of course you will,' she grunted. 'Why not just take them off me?'

'Because you're not a child.'

The irony of that made her laugh. 'Thanks for noticing.'

'My job is to create an environment that limits risk, Sera. I'm your protection, not your parent. You already have one of those.'

Again, the flash across her gaze. But while her irritation was real it didn't seem directed at him.

'You can't work around the clock, Brad,' she said, and he got the sense that the idea was genuinely troubling her.

'You'll barely know I'm—'

'I'm not worried for me,' she interrupted. 'It's not fair on you. I'm sorry that you have to be inconvenienced for something that won't even be happening. I had hoped that no one would be put out by me this Christmas,' she muttered.

Was it his imagination or was there an extra subtle leaning on the word '*this*'? But curiosity belonged between them about as much as empathy did.

Indifferent acquiescence...

'It's not an inconvenience. It's my job. Besides, personal protection isn't exactly taxing,' he said.

'Until it is?' she guessed.

Again, that sharp mind at work.

'Nature of the beast,' he murmured. 'It's all waiting around and watching until it blows up.'

'Well, it won't be blowing up because of me,' she vowed with determination in her eyes. 'No matter what my father thinks. I'm afraid it's going to be a dull month for you.'

Yeah... The road to hell was paved with good intentions. 'Did your last protection detail buy that gentle sincerity?'

Right before he got reassigned over the whole research-lab debacle.

He deserved her annoyance, but the flush he got instead was shame. It peaked high in her cheeks and cast her eyes downward.

'I'll be all right,' he assured her in lieu of apology. 'I'll take my downtime as I can.'

'I just want you to know that I'm okay with the idea of personal space,' she murmured.

He couldn't help the laugh then. 'I'm sure. Unfortunately, I'm required to intrude on yours quite a bit.'

She sighed and moved to the bedside table to collect her key. 'Well, we might as well get on with it, then. The resort schedules a complimentary spa session for anyone who has come in on an international flight. Mine's in half an hour.'

Back on the job. 'I'll call up the buggy.'

'I'd like to walk. To get some pictures before the spa,' she said. 'Then perhaps some more shooting after lunch.'

It wasn't a request, no matter how politely delivered.

Here was a woman who'd been negotiating with protection details her whole life, though, while she was good at it, her tension told him she didn't enjoy it. Fortunately, he did. Clear, confident directions boded well for a client who would accept his daily intrusions into her life.

'Sounds good,' he said.

In reality, protection details were dull more often than they were *good*. The trick was in staying alert and on your game while your mind turned to mush watching some client reading a book or watching their kid at a ball game or catching a movie. The consequences of losing focus could be bad. And prevention was a whole lot better than cure.

As he knew from experience.

Sera grabbed her camera from her luggage and a wide straw hat from her bedhead and turned for the door.

'Let's go.'

'Did the floor say something to offend?' Sera asked him, her voice husky from an hour of languorous spoiling in the spa. The rest of her was buried in her oversized robe, enjoying the dazed, spaced-out, post-massage moments.

Brad's grey gaze shot upwards as he pushed to his feet. 'Sorry, what?'

Her smile was as slow to form as her slurred words, but the uncomfortable expression on his face as he looked her over made her want to double-check that the robe was closed everywhere it should be. It made her want to fix her just-massaged hair, too, but she resisted the urge.

'The floor,' she clarified. 'You're frowning at it pretty severely.'

'We, uh, disagreed on a few fundamentals.'

His gruff chuckle did more for undoing the stresses of her arrival in Umm Khoreem than the hour-long rubdown she'd just enjoyed. Or the good, cathartic cry she'd had in the pool. A laugh, on this man, was as surprising and rare as the light out here.

'Feel good?' he said, dragging himself up into professional guard stance.

'Amazing.' She smiled.

Her new favourite word. The desert was amazing. The suites were amazing. The massages were amazing. For someone who so easily found the beauty in the visual, her grasp of the verbal was taking a real hit this trip. It had to be connected to those eyes.

She never should have ordered him to take his sunglasses off.

'I'll wait by the door,' Brad said, nudging her towards the changing room. She stumbled forward in her half-drugged state.

The Sera that emerged from the change rooms fifteen minutes later was more the woman she liked to present to the world. She'd taken her time redressing and scrunching her hair into something vaguely stylish—using every complimentary product in the place and delighting in the complex, Arabian smells—and her bare arms and throat practically glistened from whatever oils her masseuse had used on her. She felt spoiled and mellow and fresh.

She signed her tab at the spa's reception desk and then turned and floated out the door. Brad trailed behind her, playing Sherpa to her camera gear.

'Don't forget to eat,' he murmured. 'One banana isn't going to keep you going for long, no matter how delicious it was.'

'After that massage I'm ravenous. Let's go get lunch,' she said. Sometimes—just sometimes—it was nice to have someone to do your thinking for you.

They headed for the resort's pretty hub, stopping only once to take a photograph along the way—a leggy young gazelle standing in the sand, its little tail waggling madly. Sera captured its markings, coat colour and the deep, watery depths of its eyes. Then she remembered her growly stomach.

Brad had ditched the suit in favour of dark jeans and a light shirt, but he'd kept the pricey glasses firmly in place and added a neutral baseball cap for good measure. Totally Secret Service now. Did he imagine he blended right in with the other guests? Given how he carried himself, he probably blended in nowhere outside some elite force of Arab mercenaries.

It was all very distracting.

She forced her focus back onto the landscape as they wandered along the winding stone pathway criss-crossed by the traditional watercourse that ran through the whole resort. The light was gorgeous even in the middle of the day—textures, colour—and everywhere she looked were images worthy of capturing later. The wind ripples on a bank of sand that looked otherwise completely solid. Plants she'd never seen. Birds she'd never seen. A crazy little side-winding lizard that took its twisty time cutting across in front of her.

But right now she was all about eating. And partly about ignoring the man tailing so close behind her.

He followed her over the doorway plinth into Al Saqr's heart—literally over it, all doors in the resort were cut into a much larger timber frame to keep the sand out—onto the plush rugs scattered across the stone floor. The heat and glare immediately dropped off. It took a moment for her eyes to adjust but only a moment longer to scan the entire space. The restaurant hanging off the back of the main building offered darkened, delicious-smelling dining indoors, or decorated, shade-covered tables on its deck, peering over the desert waterhole below.

'Outside, I think,' Sera said, when asked for her preference.

A minute later, she was seated on the edge of the deck, looming over the desert, her favourite juice on hand and a jug of icy water delivered. They seated Brad a few tables back, out of her view but presumably where he had a good clear outlook over the whole area. If she were her father, there was no way his security would have let him sit here, so exposed to anyone bedded down in a distant dune. But the kind of obsessive crazies The Ravens' gothic music occasionally attracted and the kind of pathetic try-hards *she* would attract were totally different creatures.

The only shot someone was going to take at *her* would end up in the tabloids, not in a morgue.

There were six other diners also having a late lunch, all of them in couples and looking very loved up. This was exactly the right sort of resort for honeymoons or anniversaries. Or romantic Christmases, as it turned out. On balance, though, it was still better to spend the festive season here than back home. Alone.

Even if she was in disgrace.

Her meal came, and right behind that Brad's did. They each ate in silence, the occasional clink of his cutlery a kind of Morse code reminding her he was close by. Sera never once turned to look at him but his presence almost *hummed*; the silence was thick with it. It dragged her attention off the gorgeous view and the delicious cuisine until she might as well have been eating airline food.

When the staff came to remove her first-course dishes, Sera pushed her chair back, turned and marched towards him.

'This is crazy. Come and join me.'

'I'm on the job,' he declined. 'But thank you.'

'Okay, you've said what your employer would want you to say. Now, please join me.'

His eyes didn't quite meet hers. 'Let's just keep it by the book.'

His manners did little more than irritate her further. Partly because she wasn't getting her way. Mostly because she was supposed to be off men—she shouldn't want his company.

But she did.

'What's problematic about having a conversation while we eat?'

His grey eyes turned wary. 'I'm paid to shadow you, not monopolise you.'

'I don't feel monopolised,' she said, low, glancing around at the other diners. 'I feel conspicuous.'

'You're not used to dining alone?'

Was he kidding? She was mostly alone, even when she had company. A nanny had always eaten with her when she was younger but it was always a very...functional exercise. Any conversation they'd had was mostly limited to which hand she held her fork in or whether she had to eat all of her beans. 'In case it's escaped your notice this is a very *coupley* resort.'

His gaze scanned the pairs dotted around the restaurant. 'You want it to seem like we're together?'

Her hiss of annoyance drew more than one curious look. 'Look. I'm the client, asking you to join me for—' she glanced around for inspiration '—my safety!'

He wasn't the slightest bit moved.

'Okay, forget it. I'll just go back to my gorgeous view and have no one to talk about it with.'

With that, she turned and flounced back to her seat, taking an oversized gulp of her dewy melon juice and sinking lower than before into her padded chair.

Stuff him—she was not about to beg. She'd never begged for someone's company in her life.

No matter how tempted she might have been.

The first Sera knew that Brad had moved was the scrape of the chair opposite hers. He stepped into the gap he'd created, placed his iced water on the table and sank down in front of her.

'The reason we don't do this,' he said without waiting for any kind of response from her, 'is that it sets up awkwardness later. What if you want to dine alone in future?

What if I do? This way there's no pressure or expectation on either side. Everything remains easy.'

She turned a baleful glare at him. 'You think I'm going to *expect* you to dine with me?'

He held his mettle and her gaze. 'You wouldn't be the first female client to misinterpret the terms of service for their protection. The rules exist for a reason.'

'If you can't handle yourself with some cougar, Brad, that's on you.' She turned back out to the desert.

His voice next came quietly—amused but slightly disappointed.

Oh, well...join the queue! Her father had communicated more disappointment in the past few months than any other sentiment all year.

'You didn't strike me as a sulker.'

'I'm not sulking,' she gritted, forcing patience she didn't feel. 'I wanted to... I don't do the reach-out thing, normally.'

Because reaching out just wasn't worth the potential rejection, in her experience. Which begged the question: Why bother, now?

'But?'

'But...even if some newspaper did track me out here into the middle of all this nothing, those gigantic fences and armed guards mean there's no chance of a picture ending up in some tabloid with a fabricated story. I just hoped that maybe I could ease back a bit on the rules this trip. Since no one knows who I am out here. You know, relax.'

His steady regard made her fingers twitch, and she curled them subtly into her fists. It only seemed to drive the flutters inward, just below her sternum.

'No one here knows you,' he said, still without blinking, 'but everyone knows me. These are my colleagues.'

The flutters fell to the floor of her gut and died there. That was right. Her plea for some latitude was essentially asking Brad to compromise his professionalism.

Remorse congealed in her blood.

'Sorry, I wasn't thinking.' Well, she was...but not about him. 'Maybe you should—'

He stopped her before she could send him away.

'Leaving again is going to draw more attention than me staying,' he murmured. 'Let's just finish lunch, yeah?'

But having achieved the company she'd set out to secure, Sera suddenly found herself struggling for a single fascinating thing to say. And he was apparently not about to help her out.

'So, you're ex-military?' she finally guessed, though she wouldn't win any prizes for intuition. Everything about him screamed Defence Forces.

'Ten years in the Specials.'

Ten years? She was just a kid when he was first heading into danger. Was that why she felt so breathless around him? Like some sixteen-year-old? She *was* a mere teen, compared to his life experience. 'You seem to know a fair bit about deserts.'

He paused, his fork halfway to his lips. 'More than most.'

'Were you posted to the Middle East?'

'My unit provided support to the United Nations. Mostly based in the capital. But I got out in the sand often enough.'

That brought her eyes back up. 'That sounds interesting.'

'If by "interesting" you mean political and volatile, sure.'

'When did you leave the UN?'

His eyes darkened over. 'Two years ago, now.'

'What made you leave?'

His eyes flicked out to the horizon.

'A mistake,' he murmured, discomforted. 'My mistake.'

She wanted to quiz him further but every question she posed made her feel like that cougar that he'd mentioned; the rare Snoopy Desert Cougar.

'And you've worked for the Sheikh since then?'

'As soon as the opportunity came up. I held out for his team.'

'Why?'

He shrugged massive shoulders. 'They're the best.'

'Must have been competitive,' she murmured.

'So am I.'

Did he have any idea how intriguing that twisted thing he called a smile was?

'And you're always based out here?'

'Not always. But Al Saqr is the gem in Sheikh Bakhsh Shakoor's crown. All his guests come here at some point, which makes for pleasant work.'

She leaned back in her seat and smiled. 'How many of *them* couldn't leave again without risking deportation?'

He fought a proper smile, but failed. As with the last glimmer she'd had of it, it transformed his face. 'You have the honour of being the first. *My* first, anyway.'

The idea of being Brad's first *anything* resurrected all those butterflies lying prone in her gut and they lurched back to life. She fought to focus on their conversation.

'Who was your most challenging client?'

'It would be unprofessional of me to comment.'

'No names, obviously.'

He stared in silence. Until she realised.

'Truly,' she gasped. 'I'm your worst?' How few had he had?

'You didn't say worst,' he was quick to reply. 'You said challenging.'

'We've been here three hours. How can I possibly challenge you already?'

For the first time, she got the sense that he wasn't saying exactly what was on his mind. 'Do you think I improvise immigration incidents every day?'

'Well, you didn't seem the slightest bit troubled by it.'

Irritated, yes...

'It's my job to appear in control.'

Seriously? Did he have to remind her every five seconds that he was paid to be here?

A beautifully dressed young woman appeared at their table with two flat stone platters dotted with pretty little desserts. She placed them down with a gentle smile, enquired after their needs and then tiptoed off again. Brad's eyes glanced after her.

For no reason at all that made her grumpy.

'So, are we okay to get some photos this afternoon?' she said, drawing his focus back to her. 'Once it starts to get cooler?'

'Whatever you need.'

He inclined his head, waiting politely for her to lift her dessert fork. She was happy to oblige, tucking into a mysterious, bluish sticky morsel—totally foreign to her but scrumptious—and the next ten minutes were all about eating in silence. Until he broke it.

'What's the story with the photography?' he asked. 'Hobby or job?'

Here we go. He wasn't the first person to assume that someone with money didn't want or need to work.

'I don't know that I've sold enough shots to truthfully call it a job,' she said. 'But I take it much more seriously than a hobby. Maybe we could settle on it being a...pastime?'

'How'd you get into it?' His interest seemed more than just polite.

'I don't remember whose idea it was, but I remember the excitement of the day my tutor took me shopping to buy my first equipment. And Friday afternoons when a professional photographer came out to teach me how to use it with any skill.'

'Do you remember what your first photograph was?'

Did she ever.

'A picture of Blaise. I ended up framing it on the wall.' But not because it was good—which it wasn't—it was so she could see her father every day. 'Then it was endless semi-skilled portraits of the staff who looked after me.'

She'd cheerfully showed them the good ones—hungry for their praise—but it wasn't those images that she'd kept. Instead, she'd papered her room with images of them captured unawares or unprepared; tidying their hair for the real photo or glancing at each other before posing properly. Laughing. Smiling. Pulling a face. Natural. As though her everyday life were simply swimming in such unguarded moments. Photography let her rebuild her world the way she wished it were...instead of how it actually was.

Who'd want to look at an exhibition of images of people carefully keeping their distance?

'Once I photographed my first London stray, though, I was all about animals. And how they intersect in the city environment. That's where I really had the best result. I don't think people are really my thing.' In so many ways. 'That led me to photograph shelter animals, to help get them new homes. I enjoyed that.'

'Not too many strays out here,' he murmured.

She thought about that. 'Stray is merely what we call "wild" in urban areas. Not much of a distinction. And the wildlife has plenty of opportunities to interact with human environments out here.'

Brad studied her close, and seemed to be wrestling with something. Finally he spoke again.

'Can I ask you something else?'

'Depends.' She smiled. 'Will it lead me to bore you to tears about my photography?'

But he didn't smile at her joke. On the contrary, his face sobered up until it was the professional mask again. 'Is there anything I need to know? About earlier... In the pool?'

Every muscle in her body coiled tighter. She shouldn't be surprised he knew about her big cry-fest. He was trained to know. But how did you tell someone you'd just met that you'd been waiting all year for that cry? That you'd been holding on to the indignity of your arrest and the disappointment it had brought your father since it had happened, knowing that, while the family lawyers had kept the actual arrest quiet, the court case was always going to be public and a total media circus. How knowing that still hadn't prevented the *other shoe* thudding down onto your heart like a steel-capped boot when the conviction had finally gone public a fortnight earlier.

And, with it, your boyfriend's betrayal.

Though really she'd lived with that since the day it had dawned on her what Mark had done. And why.

He'd officially ended their four-month 'thing' while sitting in the arraignment waiting area at courtroom number four. As redundant exercises went it was pretty spectacular. What—other than his enormous male ego—made him imagine for a moment that she would want to be anywhere near the man who had set her up for arrest? The man who had betrayed her trust and used her for the publicity her name would bring to his animal-rights cause.

Though, truthfully speaking, she'd set *herself* up. She with her hopelessly optimistic expectations and lousy judgement. He'd just sealed the deal by holding the metaphorical door open for her to walk into the arms of the authorities.

'Crying is good for you,' she joked. 'Better out than in, right?'

'So that was...catharsis?'

'It was decompression. I've had a rough couple of months.' She struggled to keep it light. 'To be honest, you're lucky it didn't start at the airport. It was touch and go for a while there.'

He didn't understand. The three little lines between his eyebrows said so.

She tilted her head and studied him. Men were such alien creatures. 'I guess crying is unprofessional, too, huh?'

'I've cried,' he said, before thinking about it. A dark flush streaked up his jaw but he didn't shy away from the topic. 'But it didn't feel good.'

He struck her as a man who wouldn't appreciate her pity. Or her curiosity. So she didn't ask.

'I'm not in any trouble,' she confirmed instead. 'But thank you for the concern.'

It seemed so genuine—even if it was reluctant—Sera had to concentrate on not letting it birth a warm glow deep inside. It was his *job* to care. It wasn't personal.

It never was.

Grey eyes bored into hers, but then he must have decided to trust her. 'Okay. But remember—'

'I will come to you the moment I'm in any real need,' she pledged. 'Rule four. I haven't forgotten.'

He meant *risk* kind of need, of course. If she felt in any kind of danger. But it felt lovely—just for a moment—to think that she had someone to go to if her heart hurt or her head wanted to explode or something just really messed with her mind. An emotional storm home.

Usually she went to herself with that stuff.

'So what do you want to photograph today?' Brad asked, bringing them back onto a safer footing and dragging his gaze from hers back out to the desert.

Probably a good idea. How had things turned from get-to-know-you chat to peering-into-your-soul chat so very quickly?

Sera pushed up straighter. 'Everything. Maybe we could start by exploring the grounds, do a bit of reconnaissance?'

He smiled at her clumsy attempt to speak his language. 'The entire fenced reserve is Al Saqr's grounds. It's fifteen per cent of all of Umm Khoreem. That's a lot of exploring. Wouldn't you rather take it a bit easy?'

'Nope. I plan on keeping nice and busy.'

'Most people generally relax over Christmas,' he hinted.

'I'm not most people.' But she reminded herself again that although he was a man he wasn't her father and he wasn't Mark. He didn't deserve her tension. He was just doing his job. 'And we have a whole month. Plenty of time for downtime, too.'

Then he asked her another question about her photography. And another. Pretty soon lunch was well and truly over, everyone that had been there when they arrived had left and a couple of new faces had arrived.

More couples... Ugh. How was she supposed to ignore the fact that she was alone during the holidays if Al Saqr kept throwing happy, lovey-dovey people in her face?

'If you want to get your camera out,' Brad finally said, standing and stepping to pull her chair from behind her as she did, too, 'we'd better get moving.'

She happily followed him.

This place was far too beautiful and bright to waste on thoughts of lonely Christmases and self-absorbed men.

CHAPTER FOUR

BRAD TRAILED CLOSE behind her, failing miserably at being invisible as Sera pottered about getting a feel for the late-afternoon light and the quality of images her tests were creating. The architecture, the exotic plant life, the wildlife. Aqil had warned her that the various hoofed creatures of the desert had free range within security fencing and they certainly let their curiosity off the leash by coming up here into the world of man. Not too close—smart things—but certainly close enough to photograph.

It took her nearly an hour to move the first one hundred metres from the restaurant.

Brad didn't complain once, though she saw him shifting his weight from foot to foot occasionally and each time he did she would self-consciously move a little farther along before becoming captivated by something else and halting again.

She moved off the paved pathways and onto the sand, wandering up and over the nearest dune to give herself the illusion of privacy from the other guests that occasionally passed by. Then her footprints—and the cascading patterns they created on the sand—kept her lens busy for another quarter-hour.

'Leave yourself something for tomorrow,' Brad murmured, out from behind his sunglasses.

'These are only test shots.' She smiled. 'I'm just getting a feel for how the sand and light work together.'

He nodded in the head-toss equivalent of an eye roll.

'You're welcome to go back to your pool, if you like,' she said.

That earned her a grunt, which she ignored and she kept

right on photographing. The sun sank lower and lower and the light grew more and more gorgeous. But on the wrong side, really, to make the most of the intricate shapes drawn by the wind in the golden sand.

Morning. That was when this setting was really going to come alive.

It was only when she felt the little thrills spidering through her system that she realised how long it had been since she'd let herself be really excited by her photography. That had pretty much stuttered to a halt when she'd found herself in a fingerprint-processing queue.

'Okay, let's head back,' she said. 'I could do with another swim.' Something told her she'd be spending a lot of time in that pool.

It took just minutes to get to the suite because, despite spending hours taking pictures, they'd ended up just fifty metres from her door. Brad let her open it but pressed politely past and cleared the room before allowing her to enter.

It was hard not to grin as all that hard muscle squeezed past, brushing against her.

'What happens if someone kidnaps me out here while you're inside clearing the room?' she called in to him casually as he checked each of the outside-facing glass doors. Taking pictures was one way to pass the month ahead—messing with Brad's mind was another.

A girl had to have a hobby. And just because she didn't want to *touch* didn't mean that she couldn't sneak the occasional *look*, right?

'Calculated risk,' he called back from inside. 'Most people prefer to conduct their crimes in private. Anyone could walk past here and see you being bundled onto a getaway camel.'

Her lips twisted despite herself. There was something almost alluring about the idea of being whisked away from the world on camelback—or on the powerful Arab horses that got their name from this peninsular—across all this sand, by some swarthy hottie. If he was built like Brad, she might not even scream for all that long.

He returned, waving her into her suite, and Sera plastered an innocent expression on as she stepped past him into the cool. His eyes narrowed immediately.

And that's why God invented fantasies. Because something told her flirting openly was most definitely outside procedures.

'I'm going to have a bit of downtime until sunset, then dinner as soon as it's dark,' she said not very subtly. Maybe a bit of healthy time apart would get her hormones back under control. Besides, jet lag was starting to catch up with her despite the restorative massage.

'Why don't you get something delivered here?' he suggested, reading her mind. Or maybe her body language.

Ooh. That was a good idea. A delicious meal on the pool deck.

He crossed to the writing desk and returned with the glamorous menu folder. 'I'll call it in while you change for your swim.'

She pushed it back at him. 'Surprise me.'

One of the things she'd been looking forward to most about this trip was making fewer decisions every day. And trying new things.

She closed herself into the luxurious bathroom to slip back into her blue swimsuit. It had dried in about nine minutes flat after she laid it out on her deckchair, courtesy of the moisture-desperate desert air, and so now it was crisp and almost just-laundered fresh. Then she pulled out her hair ties and let her hair fall down her back.

One of the greatest joys of having long hair was feeling it hanging down your back, heavy and wet. It was just so…reassuring. Like a kind of hug.

Not pathetic at all, a tiny voice sniggered.

Needs must. When you grew up without your mother

and were abandoned for months on end by your father, you
took your intimacies where you could find them.

'Sera...?'

Speaking of intimate... Brad's voice sounded so close
and so clear you would never know there was a thick, ornate, timber door between them. 'You want dinner on the
deck or in the suite?'

Well... Wasn't that a cosy kind of question? Suddenly
this whole set-up started to scream *couple*. The natural
way he just integrated himself into her day, anticipating her
needs. The way she'd adapted around him already.

On less than twenty-four hours' acquaintance.

'Deck, please. At sunset.'

His deep voice murmured, repeating her request for
Aqil, presumably, and a wild thought rushed into her head
about what that voice would be like breathing hard against
her ear.

And just like that she tripped neatly across the line in
the sand. The one between harmless imagination and dangerous indulgence.

'Just for one,' she called more urgently, stumbling over
the phrase like the clunky, over-compensatory thing it was.
The resulting silence screamed.

She froze, wincing, and caught her lame facial expression in the bathroom mirror.

You're the client, she told herself silently, giving herself
a stern look. *You ask for whatever you want.* He'd painted
such an unflattering image of women who got too attached
to their personal security—well, okay, he'd only sketched
an outline and she'd gone to cougar town with the image—
she didn't want him thinking that lunch today was anything
other than some convenient company.

She wasn't desperate for his. She'd eaten alone plenty
of times. Plenty.

It was pretty much the norm.

Still, she couldn't help trying to undo any offence she'd

caused, calling out, 'I've got a date with some golden sands and a whole lot of silence.'

Her breath stilled while she waited and she refused to look at herself in the mirror again. Bad enough being a social klutz without watching yourself do it.

'It's okay, Sera,' Brad murmured, low, from beyond the door.

And it was. His voice said it was. He knew all along why lunch hadn't been a good idea and she was just slow catching on.

Okay, so his protocol was right.

That was awkward.

Brad helped himself to an off-duty beer from his minibar and flopped down on one of the two comfortable lounges on his deck.

The hotel staff who'd brought him his dinner had also taken the opportunity to draw every thick curtain in the place, creating a warm, cosy little nest for the night. The moment they'd gone and he'd quaffed his meal, he'd flung them all open again, inviting the darkness in. This was the part of working at Al Saqr that he loved the best. The vast skies at night. The darkness that only came with complete absence of the ambient glow that metropolises generated.

At least until the moon got higher.

He flicked his pool lights on, casting random little shapes on the canopy above his head as the cool night breeze played across the water's surface. It gave him about six feet of visibility beyond his pool.

To his left, a door closed loudly in the heavy silence, and it drew his busy mind to his neighbour.

Sera was a paradox, as clients went. Usually, it took him about a day to get a general lock on the personality of whoever he was watching, but she shifted as much as those sands out beyond the darkness. Confident and all about eye contact one moment, weeping in private the next. Sharp and bright in the SUV but sleepy and downright desirable with her mussed-up hair straight out of her massage. A clumsy kind of brittle when she'd told him she'd be having dinner alone, then full of awkward distress and kindness in trying to make good afterwards.

It was almost as if her tough exterior was at war with her softer, true self.

He dug around inside trying to identify the uncomfortable sensation and surprised himself by finding it. Wounded pride. Why? He never ate with clients; it was a chore he was thankful the rules prohibited. He watched clients while they ate, all the time. He inhaled a quick snack while they were in meetings or even the bathroom. But whole meals... He did those as he did most things— later and solo.

So why the bruised sensibilities just because a woman opted out of a second round of his tremendous company? Had he really grown that soft?

Or was he a little bit too intrigued by the paradox?

He placed his empty bottle onto the deck with one hand and peeled off his T-shirt with the other, then waded into the small, heated pool in his board shorts and let the water wash away the thought. The further the winter sun sank beyond the horizon, the faster the desert cooled around them until a layer of mist rose from the water and evaporated in the darkness.

Underwater, even the desert creatures were silenced, and he held his breath as long as he could to let the warm, watery cocoon leach the tension out of him. With the survival training he'd received in the Specials, that meant a long time.

He'd sought out the Sheikh's personal guard with an expectation that he'd get to be involved in some top-end protection tasks. Something that really exploited the skills he'd perfected in the military. Short bursts, complete strangers. Business types who were happy to treat him like a ghost.

Or a shadow. Who relied on him for their safety but not for anything else.

Clients and short rosters that meant no chance of forging bonds.

That strategy had served him well these past two years. It had almost undone the damage of that day in Cairo. The day he'd learned the hard way not to get involved with clients.

Indifferent acquiescence...

Maybe he should get that tattooed somewhere prominent.

But four straight weeks of close contact with any client made things a whole heap tougher. And someone like Sera... Someone who pushed all his buttons. The one labelled 'intrigue'. The one labelled 'empathy'. The one labelled with a big red question mark...

Yeah, he needed to stay right away from that button, particularly.

Survival instinct forced him up above the surface eventually and he rolled onto his back and floated there, breathing deeply, losing himself in the changing shapes on the canopy above before finally hauling his dripping self out, towelling off and taking his empty bottle inside in search of a refill.

Sera witnessed the start of the oryxes' nightly migration as the sun started to sink below the dunes behind her suite. A little group of them had been lazing in the near distance all day in shallow, hoof-scratched divots in the sand around a waterhole but as soon as the shade vanished, so did they. They hauled themselves up, dusted off and began the long trudge...somewhere.

Over the hill and far away as the nursery rhyme went.

It made sense that oryxes and gazelles did all their resting during the heat of the day and their busy work in the cool of the night, and that changed things if she wanted to photograph them. But it also made night-time a good time to head out onto the sand to explore without having to worry about the enormous, sharp-horned beasts lurking around the resort waiting to skewer themselves a Sera kebab.

She amused herself just metres from her darkened suite, photographing the extraordinary field of stars stretching out overhead—as if someone had spilled a tub of silvery glitter over the blackness above. More stars than she'd ever been able to see anywhere. It wasn't easy finding somewhere steady enough to stand her gear, and she'd dashed back inside to return with a field guidebook, a folded magazine and the empty plate that her stuffed date snacks had come on to wedge into the sand under her tripod's three feet. Then she'd settled down on the dune a metre or so away from her equipment as it took long, open exposure shots. They would be fun to play with on her laptop when it got too warm to be out on the sand.

A busy mind was a sane mind.

The longer she sat there, and the higher the moon climbed, the more her diminished human eyes could see. All around her, she was sure, were creatures that could see her as clearly as if she stood in daylight, while, to her, they were barely even shadows. Eventually she braved a bit more distance, getting a range of pretty night shots, including back at her own suite. She immediately regretted turning all her lights out because the gentle glow pouring out of suite eleven made for really pretty composition, but traipsing back up the dune to illuminate hers seemed like unnecessary hassle when Brad's fully lit and completely identical suite was empty. She could get some practice shots now and shoot hers tomorrow night.

She released her DSLR from the tripod, left her gear in a tidy pile in front of her pool and waded through the thick sand twenty metres to the left to frame up a shot of Brad's suite. A quick double-check through the zoom lens confirmed he wasn't resident, though he'd left a beer bottle out on his deck. He'd probably had a drink before heading up to the restaurant for his evening meal.

Meal for one, as she'd so clumsily stipulated.

Ugh.

With social skills like hers it was a miracle she'd ever managed to make friends at all. Let alone keep them. Though, some friends were more willing to indulge her social clunkiness, as it turned out. When it suited them. When there was something in it for them. That was as true in adulthood as it had been in childhood.

Clever framing meant you couldn't see the bottle in her shot, only the stunning little pool and the softly lit suite beyond it. Green décor inside, where hers was themed blue. She framed up the shot and clicked, then tweaked a few settings in her camera and readied to click again, trying to maximise the saturation. But as her finger depressed the shutter, the pool's still water shifted, then bubbled, and then erupted with wet, male flesh as Brad surfaced.

Not vacant at all!

She caught the yip of surprise before it grew audible and dropped the camera down away from her eye. But that didn't stop her seeing a more distant Brad roll over onto his back in the water of his pool and just…float. All peace and serenity. Nothing like she'd seen him up until now. She half spun away on polite instinct but her eyes were slower to leave than her torso as Brad hauled that big, tanned body out of the pool—water streaming down his back—and engulfed it in one of the resort's massive towels.

Finally, her shoulders forced some decent manners on her and she sank onto the sand, her back turned, and stifled a giggle as the adrenaline dumped from her system.

Trespass charges not enough, Sera? Looking to add 'stalker' to your criminal résumé?

Sheesh.

He hadn't seen her lurking out here in the dark. How

could he? Not that *not* getting caught made her peeping any less Tom-ish...

Behind her, she eventually heard the clunk of Brad's suite door closing. Even at this distance, the silence amplified the simple snick as he went inside. She glanced back, sheepishly, when she heard the door again and caught him lowering himself back down onto the deck lounge, now dried and in loose jogging bottoms and a sweater, a fresh beer in one hand and a book in the other.

Oh... He was a reader.

Why did that throw her so much? Clearly, the man had to have an education to have come as far as he had in life. But being *able* to read didn't necessarily mean someone *liked* to read.

Brad did. And she hadn't expected that.

Though she wasn't sure what she had expected—she just wasn't used to getting to know much about the people who worked with her.

For her.

In the darkness, she twisted to her feet and returned to her camera equipment, where it still lay in front of her own suite. It didn't take long to become newly fascinated by the way the increasing moonlight slashed across the sand, highlighting the wind ripples that scarred all that eroded smoothness in a way that was totally different from the daytime. But while her fingers worked automatically, her mind struggled to engage. It was far too busy thinking about the momentary glimpse of Brad and his wet skin as he'd emerged from his pool.

On duty, Brad moved like a man on a mission. Every step considered, always scanning their surrounds, always as if he had somewhere important to be and was already late. Perpetually irritated. But off duty Brad just kind of...sauntered. He'd risen from the pool and then came back through those doors like a man who had nowhere better to be but on a deck drinking a beer and flicking through a crime novel.

She kind of liked it.

And she kind of wished she was on the deck lounge next to him doing the exact same thing. Just sitting in silence reading together. Chilling.

Then again hadn't she been wishing for much the same thing her whole life?

Don't get attached, her father would have cautioned; and wasn't that the pot calling the kettle a very gothic kind of black?

As if she needed to be told. As if she hadn't already learned not to attach to anyone, just in case. In her world, people came and went and always did their best but never, ever stayed. It was the nature of the beast. People who were paid for their services generally and eventually left for something else. They were staff, not friends—

'Sera!'

Mid-thought, hard hands spun her around and she faced a furious, puffing Brad.

'I'm less than a minute from the suite,' she automatically defended.

'In the dark. Alone!'

'I could see you,' she said, then flushed horribly at the admission. 'No way you wouldn't have heard me if anything had happened.'

'*Anything* could have happened in just the time it took me to get here,' he growled.

'Come on, not the getaway camel again.' Did he seriously think bad guys would turn up and drag her off into the desert?

'Vipers. Scorpions. One minute for me to get down here and two to carry you back up. That's three of the six minutes you get to live if bitten. This may be a resort but it's still wild habitat, skittering with things that can kill you.'

'Oh.' *Right.* She glanced down at her shadowed feet in the darkness.

'Why are you so resistant to simple instructions?' he gritted, fuming.

'They might be simple to issue but they're a lot harder to live by. I just wanted to get some night pictures.'

'Then you call me.'

'You're not my lackey, Brad. You've earned your down-time.'

'Then you get your night pictures tomorrow night and I take a few hours off in the middle of the day in lieu.'

Sure, it made sense when said like that. 'It doesn't work that way, Brad. When inspiration strikes...'

'Something tells me inspiration is always striking with you, Sera. My job is to keep you safe. Not to let you go traipsing off into death-infested sand dunes.'

'A little exaggerated, don't you think? I'm within a hundred metres of the suite. Give me a little credit.'

'I really want to, Sera, but we're not doing so well so far.'

There it was... The disappointment. Her father's judgement coming out of Brad's mouth. It never mattered what her intentions were...

'It's ninety seconds from safety,' she repeated, angrily, gathering up her gear and heading off back up the dune towards her suite.

Though, the ninety seconds it had taken to go downhill *did* take a lot longer in the cascading, scrabbling sands of uphill. By the time she reached the top and the little stony path into her suite's garden, she was puffing with more than just umbrage.

'I'm staying here,' Brad announced as she stepped up on deck and struggled to open her door with arms full of equipment. He pushed in and opened it for her.

'No, you're not,' she said as she squeezed past him. 'You have a perfectly good suite right next door.'

'Which I'll use when I'm confident that you're not going to make bad decisions.'

'You might as well pack your bags now, then, because

I make bad decisions all the time. Apparently I'm on the perpetual verge of disaster at any given moment.'

If her father was to be believed, anyway.

He followed her into the suite until she spun back on him. Both her hands shot up between them and he walked straight into them. With only a thin sweater on, his chest felt every bit as hard as it had looked through her lens. She jerked her fingers away.

'You weren't serious?'

Grey eyes pinned her. 'Utterly.'

'You can't stay here.'

'Why not?'

Inspiration struck. 'Because it's against the law!'

It was the truth. And good luck convincing Arab authorities that a healthy, single man of his age took the sofa when spending the night in the suite of a healthy single woman of her age. Her eyes drifted to the massive bed just begging for two.

But her words definitely gave him pause. 'On your deck, then.'

'All night?'

'If it means I'm here the next time your muse calls, sure.'

The barely muffled hiss of air between her lips should have told him exactly what she thought of that idea. 'What's going to stop me simply going out the front door?'

He crossed to her dresser, took the oversized key from there and locked the front door from the inside, then pocketed the key.

Are you kidding me? First she was a prisoner within the resort and now within her suite.

'What if there's a fire?' She glared at him.

'I'll save you,' he shot back.

'How heroic.'

'I live to serve.'

Her camera bounced on the expensive mattress as she

tossed it there. Behind her, he turned and moved towards the door.

'How am I going to sleep with you lurking out there?' she said, suddenly tired.

'Safely,' he barked.

He closed the glass door behind him, signalled at her to lock it from the inside, and then flopped himself down on the same deck lounge he'd been in one suite over when she'd gone all stalker on him. Automatically it became *his* lounge in her mind. She stood, glaring out at the back of his head, then gave up when it became obvious that he couldn't feel her irritation any more than he could see or hear it.

Fine. If he wanted to really play GI Joe, then he could. It was Arabia at the start of winter; he'd be cold overnight but he wouldn't freeze to death. Even for an Australian.

She snagged her pyjamas up as she passed the bed, took herself into the bathroom and changed, brushing her teeth and hair. As she came out, her glance went to the grumpy silhouette out on her deck rubbing his chilly hands against his jogging bottoms. He turned as she emerged onto the deck, a cushion in one hand and a woven throw from her sofa in the other. Without a single further word, she dumped both into his lap and then withdrew back inside, locked the door, yanked the curtains across and tried to block him from her mind as effectively as the curtains blocked the moonlight from the room.

CHAPTER FIVE

THE WHOLE NIGHTS on the deck thing became Brad's habit over the following week. Al Saqr was high-end enough that even the outdoor furniture was comfortable enough to fall asleep on. He'd lain on far poorer in his time. At least from the deck he could catch Sera the next time passion struck hard enough to draw her out of her suite on the quiet.

Not that it had happened again. Clearly, his presence was some kind of passion-killer.

Meh. He'd been called worse.

Over the days that had passed since he'd looked up from his book and seen a slight silhouette standing alone out in the moonlit desert, his nightly arrangement had grown from spare cushion and sofa throw to one of Al Saqr's fat European pillows, woven wool blanket, single beer, book and reading light. So, clearly, Sera had accepted that he was staying put. And her heart was too soft to let him just rough it.

No matter what she wanted him to believe by daylight.

Between her constant activity and cool aloofness by day and the staunch arm's length he'd been working so hard to maintain, it was amazing they managed to even meet each other's eye. Yet, by night, out came all the silent, borrowed comforts of home and Sera gave her true nature away.

Not brittle and sarcastic and angry all the time. There was compassion and empathy in there, too.

He shifted in his half-doze in the cold morning air and flipped onto his left side. A bare moment later, something drew his eyes open. The tiniest sound. A guttural kind of chuff. He squinted blearily in the golden glow that heralded sunrise.

Squinted and then blinked in astonishment.

A unicorn drank from the infinity edge of Sera's pool, white and luminous in the rich morning light, hazily obscured by the steam coming off the heated pool, shadows cast along its angular face, its long horn spiralling upwards to a deadly point.

Beautiful and completely impossible.

Brad cranked his head up away from the pillow, and the unicorn's shadowed eyes flicked in his direction. He froze. It kept right on drinking, though it didn't take its focus off the unexpected human. They went on like that—him freezing, it drinking—for minutes, and in those minutes the sun peered its wintry face over the horizon and the dawn light completely changed.

Those weren't shadows down its long, horse-like face—they were black facial markings. As if the light desert dew had spiralled down its black horn and stained its pristine face. And as it shifted more front-on he saw it was not one horn at all, but two. Just as long, just as sharp.

If the oryx was surprised to find a man sleeping on a pool deck at its favourite watering hole, it didn't show it, but when its eyes flicked away from his and locked firmly behind him, Brad couldn't help but follow their gaze back over his shoulder.

Sera stood there, half asleep and fresh from bed, her long fingers pressed up hard against the breath-frosted glass of her suite door, a look of childlike wonder on her face.

He should have been noticing her long, bare legs, or the shape of her breasts under her cotton pyjamas pressed hard up against the glass, or her just-woken bed hair. But—just like the oryx—he couldn't take his eyes off hers. The pure joy that glowed in them. She didn't run for her camera or even the sketch pad that sat on an easel near the door. She just...smiled. And stared. Radiant and transfixed. Completely oblivious to Brad's presence. Woman watched beast.

Beast watched woman. And man watched woman. Even though he knew he shouldn't.

He really, really shouldn't.

Yet he didn't look away even as he acknowledged that thought.

Eventually the oryx wearied of her fascination and slurped its last mouthful. Brad only knew that from the shifting focus of Sera's mesmerised gaze as she followed the animal along the front of her garden and craned her neck to watch it disappearing over the edge of the dune, all watered up for the day. Only then did she turn her eyes to him, complete joy radiating from her face. The smile she threw him actually hurt his heart. She looked young. She looked alive.

She looked as beautiful and mystical as the unicorn.

And for that half-moment before she remembered she should, she didn't care that a virtual stranger was looking at her in her pyjamas. She just wanted someone to share the magical moment with.

Then, the real world intruded, the joy faded slightly and she seemed to shrink away from the glass, reluctantly—almost against her own will—until all that was left of her was the opened curtains where she'd stood and the rapidly evaporating hand marks on the glass.

And all Brad was left with was the vague feeling that mornings would never quite be complete again without at least one unicorn…and without that gorgeously dishevelled face.

Sera was emerging from the bathroom when Brad's shadow fell across the deck doorway. He tapped on the glass first and then his watch. The doors, when she pulled them both inwards, invited the fresh, dawn air inside. It smelled as golden as it looked.

'You're still up,' he said.

Thank you, Captain Obvious.

'The falcons are on at seven a.m.,' she murmured. 'That's why I got up early in the first place.'

Up in time to see the oryx drinking at her pool.

'Glad you did?'

Okay, so he'd seen her in her brief PJs, unmade up, ungroomed and with sleep-encrusted eyes. Nothing she could do about it now. 'If you'd told me that was happening every morning I would have made more of an effort to be up for it before now.'

And be dressed.

'First time for me, too,' he admitted, stepping inside. 'Kind of cool, huh?'

That unexpected wildlife moment was to 'kind of cool' what these deserts were to just 'okay'.

'It didn't look that surprised to see me there,' he said. 'My guess is that he's been coming up in the dark each morning and stealth drinking while I've slept through it.'

'Why? When there's your empty suite next door? And the one on the other side.'

'Creature of habit, maybe? Different humans might come and go in it but this is *his* pool...'

He certainly sauntered away from it with entitlement enough. In fact, he moved with the same kind of deliberate control that Brad did.

'Your buggy pickup will be here in ten minutes,' he said. 'I'm just going to run next door and change. I'll meet you at the front.'

He passed her the door key that he'd continued to hold on to and then jogged out the back, down past her pool and around the brush fencing between their suites.

If he took the full ten minutes, she didn't know it. She emerged from her suite as Eric pulled up in the courtesy buggy, and Brad was already standing at attention by the front door, casually but professionally dressed today in cargos and a light shirt.

'Morning!' Eric said to her cheerfully and with much

more professional focus than the silent nod he'd just exchanged with Brad. 'How did you sleep?'

'Like the dead,' Sera admitted. 'Either it's the beds, the darkness, or you're drugging the water. I've never slept as well as I have here.'

Eric laughed. 'We try to keep guest-drugging to the minimum.'

'So, any chance that you'll be easing back on this crazy pace any time soon?' Brad murmured to Sera as they whizzed through the silent dawn towards the resort's heart. It was a reasonable question. She'd done half the resort's activities already—some of them twice—and filled every other waking moment with photography-related tasks.

'I've relaxed. Taken naps. Swims.'

He frowned. 'Taking photographs from the pool is not swimming.'

'But it is fun. And fun is leisure, right?'

From his grunt he was in no way convinced. 'I'm asking myself when you're going to stop pushing so hard. I'm also asking myself why?'

Why wasn't a conversation she felt like having before coffee. Or with a man who liked to be in charge so much.

She twisted to meet his gaze more directly. 'I'll stop pushing hard when this place and this desert stop being so interesting.'

'Right,' he muttered. 'So no time soon, then.'

They arrived at the centre of the resort and then Eric led them on foot to a mini amphitheatre set up on the sand. There, several birds of prey and a group of other guests waited for the daily flying demonstration. Customs confiscations of the bird variety, Eric explained as his colleague prepared the birds to fly. When someone tried to smuggle a trafficked bird in or out of the country and was caught, the bird was retired to Al Saqr. There, the valuable birds got to stretch their wings twice a day in training and lived like rock stars in between.

'They even have their own security,' Eric said for probably the hundredth time.

The smattering of other guests there all chuckled, but Sera couldn't help feeling self-conscious since her own security loomed like a bird of prey himself, two rows back from her on the richly carved wooden seating. She hoped Brad wasn't looking at the other guests with the same beady-eyed assessment that the bird did when its hood came off.

'This is a saker falcon,' Eric announced. 'The species after which Al Saqr takes its name. These birds have been flying desert skies for three millennia.'

They were, as she had expected, stunning, strong birds. Bullet fast. Each one went through its paces and showed off its strengths free-flying in a far arc around the amphitheatre and returning to try and snaffle their handler's fleshy lure. She learned about bird biology and habits, the valuable breeding efforts, the long history of falconry in the desert, and their personal history while each bird flew high up into the endless, blue sky, wheeling and turning, staying focused on its job. None of them tried to fly off although the tracking device clipped to their tether suggested they could have at any time.

Best of all, between each bird coming off its perch, Sera and the other guests got to take as many photos as they liked. *Boy, did she like.* Fortunately, her lens was long, her camera was digital and her memory card emptied so there was almost no limit to the number of up-close photographs she could take in the air or on the perch.

And then she met Omar.

'Omar is an eagle owl,' Eric narrated for the crowd, raising a healthy, solid, brown bird tethered to his gloved arm. 'He came to us as a chick and was hand-raised right here at Al Saqr. He never knew his parents. In fact, he's never really met another owl.'

Instant affinity formed in her heart for Omar.

She'd grown up in the care of others, too. She saw one parent several times a year—which was more than Omar could say—but even her father had only known her groupie mother for the time it took to get her pregnant midway through a European tour. Forty-two weeks later his lawyers had taken delivery of a squalling, infant Sera. He'd done his actual best and thrown all the money and personnel needed to raise a child at her, but touring half the year and recording offshore for much of the rest tended to put a crimp in any serious father-daughter bonding time. To give him credit, he'd worked hard to make the most of the time they'd had together but, when it was over, he went back to his busy, exciting life that passed in a flash, while she went back to her quiet, empty room to wait out the endless weeks until she got to wrap her spindly little arms around her daddy again.

'Omar looks like an owl, but he behaves more like a buzzard because that's who he grew up sharing an aviary with.'

Eric might have been talking about her. Except instead of growing up half buzzard, she'd grown up half…well, half grown-up. Even as a little kid, she'd been more like a miniature grown-up because that was who had raised her. A string of professional, well-trained adults out on her father's expansive country property. Big enough for a little girl to never tire of exploring and remote enough to satisfy her father's security concerns. Such was Blaise's fame at the peak of his career that even his young daughter was considered a credible target.

'He can't hoot,' Eric continued softly, curling a finger along Omar's glistening feathers, and earning sad sighs from his audience, 'because no one ever taught him how.'

Something in her fractured just a little bit.

Poor, hootless Omar.

When she'd finally hit thirteen and her father's obsessive popularity—and security concerns—had waned a little, she'd got to set foot for the first time inside an *actual* school filled with *actual* other kids. A reclusive, home-schooled rock heir fitted about as well there as Omar did amongst other owls. She'd had no real idea how to be a regular teen. The end result was a girl heavy on academic achievement but light on healthy friendships.

'He's had the best care here,' Eric assured everyone, on a charming smile, 'but we've all had to be super careful to make sure he didn't imprint on us. Because we could move on at any time and then where would he be if he'd cast one of us in the primary carer role? So he imprinted instead on the buzzard.'

The thing inside her that had fractured on discovering Omar's inability to sing the song of his people threatened to break even more. Break and spill out everywhere. Instantly, her body tightened up in anticipation and her pulse began to hammer. She shot to her feet, and Omar—with his super hearing and massive peripheral vision—flinched and ruffled his feathers in surprise. Eric threw her a concerned look.

Brad was there in a heartbeat, murmuring her name from just behind her ratchet-straight back.

'Headache,' she said for the benefit of the other guests who were starting to look at her. She mouthed an apology to Eric, who smiled and nodded and went back to his presentation. Then she climbed down off her seat and quickly scuttled away from the amphitheatre.

'Sera?'

Brad was right behind her. Of course he was. Perfectly positioned to witness her humiliation.

'Headache,' she repeated. Because lying was easier. How could she explain that a captive bird had opened up a sore spot in her chest. Clawed it open, really, with those big, taloned, completely innocent feet.

The sand dunes were steep just there, where the resort's main building towered over everything around them, and she sank as much as she climbed but, eventually, she neared the top. Her puffed breath wasn't made any easier by the fist twisting hard within her chest.

'Sera?' Brad jogged up closer. 'Are you upset about the show? The birds?'

'Why would I be?' she tossed back over her shoulder.

'I thought because of your thing for animals…'

She turned on the spot. 'My "thing"?'

'Your interest, in animal welfare…'

She could hardly blame Brad for the assumption. She'd happily made her own bed when she'd innocently started photographing strays and waifs. And she'd more than lain in it when she was gullible enough to let Mark's PR-loving animal-rights group draw her into trouble by photographing the lab animals.

The tabloid headlines flashed before her eyes. *'Brazen Blaise…' 'Rock Heir Faces Charges…'* And her favourite: *'Chip off the old Rock…?'*

That last one was the most ironic. Her father had spent his career bringing all manner of social injustice to light through his music; you'd think he would have been more supportive when she tried to do the same.

What did a girl have to do…?

'One bird didn't want to return to the wild and the other two couldn't make it. No, it doesn't bother me that they're living here, instead.'

'Then what's—?'

'Headache!' she shot back at him.

He clambered up the dune behind her. There was probably an easier path out of here but, right now, she just needed to be away from all the prying eyes—stat.

'Why don't we get you something to eat and drink?' Brad suggested, clearly at a loss for any better way of dealing with a neurotic female than feeding her.

The dark, quiet restaurant…with bathrooms. The female

half of which was one of very few places in this whole resort where Brad could not follow her.

'Okay, yes.'

Near the dune's top he climbed past her, reached back
and took her hand, hauling her up over its edge when her
legs started to protest the steepest part. At the steps to the
restaurant's deck she excused herself and didn't wait for
his consent, plucking her fingers free of his.

'I'll just...freshen up.'

The facilities were as elegant as the rest of the resort
and furnished just as authentically. The plush room smelled
like a spice souk, which was a pleasant surprise given its
usual purpose, but the delightful scent did nothing to ease
the thoughts whipping around in her mind. As every other
person in the resort was either still asleep or out on one of
several early-morning activities, she had the whole place to
herself, so she sagged down onto a padded chair recessed
neatly off to one side and let her face fall into her hands.

*We've all had to be careful to make sure Omar didn't
imprint on us.*

Was that how it worked? Enough love and affection for
the bird's basic needs but not so much that a young Omar
might have started growing attached.

*We could move on at any time and then where would
he be?*

Right, because it was a job to them. And jobs changed.
Thanks to her father's endless bank account and a revolving door of expert personnel, she'd made it to adulthood
in one piece. Very nice people—professional and dedi-
cated—but, ultimately, not hers to keep. In the same way
that the staff at Al Saqr cared for Omar but took pains that
he didn't come to *need* them. To rely on them. To *love* them.

In case they had to leave.

Having her life summed up in such matter-of-fact terms
this morning... Looking at Omar's sweet face and hunched
over body—*poor hootless Omar*—it had just felt too raw.

A quiet knock sounded on the door.

'Coming!'

Sera shot to her feet and crossed to the row of sinks and flicked on one tap. It took only a moment to wash her hands and rinse her face. A moment longer to dry them on a scented, fluffy towel that felt too good to throw straight into the waiting hamper. She took a few more moments, steeling herself before emerging to Brad's intent stare. He shepherded her into the restaurant and pulled out a chair for her at a table on the deck. Seeing the golden sands and bright morning light made her feel a little better, but seeing the people streaming away from the finished bird presentation at the foot of the dune below made her feel a little worse.

She'd missed out on photographing Omar.

Brad pulled out the chair opposite her.

She took a long breath. 'I'd like to—'

'Eat alone,' he finished for her. 'I know. I'll move as soon as I'm sure you're okay. Do you need a doctor?'

In fact, she'd been about to say, '*I'd like to apologise...*' For her rapid departure from the falconry display. And her general neurosis. And her crankiness all week.

'For a headache?' The lie was catching up with her and shame was close on its heels. 'It's just the sun.'

'It's only just gone seven.'

'Then I guess I'm tired.'

'You told Eric you slept like the dead.'

'Brad—'

'Sera?' His grey eyes bored into her. 'Come on. I'm not leaving you until I know for certain that you don't need me.'

She stared at him, trying to decide how much to share. Hadn't he said she should come to him? This might not have been what he'd meant but right now it was exactly what she needed.

Someone to confide in.

* * *

'Omar,' Sera started, lines of tension forking at the corners of her eyes.

It took Brad a moment to realise who she meant. 'The owl?'

'I just… His story got under my skin.'

An *owl* had caused the dramatic public exit? Though staying and bursting into tears would have been more dramatic and that still looked like what she wanted to do. Did her emotions always run so close to the surface?

'His situation resonated for me,' she continued.

Brad frowned back at her. 'What about it, particularly?'

'No one taught him how to hoot.'

He took the menus from the young man who presented them but placed them straight down to focus on what she was saying. The waiter took the hint and dissolved into the background.

'He seems to have survived well enough without it,' Brad said, scrabbling desperately to connect the dots.

'He's an owl, Brad. He's supposed to hoot.'

Somewhere in here was a point she was trying to make if he could just find his way to it. 'Sera, he doesn't know any other owls, so he doesn't know that owls *should* hoot. I doubt he feels any kind of deficiency.'

Her brown eyes bled indecision back at him. But then they seemed to clear, and she took a deep breath.

'Has anyone stopped to think that they've raised a bird bereft of a personal attachment to anyone at all? Not just to them.'

His chest tightened. 'Okay…?'

'The way I was brought up—by nannies and tutors and bodyguards… Do you think any of them stopped to think that if they weren't teaching me how to hoot then no one was?'

Oh. This was about her childhood.

'Maybe they were looking out for your best interests?'

he said tightly, because he *was* one of those people she was talking about. And he knew all about the firm line in the sand that they weren't supposed to cross. He'd juggled it his whole working life. So a crack at them was a crack at him.

'How exactly is it in a child's *best interests* to be kept at arm's length?' she argued.

How? He could tell her some stories. One in particular…

'If they got too attached—'

'Oh, don't get me wrong,' she hurried on, 'I eventually came to appreciate the professional distance. When I was old enough to understand it. It meant my heart didn't get broken every time I said goodbye to a paid staffer.' She took a deep breath. 'But try telling seven-year-old me that.'

He fought to keep his jaw from locking up, it was that tight. He could understand what it must have been like for her when she was a kid. But she had no idea what could have happened if any of her team had let themselves get too close. And why they didn't.

Or weren't supposed to.

'What if I'm like Omar?' she tried again. 'Deficient without realising it. What if there are things normal women do that I don't know I should be doing?'

Like hooting. It was then that he finally realised what she was getting at.

'Normal women?'

She waved a single hand. 'Women raised in normal families. By normal parents.'

'Instead of being raised by rock-star millionaires in rambling rural retreats?'

Her laugh scraped like steel wool. 'Instead of being raised in a bubble by paid professionals.'

She leaned in over their unopened menus. 'You must have dated loads of women…'

Okay…enough. He needed to put this to rest. 'Sera. Normal doesn't exist. People are different. That's what diversity is all about.'

'But on a scale of one to ten. How do I rank?'

He lifted one brow. 'Against the ocean of women I've apparently been with?'

But she didn't waver. She truly thought that her upbringing had turned her into something...broken.

He sat back, frustrated. 'You want a number?'

'Yes, please.'

He pursed his lips in exaggerated thought. 'I'd give you a...four.'

'A *four*?' Her shocked cry drew the waiter's eyes. He stepped forward then froze again as the privacy of their discussion dawned on him. 'Out of ten?'

'Maybe a five on a good day.'

All she could do was blink at him. He leaned forward earnestly.

'Your talent as a photographer isn't normal,' he said. 'The way you can switch between personalities in the space of a breath isn't normal. The way you are put together is a mile from normal.' *God knows!* 'Your interest in the most invisible details of life isn't normal. Your ability to have a discussion like this and then go right back to polite strangers isn't normal.'

She frowned at him, probably trying to decide whether she was being insulted or not.

'I've known women who didn't get passionate about anything. Ever. Or they faked excitement in things that I liked to make themselves more appealing. They could look at this desert and see nothing more than sand and sun, and this trip as nothing more than a chance to get a tan. You want me to rate you against them?'

She blinked at him. 'Why are you so angry?'

Good question. But there was something incredibly disturbing in the idea that anything those people did raising Sera might have turned such a strong, accomplished woman into this uncertain, weepy mess.

Because he'd *been* one of those people. And he'd had his own little Sera.

'I've known women who are the most extraordinary mothers and who would give their lives for their children. Or battlers of terrible diseases. You want me to rate you and your privileged life against them?'

Her lips tightened. 'Privilege is not all it's—'

'How about the women soldiers who can shoot a man in the face without blinking?' he barged on. 'Where should I rank you against them?'

Her arms curled around her middle. 'Look, forget I—'

'There is no normal, Sera,' he said, softer, seeing the impact his frustration was having on her. 'There is no scale. The only way Omar the owl would know that his inability to hoot is a *deficiency* is because we tell him it is.'

'And it isn't?'

Brad shrugged. 'What's he going to do with a hoot? Use it to call for an owl girlfriend he'll never get to meet? Use it to defend territory that's already protected for him? Omar's life is what it is and, in his life, a hoot is an optional extra. He's getting along just fine without it.'

The pinch of her face got tighter and he thought for a moment that she was going to splinter.

'He's not broken, Sera, or disabled.' *You're* not. 'Being different is what makes him so memorable to all the people who meet him. Who do you think they go home and tell stories about to their families and whack on their social-media pages? The other birds? It makes him more special, not less.'

Something in his words pulled the plug on all the morning's tension and it just poured out, over the deck and down onto the dune below them like so much sand.

'He's not hootless.' She sighed, finally getting it. 'He's just... Omar.'

'Exactly.'

Which meant Sera wasn't necessarily deficient either.

Despite her upbringing. She just...was. And he really needed that to be true because God help him if his actions had caused this kind of distress to the boy he'd been responsible for.

Sera's brows dropped. 'Have I annoyed you?'

He took a deep breath and marshalled his emotions. 'No.'

'Then what is that face?' she challenged.

He considered her, long and hard. Whether or not she was up to hearing any more of his potted wisdom.

'Everyone has baggage, Sera. Everyone. We are all products of our upbringings, but those things shouldn't steer our actions forever and they're not excuses for whatever mess we might have made of our lives.'

She sat back straighter, and a coldness whipped around between them even in the warmth of the desert morning. The chill of his judgement.

'Tell me about the trespass,' he demanded, out of nowhere, and he suddenly realised that he really wanted to know. Needed to know.

Her eyes narrowed slightly. 'Tell me about your interest...'

But he couldn't. Not when he didn't understand it himself.

He placed his hands flat on the table, readying himself to get up. 'You're right. It's none of my business. I'll leave you to your breakfast.'

'Don't.' The word shot out of her like a bullet. 'Sit. Stay.'

He glanced back down at her. 'So, I'm your dog now? Maybe I should get you a whistle?'

'Stay,' she repeated, more softly, and her chocolate eyes filled with remorse. Long fingers reached across to his side of the table and pressed there. 'Please.'

He did, though it took him long enough to decide.

The hovering waiter seemed relieved to finally secure

their order and it wasn't long before Brad's protein-rich breakfast was delivered, steaming, along with her platter of local curiosities. In between mouthfuls they talked about the oryx from this morning, the beautiful birds they had just seen, and how she could go to the bird-of-prey training every day for the rest of the month if she wanted to photograph Omar properly. At first, it was a bruised kind of conversation—as though both of them were a bit raw and confused as to how things had gone so awry just moments before—but the longer they went, the easier it became.

Though, *easier* wasn't the same as *easy*. Something about Brad kept her always just one step shy of relaxed.

'I thought we were working towards rehoming ex-lab animals,' she suddenly volunteered as the waiter who refreshed their final coffees departed. 'Legitimately.'

He had no trouble keeping up with her sudden tangent. And she thought he looked relieved that she hadn't entirely dismissed his interest. Even if she didn't understand it. 'You didn't know you were trespassing in an unauthorised space?'

'I should have. I accept that as my responsibility.' She shrugged. 'I mistook politics for passion.'

'Explain that.'

Technically, he had no real right to ask—it had no bearing on his ability to do his job—but the past half hour had earned him at least one indulgence. Even if it was to discover her least fine moment. But boiling months of sorrow down to twenty-five words or less wasn't easy.

'I trusted the wrong people. Friends. A lover. And it turned out they were more interested in my connections than my photographic abilities. The end.'

'A lover?' Trust him to grab onto that. 'Mark Ryder?'

Hearing his name still made her heart twinge, but not for good reasons. She squirmed against the necessity to reveal her own naïveté. 'How do you know about Mark?'

'Your file,' Brad said, simply. 'He was underlined. Twice.'

'That's more prominence than he deserved, as it turns out.'

'What happened?'

'He thought there might be some PR advantage in being with me. For his animal-rights cause.'

'He was right,' Brad murmured. 'That story went global. Effected real change for those animals.'

Air struggled to push past the fist in her chest. 'Yes, it did.'

Though at her cost.

'And now you're lying low in the desert while it blows over?'

He made that sound so cowardly.

'The timing was not good,' she muttered. 'The band was launching a new album for the Christmas market—'

'Wait...' His large hand came up and his grey eyes turned stormy. 'You've been exiled here, practically under guard, because your father doesn't want his downloads impacted by bad press?'

'"Upstaged",' she quoted. 'And it was more his music label's idea...'

But the defence sounded weak even to her ears. There had definitely been more than one point where she'd hoped her father would have backed her. Even against the label's powerful executive. She'd only ever wanted his respect, but it was getting harder and harder to capture that. If she ever had.

'Dad asked me to do this. So...here I am. Trying not to disappoint him.' She took a deep breath. 'Though your presence unfortunately means that he doesn't trust me not to.'

If he had, he never would have had their London security arrange protection here in Umm Khoreem.

Brad flopped back against his seat. 'No wonder you

haven't exactly warmed to me. I must be a daily reminder of that.'

Hourly.

'I'm sorry if I've been…un-warm,' she murmured. 'It's really none of your fault.'

He laughed. 'I was so sure I was a likeable guy. Is it wrong that I'm relieved?'

She smiled at him, then lost time as his laugh sobered into a warm gaze. But he dropped his head and made busy with folding his table napkin, which meant she could breathe again.

'End of day, his people wanted me out of London while the media attention blew over and I was happy to go. I'm not a big fan of Christmas anyway, but this year The Ravens have been booked to perform for some US millionaire.'

'So your father is spending the holidays with someone else's family?' Brad shook his head.

'And doing a New Year gig in New York while they're over there.'

'That sucks.'

The succinct truth drew a laugh out of her. 'Nice summary.'

Though, in reality her father only ever made it home one Christmas in three, anyway. But when he did, everything else was forgiven. Apparently she was still seven years old at heart.

'Is that why you picked an Arab region to lie low in? Because December twenty-fifth is just another day?'

She couldn't hold his eyes then. She turned hers back out to the golden sands. 'That was the plan.'

'Well, London's loss is Al Saqr's gain,' he commented. 'Though I should warn you they don't completely ignore it here thanks to the overseas visitors. There will be festive menus at the very least.'

Her laugh tinkled as much as the cutlery of diners

around them. 'If it's not "Jingle Bells" on the radio and heart-warming movies on the TV, I'm happy enough.'

Brad considered her for an age, until she started to squirm under the scrutiny. 'What?'

'Just trying to imagine what happy looks like on you.'

Anyone could be forgiven for confusing the heated glow spreading out from her solar plexus under Brad's close regard for happiness. Or the look in his eye for something more than just empathy. But she wasn't that easily fooled.

She folded her napkin and laid it quietly onto the table.

'If you do see it, let me know. We can be amazed together.'

CHAPTER SIX

THE HEAD OF Security was going to kick his butt. His boss was starting to get twitchy at the latitude Brad was employing in watching over Sera—the cosy dining, the nights on the pool deck—not because he couldn't see that he was doing what was necessary for the job, but because he'd never known Brad as anything but the poster child for discipline. The guy who coloured strictly within the lines.

Then again, Brad was getting twitchy himself. He'd learned the hard way not to get friendly with his clients. But every day with Sera made it more and more difficult not to bend rules.

Try telling seven-year-old me that, she'd said and painted such a vivid picture of her lonely childhood, he'd struggled not to see another little face superimposed over his image of seven-year-old Sera. The last thing he needed was to be drawing comparisons between Egypt and Sera. Or to empathise for the situation with her father.

Empathy led to compassion.

And compassion wasn't going to get this job done.

He moved up behind her as she stepped over the threshold into the resort's heart to meet her guide. Standard procedure even though they'd been here long enough now to know where to go to meet Eric for just about anything. Today it was camel riding. She'd been waiting for a quieter guest day when she'd have the sands—and the camels—more to herself. He guessed that getting the kind of shots she wanted wasn't easy when there was a dozen pairs of feet trampling over everything. It took a full week and a half before a day fell where only one other couple happened to book a desert sunset ride.

That was about as good as it was going to get.

'Well, hello...!' Sera gushed.

You'd think she was greeting a pack of puppies. The cud-chewing camels knelt in a five-long, curved train, and a loose one stretched out in the sand just beyond them like a gangly, oversized dog. The four in the middle were fully kitted up in the camel equivalent of saddlery complete with patterned woven throws and bright, woven muzzles over their mouths. The front camel and the reclining one had no saddles at all, just a thick wad of rugs folded onto themselves and held on by a couple of girth straps. At first glance, the camels all seemed to be identical—pale, leggy ships of the desert. Up close, they were distinctly different: Sera's was honey coloured where the one behind was more wheat. His had a stately head where its neighbour's head was longer. All of them had the deep, silently considering eyes of their species. With supermodel lashes.

Eric took all four of them through a basic safety talk and then gave Sera his arm to help her mount. With her camel kneeled, she barely needed the assistance. She grabbed the saddle, pushed up onto her elbows and swung her for-ever legs over the pommel like a gymnast. Brad waited while she got herself comfortably secure, passed her camera pack up, then walked behind to his own animal and hiked himself on.

Salim, the camel driver, worked his way down the line checking everyone was secure. When he got to his side, Brad caught his eye and murmured, 'Extra care today.'

Salim lifted one brow, glanced at Sera and nodded.

'Relax, Brad,' Sera quipped, misreading his tension. 'If anyone tries to steal me away on their camel I'll just out-run them on mine.'

Behind them, Eric nudged his sleeping young animal onto its feet and leapt on as if he'd been born to it. Salim *was* born to it, and he did the same up front, sitting way back on his mount and half hooking his leg around its blanketed hump in a relaxed side-saddle that lent itself best to his traditional robes. Immediately behind Salim, the couple got all settled on their shared animal.

Poor Sera…*another* couple.

The thought came before he could shut it down. There was no 'poor' Sera. Or happy Sera. Or cranky Sera. For his own sanity there could only be client Sera. That was just how it had to be.

And how he wanted it.

Salim gave a whistle and all five animals in his train stood, back ends first.

The best part of riding a camel—their legs seemed to be jointed the wrong way and they pushed up with their knees while taking their weight on their elbows, then righted their front halves. Except they took their sweet time about it. Salim gave Sera's camel a shout when it lingered just a bit too long in elbow phase and she and her expensive camera gear wobbled precariously. Brad's eyes instantly went to the soft sand below and he started thinking about impact consequences until the surly beast stood up fully and she was able to release her white-knuckled grip on the pommel behind her.

Her feet sought around for something to brace in and eventually give up at the lack of stirrups and just dangled uselessly. He knew the feeling. Stirrups gave you balance and strength and the ability to leap off responsively if you had to. You were a *participant* in stirrups. You were just a passenger without them.

The only power no stirrups gave you was the power to tumble off into the sand face-first.

The couple squealed a bit and then they were off, Salim urging his lead animal to a comfortable lope and all others following lazily. Eric gave the train a moment to straighten up then jogged up from behind to ride next to Sera. Every muscle fibre in Brad's body tightened, even as his brain told him it was just Eric and he was paid to engage her.

And even as his brain assured him that the only reason he was getting tight-chested about it was because *he* was paid to do so.

He was her protection. He was supposed to feel protective.

But not possessive, a tiny voice judged.

'It's so beautiful,' Sera called back to him once Eric had finally trotted off, gripping tightly with her knees as her camel swayed from side to side in its exaggerated gait, so that she had both hands free to wrestle her gear out of its bag. Along the train, their fat-filled humps lolled in syncopation but once they hit a rhythm he saw her relax and enjoy the journey out into the dunes as the sun sank ever lower on the horizon. Conversation wasn't really an option given they were all facing the front and spread along the train, but that didn't stop Sera turning and smiling back at him at regular intervals across the twenty minutes it took to get out to their break point.

He hardened his heart against every one.

On arrival at the base of a massive dune, Eric and Salim helped the couple up front until they stood beside their now kneeling mounts. Brad gave his camel a hearty pat on its thick hide and then strode forward to relieve Sera of some of her camera gear so she could climb down.

'You really need to get yourself a little point and click,' he murmured, wrangling the heavy gear.

She turned her outrage down to him. 'Wash your mouth out!'

But then her pleasure in the journey spilled over in a tinkling laugh as she sprang to the ground. 'Come on.'

As he trailed her past the front of the camel train his eye line collided with Salim's. Both of them tore their focus away to something else.

The dune ahead was hard and compacted at its core but as loose as the sand around the resort on its surface. That made scrabbling up the outside a heap trickier than a regular hill climb, so that when they arrived midway up where a catering station had been set up for sunset drinks they were both out of breath.

'Water or sparkling wine?' Eric asked Sera, easily slipping from guide mode to host mode and holding one of each up in his hands.

Sera reached for the frosty-glassed champagne.

Eric tossed the bottle of water to him.

'I think that's the first drink I've seen you have since you got here,' Brad murmured. He'd assumed she didn't drink, but maybe she was actually worried about the local prohibitions. None of which applied within Al Saqr's fences.

'We're standing in the middle of the Arabian desert,' she said on a long, relaxed breath. 'The sun is setting and stars are going to start twinkling. Can you think of a better time to enjoy a quiet glass of bubbles? Besides, weren't you the one who wanted me to chill out a bit?'

'Yes, I was.' He laughed. 'Maybe I should get you a second glass.'

He glanced at the couple who were already in full romance mode, making their way to the top of the dune, champagne in hand. Sera took a sip and then started to make her way to a sunset-facing point about three-quarters of the way up the dune.

Brad set off after her. 'Here…'

He relieved her of her glass in exchange for her camera gear he still carried, and she thanked him with a comfortable smile then got busy taking her first test shots. The sun still had a reasonable way to go before it hit the horizon but the light changed fast out here, meaning constant adjustment of the settings on her camera. So, she was right to hurry. Every now and again, he passed her the wine and she took a grateful, sighing sip before getting busy behind the camera again.

'Is that pollution?' she asked, looking up at the fine haze way up in the troposphere that cast an ethereal pink glow over everything as the sun drew closer to the distant horizon.

'It's sand,' he explained. 'It blows out to sea by day but returns on the evening currents. The price of living in a desert nation.'

Her smile, then, rivalled the sunset that bathed her in its beautiful light, and he had to take a long, strong breath to settle his pulse as she turned back to her work. 'It does great things for my photos.'

A dozen glowing, golden dunes stood between their vantage point and the distant resort and each one of them began to change shape as the sun sank towards the horizon. The closest ones almost rippled with the wind-born striations across their surface. Easy to see why people called it a sea of sand. Beyond those, the tiny Bedouin-style suites of Al Saqr and—beyond those—the blazing, enormous sun as it kissed the western horizon. Sera's camera whirred away, capturing all of it. She photographed down low, she photographed from the highest dune point, she photographed the straggly fire bush that was home to the creatures that wouldn't come out until dark. She forgot all about her champagne as she grew more and more engaged.

Up on the top of the dune, the couple that rode with them on the camel train stood silhouetted, in some intimate conversation. Sera surreptitiously turned her camera and fired off a few shots against the gentle pink twilight before the two strangers wrapped each other in a long, enduring hug.

And then the sun was completely buried in the sands of the horizon. And everything changed.

What was previously pink washed over with a purpley-blue and the definition all around them diminished. The man staffing the drinks stand fired up a pair of bright brands that flickered and burned and, from nowhere, he produced a platter of delicious hors d'oeuvres.

Brad laid a hand on Sera's lens and lowered it.

'Enough,' he said mildly. 'You're missing all the good stuff.'

She didn't protest, glancing around behind them at the changed desert as if she'd just awakened from a nap. She packed her gear away in its bag, took back what little was left of her champagne and followed him back down to the food-station area where delicious aromas of goat's cheese and onion, sizzling meat on mini skewers and a trio of earthy dips and salted bread awaited.

'I'm going to email you a couple of images to the resort's address,' she said quietly to Eric, glancing at the silhouetted couple. 'Could you please make sure they get to them? They might like a memory of the proposal.'

Eric nodded and smiled and then drifted off again.

'That was a proposal?' Brad asked when he was gone. 'How could you tell?'

She turned and glanced at him strangely. 'How could you not?'

Okay, so…yeah. It had been a pretty schmaltzy scene and these views would be hard to top as proposal memories went. In fact, with Eric and the couple's guide tactfully withdrawn, the fire brands of the food station flickering like oversized candles, and Sera no longer otherwise engaged with photographs, the whole thing suddenly took on a whole bunch of extra meaning.

Extra awkward *romantic* meaning.

'So what's the plan for tomorrow?' he said a bit louder than necessary.

Sera just smiled at him as if she knew exactly how uncomfortable he'd just become, but she wasn't going to buy into his idiocy. She squeezed his forearm and moved past him to the catering table to nibble on some of the goodies there. He did his whole standing-to-attention thing not far behind. But with the guides keeping polite distance and the couple immersed solely in each other, Sera had no one to talk to if not him.

And suddenly he got a vivid flash of what her childhood might have been like. When the only people around were there because it was their job to be. When she had no one to share experiences like this with.

Don't be a jerk, Kruger. Talk to her.

'Want to go meet the camels?' he asked instead. It wasn't ideal but it was a reasonable compromise between too alone and too together.

Her eyes brightened in the glow from the brands and she nodded enthusiastically. A soggy kind of satisfaction swelled in his gut, and he realised that it pleased him to please her.

He took her gear again so she could finish eating the few nibbles she'd grabbed and walked beside her as she picked her way carefully down the dune face. Salim had lit the brands at the foot of the dune, too, and his animals were bathed in a rich red glow. As they approached, two camels grunted in protest.

'No, we're not getting back on yet,' Sera reassured them loudly, warmly. She crossed straight to Salim.

'Would it be okay to say hello?' she asked him.

Salim glanced at him for only a moment before rising from his rest on the warm sand and replying.

'They would be delighted.'

Meeting the camels formally was lovely but wouldn't have been nearly as notable if Brad hadn't dropped back and given her and the camel driver so much space. Normally he trailed her like a conjoined twin, but out here—where there had to be more risk, not less—he fell back into the night's shadows while the camel driver introduced her to his charges.

And his absence got her attention.

'Do they have names?' she asked.

Salim pointed at each animal in turn and rattled off their Arabic names as well as discussing their personalities and then answered a few more of Sera's questions about their care and management.

'Your accent is very good,' she commented when he finished.

'I was raised speaking it as well as the language of the Bedu,' he murmured with another anxious glance towards Brad.

Sorry, friend, looks like he's leaving us to it.

Salim bowed politely and backed away, looking quite relieved and leaving her to commune with the camels. She wove in between each kneeled animal, patting their long faces and looking deep into their thickly lashed eyes, chatting lightly to them and making mental notes for images she might be able to get on a future desert trek. Her treads in the thick sand were silent and so, as she came quietly around the back of the camel nearest to Brad, she caught him and the camel driver, heads down, in private conversation.

They practically sprang apart when they saw her. It was the first time she'd seen Brad even slightly off guard. But before she could speak, voices began to filter down the dune towards them.

Moment lost.

But her curiosity blazed as bright as the torches poking up out of the sand.

It took about ten minutes to get the reluctant camels back on their feet and everyone mounted in the dwindling light. Brad seemed conscious of her speculative gaze falling on him—and, occasionally, on the camel driver—but, finally, she was mounted up between them and couldn't plague either of them with her curiosity.

The wide rocking motion of the camel helped to dislodge some of her inquisitiveness on the return journey, but it came back in force as soon as they got back to the resort. Sera warmly thanked the camel driver—who only met her eyes for the moment it took to be polite—then farewelled

Eric. Brad stood silently at guard throughout. He did a cracking impersonation of the camel driver's averted gaze.

Okay, what was going on...?

She headed back up towards the suite, glancing at him repeatedly. But his face was closed and his forward-facing eyes kept her firmly out. Eventually she sped up to get a little ahead of him, spun and planted her feet in front, saying nothing, just staring with eyebrows raised.

'So...that was rude,' she began. Not really where she wanted to start the discussion but it was as good a lead-in as any.

Tension seemed to make him taller. 'What was?'

'Your failure to thank the camel driver. Or even acknowledge him.'

Brad's night-darkened eyes narrowed. As if he knew when he was being played. 'He'll survive.'

'Anyone would think you had an issue with the man.'

'Are you truly calling me on my cultural sensitivity, Sera? The woman who arrived in the country wearing a glorified table napkin and scandalised half the arrivals lounge?'

'Technically, I'm calling you on your shadowy secrecy, but clearly you aren't getting that.' And she knew Brad well enough by now to recognise deflection when she saw it. 'Come on, what gives?'

She'd meant this interaction to be playful teasing but the sudden defiance in Brad's expression turned it very quickly into something a whole lot less fun.

'What gives,' he repeated, 'isn't really any of your business, Sera. Like most of the questions you ask.'

She stumbled back half a step and then steadied. 'Right you are.'

She turned back towards the resort's hub, powered past it and headed to their suites. On arrival, she waited silently while Brad opened up and cleared the room, then brushed past him and laid her camera gear down.

'I'm going to skip dinner,' she announced, trying to keep her body language loose to beat his stupid specialist training. She'd grazed on the table out in the desert and she had a bowl full of fruit in here. She wasn't going to die overnight. And he wasn't her keeper.

'Okay,' he murmured. Making no effort at all to keep her.

'I'll see you tomorrow.'

His grey eyes turned steely. 'All right.'

But he just stood.

And she just stood.

One of them had to move first.

'I'll leave you a beer on the deck,' she tried again. As hints went, it was not very subtle.

That drew his eyes to the curtains the service staff had pulled closed. Something told her tonight would be the first night she left them that way. Speculation bubbled across his expression, followed by exasperation. But he knew his professional manners and—boy—was he ever master of his emotions.

'Okay, Sera. See you in the morning.'

The moment he left, shame flooded her body. Snoop's remorse. Brad was right, it really was no business of hers what stood between him and the camel guy. Her curiosity was piqued but she was hardly going to lose any sleep over it. There was just something so…*unjust*…about his expectation that she would bare all in their conversations and yet he would remain such a closed book. The harder he fought to keep his secrets, the more she came to resent them. On principle.

She didn't even want to know what they were. She just wanted him to trust her with them.

Is that it? a little voice challenged. *Or do you just want to know that* you *can trust* him?

You'd think that she would have sworn off that by now. She'd trusted Mark and his friends and it had turned out they were anything but worthy of her trust.

Worthy...

The word echoed around her brain. Was that what she was doing with Brad? Testing his worthiness? The aspects of him that he wasn't already paid to deliver? Pushing him to see how he stood up? Why, when he was around for only a few weeks at best?

She sagged.

She really had learned nothing since her childhood.

The woman was infuriating.

Brad sank down onto the deck chair and tossed back half of a beer he didn't really even want. But keeping his hands busy would stop him from going back in there and picking a fight. So if nothing else it served that purpose.

The more he tried to keep Sera at bay, the harder she seemed to work to wiggle her way under his defences—consciously and unconsciously. As if a woman who'd been neglected by her father and been thoroughly betrayed by her jerk of a boyfriend needed any help at all in garnering his empathy.

Now she had him feeling like a louse for maintaining the boundaries he was *required* to observe.

Visiting Salim's camel train had been a bad idea; putting the two of them in the same space for any amount of time was always going to lead to questions—on both sides—but desperate times called for desperate measures. In that moment, it was find a solid distraction or haul Sera into his arms for a hug. She'd just looked so lost and so lonely standing there on the dune side.

Not the first lost, lonely soul he'd carelessly let himself soften to.

How exactly is it in a child's best interests *to be kept at arm's length?* Sera's words on the day of the flight show returned to him just as hard now. Like a punch to the guts. He'd been burning to tell her that it wasn't necessarily in a child's best interests for them to be drawn close either.

It wasn't good for a kid named Matteo. It nearly got him killed.

Building a friendship with someone who was only going to be in your life for a nanosecond wasn't going to do Sera any good either. Not with the kind of childhood and revolving door of caretakers that she'd had. Her comment on the drive out here—*'just so I know you're real'*—made a whole lot more sense given the supposed friends who'd roped her into their animal-rights protest. Who'd used her celebrity to get themselves some publicity. And all the people she'd been raised by who all kept a professional distance.

But, clearly the whole *indifferent acquiescence* thing wasn't really working out. Sera was under-skilled in acquiescence. And apparently he was under-skilled in indifference.

Still.

CHAPTER SEVEN

THE GENTLE SPLASH of a big body moving in the pool was easy to hear even though Brad worked hard to keep it quiet. Sera stood by the closed curtains, thinking. She owed him an apology but the bright light of morning was probably the right time to extend it, right?

Although, he was still up… And she was still up…

And he'd already seen her pyjamas.

She reached between the curtains and quietly unsnicked the lock, then slipped the rest of her body through as she opened the door. Brad hung off the wall at the far end of the pool, staring out into the night, steam from the heated water shimmering up and away into the cold desert air, oblivious to her presence. But when she turned back from closing the door behind her he wasn't oblivious any longer. He twisted, still hanging there in the deep, wordless, his guarded eyes watching her emerge. She took a deep breath and moved to sit on the corner edge of the pool, her feet on the second step. The water's temperature was virtually the same as the warm bed she'd just left, but its wet caress felt gorgeous, like warm silk, and its temperature soaked up to the part of her that was exposed to the winter desert air and warmed her through.

Or maybe that was just the sight of a semi-naked Brad.

'Can't sleep?' he murmured from the other end of the pool. Making nice.

Nope—her mind was too busy. But she just shrugged.

Brad reversed his position, his bent arms spread like powerful angel wings behind him, supporting his body in the deep end so he could face her. It was simultaneously casual and on guard but it did nothing to diminish his strength. If anything, the sheen of the water glistening on all those muscles just amplified their power, making it hard to look away. It was the desert stalking all over again.

Except this time she wasn't lurking in the shadows.

'I wanted to apologise for the silent treatment earlier,' she said, loud enough to be heard above the water cascading over the pool's edge into its collection area, but quiet enough to be personal.

He masked his body language. 'You don't have to be any particular way with me. And you don't owe me any apologies.'

'Because it's your job?' she asked tightly, staring at the water. Or because he didn't care? And why did that make her feel so miserable?

'Because it's none of my business,' he clarified.

That brought her eyes up. 'What if I want to make it your business?'

Those big shoulders shrugged but it was far from easy. 'Then I'll listen.'

Could he sound any more reluctant?

She studied the ripples spreading across the surface of the water from her submerged calves and tried to find a place to start.

'I know it's not reasonable of me to expect you to open up to me on command—like what the deal is with the camel driver—I just feel like...' Her waving hands tried to grasp the words she needed. 'I've trusted you with some of myself—I think I wanted it to be reciprocal. Like...friends.'

God, it sounded pathetic aloud.

'You're a client, Sera,' he said carefully.

One leg kicked out, destroying the pretty water rings on the water's surface. 'I know. I have no right to expect anything more from you than your protection. I just thought getting to know you was a way to be more comfortable around each other.'

His brows dipped. 'I make you uncomfortable?'

'No, not... That sounds worse than I meant it. We have weeks yet together, Brad, and it would be nice not to be on eggshells for that. But I can't be at ease when I know nothing about you.'

And then she might as well be here all alone...

'I've answered your questions.'

Yes, like a good employee. 'You've told me facts. Some. But I don't feel like I know you any better.'

"'I'm your responsibility, but not your friend",' he murmured gently. 'That was your ground rule.'

He pushed away from the pool edge and swam out into the middle. Small as it was, that put him much closer to her but he didn't come too close. He just drifted there, sinking up to his nose in the heated water so that only his veiled eyes looked back at her.

'Yes, I did say that.'

'Did you not mean it?'

'I did mean it.' At the time. But somewhere in the past ten days, things had changed.

He surfaced long enough to say, 'So where's the problem?'

Some noise out in the desert drew her eye but really it was just an excuse to avoid his question long enough to think of the best way of wording her answer.

'Shouldn't I trust you? As my protection? Isn't that important?'

He slowly pushed up out of the water, eyes steady. And concerned. 'You don't trust me?'

'I barely know you. Meanwhile you know all about me. Including things I probably don't even know.' Who knew what else her file had in it? 'It doesn't feel balanced.'

And she was hardly someone who needed barriers to trust.

'So you're looking to even up the score a little?'

'I'm just looking to get to know you, Brad.'

Wary grey eyes pinned her. 'Why?'

His see-all focus made her intensely uncomfortable and snappier than she'd meant to be when she'd come out here with apology on her lips.

'Because we're living in each other's pockets.'

'From what you've said, I'd have thought you'd be used to people maintaining a professional distance.'

A fist squeezed deep down inside and she replied, 'I am. Entirely.'

His big hands paddled him a little closer. Just a little. 'But you don't like it.'

Some questions weren't really questions.

His voice, when he spoke next, was rich with caution. 'You know we can't hook up, right?'

That brought her head up with a whip-crack. She practically reared back. 'I wasn't offering a hook-up. I was just wanting to get to know you a bit.'

Which was starting to feel like a really dumb idea, now.

She pushed up from the edge of the pool, but one powerful stroke had Brad there in time to grab her ankle and tug her gently back down to the tiled edge, now wet with spilled water. Her calf brushed down his smooth chest and tingled the whole way. The spilled water soaked into her behind as she sat back on the pool edge. But she didn't care. She almost didn't notice.

She was all about his hand on her leg.

'Relax, Sera,' he said, releasing her. 'Just a reminder of protocol. What do you want to know? If I can tell you, I will. Within reason.'

She stared as the umbrage started to drain back out of her. Did she look as wild as her hammering heart suggested? Okay, so maybe coming out here in the middle of the night in her pyjamas wasn't the *least* loaded way she could have done this. But she trusted Brad was above tacky scenarios.

'What is the deal with the camel man? All the secrecy?'

He stared at her, his busy mind turning over.

Really? He couldn't even—?

'Salim and I don't acknowledge each other in the work context. It's an etiquette thing.'

'He's your friend?'

'He's my uncle,' Brad shot back. Then, as she flared with the surprise, 'Honorary uncle, at least. My mother's cousin.'

Astonishment stole her words for a few moments. Brad was half-Bedouin? 'What's he doing at Al Saqr?'

'His job. He's worked the camels here since the resort opened. It sits on the edge of his tribal lands. He gave me the in with the Sheikh's security team.'

A camel-driver...?

'He must be well regarded. If his recommendation goes that high.'

'Bedouin are not judged by the task they do, but by the men they are. Salim's family is older even than the Sheikh's.'

'And when you're at the resort, you pretend not to know each other?'

He shrugged. 'It's not a secret, but we just don't flash the connection about. Upper management knows, of course. But no one else. Salim's call, and I respect it.'

Sera blinked at him. 'Your mother's cousin. So she's where you get your dark colouring?'

His chest expanded hard, bringing him up out of the water a little, then he sank back down again as he breathed out. 'She grew up just over the border.'

'And so your father's side are Australian?' His half-submerged head nodded. 'And you grew up there but now you live here?'

He emerged from the water, carefully. 'I work here. Like thousands of other ex-pats.'

Immediately, she wondered which he identified as—Aussie or Arabic. 'Away from your family?'

'I have plenty of family here.'

'But your parents...?'

'There's a big wide world out there, Sera. Most people leave home by their twenties...'

She was glad for the soaking her rump was getting on the pool edge because it helped to offset the flaming heat of her embarrassment. She'd often felt like she lived in a bubble, but how had it never occurred to her simply to *burst* that bubble? Move away.

Was she too unprepared for the real world?

'Your knowledge of Arab culture. That comes from your mother?'

His eyes grew shadowed. 'My mother surrendered much of her culture when she married my father. Her choice. So everything I know—and there's still a lot that I don't—comes from my uncle.'

Something occurred to her. 'That's why you understood Omar so well. Because you were raised just fine outside of your culture, too.'

'I was raised how I was raised. If Mum had practised her culture then I guess I would, too. But she didn't and so I don't. I'm not broken.'

And I don't need fixing. The subtext was clear.

She let some silence flutter down onto the extra heat her questions had caused. Breathing space for both of them.

'I can't tell you what I'd give to know both sides of my family...' She sighed.

His eyes softened and they filled with something that might have been understanding. Or even regret. 'Yeah, I get that. I was nearly adult before I met Salim and his family. I'm treated more like a son there. Instant siblings.'

'I could have brothers and sisters,' she murmured after a long pause, 'and I wouldn't even know it.'

Brad peered up at her. 'If you asked your father would he tell you?'

'He would, I'm sure. But he doesn't know either.' She felt shamed, as always, at the tawdriness of her conception. 'He didn't even know her last name.'

That brought Brad's head up. 'Wait. So he took a tiny baby from a stranger and just trusted that it was his?'

'She acted anonymously through a lawyer. And she sent DNA test results, which he had verified. But he didn't need them. He said I was the spitting image of him as a baby.'

Doubt soaked his face. 'I've seen your father online. I can't imagine you and he looking anything alike.'

'Stage make-up.' She shrugged. 'It's all smoke and mirrors. He can walk down the high street and hardly anyone recognises him. Except as their neighbour. It's kind of cool.'

His eyes narrowed. 'Answer me this, Sera. Is all your agitating an attempt to get his attention?'

Lord, he made her sound as if she were still ten years old.

'My agitating?' She laughed. 'I've marched in a few protests and raised money for causes—'

'And been arrested in a secret research lab. I'm just wondering if you were always so...social-minded.'

She studied him and wondered what he would think of her endless attempts to be exceptional as a child. 'I was a good student, a good worker. I didn't smoke, or drink or party. I studied hard and excelled academically.'

'Not exactly the way to win friends and influence people when you're a teen.'

'I wasn't interested in winning friends. I wanted respect. My teachers, my carers—'

'Your father?'

'Of course.'

'Did it work?'

'Not really. He didn't notice the good girl, but I was too good at heart to be a convincing bad girl.'

'And so the causes.'

She inclined her head. 'I thought it would please him to see that I'd inherited his sense of social justice.'

'And did it?'

'No. I think that was more his thing. His brand. Maybe more of a construct than I realised.'

Certainly, his PR firm were less than happy to see her treading the same path. Stealing focus.

'You know, you're pretty resilient, considering.'

Resilience. Desperation. *Potato...potahto.*

A laugh barked out of her. 'No, I'm not.'

Brad's hand slid onto her foot and just pressed there as though it were her hand.

'You are. More than you think.' He said this with such confidence she almost believed him. 'Or you wouldn't be looking to trust someone again so soon after the whole lab thing.'

'You mean Mark.'

'I'm sorry that happened to you, Sera. You don't deserve it.'

'I walked into it. With my eyes wide shut.'

'You blame yourself.'

'Of course.'

'Getting close to you to leverage your fame was an incredibly low act. It says more about your lousy ex than it does about you. Give yourself points for picking up and carrying on.'

She didn't want his words warming her. And he wouldn't want that either.

'Lying low, I believe you called it.'

'Healing.'

She peered out at the beautiful night. 'If there's a place for that, this is certainly it.'

Brad circulated the water around him gently, keeping it—and the mood—carefully moving.

'So look at us having a regular conversation.' She chuckled.

His smile—so broad and so white against the comparative tan of his skin—lit up the pool. 'Pretty painless, really.'

And just like that, her ability to speak completely dried

up. Something about his strong hand on her foot, that twisted smile and those bottomless grey eyes peering up at her from the pool steps... Words completely failed her. Because you needed breath to make sounds, didn't you? The only part of her that could function was her eyes, and those seemed drawn in to his like a tidal current.

Such inscrutable, unfathomable eyes.

Thick lashes rescued her by falling down over Brad's gaze and severing the tractor beam drawing her towards him. His hand slid away from her foot and he pushed against the pool wall and drifted back to the safety of its deep middle.

Back to a professional distance.

'Do you do Christmas?' she blurted without realising she was about to.

'Do I *do* it?'

'You know—family, gifts, food.'

'If that constitutes Christmas, then, yeah, I do that. With Dad's side of the family. Not this year, obviously.'

Because he was babysitting her. 'I'm sorry.'

Those big shoulders shrugged. 'I'll call home, video chat. Maybe put on a candy-cane tie to mark the day.' But his eyes narrowed. 'Unless you have other plans for the day?'

'Lord, no.' She shook her head. 'I don't want to impact on your Christmas at all. I've done quite enough of that in my life.'

He studied her through the slight mist rising from the warm pool water. 'What were your Christmases like?'

'Quiet. Unless we had ourselves a bona-fide miracle and Dad made it home. Then it was anything but. He filled the house with his muso friends. It was crazy.'

From one extreme to the other.

Brad's lips thinned. 'So even when he was home your father still managed to ruin your Christmas?'

God, when had she ever laughed about this? But there it was...an actual chuckle. Brad had a gift for easing her worst ouches. Smoothing them over the way his big hands skimmed the water's surface right now.

'What about when he wasn't?'

'I asked for a roster,' she admitted. 'So that no one lost their whole Christmas Day to looking after me. Nanny in the morning. Tutor in the afternoon. Security at night. Same on Boxing Day. It worked well. I got to see just about all of them over the holidays.'

'That's something, I guess.'

'Except that it meant I was taking three people away from their tree or their roast or their *Miracle on 34th Street* so they could sit with me instead. I still didn't like that.'

'Doing to some *other* kid what your father's music did to you?' he murmured.

When had anyone *got* her quite so easily?

But as they stared at each other—as they *got* each other—Brad's eyes lost their warm kind of interest and flattened out. She felt the chill immediately.

'Well, don't worry on my account,' he joked, bringing the conversation back into the shallow end even as he pushed out deeper in the pool. 'I'm just as happy to let this one slide. I'm still working off last year's turkey in the gym.'

Dismissed.

Suddenly, tiptoeing out here to make good on her earlier rudeness looked a whole lot more desperate and intrusive. This might have been her deck during the day, but while he was sleeping out here, it was virtually his bedroom. And she'd let herself into it without knocking. And while he might have been kindly willing to humour her get-to-know-you questions, he was under zero obligation to indulge her swilling hormones.

He cleared his throat. 'Do you think you will be able to sleep now?'

She tucked her wet feet under her on the edge of the pool. 'Yeah, I think so. Thank you for the chat.'

He nodded once—very military, very proper. She missed

the Brad of moments ago already. But if nothing else, at least she knew he was in there. Lurking.

She pushed up onto her feet. But as she did, the talc-fine sand that covered everything out here mixed with the pool water into a treacherous slime and she felt her weight-bearing foot slip out from under her. There was no graceful, Hollywood tumble into the waiting water. There was no dramatic cry even. Just the awful, spine-jarring *grunt* as her bottom hit the pool edge, the pain of her tongue caught between her teeth as they slammed shut, and the inelegant face-first slam into the shallow end.

Whereupon she flailed around like a kid who'd never learned to swim, sucking down water, until strong hands wrapped around her and helped her to right herself.

'I've got you...'

Brad pulled her to her feet and steadied her as she spluttered and coughed and pushed the soggy hair out of her face. Spears of pain shot outward from her lower back and, as soon as she had enough breath, she wasted it on a very unladylike curse. But it was only as she wiped the saline water from her eyes that she glanced down and saw the real humiliation—her flimsy pyjamas glued to her naked breasts like a plaster-cast moulding. She ducked back under the protection of the water with a tiny squeak.

'Are you okay?'

She was still too winded for actual speech so she just nodded and concentrated on taking some shallow breaths. His hands were all over her then, checking her limbs and tipping her head back to examine her pupils. She stood, compliant, under his examination but didn't rise above water level.

'You didn't hit your head?'

She shook her head and nothing rattled so...no.

'Okay, let's get you out.'

She tried to shy back from him but movement under water was slow and it took him a moment to notice her full-bodied resistance. He frowned as she disentangled herself from his arms.

'I can't...' she gasped past her breathlessness, glancing down.

That was when he noticed how transparent her pale blue pyjamas had become, even though she still had everything important carefully obscured under the water. A flood of colour ran up his jaw.

Who knew they even still made men who could blush?

'Okay, hang on, I'll get you a towel.'

He hauled himself up the stairs—and she wasn't so shell-shocked from her tumble that she didn't enjoy the up-close view of that from below—and then he grabbed up one of the oversized guest towels that the resort staff replaced every day, apparently regardless of whether they were used or not. He shook it out and held it up, carefully and strategically, between her see-through PJs and his gaze.

'Come on out. Use the safety rail.'

After her slip of moments ago you bet she would! She pushed her wobbly legs over to the far edge of the stairs, wrapped her hand securely around the rail and gingerly pulled herself up the four steps to the timber deck. The pain increased with every step out of the zero gravity of the water.

Brad turned slightly to respectfully orient the opened towel in her direction and she walked into it exactly as if she were walking into his arms. And when they closed around her all warm and strong it was like the hug she desperately needed.

He pulled her into his chest, wrapped the towel tight. 'Do you think you've fractured anything?'

It was hard to remember his concern was purely professional as she stood here wrapped in warm towel and wet man, but she managed it, barely.

'I think I've bruised my—' *pride* '—coccyx.' The crack

she'd heard on landing on the tiled edge of the pool certainly suggested so.

His hands rubbed her limbs through the towel like a soggy child, and the contact made her feel anything but. He moved out from behind her, holding the towel pinned closed so that she could turn in its circle and grasp its edges together herself and maintain her own modesty.

'Take a quick shower and then I'll take a look.'

'You will not!'

'I need to know if it's fractured, Sera.'

'Unless you have X-ray vision, I don't think you're going to be able to do that by looking.'

His consternation was immediate. 'You're right. I'll call Reception—'

'No!' What was it? Nearly two-thirty a.m.? 'Look, just... come in. We'll sort it out in here.'

She dripped on the tiled floor and the ornate rugs as she crossed into the bathroom. Brad rummaged her up some clothes, and she tried really hard not to wince as big, masculine hands passed her own lacy smalls along with something dry to wear in to her through the bathroom door.

'Be careful.'

'It was just a slip, Brad. I'm not an invalid.'

Though truth be told she really felt like one. The jar on her coccyx was still resonating through her wobbly legs, especially as she bent to peel soggy pyjama bottoms and underwear off. But a hot shower freshened her up a treat, and after, she pulled herself into the T-shirt and leggings that Brad had grabbed for her. Totally mismatched, but that was a man for you. At least they weren't transparent. She combed her towel-dried hair, scrunched it a bit to give it some body and moved towards the door. At the very last moment, she stepped back to smudge some kohl around her lashes and patted on some clear lip gloss.

Just because she *was* a certified disaster zone didn't mean she had to look like one.

Brad shot to his feet from his chair, oblivious to her face, making her efforts as *in vain* as they *were vain*.

He thrust something towards her. 'I made you an ice pack.'

Because that was what you really wanted after a nice hot shower—the block from your minibar freezer. But she took the folded package gratefully and dutifully reached around behind to press it on her lower back.

Her groan was immediate. Yeah. That felt a bit too good. Maybe it was a fracture after all?

'On the bed,' Brad ordered, frowning.

Any other time... The thought made her giggle and he glanced at her with concern as she hoisted herself up gingerly onto the *Princess and the Pea* bed.

'I'm *fine*,' she urged. 'No head injury.'

He helped her to arrange the multitude of pillows and cushions in such a way that she could lie on her side and not on her offended flesh.

'I'm just going to lower your underwear.'

The giggles came back in force.

'I'm serious, Sera.'

'I know, that's what makes it so funny.'

He muttered something under his breath, then, 'I'll laugh when I know you haven't fractured your spine on my watch.'

'It's my bum, Brad. It was built to cope with impact.'

The giggling returned because that sounded way dirtier than she'd meant it—maybe it was a delayed kind of shock, after all—but his serious hands simply rolled her more fully onto her side and relieved her of the ice pack. Then warm fingers tugged her leggings and underwear modestly down and got busy gently pressing on and around the base of her spine.

Could a man ever look you in the eye again after studying your *pants cleavage* close up?

They were about to find out.

His touch was both gentle and a little bit too interesting, and he misinterpreted every flutter of her flesh as pain. Necessarily the inspection took twice as long as it needed to before Brad finally offered his verdict as he eased the ice pack back on.

'I don't think it's fractured.'

'How much experience have you had with busted coccyx?'

'I've assessed other fractures in the service,' he muttered. 'I'm sure the principles are transferable.'

And suddenly her mind was full of military Brad, deep in some awful conflict zone, dirty and sweaty and besieged, urgently doing first aid on a mate covered in blood and broken, shattered limbs. The giggles dried up completely.

'Thanks for checking,' she said, her voice low.

'No problem.' He kept the ice in place with the reliable pressure of his hand, and she gave up her futile attempts not to roll back into the mattress sag where he sat next to her and just let herself relax against the warm heat of his thigh and hip. After the warmth of his enquiring fingers, the cold of the ice was a tantalising contrast.

'Sorry about all of this,' she murmured. Clumsy, clumsy Sera. 'It wasn't intentional.'

The bed shook slightly with his rumbly laugh. 'If I thought it was a ploy to get half-naked in my arms then you'd be the lamest femme fatale ever.'

Suddenly the memory of being in his arms with nothing but a towel and her wet PJs between them returned in full force and she ducked her face to prevent him from spotting her flush. But it wasn't embarrassment causing it. He shifted the pack again and used his fingers on her hips to hold his hand, and the pack, in place. Then he shifted slightly, leaning over her, and retrieved a glass of water from the backlit wall niche above the bedhead.

'Here, take these. It's probably going to get worse before it gets better.'

Generally, she avoided painkillers but something told her he knew a thing or two about injuries. She pushed up onto her elbow to toss the little white pills in and then took a healthy swallow of water to wash them down.

He relieved her of the glass, and she sagged back against his solid strength.

'I'll keep the ice on until you fall asleep,' he murmured. 'Just close your eyes.'

Lord, that was tempting as all his heat soaked into her. 'What if you fall asleep, too?'

'Then the thump of me hitting the ground will wake us both and you can hold an ice pack to my butt instead.'

The idea of holding anything against all that muscle brought a dreamy smile to her face but she was in no mood for conversation. She squirrelled down against him on a happy sigh and let her eyes drift shut. Distantly, very distantly, she felt the heavy heat of his other hand on her head and a moment later the gentle brush of his fingers as he singled out a length of hair and curled it around his fingers, then pulled it out gently.

Over and over.

He probably thought she was asleep. Ten seconds more of this and she would be. Maybe it was the drugs, or the pain—or the excruciating sweetness of the gesture—but she couldn't help the fat tear that squeezed out from under her lashes as she lay there under Brad's gentle touch. But as long as she was turned away from him, she was free to enjoy his secret caress—and indulge her tears—as much as she wanted.

And so she did. Until darkness claimed her.

CHAPTER EIGHT

WITH NO ONE to wake her to go and learn archery or participate in an early-morning wildlife walk or watch the sun rise from a hot-air balloon, Sera slumbered right through dawn, right through the return of their friendly neighbourhood oryx, right through her scheduled dune-drive and right through breakfast.

As soon as she'd nodded off, Brad contacted the resort's night staff to cancel their morning activity and confirm suite delivery for a very late breakfast instead of the restaurant for an early one. Whatever Miss Independence thought she'd be doing today she was in for some disappointment. She was staying in and he was staying with her to make sure she cooperated. He might have finally been persuaded that she hadn't hit her head but even *his* teeth had rattled with the force she'd hit the poolside, spine-first.

Sera was going to be really sore today. She was probably due a down day, anyway. Between her endless photography, array of activities and thorough desert walks, she'd been running on full speed since they arrived. Not exactly R&R.

Though, with what he'd learned about her Christmases past that was starting to make more sense. As was her general uptightness about…pretty much everything. Little Miss Clumsy had ridden her share of rubbish waves in life.

Brad eased his weight from his left leg to his right against the far wall of the suite. He'd only left her for as long as it took to run next door and get some dry clothes at about three a.m. Since then he'd stood guard as far from her bed as he could manage and still do his job. Something about watching her sleep made him feel like a creep—even if he did have good intentions.

If not for him, Sera wouldn't have hurt herself at all. If not for his determination to keep her safe she would have been tucked up in bed comfortably asleep last night instead of zonked out on painkillers.

What was it with him that the more he tried to keep someone safe, the worse it ended up for them?

What he should have done was send her back inside the moment she stepped foot outside her suite. Or made some excuse and left, himself. What he *shouldn't* have done was let himself be drawn into her gentle questions. To convince himself that keeping client relations positive was more important than keeping a professional distance.

Distance existed for a reason.

Had he truly not learned that from Cairo?

'Ow…'

A muffled curse came from under the goosedown quilt. He'd lowered the temperature in her suite to make sure she really snuggled into all those covers, and it had helped her tumble into the very deep slumber that followed. Shambolic hair emerged first and then the squinty eyes gone full panda with the eyeliner she'd put on after her shower.

As if her chocolatey eyes needed the adornment.

'Morning,' he said cheerily, but mostly so that she knew immediately that he was still in the suite. 'I thought you were never going to wake.'

Total lie. He'd sat here in silence, hoping she'd sleep as long as possible. The only reason he'd thrown open the curtains now and let the bright light wake her was because their brunch was arriving in fifteen minutes. And it was almost lunch, really.

She pushed upright and then gasped audibly as she sat on her forgotten injury.

'Here…'

He crossed straight to her and piled her pillows the way he had last night. He'd even found two spares in the cupboard and thrown them on for good measure. But she

started fighting him immediately, batting his efforts away
with her hands, and rolling unhelpfully where he was trying to engineer a bank of pillows.

'I need to...' One hand waved vaguely at the bathroom.

His job became demolition, then, and he tossed all the
barriers to her getting out of bed to the foot of the bed, allowing her to ease onto her feet and inch her way into the
next room. The little cry of despair that followed could
easily have been about the panda eyes as much as the pain
of lowering herself onto the toilet with an injured coccyx and—sure enough—when she emerged a little later
her hair was brushed and the smeared eye make-up was
wiped clean.

She still looked gorgeous. Just a different kind of gorgeous.

And he wasn't allowed to appreciate either.

Sera frowned at the bright light piercing through a gap
in the suite's thick drapes. 'What time is it?'

'Time for brunch,' he said. 'It'll be here any minute.'

She grabbed up her robe and shrugged it carefully on
at the discreet knock that sounded at the door. It was their
breakfast—with a generous side serve of official guide.
Eric looked both unsurprised and unconcerned to find him
in here with her.

'I heard about your injury,' he said, walking in behind
the room service who got to work immediately setting
breakfast out on the deck dining area. 'Are you okay?'

'I will be.' Sera smiled, though it was thin, and Brad
guessed she was in dire need of another dose of painkillers.

'Good call cancelling the dune drive today,' Eric said.
'Two hours bumping up and down sand dunes would not
have been fun for you. Though the photo ops might have
distracted you a little.'

Dark eyes came straight to his in silent thanks, then returned to Eric. 'I hope I can book again. I was looking forward to it.'

'Any time. I'm always happy to go up the big dunes.'

'Thanks for checking up on her,' Brad said when conversation dwindled to awkward silence.

'Actually, I come for another reason.' The vaguely uncomfortable expression on Eric's face piqued both their interest. The first time the unflappable guide had looked anything other than totally in command all week. 'An invitation.'

Instinct stiffened Brad's spine. No, no…

'Who from?' Sera asked, stepping forward.

'Actually…' Eric frowned. 'It's from Salim, your camel driver from last night.'

Sera glanced his way for a heartbeat, just in time to catch his glare. 'Oh? That's…unexpected.'

That was what his uncle had grabbed him to murmur so briefly on the sands last night. A family gathering. But to invite a client… This client…

What the hell was he thinking?

Eric looked as curious extending the invitation as he did uncomfortable.

'Here's the thing…' he said, glancing at the wait staff still setting up breakfast on the deck and lowering his voice further. 'Salim is a good man. He could get in a lot of trouble for this, but an invitation in Bedouin culture is a really big deal. So I promised him I would bring it to you personally. To keep it quiet.'

He stepped forward to hand her a slip of paper with the details on it, but Brad got there first.

'If you wanted to protect him, why didn't you refuse his request? This is against policy.'

Which made the gesture as crazy as it was incomprehensible. Though his uncle never did anything without consideration.

But rather than answer him, Eric turned his gaze back to Sera. 'Salim loves what he does and Al Saqr's guests love the experience he offers—no one would win if he was to be removed from service here. His enormous family least of all.'

'You're asking me to keep it secret?' Sera murmured, glancing his way again.

'I'm…' Eric sighed. 'Yeah, I guess I am. I can tell Reception that you have an activity in Kafr Falaj tonight. I can drive you to Salim's camp and back myself.'

Except that Aqil knew Sera couldn't go outside Al Saqr's fences without deportation. So that would only raise suspicion.

'That won't be necessary,' Brad began. 'Sera's too injured to attend.'

Dark indignation swung his way. 'I'm not too injured to sit in a luxury SUV and then have dinner,' she argued. 'He's hardly going to send camels to collect us.' But then the idea seemed to grab hold of her and she turned back to Eric worriedly. 'Is he?'

Brad tried a different approach. 'You don't know him, Sera—'

Never mind that *he* did…

'That's what dinner invitations are for, Brad,' she said sweetly. 'To get to know people.'

'Bedouin hospitality is second to none,' Eric urged. 'It's how their tribes traditionally gathered information to help them thrive. It's practically in their DNA. It really is an honour to be asked.'

'So we're to be held hostage by cultural niceties?' Brad growled at Eric.

But he knew what was really going on. His uncle had excellent networks within the resort; he must have heard about all the cosy meals he'd been sharing with Sera, the whole sleeping-on-the-deck thing. Obviously, he wanted a legitimate opportunity to check things out for himself.

'Please extend our regrets to—'

'I'd love to accept, Eric. Thank you—'

Brad snapped his gaze to hers. 'Sera…'

'—but I can't leave Al Saqr's grounds, so I must very regretfully decline.'

She looked pleased as Punch to have found a tidy way through this dilemma. Except it solved nothing.

Eric's face brightened. 'Salim is an elder of the Bani Khalid tribe. Their lands once included these deserts, so he has traditional land rights.'

She turned her confusion to Brad.

'Salim's traditional camp is inside the fences.' He sighed. 'Over on the far boundary.'

'Well, then…' Her smile was both slow and brilliant as she turned to Eric. 'Please tell Salim I would be honoured to attend.'

'Sera—'

'You don't have to come if you don't want to, Brad.'

'My job is to ensure your safety.'

'Good, then.' Her gaze twinkled way too much for someone who was still in pain. 'I'm sure you'll also be very welcome. I'll vouch for you,' she teased.

The service staff returned from the pool deck and nodded to Eric that breakfast was ready to go. Then they took their leave. A few moments later their crowded little suite was quiet again.

'Curiouser and curiouser,' she said, all innocent Alice, limping past him towards breakfast.

'Why did you say yes?' Brad gritted.

She turned back in feigned surprise. 'Because an elder of the Bedouin asked me to dine. And because I'm unlikely to get an opportunity like it ever again.'

'It wouldn't have anything to do with getting to snoop inside my family some more?'

'Gosh, someone has tickets on themselves,' she muttered, just loud enough for him to hear. But her grin gave her completely away.

'Sera—'

'Oh, Brad, relax. You'll be perfectly safe there. An entire tribe to protect you from my rampant curiosity…' She plonked a pillow onto her seat at the outdoor table and eased her bruised spine down onto it.

Relax. As if that were going to be at all possible once Sera was surrounded by his family.

'That's not exactly what I'm worried about,' he gritted.

Though he couldn't begin to tell her what he was truly worried about. That seeing her immersed into his family's life was hardly a good way to toughen his resolve against her.

She lifted her tired eyes to him and they were filled with offence. 'Your secret is safe with me, if that's what you're worried about. Besides, refusing would have to draw more attention than going, don't you think?'

He sighed. 'The Bedu are interconnected, Sera. Everything I do reflects on my uncle and vice versa. I just don't want the lines crossed. I don't like this.'

But Eric was right about one thing. An invitation was a very big deal. Still, first opportunity he got he was going to call his uncle and find out what the hell was going on. Sera had seven hours in which to discover she really was too sore to go. Maybe sense would win out over stubbornness.

And maybe an inland sea would spring up in the desert overnight.

The desert sun sank just after five p.m. at this time of year, but there was more than enough light as Brad drove them into his uncle's compound to showcase the array of traditional camp tents with their tall, woven roofs and open fronts. With the sun low in the west, the shadows cast by the large tent tops matched almost exactly the geometry of the dunes in the distance behind it, like a model version of the real thing. Interspersed with spotless, late-model four-wheel drives.

'Does Salim's family live here?' Sera asked, craning

from her seat to get a better look at the little tent village. 'In the desert?'

'Some Bedouin have fully assimilated into modern culture,' he said, rubbing at the tension in his neck, 'and others have rejected it. My uncle's tribe straddle both sides; they work and earn a living on the fringes of contemporary society but spend every other waking moment out here on their traditional lands. Today was a rest day for my uncle and his brothers so they headed up-country as soon as they were free to. It's where they can breathe,' he finished, almost sadly.

Sure enough, a half-dozen robed and sandalled men with heads comprehensively wrapped in earth-toned fabrics milled around under the biggest of the shelters, while around the camp scuttled dozens upon dozens of boys and girls.

'Ordinarily, Bedouin women over sixteen retreat to a separate tent when strangers come,' he said, guessing the direction of her thoughts, 'but they do come together on special occasions. My uncle understands I cannot let you out of my sight, so tonight the family will mix. It's practically a festival,' he murmured.

Sera couldn't help the instinctive frown.

'Don't feel too sorry for them.' Brad chuckled. 'Aaliyah says the conversation of the men is intensely dull compared to the quality gossip in the women's tent. I doubt they'll be hurrying to emerge, except perhaps to meet you and assuage their curiosity.'

'Aaliyah?'

'My cousin. A bunch of times removed.'

'How many children does your uncle have?' she asked.

'Three daughters and four sons,' he replied.

That brought her eyes back from the camp around them. And a heart-squeeze with it. Who might she be if she'd grown up with that many siblings? That much noise. That much company.

'That's a lot of mouths to feed.'

'Family is everything in Bedouin culture. Bloodlines are fiercely protected.'

Their SUV bumped along the well-worn sand track and finally pulled between dunes into the heart of Salim's tent village. The man himself strode towards them, arms outstretched.

'If anyone gives you anything, take it,' Brad muttered as she undid her seat belt. 'And eat whatever is put before you.'

She flooded with sudden nerves. Of all the timing…!

'Welcome, my friends!'

Salim offered Sera a strong, weathered hand to help her carefully down from the four-wheel drive. He seemed a completely different man from the one who'd wrangled the camels for them a night earlier. Totally commanding.

'I am sorry to hear of your injury. We will make you very comfortable with us.'

'Thank you for inviting me, Salim. I am…honoured.'

Brad saved her from the awkwardness of the clunky formality by jogging around from his side of the four-wheel drive as her feet touched the sands of Salim's camp.

'Welcome also to my home, Mr Kruger.'

'Save your breath, Uncle. She knows.'

Shrewd black eyes swung back her way.

'Does she indeed? Well, that will make things simpler for everyone. I had little confidence in your youngest cousins.' He snorted. 'They can barely keep their *own* secrets…'

Salim turned back to her. 'Come. Meet my family, Miss Blaise.'

'Please, call me Sera…'

It was such a novelty, being the centre of attention, but not because of who she was or who her father was. Dozens of dark, curious eyes watched her every move. And Brad's. Then a stunning young woman in layers of beautiful fabric approached.

'My eldest daughter, Aaliyah,' Salim introduced. 'She will translate for those in my family who do not have such fluent English.'

In the distance, several shorter, rounder women emerged from a side opening in the tent, fully garbed in darkened robes, and hovered towards the back of the gathering crowd, but Aaliyah was spectacularly dressed in layers of the most stunning green and blue fabrics, with a rich veil of the same kind of intricacy as dragonfly wings draped over her dark hair and curled around below her chin. Two generations of Bedouin women looking vastly different— three if you counted the little girls running around in T-shirts and cut-off denim.

Did Salim mourn the changes to his culture or did he accept that they shifted as steadily as the sands all around them?

For a desert people, the skin of their younger women was luminous, and Sera immediately felt self-conscious both for her height and for the comparative plainness of the scarf that she had purchased in the resort's gift shop to drape around her hair.

The next twenty minutes were a crazy barrage of faces and names she would never remember as they inched their way from their vehicle into the main tent. It was closed on two facing sides and open front and back to promote air-flow, and huge woven mats laid directly on the sand created a soft, comfortable floor. Five low tables surrounded by cushioned seating filled the space and bunched and tasselled rags lined the welcoming face prettily.

It was all very inviting.

The greatest pile of pillows was reserved for her and her wounded coccyx, and she sank into them gratefully. She'd taken pain relief again in the morning but nothing since then. A fully cloaked woman approached and folded a small pot into her hands with her own surprisingly soft ones murmuring in Arabic as Aaliyah translated.

'My mother wishes that you would use this on your injury. It will ease your pain as you sit here with us this evening.'

Salim's wife clearly had little English but gratitude needed no translation, it seemed, and Sera's effusive gushing got the message across. A few moments of mime told Sera what the woman wanted her to do—rub the unguent directly on her lower back—and Aaliyah and her mother stood more closely together so that she could do it discreetly in the mixed company. Pillows to her back, a human screen to her front.

'*Mukhaddir...*' the mother urged.

Sera opened the fragrant pot, took a quick whiff and then scooped a couple of fingers' worth as though it were commercial chest-rub. Then she reached around under her long shirt where no one could see, snagged her trouser band with her clean fingers and tugged it down to apply the sticky mix directly to the base of her spine. Other than a pleasing, cool tingling, nothing much happened at first, but after only moments she began to feel the full effect as the whole area numbed over.

'It is made from *ruta* and pomegranate pulp,' Aaliyah murmured as Sera sighed with relief. 'My family uses only natural medicines and foods. The land gives us everything we need.'

The talent it must take to find much of anything in these sandy mountains...

'Please, thank your mother. I'm so grateful.'

She glanced around for Brad and found him surrounded by the male members of Salim's family, who were all chatting at a pace. But he caught her eye and started easing his way back towards her, strain easy to see in the tautness of his carefully neutral smile. The stiffness of his posture.

Was he still worried for her safety? Even here amongst his own family?

'Are you okay?' she murmured, leaning briefly towards

him as he accepted Salim's invitation to sit and sank down onto the cushions next to her. Immediately people rushed forward with timber platters covered in fragrant, earthy morsels and a big goblet filled with fresh juice.

'I'm fine,' he lied.

Guilt immediately washed over her that she'd forced his hand in coming tonight. Insinuated herself into a part of his life she had no fair right to. Somewhat disguised between the cushions, she stretched her little finger out and brushed it against his in apology. He snatched his hand back reflexively.

Sera straightened and disguised her flush by focusing on Aaliyah's efforts to recall the lingering children into another tent for the evening. But when Salim merely raised his eyebrows in their general direction they all scattered like sand beetles and disappeared behind the intricate weaves. From where they sat, Sera had an excellent view out of the open front of the tent over the golden desert as the sun cast its last light over the sands and it did not take long to soothe the wounded pride out of her.

As soon as the sun vanished, a dozen braziers replaced its warmth inside the tent and fragrant torches were lit outside, and one of Salim's family began to pluck away at a gorgeously carved stringed instrument. The authentic desert music made the perfect backdrop for their conversation. Aaliyah translated all Sera's questions and her family's answers, and made sure she knew what each dish contained as they came out. A cinnamony camel's milk entrée, meat dishes of lamb and antelope, and a constantly refreshed supply of aromatic coffee spiced with cardamom.

'My family are horse and camel-breeders, primarily,' Brad explained next to her. 'That's how they make their staple living. Salim is well known for his talent with difficult horses.'

'You must ride one of my Arabs in the big sands,' Salim announced loudly. 'I will pick you one personally.'

She glanced at Brad, who watched her intently, and suddenly felt the weight of any social slights she might accidentally make. She didn't want to damage the obvious rapport between uncle and nephew.

'I would like that.' Sera smiled. 'As soon as I can sit without wincing. Perhaps you have one that is gentle and patient.'

'We will find one that is also beautiful and courageous. Like its rider.' Salim had the same impenetrable poker face of his nephew and he turned it on him now. 'Do you think that would suit, Bradley?'

Brad looked completely lost for words at his uncle's happy manipulation. Though, he managed one word, at least…

'Certainly.'

Sera sagged back against her cushions, perplexed by Brad's reluctance to pay her any kind of compliment, but more entertained by the obvious mischief in Salim's eyes. Since he wasn't expending it on her. Was it wrong to share this little bit of sport at Brad's expense?

The next half-hour degenerated into a fast and engaging discussion between the men on the relative virtues of four-wheel drives generally and their various models specifically. Then there was a raucous tour outside to the cluster of near-new vehicles parked there including Al Saqr's top of the range SUV.

'The way to a man's heart is through his vehicle,' Aaliyah said as they watched the men go. 'Once, it was camels that were so greatly prized. When our lives depended on them and not on machines.'

The thought of getting caught out on the sands without one ship of the desert or another definitely did not appeal. The sand and sun could suck you dry of all your moisture in a day and leave you no more than a desiccated husk.

The men returned, yet more food was served—this time a delicious meat wrapped in flatbread half-leavened in the ashes of the fire—and loud conversation resumed. Much of it was in the language of the Bedouin and although Aaliyah did her best to keep up she eventually resorted to simply translating the parts that were directed at or about their guests. That gave Sera a chance to breathe. And to just listen. Vigorous argument, cracks of laughter, teasing. She relaxed back against the cushions and enjoyed the energetic vibe.

'Your family are amazing,' she said. 'I've never been to anything like this. There's so much…'

Affection. Intimacy. Love.

'Food?' Brad volunteered, coaxing a laugh out of her.

And as he did, yet more courses were thrust their way—fresh, delicious and mysterious. Sera stopped wondering what was in each dish and just leapt, bruised coccyx and all, into the full cultural experience. She trusted Brad to stop her from eating something she would regret.

Trust.

The thought took her by surprise but, yes, there it was. Actual, earned trust. With her safety, with her diet, and with her bruised bones. She might not know a whole lot about Brad Kruger but some time in the past twenty-four hours it had sprung up between them.

On her side, at least.

'What is this one?' she murmured to Brad as yet another dish was laid before them.

'Lightning,' he murmured.

She turned her confusion to him.

'It's *fagah*. A kind of desert truffle. It is said they form during electrical storms wherever lightning strikes. The electricity changes the very nature of the air and sand and *fagah* are born. The greater the number or severity of desert storms, the greater the resulting harvest.'

It was impossible not to be seduced by his low voice and evocative words.

'Children get intensely competitive hunting for the biggest ones,' he went on, leaning closer into her to be heard over the noise of conversation, 'searching for the telltale fissures in the sand and digging madly to uncover the dessert gem below. In serving *fagah*, the Bedu capture the very lightning to gift it to their honoured guests.'

His words were as close as she'd ever come to the visual richness she experienced in photography. In fact, his vivid descriptions *became* images in her mind, and she longed to go and dig through the sands herself.

And to stay out here forever.

'Beautiful legend,' she murmured as she raised her fork. 'And beautiful food.'

His gaze touched on her like heat. And stayed there. 'So much of this culture is beauty.'

Around them, a passionate discussion sprang up over what had caused more ruin to the Arabian peninsula—the coming of oil, the coming of water or the coming of tourism. Salim eventually murmured to Aaliyah, who stood gracefully and moved to the rear of the tent where another woman met her. Together, they sat on the rugged floor beside the musician as an adolescent boy came out to join him with a piped instrument. What followed was a beautiful four-part song—string, wind and two voices—that needed no translation to hold Sera enraptured.

Afterwards, a less weathered version of Salim stood on his left and began to speak in Bedu, deep and resonant. Without Aaliyah at her side, the words went untranslated but the cadence of the man's speech made Sera think it must be a traditional poem. She let herself sink into his rich tones regardless of her comprehension.

More music followed. Then more stories. Aaliyah returned as Salim himself stood and told a tale in his native tongue. Celebrating the long history of his tribe and how the Arabian deserts were the true homelands of the Bedouin. How they migrated between scarcely fertile areas then moved on and left them to replenish only to return years later. It wasn't hard to imagine this very feast happening out in the middle of the expansive desert. Except perhaps then the dining would have been more meagre. A desert culture was all very romantic until you remembered how close to starving the original Bedouin perpetually were.

Brad gently touched Aaliyah on the hand and took over the responsibility for translating, bending low and close to her ear so she could hear him without disturbing Salim's oratory.

'He's talking about the Bedouin honour code now,' Brad breathed against her ear, causing tiny flutters up her neck. 'It's the basis for their entire social and justice system.'

Sera glanced sideways to watch Brad, whose eyes were on his uncle as he continued. There was respect there, and affection. It glowed rich in his dark eyes. It wasn't hard from there to let her eyes wander over the strong lines of his bearded jaw, over his lips…

'Me against my brothers,' he murmured as Salim postured grandly, clapping his actual brothers on their shoulders. *'My brothers and I against my cousins, but my cousins and I against strangers.'*

Everyone present cheered, and Brad turned back to her and whispered, 'Family is all to the Bedu.'

Then, in a very determined way, Salim turned to Brad and muttered a few more words directly to him.

Ibn 'amm.

Brad pushed to his feet and clasped Salim's right forearm with his left one. The gesture was at once incredibly masculine yet rich with affection.

Sera leaned across to whisper to Aaliyah, 'What did he say?'

'Ibn 'amm means "son of my uncles". He is acknowledging Brad as family.'

'Hadn't he already?'

'Yes, but *ibn 'amm* is more…intimate. He is acknowledging Brad as a kind of son. A son of the Bedu. As my brother.'

Brad's eyes glittered with emotion as the fierce gesture became a manly kind of hug. Everyone around them cheered again. But Sera couldn't join them.

She would never know this much love. This much belonging.

The ache in her heart swelled out through her whole chest.

The shisha came out and the tent filled with the aromatic pleasure of apple-scented tobacco. Right behind that were final coffees. As aromatic and lovely as both were, Sera's enthusiasm for the night had evaporated when Brad had stood and walked to his uncle.

Salim's cue was subtle enough that she completely missed it but everyone else seemed to understand the exact moment the evening was over. Brad helped her gingerly to her feet and suddenly it was all farewells. Sera clung to her little pot of unguent and then found herself loaded down with items to take back to the resort. Some still-warm bread wrapped in plain cloth, a mat woven in the same style as those in the tents, and—from Aaliyah—her scarf.

It was the one thing she baulked at. Even remembering Brad's warning, and even here where beautiful fabrics were so common—such a scarf was too, too precious.

'The only thing that brings the Bedu more pleasure than having a beautiful thing is to gift it to someone else,' Aaliyah assured Sera, unravelling the scarf from her head, pushing it firmly into her hands and folding her fingers over them. 'Sharing our pleasures and hospitality is our greatest pride.'

And then they were off bumping back across the dunes—like Alice scrabbling back up the rabbit hole, or Dorothy waking from Oz—though the road seemed invisible to her in the moonlight. She sagged into the comfortable passenger seat of the SUV and tried to ignore the occasional brush of Brad's knuckles on her leg as he changed gears in the sands.

'Such an extraordinary evening,' she murmured when the comparative silence of the SUV grew too oppressive. Suddenly she had an inkling of how suffocated the Bedouin might feel within the walls of a conventional house. How was she going to eat at a regular table ever again? 'Nothing like I was expecting.'

'What were you expecting?'

Who knew? She couldn't imagine him in any other setting now.

'Your uncle is quite the politician.' She chuckled.

'It is an insult to direct a command to a Bedouin,' Brad murmured, 'so Salim has learned to lead through a careful balance of diplomacy and generosity. He has earned the respect of his people.'

'And his nephew.'

'It is hard not to. He is progressive despite the simplicity of his culture. He believes his children are as much tools of his trade as his animals and sees no reason to let half his tools go blunt by not educating his daughters. Aaliyah is a good example of the wisdom of Salim's approach. She's inherited her father's gifts with horses. Her beauty and her brains will set her in good stead.'

'Good genes obviously run in the family.'

She'd hoped the compliment to earn her a wry smile but it only added an extra line to the fork between his brows.

'Thank you for taking me, Brad,' she said to stop the lingering warmth between them from haemorrhaging out of the vehicle like oxygen from a vacuum. 'It was eye-opening.'

And thought provoking. And it made it a whole lot harder for her to *meep* about her youth when she saw how other young girls were living theirs in this world. They just...got on with it. They accepted the kind of responsibilities they had to their families and let their ambitions align with it. There was a certain desert pragmatism in that that she really liked.

'I didn't *take* you, Sera,' Brad said carefully. 'It wasn't a date.'

Fierce heat flooded her cheeks. 'No, I know that. But you allowed it.'

'The invitation was for you. It wasn't up to me to allow or disallow anything. I'm not your keeper either.'

She turned to face him and spoke carefully. Why was he forcing such distance between them all of a sudden? 'No, you're not.'

His eyes didn't stray off the road ahead once.

'Brad, what's going on? You've been weird since Eric gave me Salim's invitation.'

'Nothing's going on.'

'You were tense tonight. And it can't have been the company.' He must have had dozens of such nights in his years in Umm Khoreem.

But she caught the sideways flick of Brad's eyes. Towards her.

Oh... Unless it *was* the company.

'You're still angry that I accepted?'

'I'm not angry, Sera.'

'Then what—?'

'They are my *family*,' he burst out. 'You invited yourself right into my family. Without a second thought.'

Defence came naturally to her. 'I didn't invite myself, your uncle invited me. If you didn't want me to go you should have said.'

'I'm pretty sure I did say.'

Guilt rushed up under her collar. 'You're reacting like I'm some kind of stalker,' she sputtered. 'It was a dinner invitation, Brad. That's it.'

'It's my family, Sera. You couldn't really have inveigled yourself any deeper in my personal business.'

Inveigled. That was a pretty horrible way of putting it.

'I get that Bedouin propriety means you couldn't order your uncle not to invite me, but it's hardly my fault that he did.'

'You accepted. Even knowing I wanted to keep professional boundaries between us.'

'Oh, please… What is it that you imagine I'm going to do with this new-found intimacy, Brad? Force myself on you?'

Something ground visibly high in his jaw. 'I'm a professional, Sera. I don't get involved with clients.'

'So you keep saying.' Ad nauseam. 'I'm beginning to wonder who you're trying to convince.'

His lips pressed shut and his eyes remained firmly glued to the road ahead.

Conversation over.

Sera turned to study the dark desert outside the passenger window as humiliation swilled through her. She'd just wanted a chance to see the culture up close, when it wasn't on professional show for guests of the resort. And it would have been rude not to accept.

At least, that was what she'd told herself, but Brad's words sat like a heavy meal in her gut. Dense and uncomfortable.

Was she so eager to belong somewhere—to someone—that she had insinuated herself right into his world?

It was hardly a flattering image.

'Just take me home,' she murmured, leaning her hot cheek into the cool leather and staring miserably out at the beauty of the desert at night.

Home.

Funny how that could be a country so far from her own. A resort. A suite.

Or a person.

CHAPTER NINE

BRAD PULLED IN to Al Saqr's vast welcome driveway and leaped out to open her door—because he was paid to, certainly, not because he wished to extend her any kind of courtesy—but her feet found the dark ground well ahead of him.

'I'd like to walk back to the suite,' she said to the night air, not waiting for a response. Or the courtesy buggy. She set off in the direction of home, limping hard and fast.

Brad assumed his usual position—behind her and to her left, a dark shadow in the night. Business as usual, despite the fact they'd sat together and talked and laughed and shared something special this evening.

For her anyway. Maybe nights like tonight were ten a penny to him.

She marched down the gently lit path, ignoring the pleasant night air, wishing she were still ensconced amid cushions and romantic tales and the delicious smell of apple tobacco instead of stumbling awkwardly ahead of a man who believed her to be trying to wheedle herself into his world.

Like some kind of sad cuckoo shoving its way into a nest.

When they arrived at her suite, Brad cleared it silently and then stood back to let her in. The whole room glowed with the gentle light the night staff had left on after preparing her room for the evening. None of the overhead lights were on, only those few built into the wall niches and designed to showcase the interesting artefacts standing in them. The pale colour of the closed drapes reflected the low light around the room while its fabric made the whole place cosy and warm.

And incredibly romantic.

Which only made the sting of the earlier conversation more profound. Would he blame her for this, too? Suspect her of setting some kind of seduction scene?

Silent awkwardness soaked the room like the rich, spreading light.

'I might have my coffee in the pool,' she said just for something—anything—to change the subject. 'My back could use a warm soak.'

He offered no opinion, and no argument. Like a good little bodyguard. 'I'll be right back, then.'

Sera loaded the coffee machine with fresh-ground local coffee and set it to run before padding to the bathroom and changing into her swimsuit. When she emerged on the back deck, steaming coffee in hand, Brad was already there—changed into board shorts and a T-shirt.

'That's going to be chilly tonight,' she commented, glancing at him.

For no reason, she grew instantly self-conscious about his presence. He'd seen her in the pool plenty of times and climbing out of it a few. He'd even *carried* her out of it a dozen short hours ago, but this was the first time she'd had to disrobe in front of him, even if that only meant shrugging out of her wrap. Suddenly the simple act turned into some kind of dance of the seven veils.

Would he accuse her of doing it too provocatively?

'I don't think you have to sleep out here any more, Brad,' she started as he laid out his stuff on the deck lounger he'd been calling his bed. 'I'm not going to go on any more midnight expeditions without letting you know first. I've learned my lesson.'

And she was tired of the energy it took to be around him so relentlessly.

'It's not about that any more,' he murmured. 'I can just be more responsive from here.'

She dipped a toe into the water to test its temperature,

stalling terribly. It was nice and toasty against the cold night air. 'What is it you imagine you're going to need to respond to? Murderous plots? Attempts to abscond? Surely I've earned a little faith by now?'

What the hell did she have to do in this world to earn the respect of men like Brad? Or her father?

'I'm good out here,' he said with some finality, perching on the end of the deck lounger and watching her.

Except that she was good at last words, too. 'And if I insisted? If I *ordered* you to go back to your own suite?'

'I might grow suspicious as to why you were trying so hard to get rid of your protection. And then I wouldn't be doing my job if I left.'

Your stupid job, she said in her head. Aloud, she just muttered, 'Whatever.'

She failed miserably at removing her wrap in an unconcerned way and felt as if she'd only managed to draw *more* attention to herself as she peeled it off and let the long fabric pool onto the deck.

Lamest striptease ever.

She was up to her neck in warm water when she heard him wade in behind her.

'If you go A over T again you could do more than just bruise a few muscles,' he said when she turned to gape at him. He settled himself comfortably on the pool's lowest step, a respectful distance from her.

Being treated like a child had always grated. When she *was* a child it was because people expressed their professional care and concern that way rather than in the good old-fashioned way—loving her. And as an adult... Well, no one liked to be patronised.

'I think I can manage to float in the pool without incident, Brad,' she gritted past her suddenly tight chest. Being angry at him wasn't going to be helped by all that bare, hard flesh.

He shrugged his broad, wet shoulders, and she tried

not to dwell on how the water streamed down them. 'I'm in, now.'

She rested both elbows on the infinity edge of the pool so her spine hung straight and flat, and the deep water supported her as she stretched out her sore muscles. Her fingers stroked the tiles of the infinity edge as though it were Brad's olive skin. Smooth and just as soothing.

'If you're staying, then I want to talk about tonight,' she said, half back over her shoulder.

That should get him running.

Somewhere in the distance a bird shrieked into the night.

'I don't particularly feel like doing a post-mortem on the evening,' Brad finally said. 'But if it's still bothering you go ahead and commence the inquisition.'

That was man code for back off. So, naturally, she stepped forward.

Or turned, in her case. Hanging from stretched arms along the far edge of the pool.

'Of course it's bothering me. You implied that I was some kind of stalker simply because I accepted your uncle's invitation. Like I'd coerced my way into your life on purpose.'

'Didn't you?'

'I didn't go because it was your family, Brad. I would have enjoyed it just as much if it was Aqil's family. Or anyone else's.'

'It wasn't theirs, it was mine.'

Sadness washed through her. 'I thought we'd become friends enough these past few weeks to give each other the benefit of the doubt, at least.'

'We're not friends, Sera. It doesn't work that way.'

'It was working just fine from my point of view.'

'For me, then,' he said, pushing to his feet and stepping towards the pool's middle. 'Is that what you want me to say? It isn't working for me. It's distracting me from my job.'

'How? Nothing has happened. You're doing your job just fine.' Too diligently, at times.

His brows folded down. 'I've seen it before, Sera. Affection is...an emotional distraction. I don't need the complication.'

Before? He'd been in this situation once before?

'A complication?' she challenged, trying hard not to be jealous about whoever it was that earned his affection in the past. Apparently, *they* were good enough to bend the rules for.

'Honey, you are nothing but complicated.'

A tease of hope burst through her. That didn't sound like the words of a man who was *un*affected. She pushed off the pool edge and stroked towards him.

Immediately, his eyes grew wary.

'Tell me about her,' she said as her feet found the tiles on the pool bottom.

'Who?'

'Whoever you got involved with before. Did it end badly?'

Caution closed his face. 'Really? You're wanting into my personal life again?'

'I just want to understand you.'

He rolled his eyes heavenward but it wasn't irritation. He was searching for something. An escape, maybe? 'Why can't you just step back and let me do my job? Why can't you just be a normal, respectful client?'

'I don't really *do* normal, Brad. I thought we'd established that.' His gaze steadied and locked on her. Full of defiance. She drifted forwards again. 'So who was she?'

Impatience singed his tone. 'There was no "she".'

'A "he" then?' She grinned. 'Go you!'

But his grey eyes weren't the slightest bit amused and their seriousness stopped her in her watery tracks. 'Wait... Really? A he?'

Wow. She'd not seen that coming.

'A child,' he was fast to correct. 'Matteo. The seven-year-old son of a diplomat family I was assigned to in Egypt. He and I became friends. A big-brother kind of deal. He looked up to me.'

As any kid would. Strong and brave and exceptional. What was not to love?

She stumbled over the word even though it was only a thought. No one needed to be thinking about *love*…

'What happened?' she asked instead.

'He got hurt. Because I was off my game.'

'Did you miss something?' Hard to imagine. He was so thorough.

'No.' His gaze shadowed over. 'Both his parents were embassy staff, with a contingent of diplomatic security as well. That meant I reverted by default to Matteo's cover most of the time. When he was at school. Out playing. Everywhere.'

'That's a lot of together time.'

He nodded. 'Attachment is always a risk with close contact. He was a good kid. He had a bit of hero-worship going on.'

The affection in his gaze—despite being mingled with pain—made it easy to imagine Brad as the father.

Whoa. She pushed that little piece of deluded thinking aside.

'You're referring to him in the past tense,' she said instead.

'When the unrest got too bad, the UN pulled their diplomats out. But not their forces. We stayed behind to defend the evacuated compounds and facilities.'

'So you had to say goodbye to Matteo?'

'I didn't know how hard he had bonded. When it came time to bug out he just…wouldn't go. He wouldn't leave me behind in danger and my orders prevented me from going with them.' His big body sagged. 'He ran off to prevent the car from leaving. As the rebels were swarming towards the embassy.'

'Oh, Brad...'

He knew where her mind had just gone and was fast to correct her. 'No. I found him. But I had to manhandle him into the SUV. Force him in, screaming. I hurt him, Sera. It was...'

Bad enough, apparently, that he couldn't find a word for it.

'But he made it, yes?' She held her breath. *Please say yes.*

He cleared his throat. 'Sixty seconds longer and he wouldn't have. The shooting started. It was a week before I got confirmation that the whole family had made it out.'

What a week that must have been. Wondering... Fearing.

'I thought I'd gotten them all killed,' he gritted.

'But you didn't.'

He took a moment to control his choppy breathing. Then another.

'It doesn't matter. I learned my lesson that day. The rules exist for a good reason, Sera.'

He stood in the shallow end, rolling his hands in and out of the warm water in a figure-eight, letting the rising steam brush across his skin. It reminded her of the way he'd stroked her hair until she'd fallen asleep last night.

Total contrast to Brad, the tough guy.

'I doubt Matteo would agree with you on that point,' she risked saying. 'I was raised by the book, Brad. It's a pretty lonely way to grow up.'

His frown deepened. 'Sera, just because they kept a professional distance didn't meant they didn't care for you.'

'People can't just opt out of their feelings.' God, how much difference would that have made to her childhood if it were true?

'They can opt out of *showing* it,' he bit out. 'If someone is not theirs to care for.'

Silence settled amongst the mist on the surface of the pool.

'Are you wishing that's what you'd done with Matteo?' she finally murmured, stepping towards him far more gently than her hammering heart demanded. 'Or are you saying that's what you're doing with me?'

He backed away two paces. She felt each footfall as if it were landing on her ribs and not on the bottom of the pool. Story of her life, really…

'Let it go, Sera.'

Did he have no idea how difficult this was for her? To expose herself like this?

'I don't see you climbing out of this pool,' she pointed out on a deep breath. Could he hear the thrum of her heartbeat in it?

Another backward step. Another slam against her chest.

'My job—'

'Is to stand up there in the corner of the deck and watch our environment,' she interrupted. 'Yet here you are, in the pool—' she swallowed '—watching me.'

A dark flush chased above the waterline. 'That's easily fixed.'

But before he could move she cornered him in the shallows, blocking his exit with her body. And like any desert creature, he didn't respond well to being cornered.

'You're not really one to take no for an answer, are you, Sera?'

She held her ground, though every part of her quailed. Some instinct pushed her onward. An instinct she normally ignored.

'Or are you just trying to show everyone in your childhood how wrong they were?'

That knocked her focus. 'What do you mean?'

'That you were worthy of their affection all along.'

A pulse hammered in her throat but it only seemed to flush her blood away from her face. 'Are you saying I'm not?'

'I...' He sighed, trapped in his own desperate scrabble. 'No, that's not what I'm saying. Of course you're worthy of it.'

Her gut clamped down. 'But just not worthy of you?'

'I'm nothing special, trust me.'

Au contraire. 'You think I'm just looking to exorcise a bit of childhood angst by flirting with you?'

Though, really, they were so far beyond flirting...

'I think you need to be honest about what it is that you're proposing here.'

'Do I really need to explain it?'

He'd run out of pool to back into, and she slid her arms up around his slick shoulders and used his own strength to hoist herself up closer to his lips. His Adam's apple practically danced beneath the prickle of dark beard that grew down his tanned throat.

'Do I really need to explain how tired I've grown of fighting the thing that zings around between us?' she murmured.

'Sera—'

'Or how I don't think I've ever felt a connection like this with anyone else...ever? Is that the kind of honest disclosure you are recommending?'

She breathed against his mouth, conscious of every place her long, wet body melded into his warm, hard one. She pressed her lips against the corner of his mouth even as he stood like a stone pillar, completely non-responsive. His mouth tasted of salt water and defiance. Though his lips were lusciously full and soft.

'Do you have any idea how hard it is for me to lay myself open like this? Like a skeleton out in those dunes?' She peered up into his dark eyes. 'Or how it hurts to see you stumbling back away from me?'

Regret blazed across his gaze, but she was not about to accept his pity. She hung there—lifeless—for a moment longer, then used his bare chest to push herself off him and back into the water.

'If one of us has to have a good honest look at their motivations,' she said as she turned away from him towards the steps, 'I don't think it's me.'

'Stop!'

No. She was through hearing his greeting-card thoughts on what she needed to do.

Or be.

Her foot found the middle step, but before she could haul the rest of her sore body up onto it, strong arms banded around her waist and pulled her back into the pool. Like a zero-gravity tango-dip. Water sloshed around her hair and face but Brad wasn't about to let her sink. Besides, you had to swallow water to drown and her lips were too sealed by the astonishing press of his for that to happen. They were firm and whisker-sharp, not a particularly good fit, but even someone as kiss-deficient as she was didn't want an angry—or, worse, *a pity*—kiss.

Both heels of her palms pushed against the slick curve of his shoulders to set herself upright, but he didn't let her go.

'I wasn't backing away to stop *you*, Sera,' he vowed, low, helping her find the pool bottom. But when she did, he still didn't release her. 'I was backing away to stop *me*.'

Helium seemed to fill her body, taking away her pain, even her weight.

'I was stopping for both of us,' she reminded him. 'I was getting out of the pool.'

His grave face pinched. 'I know.'

And then his head dipped towards her again and this time his lips fitted perfectly, they moved perfectly. They stole her breath and thickened her blood *perfectly*. Even the rasp of his trim beard teased her flesh enticingly. Whether from the tight curl of his wet arms around her, the glorious heat and taste of his mouth against her cold flesh, or the sheer shock and exultation of his endless kiss, Sera started to see dark shapes on the edges of her vision. She pulled free and gasped in a life-preserving breath. Then she rejoined him the moment her lungs were replenished. His hands forked up through her dripping hair, holding her face still for the welcome assault of his mouth. She stretched up into his hold, held buoyant by the water, pressing her whole body against his—participating fully, imagining what it was going to be like to tumble together into that massive, cloud-like bed inside and feel his wet weight on top of her.

What it was going to *be* like.

His chest rose and fell with every tortured breath. Eventually he pulled free enough to speak.

'You are an intelligent, creative, beautiful woman,' he murmured against her flesh, and her soul sang almost as much as her skin. But then he set her a little back from him and the sudden distance got her immediate attention. 'And this is one hundred per cent my loss.'

Wait...what?

It took a second for his words to make sense, but while she was still frowning, he hammered his point home by setting her away from him. Well away.

'Go inside, Sera.'

Alone...?

Then it dawned on her what was happening. He'd kissed her. But only for a moment, and now the moment was over. He was already retreating back behind the safe pages of that flippin' book of his. It was like last night's hair stroking—something he did before thinking better of it.

Every rejection she'd ever felt as a kid bubbled back up from the depths where she'd shoved them. She wanted to argue. She wanted to beg. Or scream. Or cajole. But, no, she'd had her fill of being delightful and entertaining and trying to win some hint of genuine affection from the adults around her as she'd grown up. She wasn't about to demean herself now.

She'd already done a good enough job of that by climbing up him like a rat in a flood.

She shrank back from his roasting, cautious regard and forced her heart into that lead-plated place she kept deep inside especially for it.

'Like I said, Brad, maybe it's time for you to go back to your own place at night. I give you my word I won't leave the suite.'

'Sera, listen—'

She crossed her arms over her chest, suddenly cold despite the warm pool water. 'I'm instructing you, as your client, to return to your own suite from now on. Since your professional obligation means so much to you I know you'll comply. Or do I need to call your superiors and get them to instruct you for me?'

A dozen emotions chased behind his eyes—grief, regret, loss, confusion—and finally settled on determination. He was, above all else, a pro.

'Will you be okay?'

Have you broken me for good, you mean?

'You think this is my first rodeo?' she scoffed, though the effort cost her every bit of strength she had left. She'd faced moments like these all through her life. When she'd tried to get close. When she'd been rebuffed... 'If there's one thing I do know how to do it's a fast rebound.'

She pulled herself out of the water, threw her wrap around her shoulders and went to walk into her suite, still dripping. Gorgeous rugs be damned. She needed to be away from Brad, his opinions, and his pity right now.

Before she truly shamed herself.

As soon as the door and thick curtains were secured behind her, she let the soggy wrap fall to the floor and crossed straight to the bathroom, her trembling fingers pressed against her still-tingling lips. There she climbed into the expansive shower, cranked it up to scalding, and stood under it until all the chills had burned away.

The cascading water disguised her humiliated tears and when her sobs grew too loud, she shoved the saturated washcloth into her mouth to muffle it in case the sounds drifted on the silent desert night to the man in the suite next door.

CHAPTER TEN

AL SAQR'S SUV convoy teetered right at the top of a mountainous dune—the biggest as far as the eye could see outside the protected area—as the rising sun threw spectacular light across the entire desert. Easily the most stunning views Brad had ever seen.

Sera should have been enraptured. And her camera should have been out the whole time, clicking itself into an overheated frenzy.

Eric had worked his guts out trying to give her a quality four-wheel-driving experience, but no matter how much the vehicle tilted or how high he took her or how astonishing the vista, Sera barely even raised a brow. Brad couldn't actually see that for himself from where he was in the back seat, but he could tell from the way Eric kept glancing at her in the front and upping the scare stakes, trying to create some impact.

And from the way Eric glanced back at him a few times in the mirror, he was clearly concerned.

Yeah. He'd been concerned, too, but Sera wasn't about to accept that from either of them.

When the three-vehicle convoy finally climbed its way to the top of the highest dune for miles and stopped there for a thirty-minute exploration break, she at least took a half-hearted photo—with her phone. And that was almost worse than not taking a photo at all. Her expensive gear sat untouched in the bag in the front of the SUV.

She should have been all over this opportunity. Or maybe she should have cancelled again. Despite her injury being a day better now. The dunes lay out before them like a long, serpentine spine running all the way to the horizon but that wasn't what Sera was looking at. She only had eyes for one thing. A tiny, solitary Ghaf tree, far below them, at the bottom of this massive dune; a distant speck of green against all that golden blonde sand. Like some kind of lonely bonsai.

'Can I walk down there?' she asked as Eric stepped up next to her, nodding at the Lilliputian tree.

Eric looked to him for permission and he gave the slightest toss of his chin.

'If you follow the ridge down,' Eric told her, 'and then stay in the shade. We'll pick you up on the way down. Careful!' he added as she set off towards the dune's edge. 'It's steeper and farther than it looks.'

Brad immediately fell in behind her, and she stopped him with a firm, resolute hand. But no eye contact.

'I'll see you at the bottom,' she ordered.

He was probably supposed to argue. This was raw desert, full of scorpions and vipers and random sand monsters. But right now *he* was the most clear and present danger to Sera's well-being. So he let her go, and she started stumbling down the dune face.

'If your back gets too sore just raise your arms,' he called after her. Just as swimmers did in the oceans, back home. 'We'll come and get you in the SUV.'

If she heard him she didn't show it, as disturbed sand cascaded ahead of her. He wondered then if giant dunes could have avalanches.

'Start the vehicle,' he ordered Eric as soon as she was out of earshot, 'and if something happens we're going straight down this hill, nose-first. Be ready.'

Eric did as asked and Brad moved to the sharp edge of the dune and locked his eyes on Sera as she picked her way down the vast mountain of sand. He started to sweat a treat standing there, hatless, under the rising sun. Even in winter and even in the morning it still had bite. It took Sera forever to get down, and she got tinier and tinier, reinforcing just how high above the world they were, until finally she reached that desolate tree and sank down against its trunk.

The image was as heartbreaking as it was striking.

Tiny woman against massive world. And very definitely against him.

Being at odds with Sera didn't sit comfortably. At all.

But he only had himself to blame.

The universe had given him heaps of opportunities to do things differently with her. He could have let the authorities deport her back to London after the plane incident. He could have manned up and rebuffed her very first efforts at friendship. Worked harder to maintain professional distance every day since then. He could have stood in the shadows for every one of her meals and taken the same back seat he took today on every one of her activities. He could never have let her affect him at all.

Could have. Should have. *Didn't.*

No—he'd kissed her. How freaking inspired! He'd put his dirty mitts all over her, because that was the kind of idiot he was.

All he'd wanted to do last night was undo the pain he'd seen on her face when he'd backed away from her. It was one hundred per cent pure instinct. Did she seriously not know that a beautiful, wet, virtually naked woman with fire in her eyes striding through the water towards him was the best part of fantasy? And it had scared the stuffing out of him, in that moment, because it had been happening. Because of how much he'd *wanted it* to happen.

And then Sera had seen his hesitation. And he might as well have struck her.

Kissing her was scarcely a better plan, but what kind of a man would he be if he'd let her leave that pool thinking she had somehow repulsed him.

The kind of man that did it just moments later, anyway, a tiny voice scolded.

No. He'd been in that kiss, too. He knew how it felt. How the two of them had combusted despite all the water. He'd stopped it before it had become something much harder to come back from. And he'd stopped it before he'd really done something that his bosses would haul him over the coals for. He'd done what he did best.

Retreat. To the place where things were clear-cut and simple and defined.

No one said you couldn't *want*, just that you couldn't *touch*. His mistake had been in thinking it was kinder to let Sera know how much he wanted.

What had happened after that wasn't kind at all.

Matteo's little face flashed across the morning sky. Mouth agape in silent grief, his damp little fingers pressed to the back window of the UN vehicle as the extraction team raced him away from the embassy in Cairo. Saving his life.

He'd learned nothing from that day.

'If you want to collect any messages or emails,' one of the other guides called out to the guests roaming around on top of the dune, 'this is your last chance. We get full-signal 4G up here. We'll be heading off in a few minutes.'

Brad glanced at his smartphone and saw that he had vastly more signal here than anywhere else in the resort. Made sense since they were closer to the comms satellites here than anywhere else in the desert.

Far, far below, Sera still hunkered down at the base of that one solitary tree, her knees pulled to her chest. As alone and stoic as the tree was. They still had a couple of weeks to go out here, together. In each other's pockets. And no matter how hardened Sera thought she was, she was going to suffer for all of it. Death by a thousand cuts. Unless he did what he was paid to do...

Protect her.

Brad brought his phone up to eye level, framed it with

his keypad on the right and her distant, huddled form on its left and did the most decent thing he could.

He hit two on his speed dial.

For a big man with a heap of presence, Brad was pretty proficient at turning invisible. He tailed her everywhere his job description said he had to, but otherwise he kept a low profile all day after the duning and just let her be. He lurked in the shadows at breakfast and lunch, he left her to her thoughts in her suite, he kept a more than respectful distance when she went for walk.

Of course, proficiency was kind of his reason for being in this world, right? It was what floated his boat.

And what sank hers.

As 'it's-not-you-it's-me' speeches went, his had been pretty spectacular.

...one hundred per cent my loss...

Kissing her might not have been the most conventional let-you-down-easy technique but it had at least served to befuddle her mind enough that she didn't put up much of a fight. So in that regard it was fairly effective.

'Sera...'

He sank down in the chair across from her in the restaurant, grave focus on his handsome face, and the succulent bite she'd just forked into her mouth turned to ash. Something about his expression made her want to sit down. Except she already was.

'I wanted you to hear it from me first...'

Her breath immediately tightened. 'Is it Dad?' she croaked.

The clutch of fear and the flash of childhood memories between the thumps of her heart reminded her of how much she had to lose, even if Blaise hadn't always been the father of the year. He had his own protection detail, too, but they couldn't be everywhere, right?

'No, no,' Brad was quick to reassure and managed to look pained all over again. 'He's fine. Sorry.'

But he couldn't hold her gaze and he resorted to a kind of half-hearted scan of the perfectly secure restaurant to poorly disguise it.

Ice-cold crystals of certainty began to form in her chest cavity. Here it came...

'I've been reassigned,' he said simply. 'It's effective immediately.'

The crystals crackled with every challenging breath in and out. Did he seriously believe his lie wasn't totally transparent? That she would fail to grasp the incredible coincidence in timing? No, he'd *asked* to be transferred. To get away from the pressure she'd stupidly put on him.

Her gut balled up around the dinner she'd barely started, but he was giving her a vaguely gracious out and she wasn't going to pass up the chance to save some shred of dignity.

If it wasn't too late.

'You're in demand,' she squeezed out and hoped it came across lighter than it felt.

'It's a good opportunity,' he murmured. 'Some US corporates heading out to the Sheikh's oilfields.'

'That's a step up from babysitting.'

His big shoulders sagged. 'Sera—'

'No! It's good. It's the kind of work you prefer. Congratulations.' Consonants and vowels had never cost her so much. Nor sounded so hollow.

'My replacement arrived an hour ago. He's settling into my suite. I'll do a full handover with him tonight and head out first thing.'

'Hope he likes sharing a bed.' She couldn't quite muster up a chuckle. Her lungs wouldn't expand enough for it.

'I'll take the deck lounger one last time.'

Last time... Inner Sera whimpered. Her breath grew uneven. 'Your deck or mine?'

Grey, steady eyes bled regret. 'I wouldn't mind getting one last look at our oryx.'

Our oryx. Just how pathetic was it that she would wake early every day from now to see it, too, simply because they had it in common? And it would remind her of Brad. Until she left anyway, then what would she have?

The awful reality of what he'd just told her started to sink in. If only she'd kept her temper last night, if only she hadn't let the pain leak out all over him. If only she hadn't thrown herself at him then Brad might not be leaving now. She'd made it virtually impossible for him to stay, really, by compromising the professional integrity he valued so highly.

How could she be angry with someone for acting in accordance with their principles? Principles were what she respected most about him. His ethic and passion.

Just not when it meant he had to leave tomorrow.

It was only when her time had prematurely run out that she realised what two more weeks would have meant to her. And what the past couple weeks had. How a simple fortnight could feel like half a lifetime…when it was over. And it was only when she realised *that*, that it occurred to her what Brad had come to mean to her.

He would return to his apartment in Kafr Falaj and his schmick new assignment, and she would return to London, to whatever lingered of the press storm she'd fled, and to her father. Half a world away. And she would never see Brad again. Her only avenue to him was through the Sheikh, and the head of security for a gazillionaire royal was hardly about to divulge the personal information of one of his personnel. No matter how nicely you asked.

But asking Brad to stay in touch was not an option.

She at least had that much pride.

The futility and powerlessness of that began to gnaw. She wanted to panic but she wanted to stay dignified, too. The reality was that two weeks was *not* a half a lifetime…

it was just two weeks; and they would have faced this moment soon enough anyway. At New Year when she was due to leave. Just because a man kissed you half to death didn't mean he wanted to kiss you until he was old and grey.

They were never going to get happy ever after. Brad had just brought it forward a little.

'I'll be sorry to have to break another you in,' she said. *Don't go...*

He flashed her that twisted smile that was his speciality. 'Think of the fun you'll have messing with the new guy's head.'

'Salim will be sorry not to get to show off his horses.' *Please, don't go...*

'He'll live.'

She straightened her cutlery either side of her plate until it was perfect, then murmured to the tablecloth, 'Thank you for taking such good care of me.'

Don't leave me...

'It was my pleasure, Sera.'

Not what she'd meant. Somehow in the past two weeks Brad had done more for her aching heart than anyone in the years before it, without even trying. Despite the dismal ending. Kind of patched it over. Made it slightly better.

Or maybe that was just hope. Wasn't that what she'd started to let herself feel? Believe?

That maybe this time things were going to work out.

But then a tanned hand slid into view and over her own. It drew her gaze upwards.

'Sera,' he started, a deep, pained shadow behind his eyes. Of course he was feeling it, he wasn't an unkind man. She couldn't love an unkind man.

Oh, God...

'You're going to be fine,' he assured her through the ringing of realisation in her ears. 'Dwayne is a good operator.'

But she couldn't find the words to reply. Everything

inside her was too busy spinning at the enormity of what she'd just realised.

I think I might love you.

He pushed back from the table at her silence. 'Okay, I'll leave you to your dinner. When you wake up tomorrow, Dwayne will be on duty and I'll be gone.'

Her pulse kicked into a panic at the very thought of him disappearing into the desert, or the city or some oilfield. Of being entire oceans away from her. Anonymous and untraceable. But life had prepared her well for this moment; she'd cared for people before and watched them move on, so she'd had plenty of practice. But it still wasn't easy to not say what her head and heart were screaming.

I love you.

'Okay.'

And then—on that pathetic parting croak—it was done.

Brad was up and back standing in the shadows doing his job and she was left to hold it together while he watched. Excruciating! The harder she tried to master her breathing, the choppier it became until the intolerable fear that she'd break down in tears in front of him and everyone else in the restaurant prompted her to fold her serviette onto the table and stand up. She waved away the concerned staff, assuring them the meal was faultless as always, and hurried past them for the nearest exit. Hiding in the bathroom wouldn't do anything to quell the tornado of emotion churning through her—she needed to be free…moving… not trapped in a small space with Brad waiting outside the door.

Witness to it all.

He practically had to jog to keep up with her furious pace back along the pathway, and she couldn't hear his soft footfalls, but she didn't turn around, didn't try to speak to him. She knew he was there. Exactly when had she become able to *sense* his presence? She fumbled the key at the door to her suite but slipped in and closed it hard behind her

before Brad could step forward from the shadows to clear
the room. Then she killed the suite's nightlights, climbed
into bed fully clothed and pulled the covers up to her chin
in the pitch darkness.

As fortified as she could get in this wide-open place.

CHAPTER ELEVEN

BRAD STORMED AROUND the luxury suite at midnight, shoving his belongings into his bag as he found them. The beauty of travelling light—it only took minutes to pack again. Lucky he'd done what he had to do by phone earlier that morning, because sitting in that restaurant looking at the watery courage in Sera's eyes as she desperately tried to hang on to some dignity, he wasn't sure he would have been able to follow it through.

But he needed to be gone from this assignment.

Sera was too precious and too fragile a creature to withstand him stomping around finding his way with her. He was a soldier. Destroying stuff was his speciality. She needed someone more rock-solid to watch over her. Someone with more discipline.

Someone with some personal fortitude.

She'd been let down by every man she'd ever known. What made him think he'd be any different?

He'd already proved he couldn't be trusted with fragile hearts.

Lucky for him Sera had more strength than she suspected, because if even one of those tears she'd been holding back in the restaurant had tumbled down her cheek he would have been a goner.

He paused in the middle of the suite, staring blindly at the items he'd shoved in his duffel, his eyes locked on one in particular. A rolled-up watercolour he'd found tucked away in the back of the resort's little shop of Arabian curiosities. Some artist who had painted Omar while staying at Al Saqr. A beautiful work that somehow captured the bird's vulnerability as well as his essential strength.

It had reminded him immediately of Sera.

He'd bought it for her in one of his undisciplined moments. Because he'd wanted to give her one positive Christmas memory, at least, to hold to her heart.

But instead of saving Christmas, he'd just added to her litany of sucky associations. Future Sera wasn't going to remember the beautiful deserts of Umm Khoreem or Omar or the gorgeous light that she'd discovered this December. She was going to remember the fool who'd rejected her already bruised heart. Who'd kissed her then coldly turned his back.

He hadn't saved Christmas for her at all. He'd pretty much nailed its coffin lid shut.

Outstanding work, Kruger.

And this was why he couldn't have nice things.

Behind him, a strong fist sounded on his door just once, and he crossed to open up to Dwayne Cooper, Sera's new protection. Dwayne was exactly what Sera needed. A pro. A good and loyal operator. He'd been doing this most of his life and he'd never done anything more than his job.

Dwayne wasn't going to make Sera feel any better, but he sure as hell wouldn't make her feel any worse.

It was hours before Sera heard him again, but she was still dry-eyed and awake after Brad finished his handover with the new guy and her ears immediately heard the soft fall of his boots as he stepped up from the desert sands onto her deck. The deck lounger creaked a little as he sank down into it for what was left of the night and then all was silent again outside.

By the time the curtains started to glow with the telltale arrival of dawn, her arms were cramping and her fingers had fully seized up. She imagined their oryx—all aslosh with pool water—pootling back down the dune front to join its fellows for the day, and Brad sitting up murmuring his final farewells to it.

It was hard not to whisper a few of her own.

The deck lounger squeaked, boots gently touched down on the deck and then—just moments later—there was a soft knock at the glass door. Barely more than the scratching of some kind of wild creature. She remained frozen in her feather fortress until the scratching ceased. Then the footsteps tracked around the suite, stepped off the deck and were gone. In the heightened silence, she heard two deep voices speaking low somewhere nearby and an eternity later a pair of heavier boot falls on her deck. A heavier creak on *Brad's* deckchair. And the slurp of coffee.

He was *a slurper*, this new guy.

Inexplicably, that was what ended her emotional siege. Brad had never slurped. He just sipped. He tasted and appreciated his coffee. He valued it. He knew what mattered in life.

Unlike Sir Slurps-a-Lot out there.

'Hey!' she said, flinging the door open to a surprised stranger.

Dwayne practically tipped his coffee all over his immaculate suit in his haste to get to his feet. 'Morning, Ms Blaise—'

She ignored his greeting.

'How much trouble is he going to be in with the Sheikh for not finishing this job?' she demanded.

To his credit, the guy didn't even pause. Or pretend to misunderstand. 'None.'

Really? 'He made it seem like such a big deal.'

'He quit, so it doesn't matter what they think.'

'What?'

'He and the boss mutually agreed to wind up his contract.'

No. That wasn't right. Work was everything to Brad. Work and reputation. He couldn't just chuck it in. Not over her. She was not going to be responsible for another good man losing his job.

'What time is his pickup?' she cried, dashing back inside.

'N-now,' he stammered. 'He's going home right now.'

Home. To Australia? Somehow that felt even farther away.

'I need my guide!' she called out, hauling on a pair of jeans over her little pyjama shorts and not caring that a stranger watched. 'And his SUV. Now!'

It took Dwayne just a moment or two to discover that Eric wasn't on until six a.m. and he reported that as he hung up her phone. 'They're sending someone else to get you.'

'No time to wait for a buggy pickup. I'll meet them at the vehicle.' She hopped out of the door, tugging a second trainer on, and set off in the direction of the resort's reception.

'Someone' turned out to be Aqil, who sat perched in one of Al Saqr's SUVs like an adolescent boosting a car that was way too powerful for him.

He looked totally ready for adventure.

'Can you drive this thing?' Sera called, leaping in beside him. Dwayne climbed straight in at the back, though he didn't look entirely pleased to be there. He was probably used to taking shotgun.

'More or less.'

Good enough. 'Floor it.'

He did, but the distant dust plume that was Brad's ride was very distant and they didn't seem to be making any headway in catching it. And if he reached the highway then she would lose him because she could hardly run through the International Airport in a low-cut pyjama top. Barely in England. Absolutely not here.

Not unless she fancied a second round with the authorities.

'Can we go off road?'

'Not if you want to catch them.' Regret-filled brown eyes glanced at her, as though she was the first person he'd ever failed. 'I'm sorry.'

Once again Al Saqr's immaculate training meant their staff needed no explanation and Aqil caught on pretty quick. He fumbled with one hand in his pocket and tossed Sera his mobile phone. 'Please press four.'

The polite request was so ridiculously at odds with a woman still in her pyjama top and a bear of a man in a dark suit forcing him to drive like a getaway driver, she found it impossible not to laugh. She set the phone to speaker and pressed the keypad. Someone answered in the local tongue. Aqil fired off a reply that was equally unfathomable. A question back and again and a spray of incomprehensible but lyrical Arabic, then he signed off and nodded at her to disconnect the call.

'The security guard will hold them.'

Of course! She'd totally forgotten Al Saqr's high-security entrance. 'Oh, I could kiss you, Aqil.'

His delighted dimples flashed but he didn't slow down. He was Guest Liaison and not a guide—he probably didn't get all that many chances to drive the company vehicles like a rally pro. They bumped and bounced over the compacted sand, then onto the limestone, and finally onto the asphalt. Just moments later, the boom gate and massive fences came into view. A black SUV sat there patiently idling in front of the lowered boom, the driver and security guard leaning on the boom gate, having a casual conversation while they waited.

As Aqil applied the brakes Brad got out of the back of the SUV, a deep frown scoring his face, and turned towards them. He braced his whole weight on two slightly spread feet, ready for anything. It was only at the last minute that Aqil slowed and then pulled to a gentle stop as though they'd been out for nothing more than a Sunday drive.

'What the hell, Sera?'

His words were for her but his dark frown was for Dwayne, who followed her out of the bigger vehicle.

'I didn't get to say goodbye,' she said simply, suddenly

stunningly self-conscious about the four pairs of male eyes witnessing this scene. And her pyjama top.

'I knocked.'

'I know. I ignored you.'

He shook his head. 'So you thought an early morning heart-starter was in order?'

Her colour was high. She could feel it in her own cheeks.

'Stay,' she blurted. And it stunned him into silence. 'I'll hire you privately, to stay...here.'

With me, she couldn't quite bring herself to say.

'Al Saqr's a little out of my budget,' he hedged and the fact he did nearly robbed her of the courage she needed to spread her ribs wider.

'You can stay in my suite,' she breathed. 'On the deck or...not.'

God. She was just terrible at this. But didn't she have to take a risk at some point? Or was she going to let fear keep her cowed forever? Brad was not Mark. The way she felt when she was with him was like nothing she'd ever known before.

Tiny forks appeared at the corner of both eyes. 'I can't, Sera.'

Was he going to cite the local law at her as she had once with him? Because she was more than ready to commit another crime if it meant she got a second chance with Brad. And there was always a first time for him...

She kicked up her chin. 'I'm not worth breaking a few rules for?'

'I'm not...I can't...' Breath hissed out of him. 'I don't want to hurt you any more than I already have, Sera.'

Just when she'd felt sure her new-found courage would be rewarded. Did the universe not realise how difficult it was for her to open herself up like this? But having started, she couldn't stop. Too much rode on it.

'Then what's stopping you? Because it's sure as hell not your job. Dwayne told me you've quit the Sheikh's team.'

Angry eyes swung towards Dwayne, who very carefully kept his focus on the horizon. Like a trained pro. But when Brad's came back to hers, they weren't harsh. Quite the opposite.

'I think I'm stopping me, Sera,' he murmured.

It was the pain that got her attention; it shadowed his gaze and thickened his voice. His leaving would hurt her, but staying was hurting him. Somehow. And she didn't want to hurt him. But she had to understand. And she would never forgive herself if she didn't try just one last time.

'Some things are more important than rules, Brad. Aren't they?'

His eyes were filled with sorrow. 'Some things are, yes.' Oh.

Awful, horrible awareness came into focus the way the desert sharpened around her as the sun rose each morning.

Some things were more important than rules. But she wasn't one of those things.

The fact she was so unprepared for that answer was almost a greater surprise than hearing him say it. Had she really learned nothing from her past? The whole work cover was just to save him from having to hurt her feelings by rejecting her outright.

He'd lied to protect her.

Of course he had. That was his job.

'I'm not a good fit for you, Sera. I'm not...' Words seemed to elude him. 'I can't be responsible for your emotional well-being.'

Everything in her froze.

Was she that much of a basket case? That he didn't want to be anywhere near her? Was she just too high maintenance?

'Okay...' Her voice was deeper than she wanted.

'Sera—'

'No!' Her arms curled around her torso to rub her bare arms. God...she'd chased him. In her pyjamas. With witnesses. 'You should go, then. I get it. I'm sorry that I pressured you to stay. That was unfair of me.'

He shrugged out of his coat, transferred his wallet into his trousers pocket and draped the coat around her shoulders to give her some warmth. And some very overdue modesty.

'There's no pressure, Sera. Don't let this set you back—'

No. She could not stand here and listen to a man who was rejecting her lecture her about how to handle rejection.

She could only bend so much before she'd break.

So she just nodded. And backed away.

'We had a safe word,' she joked, miserably, trying to make the pain go away. 'You should have just used it.'

His deep eyes softened almost unbearably and his big hand came up to brush her cheek as he killed her soul.

'Capsicum,' he murmured.

It meant *goodbye*. It meant *I'm sorry*. And it meant *it's over*.

It took everything she had not to let the sob that broke within her actually come out. But her body jerked as it imploded painfully and silently inside. She didn't call out a farewell as Brad ducked his head back into the SUV. She didn't wave as the boom lifted and he set off again, airport bound. She didn't cry as all three of them bumped, slow and silent, back up Al Saqr's endless driveway because she was too emotionally hollow to feel much of anything. She just tucked Brad's coat more closely around her and buried her nose into it, letting the slight hint of his scent comfort her.

Yay. That had to be a new personal low.

CHAPTER TWELVE

HAD SOMETHING HAPPENED to the light out here? Maybe the seasons were changing as Christmas Day loomed? Eric had answered politely in the negative, and assured her that last week's light was much the same as this week's.

Except that nothing else about the past seven days was the same as the weeks before it.

Dwayne had settled easily into the role of desert protector, and she had managed to settle obediently into the role of protec*ted*. Compliant and co-operative. Dwayne must have wondered if he was monitoring the wrong woman; she was nothing like the one that Brad had probably warned him about in his handover. The two of them spoke, but nothing interesting. He smiled and laughed on cue but it was always respectfully hollow and Sera never really felt like joining him. Or teasing him. Or challenging him. Or watching him swim, shirtless. Until she wondered how much of her day-to-day interaction with Brad had actually been foreplay in disguise.

Had his leaving even sucked the golden out of this beautiful place? She flicked through the images on her laptop and tried to compare them dispassionately. On screen, the sunrises were just as blazing, the mountains loomed equally powerfully and the light was still rich and gorgeous. She flipped the lid shut on a hiss and stared out.

So it was just her, then.

'Time to go,' Dwayne said, knocking firmly as he nudged open her front door.

That was his style. He never came in except to clear the room. He never camped out on her deck. He never engaged as she undertook the daily desert experiences. Which was fine because she didn't want that from him.

But, Lord, how she missed it. The desert now felt as isolated and empty as Brad had warned her it could be.

'What are we doing, again?' she asked Dwayne distractedly as she rose and moved towards the door. He'd reminded her the night before but whatever he'd said was gone now.

'Archery.'

Good, she was just in the mood to shoot something. Lots of somethings. Fortunately for her and her terrible aim, the archery field had nothing but a big, empty sand dune behind it, so when she missed—and she surely would— her arrows wouldn't go whizzing towards anything with a pulse. Her mood wasn't so dark she wanted to start killing the wildlife she'd come to adore.

In her mind, Brad chuckled at her joke.

Sigh. There he was again.

It really didn't take much; the vaguest connection and some Brad-related memory managed to sneak through her shields the same way sand got into everything here. Never mind that she had a lifetime of memories before Brad, it seemed that her recall was firmly fixed to the two weeks she'd known him.

It was crazy. And a little bit sad. And she hoped it would stop soon.

Was this what a break-up felt like? You had to be in a relationship to break up from it, didn't you? And you had to be open to people for relationships to form. What would have happened if she'd been braver? If she'd let herself be open to the affections of others despite the risk of losing it? Maybe she'd have had more joy in her young life. Maybe she'd be married with a dozen kids by now. And maybe she wouldn't be as high maintenance as she apparently was.

Or maybe she'd just have had more loss.

There was one very obvious upside to being closed down, emotionally...

Dwayne gave her his arm, needlessly, to help her into

the low buggy that came for them but she took it anyway because she just didn't have the energy to protest. The archery range was lovely, tucked in on both sides by Sidr trees filled with the pendulous, scrappy nests of tiny birds and backlit by the morning sunrise. Dwayne retreated to a guest bench in the distance and left her with Eric, who took her through her archery basics.

She glanced at him briefly.

Eric was a good-looking guy. Maybe she could be open to Eric and maybe he'd fill that empty place inside her just as Brad had? Although Eric's job depended on his professional relationships with his guests.

Pfff... Story of her life.

She really needed to start meeting some men who weren't paid *not* to get involved with her.

'Robin Hood is total rubbish,' Eric said to her quietly while demonstrating the traditional Arabian archery technique, working hard to draw her attention. 'Carrying a quiver of arrows on your back would have been impractical and slow as you bounced around on horse or on foot. Arabian archers wore arrows at their hip and armed with three or four at a time for rapid firing.'

She should have been spellbound. It *was* fascinating. But all Sera wanted to do was get to the good part. The part that would make her feel better.

'Can I just shoot something, Eric?' she said. 'I'll come back another day for the history.'

He looked at her, long and hard, but took no offence. In fact, whatever he saw in her face put a gentle kind of understanding on his. He was out here alone at Christmas, too, after all. So, they jumped straight to the firing part. It took her no time to learn enough to get it roughly right and—just as she'd imagined—the cold, slow precision with which she loaded, drew and fired at the distant target rings suited her mood perfectly. Every distant *thwack* brought her a sore kind of satisfaction deep in her chest.

Like pushing your tongue on a toothache until you winced.

'Wow,' Eric said, staring at the cluster of arrows peppering the distant target. 'Remind me never to cross you.'

When she ran out of her own arrows—and then Eric's—Sera moved into the shade as he jogged down and collected them all back up for a rerun. Only a few of them were buried to the fins in the sand dune behind the target. That was vaguely satisfying.

'Listen,' he said as the biting sun forced them to pack up. 'You've done every activity we offer…'

He wasn't kidding—ballooning, dune drives, nature walks, falconry, spa experiences, souk visits, camel rides, astronomy, even the half-day caving special. A busy mind was a sane mind, right?

She laughed but it was empty.

'Except one,' he continued.

She turned her face up to his. 'Really? What did I miss?'

'The desert dinner.'

Instant ache returned to her gut, undoing all her positive archery therapy. 'That's a couples' thing.'

'You don't *have* to be a couple to participate.'

'I'm not going to make your staff lug all that gear out into the desert and cook for one.'

'Look, Sera, it's romantic, yes. But the desert is beautiful at night and it's Christmas Eve tonight. That's why I thought of you. You can't sit alone in your suite on Christmas Eve.'

Uh…yeah, she could. She'd seen in a lot of Christmases that way.

But the thought of doing another one like that suddenly did seem unbearable. She could fake it the rest of the year, but Christmas really put a spotlight on how alone she was. Made it very hard to ignore. Or deny. At least this way she could have a unique experience. Something to fondly look back on for future Christmases. If she ever found the courage to think of these weeks again.

'Can they do it without the towering torches?' she hedged. Giant candles would do nothing to reduce the glaring *non*-romance of the occasion.

'Not if you want to see. And keep the vipers away.'

'What about ditching the cosy camp table for two, then?' Nothing said *alone* quite like an empty place setting opposite.

'We can do that. A couple of cushions on the rugs instead. And a telescope. We wouldn't normally include it but you're such a long-stay guest, management have okayed pretty much anything where you're concerned.'

She gnawed her lip.

'In my experience,' he murmured, 'nothing heals as fast as perspective. How tiny and short our lives are compared to the great carousel of worlds around us.' He casually hiked the archery gear up under his arm. 'Anyway, think about it and let me know by noon.'

He turned and was halfway to where Dwayne now stood waiting when she called out.

'I don't have to think about it, Eric. It sounds amazing. Count me in.'

She couldn't mope forever.

Al Saqr's staff simply weren't going to let her.

Eric's smile was almost relief. Maybe a sad guest was an untenable challenge to him.

Dwayne shadowed her back to the resort's hub for breakfast and, on the way, they saw the morning camel trek returning in the distance. She'd seen Salim just once since Brad left and he'd nodded politely but not managed eye contact. As if she held no real interest now that she had no connection to Brad.

Ugh, everywhere she went…

Breakfast was stunning as always and she forced herself to dig into the plate of scrambled eggs liberally dosed with goat's cheese and red pepper. Her fork stuttered as she realised...

Capsicum.

And suddenly Brad was intruding again.

Okay, she thought, slamming her cutlery down, *this has to stop.*

Not only was it infuriating to have no control whatso-ever over her own mind but she really wanted to go back to enjoying her food.

She spent the rest of the day lounging around her suite, reading, thinking, enormous parts of it just staring at the sand and losing time. She purposefully had an early lunch since her evening meal was timed to coincide with sunset, and as the sun drew closer to the horizon Dwayne tapped on her door to rouse her for the desert dinner experience.

For one.

Eric ferried her out towards the sinking sun to a place in the sands where a number of rugs were laid out, piled high with cushions. Four torches already burned at north, south, east and west of the little camp and covered dishes sat, waiting, on a beautifully carved plinth gently surrounded by perfect glass baubles. The kind you'd normally hang on a tree. It was such a gentle and culturally appropriate nod to Christmas it was hard not to appreciate it. She reached her fingers out and brushed them along one smooth, glassy edge remembering the designer ones that had hung on her father's enormous tree back home.

Somewhere deep inside she'd hoped that travelling to somewhere they didn't do Christmas would protect her from the loneliness she associated with it. But who was she kidding? The loneliness just travelled with her. It was all she'd ever known.

And that wasn't going to change all on its own.

There were more baubles in the ornate cooler box set off to one side. Pretty carved ones this time, buried in amongst the water, wine, and the juice she'd gone so crazy for since arriving. And there was a bottle of champagne nestled in there, too.

Yeah…that wasn't going to get any love tonight.

She glanced back over to the SUV parked at a discreet distance and saw Eric and Dwayne within, each holding something that could have been water or it could have been beer. She was hardly going to begrudge them the latter on Christmas Eve. Or make Dwayne stand out on the sand, parched, while she enjoyed a lovely dinner. She poured herself a juice and wandered over to the low-range telescope Eric had set up.

The stars could be her company tonight!

She peered off into the desert's far distance with the telescope while the sky was still light, slowly working her way back in, stopping now and again for small curiosities. She saw a group of Al Saqr's guests on a guided sunset nature walk and Salim on some kind of private exercise with just two of his camels and one guest plodding through the sand beside him.

And oryx, of course, everywhere. Migrating to their nocturnal foraging grounds.

As soon as the beautiful sunset concluded, she doused the two largest of her torches—and kidded herself it was to improve her view of the heavens and not lessen the romance—then returned to her rugs and just sat, listening to the vast nothing, a woven wrap around her to keep her warm. Breathing in the natural, sweet air. Smelling the fragrant oils that burned in the remaining torches. It was all very…Arabian. She knelt in front of the plinth and uncovered all the dishes, then filled her plate with the tasty treats. Some she already knew, some were new. The sorts of offerings the three Kings of the Orient might have eaten as they tracked a bright star. Christmassy yet…not. It reminded her of the celebration at Salim's camp and she half wished for the apple-flavoured shisha and Salim's son on his twangy instrument in the background.

But eating alone never took very long, so Sera stretched the evening out by lying on the rugs between snacks and staring up at the endless starry blackness above.

Thinking.

So many stars. The closest were suns in solar systems much like our own. Some were the combined light of distant galaxies full of suns. Yet others were the combined light of galaxy-filled universes so far away it was nearly incomprehensible. She reached out a fist beside her and curled it full of sand, then let the sands escape through her fingers, luxuriating in the soft sensation as it filtered through the gaps in her grasp. There had to be as many worlds out there as grains of sand in this desert. Billions upon billions. How many of them had life that we would recognise? How many of them were home to bipedal apes who'd built civilisations and achieved space flight and conquered the diseases that constrained their population? How many of them had deserts, and teeny, tiny people having a lonely Christmas Eve dinner right now under the gaze of a trillion other worlds?

How many of them hurt as much as she did?

The heavens turned right through the delicious fruity pudding she eventually remembered to serve herself—another nod to the season. And still she lay there in the torchlight, the solid comfort of the earth at her back and the mind-bending vastness of space in front of her. With nothing but her own breath in her ears.

Except that wasn't entirely true; from beyond the visible circle cast by her torches, she could hear a kind of chuffing that she recognised from the oryx that visited her pool each morning. She slowly pushed upright. Wild oryx were less wild within the reserve's fences but they still had very sharp horns that she didn't want to get on the pointy end of.

Then, the chuffing became a grunt and she heard the distinctive plod of enormous feet on sand.

Camels.

Did they have free-ranging camels within Al Saqr's lands? She glanced over to where the SUV sat in the same darkness that surrounded her and she threw Dwayne and Eric an urgent look, trusting that they would notice.

And then the camels came…two of them, right on the edge of the torch's circle of light. All legs at first but then someone gave a whistle and the one in front kneeled awkwardly, protesting, followed closely by the one behind.

'Salim?'

She knew him by his manner with the camels and by his height on the edge of the shadows. Lovely to see him but …why? No one had told her a night camel ride was part of the desert-dinner experience? She wasn't really dressed for it.

Salim nodded but came no closer. Instead, he turned and glanced behind him anxiously as if waiting for something to happen.

Suddenly, every warning Brad had ever given her about bad guys on camels came rushing back. Where were Dwayne and Eric? Anything could have happened to them out there in the darkness and she wouldn't know. But surely if someone was going to make a grab for a celebrity's daughter they'd do it by vehicle, even here in the desert? Still, she bent her knees on instinct and readied herself for a dark, desert dash. However short-lived it might be.

God, she wished she'd paid more attention to the direction they'd come out here in.

'It's okay, Sera. You're safe.'

Lucky her legs were already bent. It saved them from buckling as Brad's voice carried to her in the half-darkness. His tall, strong silhouette followed it into the circle of light as he strode towards her out of the darkness like some kind of mirage.

Or desert delusion.

Everything in her squeezed up hard. 'Brad?'

Probably not as welcoming as he might have hoped. But that was what you got for scaring the stuffing out of someone.

'Were you expecting some other camel-mounted stranger in the dark?'

'I wasn't expecting anyone.'

'Sorry for the subterfuge,' he murmured, stepping up to the edge of the area designated by the torches.

It physically hurt to look at his face again.

'I didn't know if you'd come, otherwise.'

Even now, her instinct to protect herself was strong. All she wanted to do was fling herself at him, but she forced her feet to stay rooted in the sands within the torched area. As though light could keep her safe.

'What are you doing here? I thought you were in Australia.'

He maintained a careful distance from her. 'No. I never left Umm Khoreem.'

'But...you were headed home.' Except then it occurred to her that he'd never actually said the words *air* or *port*. 'Weren't you?'

'I've been staying out at the camp, with my uncle,' he replied with a grateful glance back at Salim, who had busied himself talking low to his beloved camels.

Questions spun around her addled mind like the wild fringes of a tornado but finally settled on the simplest one. 'Why?'

'He's been helping me.'

'No. I mean, why did you stay?'

His hands rose up either side of him and he looked as if he was struggling to find the easiest explanation, too. 'I couldn't leave.'

Old caution kept her from reading too much into that. For all she knew his passport might have expired.

He hovered, awkwardly, on the edge of the circle of light. 'Can I come in?'

Rushing forward and dragging him in was inappropriate, right?

'Sure. Wipe your feet.'

God, how she'd missed that low chuckle! Behind her, the SUV rumbled to expensive life as soon as she made the single gesture of welcome and began to reverse down the dune. She turned and stared at the slash of its headlights as Eric switched them back on.

'Neither of them were going to leave unless you were okay about me being here.'

She watched them rumble away. 'Too bad, now, if I'm not.'

'If you are not, Sera,' Salim pledged from the edge of darkness, 'then I will escort you home on his camel and Bradley can stumble back in the dark with the scorpions.'

That little show of solidarity made her Salim's for life.

'Is that why you were awkward earlier this week?' she called to the shadows. 'Because you were harbouring a fugitive?'

Salim chuckled. Or it could have been a camel... Impossible to distinguish.

Brad took another step. 'Will you sit?'

'Um, no.' This was a conversation best had standing.

'Okay.' Uncertainty stained his voice. And she'd never heard him be anything other than totally confident.

'Here,' he began, reaching back over his shoulder and gently pulling out a scroll of paper bound with a bright bow. 'I got this for you.'

Of all the things she'd imagined about this evening, camels, Brad and gifts were never one of them.

'It's a Christmas gift,' he clarified as she stood motionless.

'Christmas is tomorrow.'

'I know but... Just in case. You can keep it sealed until tomorrow if you want.'

Pfff... Did he not know her at all? She tugged on the

loose end of the bow and the pretty ribbon fell away, allowing the scroll to unspool in her hands. Then she stepped closer to one of the torches and held it up. It was a watercolour, in the deep browns and golds of the desert, filled with a very familiar face.

Her breath backed up behind the sudden fist in her throat. 'Omar.'

'I thought he'd be a good memory of your trip. Something to hold on to when you're...'

Gone.

She wanted to clutch the image to her chest and never let go, but she didn't want to mark the perfect parchment. It took all her discipline to roll it back up and retie the ribbon. But then she clasped it close.

'Merry Christmas, Sera.'

'You came back to give me this?' she finally said.

'Only in part.'

No. She wasn't going to beg. Or guess. If he had something to say then let him say it. And then let him leave again.

'This past week has been good for me,' he began carefully.

Less so for me...

'Spending time with Salim,' he went on. 'Talking. He's helped me understand...a lot.'

'About?'

'Myself mostly. A few of the wrong turns I've taken.'

'Like what?'

'Most recently... Leaving the Sheikh's service the way I did.' His Adam's apple danced. 'Leaving you the way I did.'

So...what? He'd come back to break her heart more nicely?

'Weren't they the same thing?'

His eyes fell. 'They weren't, Sera. I left my job because I let them down.' He sucked in a deep breath. 'I left you because I was afraid.'

'Of what?' she pressed.

'Of failing.'

Her heart squeezed again, but this time it was for him. For the blame she heard in his quiet words. 'Failing who?'

'People I was supposed to protect.' He took a breath. 'Matteo. You.'

There was just so much in that statement and she wasn't ready yet to face part of it.

'Matteo made it—'

'I nearly got him killed,' he urged. 'This innocent kid with so much life in him. I knew we were bonding and I let it flourish. I enjoyed it.' His eyes dropped. 'I never should have let myself grow close to him in the first place. I should have pushed him away.'

Sera took a long breath. 'By "him" you mean me, right? You think of me like Matteo?'

Like a seven-year-old child... Maybe she was. Had she really come far from the days when she would have done anything for her daddy's attention?

Dark lines—exaggerated by the sharp light from the low-burning torches—appeared between his brows. 'I thought it was going to be fine, that you were bolshie and tough as nails. I only had to worry about your physical safety. And keeping you off the internet,' he joked weakly.

'You said you didn't want to be responsible for my emotional well-being.'

Saying it out loud was scarcely more comforting than remembering the words on his lips.

'I said I *couldn't*, Sera. I didn't trust myself with anyone else's heart. If I thought for one second I'd be any good at all for you, emotionally, I would do whatever it took. Whatever you needed.'

The scarred organ in her chest began to hammer with an optimism she'd never imagined it could possibly have.

'I just needed you to stay,' she said simply.

He bundled her hands into his, begging her understanding. 'I *broke his heart*, Sera. A vulnerable little boy. I did more harm than good.'

'You might think that,' she said. 'But there's nothing good about letting a child think you don't care about them. Someone that they spend *every single* day with. Trust me on that.'

'But his suffering—'

'Would have been drawn out over months,' she urged. 'And it would have been personal. And it would have changed him forever. At least this way he had a conflict to blame for losing you and his parents to help him through it, rather than thinking it was *his* fault. That he was simply not good enough to love.'

The awful words echoed around the empty desert. Loud and sore.

Brad blinked in the flickering light. 'That's what you believed?'

'That's what I still believe.' She laughed. 'No matter how grown-up I try and be about it, it's still there in my foundations... Lurking. Because that's the message I got whenever someone kept me at a distance, whenever Dad chose his music over me, whenever some boy decided I wasn't worth the hassle. Whenever anyone used me for my connections.'

'Your father—'

'Shouldn't ever have *been* a father. I know that, logically. I suspect he does, too. He's way too absorbed in his own achievements and success. Don't get me wrong, I love him because he's my dad, but I drove myself into the ground trying to earn his respect and his love. I tried to substitute it with those around me but—wouldn't you know it?—they didn't love me either! That kind of reinforcement has a way of sticking in a kid's brain.'

She'd been staring into the low flames rather than risk seeing pity in Brad's gaze, but she looked back at him now. 'At least your Matteo had the love and respect of a man he worshipped. No matter how badly it ended. That is a *good* thing, Brad. Not something to mourn.'

Brad stared at her so long she thought maybe she was going to have to order him to blink. But, finally, he did. 'I never thought about it that way.'

'Obviously!' She snorted. 'You just leapt straight to the conclusion that you couldn't be trusted with someone's heart. The most trustworthy person I've ever known…'

Confusion washed over him. 'You're angry?'

'Yes, I'm angry. Because you've beaten yourself up unnecessarily for years over this and I'm guessing you haven't even sent that kid so much as a postcard since Cairo?'

'I didn't want to—'

'Right, so he's suffered unnecessarily for two years wondering what the hell he did wrong or whether you even survived the conflict.' She stepped up close and shoved him square in the chest, then couldn't quite bring herself to lower her hands. 'And I've suffered unnecessarily for a whole week wondering *what the hell* I have to do to be worthy of someone's love.'

'Sera—' His voice cracked.

Her fingers curled in the fabric of his shirt and she pulled herself up towards Brad's mouth. He caught her just as her lips met his. Every cell in her body celebrated. Like her, they'd thought they'd never ever taste him again. That gorgeous, rare, delicious flavour. He slid one strong arm around her to keep her fixed to him.

'Why are men such idiots?' she finally whispered against his mouth. 'We could have been doing that all week.'

'Because women mess with our minds until we don't know which way is up.'

'So this is my fault?' she challenged.

'No,' he murmured. 'I'm pretty sure you're the only sane one in this conversation. How did you get so smart?'

'Blood, sweat and tears.'

Oh, so many tears.

One of the camels snorted, and Sera remembered Brad's uncle sitting in the wings witnessing all these very *un*-politically correct displays of affection. She eased herself away from Brad a little. But he wouldn't let her go far.

'So...' She cleared her throat. 'You're back?'

Warm breath tickled her face. 'I'm back.'

She wanted to be brave. She wanted to be the confident woman that Brad would give an easy nine to on the normality scale. But old habits died hard and she had no idea what it meant that he was actually standing here. Like a mirage come to life.

'Why are you back?'

To explain himself? For a while? For good?

'I forgot to do something before I left,' he said.

Her heart recoiled into its safe little corner, preparing for the worst. But she couldn't find the mettle to speak.

'Pretty unprofessional of me, actually, to leave without fulfilling my obligation as your personal security.'

She blinked at him in pained confusion and—as she so often did—she hid behind humour. 'Something I should have signed?'

'I neglected to do my assessment report. For your file.'

Paperwork. Her head spun. *Okay...*

'Maybe I could submit it now?'

She pushed away and put a healthy pace-length of cold air between them. 'If you must.'

But he wouldn't let her go far and he held on to her fingers, keeping her close.

'Seraphina Blaise,' he recited. 'Twenty-four. Passionate and talented daughter to a father who doesn't deserve her...'

The fist in her chest shot back. Hard.

'Spent her young life developing shields to protect herself from those who should have been protecting her.' He tugged her back towards him, gently. 'Amazingly resilient and optimistic considering how often she has been let down in life, but has no concept of her true personal courage.'

She bit the inside of her cheek to keep from sobbing.

'Found her own beauty and joy in the world and then used her talent to help others. Even broke the law in defence of those who couldn't defend themselves. Was surrendered by one parent, neglected by another, used by her friends, and—more recently—betrayed by a man she trusted to protect her.'

She peered up at him. His eyes glittered with unshed emotion and behind that something else lurked. Something she barely recognised. Something she surely should not trust.

It was rich and deep and so full of the kind of promises she never, ever let herself believe.

'Yet, for all of it, she still has more love lurking in her elegant little finger than any of them have in their entire bodies.'

He drew those fingers to his lips.

'Including that man she trusted to defend her?' she squeezed out past her tight throat.

'Especially that man,' Brad breathed. 'He's beginning to suspect he never had any idea what love was really about.'

'You didn't betray me,' she said, stepping up to him. 'You just left.'

'The biggest betrayal of all. I promise never to do it again.'

In any other two people, this was where the man would fall to his knees and declare undying love. In any other two people, the woman would throw herself into his arms and they'd live happily ever after. The End.

But they weren't any other two people.

He was proud, complicated Brad. She was cautious, baggage-laden Sera. The couple on any one of those distant planets circling above them might do things differently but—in this desert, on this planet—this man standing before her knew that she needed more than just to hear the words.

She needed to *believe* them.

And seeing was believing.

He took her hands in his, then raised them out to their sides, standing open and vulnerable before her. Exposed. Truth pouring from his warm gaze. Silently offering her everything that he was and wasn't.

Weakening himself so that she could be strong.

'Oh, my God,' she choked as she stared up into his unguarded eyes. 'Do you—?'

The lessons of her childhood weren't easy to forget. Every part of her screamed at her not to say it. Not to risk it. But he was going to stand there, silently, until she found the courage to use the words herself. She dug deep and found a little faith—in Brad, who would never intentionally set her up for hurt. In herself.

And that was certainly something new.

'Do you love me?' she whispered.

And somehow it came out not as a raw question, but as a truth. Wonderful and real.

Joy flooded into his eyes. 'Apparently that's a thing I do now.'

She, more than just about anyone, had every reason not to trust that look, but... She couldn't help the massive, teary smile. 'You love me.'

He matched it. 'You say that like it's a completely impossible miracle.'

'It is!'

'Why? You're amazing.'

'Because it just doesn't happen.' Not to her.

'It hasn't happened to me before now,' he admitted. 'That doesn't make it inconceivable.'

Suddenly, standing this close to him and not touching became untenable. She threw her arms around his neck and buried herself there again, breathing him in, holding him as tightly as his sure grip.

'I think I fell for you the moment you started flirting with me on the way from the airport,' he confessed.

She chuckled. 'What part of me giving you hell did you take as flirting?'

'You were testing me, constantly. I knew that. You've been testing people all your life to see how far you can push them. Waiting for someone to care enough to push back.'

She lifted her head and blinked.

'Did I *create* the distance I was so sensitive to?'

'Maybe.' He stroked a lock of hair from her face with a soft knuckle. 'Lucky I'm so obstinate, huh?'

She shook her head. 'I thought I knew who I was...'

Brad kissed one eyelid, and then the other and the gesture turned her heart to mush.

'We have a lifetime to get to know each other,' he murmured. 'Or ourselves. Whichever is the most interesting.'

A lifetime? 'What... What are you saying?'

'That wasn't a proposal,' he cautioned. 'No pressure.'

But then he looked around. 'Although there really couldn't be a more perfect place for one. Or a night. Maybe we can come back here next Christmas Eve and have this conversation again.'

Relief washed through her. And excitement. All she could hear was 'we'.

But she kept her cool.

'You think Al Saqr will have us back?'

'I think Al Saqr can arrange just about anything we want. They're our own personal Santa Claus.'

'Do you think they would give me the real Omar as a Christmas gift?'

His chuckle rumbled against her ear. 'Not a chance. You'll have to settle for the painting.'

She sighed her disappointment but snuggled in closer. 'What about you, then?'

'Yeah—' he rested his strong chin on top of her head '—that one is definitely negotiable.'

'How is it that I feel like I've known you my whole life?' she whispered.

'Pretty long couple of weeks, huh?'

'Wonder if they'll all be that long.'

'I hope so. That'll make up for all the time we didn't have each other.'

Not *know* each other. *Have* each other.

Tears stung her eyes horribly and a fist curled tight around her vocal cords. She peered up at him again. 'You know you're the first person I've ever actually *had*?'

'Have. Hold.' Brad's eyes darkened. 'Worse. Better.'

She gnawed her lip. 'There could be a bit of worse.'

A chuckle rattled his chest again. 'To love. To cherish.'

'Until vipers do us part.'

She stretched up on her toes in the sand and met him as soon as she could. His lips on hers were better than any of Al Saqr's delicious morsels. Tastier and sweeter and the sort of thing that would linger long after it was gone. They pressed and roamed and nibbled and discovered, and hers mirrored them happily.

If he kissed her forever it would be too short.

'I love you, Brad Kruger.'

'You'd better,' he murmured against her lips. 'Or loving you back is going to get really awkward.'

EPILOGUE

Have. Hold. Better. Worse.

It was twelve months to the day before he said those words again. In the right order this time.

True to Brad's pledge, he'd brought her back to Al Saqr and the desert dinner experience to officially propose under the wide open skies. Sera had only made him sweat a little before throwing herself into his arms and they'd had the world's shortest engagement, marrying the very next day.

Al Saqr had gifted them the honeymoon suite.

Salim had insisted on the full use of his desert camp for the ceremony and made sure that only the best-looking camels were invited.

Sera glanced around at the many faces assembled under the grand Bedouin canopies: Salim's ever more numerous family, Brad's father who—just like his son—stood sure and protective over the wife who hadn't been back in her ancestral lands for thirty years. Sera's eyes tracked left. Over in the corner, Aaliyah and Eric pretended to ignore each other—but something about their body language said that Salim might have to manage another cross-cultural entanglement very soon.

Even Matteo and his father had made the long journey out here courtesy of a devilish piece of secrecy on her part.

Behind them, the traditional music of the hired musicians took a turn for the stranger as her father and his band joined in with their acoustic guitars. Possibly the first aging, Goth rock stars to ever grace a Bedouin camp and already Blaise was talking about a new musical direction featuring traditional Arabian instruments. Trust him to find a way to make her special day all about him.

Taboos were trampled, rules were bent, cultures were melded and—somehow—it all worked out just fine.

'This could have gone so badly,' Sera said softly when finally they had a moment alone together.

He took full advantage, whisking her into the shadows for a kiss. 'Never.'

'Look around you. There's a dozen international incidents just begging to occur.'

He shrugged. 'Someone else's problem tonight.'

She offered a mock gasp. 'My goodness, how far you've come, Bradley.'

His arms wrapped more tightly around her. 'It seems you've ruined me, Seraphina.'

Sera rested her head on his shoulder. 'You know what? If this is ruin, then I'm not interested in redemption.'

'How long will you love me?' he murmured.

She glanced up at the blanket of stars above them. 'Until the brightest of those burns out.'

'Good answer.' He chuckled.

'You?'

'Until you ask me to stop.'

'Stop? Are you kidding? I've waited my whole life for you.'

Those grey eyes fringed by those dark lashes… Ugh, it just melted her heart. And given what her heart had been through, that was saying something. But she'd rather a vulnerable heart to a hard one any day.

'The wait's over, gorgeous. I can't imagine ever not loving you.'

She kissed him long and hard, taking full advantage of their shadowy corner, and let the slippery silk of her traditional wedding attire slide against the rich fabric of his. In it, he looked every bit a Bedouin.

'Think Salim would mind if we borrowed one of his camels and just rode out into the desert?' she asked. The thought of galumphing along with her beautiful dress streaming out behind her and her arms wrapped tightly around his hard waist...

Brad laughed. 'Looking to indulge a few desert fantasies, Sera?'

'I have a lifetime of fantasies to fulfil,' she promised.

Brad traced the back of his hand across her cheek and drew her gaze into his own deep, dark one. 'Happy Christmas, Mrs Kruger.'

She twisted her hands more tightly behind his neck. 'Wow. That's going to take some getting used to.'

'Being Mrs Kruger?' he asked.

She pressed her mouth to his and then breathed against it. 'Being happy.'

So, this was what it felt like! As if someone had boiled up the colours of the desert into a delicious, golden tea and then given it to her to drink. It spread outward from her heart, warm and golden and immensely fulfilling.

'Are you up for it?'

With him by her side? She was up for anything.

'Totally.'

* * * * *

MILLS & BOON®

Cherish™

EXPERIENCE THE ULTIMATE RUSH OF FALLING IN LOVE

A sneak peek at next month's titles...

In stores from 18th December 2015:

- **Holiday with the Millionaire** – Scarlet Wilson *and*
  Fortune's Secret Heir – Allison Leigh
- **His Princess of Convenience** *and*
  The Texas Ranger's Nanny – Rebecca Winters

In stores from 1st January 2016:

- **Having the Cowboy's Baby** – Judy Duarte *and*
  The Husband She'd Never Met – Barbara Hannay
- **The Widow's Bachelor Bargain** – Teresa Southwic
  and **Unlocking Her Boss's Heart** – Christy McKelle

MILLS & BOON®

'The perfect Christmas read!' - Julia Williams

Jewellery designer Skylar loves living London, but when a surprise proposal goes wrong, she finds herself fleeing home to remote Puffin Island.

Burned by a terrible divorce, TV historian Alec is dazzled by Sky's beauty and so cynical that he assumes that's a bad thing! Luckily she's on the verge of getting engaged to someone else, so she won't be a constant source of temptation... but this Christmas, can Alec and Sky realise that they are what each other was looking for all along?

Order yours today at
www.millsandboon.co.uk

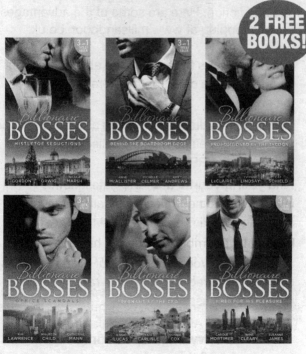